W9-AON-635

03/2020

THE Earl TAKES A Fancy

By Lorraine Heath

LORRAINE HEATH

THE Earl TAKES A Fancy

A SINS FOR ALL SEASONS NOVEL

AVONBOOKS

An Imprint of HarperCollins*Publishers*

Excerpt from *Beauty Tempts the Beast* copyright © 2020 by Jan Nowasky.

First Avon Books mass market printing: April 2020
First Avon Books hardcover printing: March 2020

Print Edition ISBN: 978-0-06-297507-2
Digital Edition ISBN: 978-0-06-295188-5

Avon, Avon & logo, and Avon Books & logo are registered trademarks of HarperCollins Publishers in the United States of America and other countries.

HarperCollins is a registered trademark of HarperCollins Publishers in the United States of America and other countries.

FIRST EDITION

20 21 22 23 24   LSC   10 9 8 7 6 5 4 3 2 1

To Katie Patterson, Executive Director of the Richardson Adult Literacy Center, and all the staff and volunteers who work to help adults striving to learn English as a second language.

To Donna Finlay, Karen Gibbs, Alexandra Haughton, Wanda Lankford, Chris Simmie, and Kandy Tobin, who are the amazing committee members for the Buns & Roses Romance Tea for Literacy, which benefits RALC, and to those who served on the committee in the past.

To the many authors who have generously hosted a table at the annual tea.

And to the wonderful readers who attend and share their joy of reading while making a difference in the lives of so many. Each year when I attend the event, I feel as though I've come home.

THE
Earl
TAKES A
Fancy

Prologue

The pain came swift and hard.

Ettie Trewlove gasped, pressed a hand to her swollen belly, and dropped the ladle filled with soup. It hit the scarred oak table, splattering her eldest as he held his bowl out toward her. It wasn't the first contraction to hit her. They'd been coming all day, but this one was definitely the sharpest, and she felt the wetness rolling down her legs. "Mick, go fetch Mrs. Winters. Quickly now."

The lad who'd been delivered to her in the dead of night fourteen years earlier didn't hesitate to dash out the door to search for the midwife. Her other darlings—three boys and a girl—stared at her with large eyes as round as saucers. She gave them a reassuring smile. "You're going to have to fill your own bowls. Have your dinner in the garden. Stay there until I come for you."

Slowly she made her way to her small bedchamber. As she began unbuttoning her bodice, she became aware of the quiet footsteps. Glancing over her shoulder, she beamed encouragingly at her daughter. "Off with you now, Gillie. Do as you were told."

"I'm stayin'." Her lips pressed in a mulish expression, she marched over to the wardrobe. It had been nearly thirteen years since, wrapped only in a blanket, she'd been left in a wicker basket on Ettie's stoop. But then all of her children had been brought to her door, one way or another. Gillie took out a nightdress and held it toward her.

Ettie sighed with resignation because her daughter was the most stubborn of the lot. "Until Mrs. Winters gets here."

By the time Mick returned, breathless and flushed, she was in her nightdress, tucked into bed, having suffered through two more contractions without screaming, but it was becoming increasingly difficult to hold her tongue.

"She's off deliverin' another babe," Mick announced with such solemnity he might as well have pronounced the midwife dead.

"Well, then." Ettie tossed back the covers. "I'd best boil some water."

"We'll do it." The stoic set of Gillie's mouth didn't hide the fear in her eyes.

"I can handle it, love."

"Just tell us wot to do, Mum."

And so she did. And four hours later, within her arms, she cradled the most beautiful babe upon whom she'd ever set eyes. Skimming her fingers lightly over the dark hair, with sorrow, she reminisced briefly about the two babes she'd given her husband, and the sweet joy they'd brought with their arrival. But then Michael had died, and shortly thereafter, so had her little ones. She'd begun taking in by-blows as a way to earn a few coins. Now she had one of her own.

"Wot ye goin' to name 'er?" Gillie asked.

"Fancy. Because one day she will not live in the squalor her mum did. But she will marry a fancy man, live in a fancy house, and enjoy a fancy life." She smiled warmly at the five children surrounding her. "You'll all have fancy lives."

Chapter 1

A man's life was bookended by two events: the day he was born and the day he went toes up. Interspersed throughout were other critical moments, but for the Earl of Rosemont, only three were of any consequence: the day he wed, the night his wife died, and the morning she rose from the grave to wreak havoc on his life.

Sitting at the desk in his library, opening the newspaper his butler had dutifully ironed, he once more read the letter that had ruined his appetite at breakfast three days earlier.

To the noble ladies of London:

It is with unheralded sorrow tempered by a great deal of hope that I pen this letter. The very fact that you, gentle ladies, are reading it today signals that it has been one year exactly since my passing. We all know gentlemen seldom observe the full mourning period of two years while women always have the more dedicated hearts and adhere more fervently to Society's strictures.

I, for one, am glad we allow such leniency toward men as I want my darling Rosemont to be saddened and without the comfort of a woman for as short a time as possible. To that end, dear ladies, I call upon you to hasten the close of his period of sorrow and bring forth his smile.

For you see, it was his smile that first drew me toward him.

It was ever so slow in coming, but when it did arrive, it fairly took my breath and softened the countenance of a man whose pride sometimes has the better of him. He is not an easy man to love and yet love him I did for I saw a side to him that few witnessed.

He has brushed my hair, rubbed my feet, and not only read me poetry with animated passion but written it as well. Ah, dear ladies, his voice is a soothing baritone, his features most comely, and his shoulder incredibly comforting when I required a haven to absorb my tears. His eye never wandered . . . well, except toward sweet shops. He does so enjoy his lemon balls.

In spite of my flaws, he remained the most loyal and steadfast of husbands. Win his heart and find yourself falling into a lifetime of happiness.

With my most sincerest regards,
The Departed Countess of Rosemont

Each time he read it, the coldhearted lie she'd meticulously penned mocked him. She hadn't loved him. Not in the least. Not with one iota of her being.

The daughter of an industrialist knighted by the Queen, Elise had been in want of a titled husband and, at only nineteen, she'd known well how to work her wiles on him. He had little doubt his smile had drawn her—that much was true—but she'd also been lured by the title he'd inherited only the year before. He'd been all of twenty-three, infatuated with her beauty and teasing eyes that promised wicked adventures and a tantalizing escape from all cares. When she'd suggested a tryst among the plants in the conservatory during a ball held at his married sister's country estate, he'd been only too keen to accommodate her. Being caught by Elise's father with her skirts up and his trousers down had resulted in a rather hasty trip to the altar. But the triumph mirrored in her eyes when they were interrupted alerted him that he'd been cast into the role of gullible fool.

It had been a hard lesson learned, a high price paid, and he'd made a solemn vow to never again be duped by anyone of the female persuasion.

A marriage based on a lack of trust was no marriage at all. During the first two years, they'd not confided in each other at all, preferred to spend their time apart, he in the country, she in the city. He'd been in no rush to get her with child. The joy of having her had died in the conservatory, and he'd been hard-pressed to work up any enthusiasm when it came to the bedding of her. The third and final year, he'd seldom left her side as the cancer had its way with her. Elise had made a point of listing all the things she'd never do. She'd not welcomed death, nor should she have. She'd been all of twenty-two, with hair that would never gray and skin that would never wrinkle with age.

Still, her letter confounded him. Why had she gone to the bother of writing it and arranging to have it published? To ease her guilt at having duped him? Knowing her deceptive ways, he couldn't take her missive at face value, so what was she striving to accomplish? Based on what he'd experienced since the message first appeared, perhaps she merely wanted to make his life as unpleasant as possible. As though the coldness of their marriage had not been punishment enough for falling into her trap.

At the approach of hushed footsteps, he glanced up to see his butler enter carrying a silver salver. The slender man, graying at the temples, came to a stop and bowed slightly. "My lord, Lady Fontaine and her daughter have come to call."

In frustration that Elise had placed him in this unenviable position, he slammed his eyes closed. His first visitors of the day. He could expect at least a dozen more before the sun finally bid its farewell. If he wasn't home to them now, they'd only return later. After carefully folding the broadsheet, he shoved back his chair and stood. "Have tea brought to the parlor."

And so it went. Day after day after day.

A parade of eligible young ladies through his front door. They had talked, talked, talked. Recited poetry. Sung on occasion. Played his pianoforte with gusto. He was invited for walks in the park as though he were a hound in need of having his legs stretched. They issued him invitations to dinners, recitals, the theater, and gatherings in their gardens. They sought promises of a waltz at upcoming balls once the Season was fully underway. They alternated between cooing over his abhorrent loss and assuring him that happiness waited around the corner if only he would march briskly toward it—and they were more than willing to become his countess and accompany him on the journey toward discovering what glories life still held in spite of the unfairness fate had already visited upon him.

It was the lemon balls that finally became the last straw. Within two weeks of the letter's appearance, he'd received so many of the damned things he could have opened his own sweet shop. If he ever smelled lemon and sugar again, he might go stark raving mad.

Hence, after having his belongings packed up and his London residence shuttered, he went in search of peace.

Chapter 2

$\mathcal{S}$tanding behind the polished oak counter in her bookshop, Fancy Trewlove read once more the letter she'd clipped from the *Times* a month earlier. The Countess of Rosemont's words regarding her love for her husband had deeply touched Fancy's romantically inclined heart, a heart she had feared would cause her—when she was introduced into Society at a ball the following week—to be foolish enough to fall for a lord who viewed her as someone to be only bedded but not wedded.

All of nineteen, she was more than aware of the realities of the world and understood fully that the circumstances of her birth would not serve her well when it came to securing her place among the aristocracy. Still, her family was determined to see her married to a noble. The man had to be titled. Not the second son or the third, but the first. A duke was preferable, a marquess adequate, an earl acceptable, a viscount . . . an outcome to be avoided if at all possible.

From the moment she'd made her entry into the world they had decided her destiny and moved her unerringly toward it, but the life they had mapped out for her seemed to lack one crucial element: love.

She yearned for love more than she wanted to breathe. Oh, her family loved her, she had no doubt about that, but she longed for the sort of devotion about which sonnets were written and poets waxed, a grand love like the one her mum had known. When

Fancy was a wee lass, yet still old enough to be curious about the absence of a man about, she'd worked up the courage to ask about her father. With tears in her eyes, her mum had explained how she'd fallen for a handsome regimental officer. They'd not been married when they'd given into passion on the eve of his departure to a foreign land, but he'd promised to wed her upon his return. However, fate had intervened, and he'd died heroically, yet tragically, on a bloodied battlefield on the Crimean Peninsula.

"But, still, he gave me the most wonderful gift of all—you." Even now, the recollection of her mum's words caused her eyes to dampen. From that moment on, Fancy had understood she was special. Unlike her siblings who had all been left at her mum's door, she had been *wanted*.

And so it was that she had a tender regard for stories brimming with romance, and Lady Rosemont's letter certainly fell into that category, serving as a talisman, offering hope that she, too, might discover a passion not to be denied.

At that very moment, with long, slender fingers, her future husband might be opening the gilded invitation that would set him on the path toward meeting her. Unlike her brothers', his hands would be soft and without calluses or scars, his movements would reflect elegance. He would have mastered the waltz to perfection, and when he took her within his arms to sweep her over the parqueted flooring, although he would hold her at a proper distance and with decorum, his gaze would capture hers and communicate his intense regard toward her, would reveal how firmly she'd already won him over. His eyes would reflect warmth and hint at his desire—

Jingle. Jingle.

As the bell above her shop door heralded the arrival of a customer, she gave a guilty start. Based on the heat scalding her cheeks, she was blushing profusely at being caught dreaming the afternoon away. It didn't help matters that the man crossing the threshold had smoothly removed his black beaver hat to reveal a handsome countenance, a face that no doubt set many ladies to swooning. Quickly, she folded the letter and slipped it into the pocket of her skirt, where she had handy access to it when she needed a reminder that love could be found among the aristocracy and that the path her family had set her on was one worth traveling.

The gent surveyed the various areas of her shop—the shelves lining the back wall, the parallel bookcases with the elaborate scrollwork standing perpendicular to it, the small tables with novels stacked on top of them, books gathered in corners. Books, books, books, everywhere he looked. She could never have enough of them, which was obvious to anyone entering her shop, whether for the first time or the hundredth.

In her youth, a lad had once told her she had a fetish when it came to books. Because of how much she read, she knew the word and that he was implying something untoward, and so she'd bloodied his nose. What she had for books was a healthy appreciation for all they offered, an admiration for those who penned them, and a gratitude to those who published them. She wasn't ashamed of it; rather she reveled in it.

She couldn't decide if her customer, who seemed absorbed by all surrounding him, was enthralled by her collection or appalled that so much space was taken up with literary works. Knowing she'd never before seen him within these walls—his mere mien indicated he was not one easily forgotten—she straightened her narrow shoulders to welcome the gorgeous stranger into her midst. "May I be of service, sir?"

He swerved his head toward her, and she became ensnared in the most striking green eyes she'd ever beheld. His black hair, a tad longer than was fashionable, every strand in place, made the green stand out all the more. Her wits seemed to have deserted her, and she knew staring into those emerald depths for the remainder of her life would be an insufficient amount of time to fully appreciate the various facets of them, of him. He seemed at once imposing, yet approachable—and she dearly wanted to approach him but remained where she was, unwilling to risk any action that might cost her a sale, or at the very least, placing a book into a hand.

"The sign on your door indicated you were closed." His enunciation, hinting at an education, good breeding, and possibly an affluent background, was posher than that spoken by most of the people who lived in the area. But it was his deep smooth voice that sent a warm shiver through her.

Interesting that in spite of the sign, he'd given the door a try. A man who obviously didn't quite trust what was before him—or perhaps one who merely needed proof that what he was told was true.

Glancing at the tall standing clock resting against the wall to her left, near her office, she saw that indeed it was ten minutes past the hour of six when she usually locked her doors. She'd been so engrossed in the letter she'd failed to even notice the chimes signaling the time. "My posted hours are more a suggestion, not a law. Nor am I one for turning away someone in need of a book. If you would like to browse . . . or I'm happy to help you find something to your taste."

He edged farther inside but only by a couple of steps. "I don't wish to impose if you were on the verge of latching up for the night."

"It's no imposition I assure you. Partnering people with books is one of my greatest joys. I can even recommend a few of my favorites if you like."

"As long as you're so graciously willing to accommodate me, I'm in the mood for some dastardly deeds. Have you the latest penny blood?"

She blinked, parted her lips—

And heard the smallest of scoffs beneath his breath. "You're no doubt too young to recall that phrase. I believe it's more popularly known these days as a penny dreadful."

"Ah, yes, over here." She skirted around the edge of the counter and approached a narrow stand of slanting shelves where she displayed the weekly publications. "I have the individual serials available here and, on this shelf"—she walked a short distance away—"I've bound editions containing all the episodes for a particular tale."

"Very good." Having approached, he leaned down to study the covers facing out revealing the title of the series represented within. He'd brought with him the scent of bay rum. Had he not lowered himself, she'd have not noted that the curling strands of his hair at his nape appeared damp on the ends, leaving her to believe he'd bathed shortly before beginning this sojourn. But he'd not bothered to shave as dark bristles shadowed his jaw. It was a magnificent jaw, strong and squarely cut. She thought it a shame to hide it away beneath a light coating of whiskers yet couldn't deny the masculinity of them. His broad shoulders also gave her pause, and she wondered if he'd come by them naturally or if his labors, whatever they were, had formed them. Those prone to leisure didn't reside in the area and seldom shopped here, so he no doubt was engaged in some occupation. He seemed an odd mixture of rough and smooth, like the brandy she enjoyed on occasion.

"Ah, Dick Turpin." A warm fondness marked his tone. "When I was a lad, I spent many an afternoon reading about this highwayman's exploits." He pulled it from the shelf. "I'll take this one."

"It's six shillings. If that's a bit of a stretch for you at the moment, I can give you credit until the end of the month if you live or work in the area."

It wasn't exactly a smile he gave her, but more a twitch of his lips—and fine lips they were, full and nicely shaped with a natural tilting up at both corners as though he were constantly amused by the world at large. "I'll settle things between us now."

"Excellent."

She wandered back over to the counter. He removed a small purse from inside his jacket, withdrew the necessary coins, and passed them over to her. She couldn't help but notice his large gloved hands and the elegant ease with which they tucked the supple leather back into place. Suddenly drawing in breath seemed a challenge as images of those hands tucking other things—hair behind an ear, a button back through its mooring, a stocking over a knee—raced unbidden through her mind. She didn't know what was prompting her to have such lascivious thoughts where he was concerned, although of late she had begun noticing the pleasing attributes of men. Her family would no doubt be horrified to learn that she'd recently started reading books banned by obscenity laws—when she could find one. She didn't want to be a complete innocent when she made her foray into Society.

His eyes narrowed as he studied the shelf behind her that housed her rare finds, some she had restored to perfection herself. They brought her such pleasure and joy, it took everything within her not to parade him on a journey through the extraordinary tomes, allowing him to carefully handle them in order to see how well preserved they were.

"Is that an early edition of *Pride and Prejudice*?"

"A first edition." She couldn't stop the bright smile from forming. "It was found in a rubbish bin of all places." Outside of a house in Mayfair. With great care, she had removed the soiled, discolored leather binding and worked with it until it was once again supple. When the book was reassembled, it gave the appearance of being barely used.

"Sort through rubbish bins often, do you?"

"You'd be amazed by the treasures people toss out."

"I suppose I would."

"However, I don't rummage through the rubbish, but some poor or orphaned children do, and they bring me their finds, in hopes of gaining a few coins." Even when the book was beyond use and couldn't be restored, she paid them to ensure they had a bit to see them through to the next day.

"You don't think you're encouraging them to steal from elsewhere?"

"Aren't you a cynic? No, I'm encouraging them not to accept the harsh life they've been dealt but to know it can be improved upon with effort, hard work, determination, and a bit of ingenuity."

"I wish you the best with that, then." He tipped his head slightly.

But she couldn't let him go without telling him more. "I once had a lad bring me a story written on bits of foolscap he'd collected here and there. He'd sewn the pages together with needle and yarn. I bought it for two pence. My hope was to encourage him so perhaps he'll grow up to be a storyteller. You might have noticed it on display in the window."

She'd taken great effort in arranging small shelves of knick-knacks in the front bay windows as a means to entice people inside. Books, a statuette of a woman reading and another of a boy, book in hand, sitting with his back leaning against a tree. One of the windows exhibited an extremely tiny desk with paper, quill pen, and inkwell—all to signify a writer at his labors.

"I did notice it. I was intrigued and wondered what it was about."

She offered him a warm smile. "Now you know."

"I do indeed."

He was studying her with the same intense scrutiny he'd given her shop when he'd first walked in. She didn't know why she'd told him as much as she had. Yes, she did. She so loved talking books. They'd been her passion ever since Gillie had first sat her upon her lap and turned back a cover to reveal the magic hidden within. She was rather certain, based on the warmth spreading through her cheeks, that she was blushing under his examination. "Apologies, sir. I didn't mean to carry on so. I'm keeping you."

" 'Tis I who have been keeping you. Thank you for so graciously remaining open for me."

"It was my pleasure." How could it not be when he provided such a compelling view? She'd only ever seen paintings of mountains, and yet she couldn't help but think he rivaled them in majesty. "I hope you enjoy the book as much as you did when you were a lad."

"I've no doubt I will."

She followed him to the door where he hesitated a heartbeat—as though he wished to say something more—before opening it and exiting her shop. Closing it after him, she watched as he halted to study her window display, the one with the miniature desk, before carrying on. A wistfulness, a sadness shadowed him. She wondered if he was without family, alone in the world.

Turning the lock, she was grateful for the sale. It would have been her first day without dropping a single farthing into her till, and she refused to be disheartened by the shortage of customers. She knew not everyone grew up in a family that cherished books as much as hers did, nor could a good many people afford them. Although for some years now, the publishing world had been working to make literature more affordable to the masses, which was the reason she'd been able to sell the one-volume collection of serials so inexpensively.

Her shop had been open for a little over a year now, and business was slowly increasing, thanks in no small part to her brother Mick's rejuvenation of this area of London. A few years earlier, he'd torn down the dilapidated ruins he'd purchased and replaced them with sturdily built brick buildings. Shops lined either side of the street. On the corner across from hers—and taking up quite a bit of the area—was Mick's crowning achievement, his grand hotel that bore the Trewlove name. While he'd not wanted to see her working, had preferred she spend her time preparing for her entry into Society, she'd managed to convince him to allow her to use one of his smaller buildings as a bookshop. All her siblings had met with varying degrees of success, and she'd wanted to do her part to make a difference, not only in her life and for her family but in the lives of others.

Walking back to the counter, she smiled as her cat leapt onto it, stretched languidly, and glared at her through green eyes. She ran her fingers through his thick fur, as white as pristine snow. He'd been scrawny and practically furless—what little bit remained in his possession had been matted—when she found him in the mews, bound up like a sausage. If she ever discovered who'd abandoned him there like that, she'd give the tosser cause for regret. It had taken a while to earn the cat's trust. "Jealous, Dickens?

His eyes were a far richer shade than yours, but you're still my favorite fellow."

He merely purred in response and began licking his paw.

Picking up her till, she popped into her small office, crossed over to a painting of a woman poised on a ladder while reaching for a book, and took it down to reveal the safe securely tucked away behind it. Tugging free the chain hidden beneath her collar, she pulled forth the key and inserted it into the lock, always feeling a bit mysterious that she had a place in which to secret things away. After swinging open the door, she tucked the till inside and then relocked the safe. The painting went back onto its spot on the wall, and she stuffed the key behind her bodice.

That chore taken care of, she snatched up her small flower-adorned hat, moved over to the oval mirror hanging on the wall, and positioned the brim just so, giving her a rather sophisticated air. From her siblings, she'd learned how she presented herself should reflect all she hoped to attain. "Half the trick is leading people to believe you've met with success," Mick had told her the day she opened the shop.

Grabbing a tiny book and slipping it into her pocket—most of her frocks contained large pockets where she could easily carry things—she wandered across her beloved shop to the door and stepped out onto the walk.

People were scurrying about, some on their way home from their jobs, others from their shopping expeditions. The fragrance of freshly baked bread wafted on the air, courtesy of the bakery two doors down. They were no doubt finishing up the order they would deliver to the hotel for the guests who dined there that evening. The elegant dining room was gaining a reputation for serving delicious meals—not that Mick would have settled for anything less than perfection. After locking up, Fancy strolled up the street.

"Hello, Miss Trewlove," a young woman with a lad and a lass clinging to her skirts called out as she hurried the little ones along.

"Good evening, Mrs. Byng. Will I be seeing you during story

time tomorrow?" Every Friday afternoon, Fancy gathered children in her shop and read to them.

"My moppets wouldn't miss it."

Fancy suspected her son and daughter favored the sweets she provided as much as the stories. While this area resembled the rookeries not in the least, she was very much aware that many of these folks had little money left over once they'd paid for necessities and it made her feel charitable to offer them something extra. Her afternoon readings provided a bit of respite to many of the mothers, especially those with numerous small tykes. She often noticed some of them dozing while Fancy worked to keep their little ones entertained. Knowing few households contained books, she liked the notion of not only introducing children to the power of reading, but possibly giving them a desire to attend school. While the recently passed Forster Education Act provided public funding for children whose parents couldn't afford to pay their education fees, it hadn't made school attendance compulsory, which she found unacceptable. Not all parents cared to see their children's lives improved. She'd grown up in an area where some had felt it was more important for their broods to work and provide coins for the family coffers than to spend a few hours each day in a classroom.

Several other people greeted her as she carried on. She would miss living here when she married, but was well aware that her future husband, no matter his title, would have a posh residence in an exclusive area of London that he would expect her to share with him. To be a proper lady, she would have to give up the management of her shop. Although Gillie still ran her tavern, it had always been understood that Fancy was destined to become a scion of Society, and that wouldn't happen unless she immersed herself fully into that culture by making morning calls, as well as hosting afternoon teas, dinners, and balls. Not to mention providing her husband with his heir and spare and a daughter or two.

But until her official introduction into Society, she was free to do as she pleased, and it pleased her to have dinner at the Jolly

Roger, a pub Gillie had opened in the area six months earlier. Because she was busy managing her tavern, the Mermaid and Unicorn, overseeing her duchess duties, and raising the daughter she'd delivered to the duke, she'd handed the reins of her new venture over to Roger, who'd assisted her at the Mermaid. The cook, who also happened to be his love, had come over with him. Hannah prepared simple fare that was a delight to the palate and often reminded Fancy of her mum's cooking.

While she appreciated having her own lodgings, she did miss her mum quite a bit, just as she had when she'd been off at a posh finishing school paid for by Mick as the first step in achieving her mum's dream of seeing Fancy well married. As a result, her manners were above reproach, her speech more refined, and she didn't sound as though she crawled out from the gutter.

Although she'd never truly spoken as though she came from humble origins. Gillie had insisted all her siblings speak well, with clear pronunciation, because she believed proper speech was essential to bettering one's life, and her first employer had educated her regarding correct enunciation. Before Fancy had ever attended a formal classroom, Gillie had sat her down and taught her how to speak like those who lived in the most affluent areas of London.

While Fancy had made the most of her time at the finishing school and understood the need to learn how to speak, walk, and eat as those among the upper classes did, she had resented the time it had required to be away from her family. Although her brothers and Gillie were much older than she was and had moved to their own lodgings before she'd seen half a dozen years, they'd remained a constant in her life, frequently visiting, taking her on outings, bringing her sweets, dolls, and other gifts. They'd spoiled her rotten—still did—and she loved every one of them for it, didn't want to let them down by not earning a place within Society that would make them proud. The magnitude of what she needed to accomplish weighed on her constantly. But she would see it through and not give her family any cause to be ashamed of her.

Enough thinking about that. She was going to spoil her dinner if all those thoughts kept rumbling around in her mind. She'd headed to the pub for the distraction it would provide. Opening the heavy door, she stepped over the threshold and stumbled to a stop, very nearly smashing her nose against the broad wall that appeared before her. Not a wall. A chest. One that had been in her shop only moments earlier. Plastering a smile on her face, she looked up. "Hello again."

"Hello."

Although undeniably handsome, if he would only sport a grin, he'd be quite devastating. "You ate rather quickly."

"I've been waiting for a table. It seems none are to be had."

"Oh." She'd arrived later than usual. Glancing around, she could see he had the right of it, but then on the other side of the room—

"Look! One at the back there is becoming available now." Two gents were heading away from a small square table nestled up against the wall.

"I'll snag it for you."

Before she could tell him that it was his by rights for being there ahead of her, he was gone, his long legs and lithe frame making short work of his edging his way between the crowded tables until he reached the empty one only seconds before the lad with a small copper tub did. Without being told, the young man who had probably seen fifteen or sixteen years began gathering up platters and glassware before using a damp linen to wipe the top of the table and the wooden seats of the chairs.

The customer who had been in her shop earlier lifted his arm and beckoned her over. She was struck by the ease with which he communicated a great deal with so simple a movement, as though he were accustomed to commanding and being obeyed without question. With no help for it, she wended her way around the tables, chairs, benches, and people, greeting those she knew as she passed by. Finally, she reached him. "While I appreciate your gallantry, you were here before me. The table should be yours."

"You'd have arrived ahead of me if I'd not delayed you in your shop."

His mien reminded her of her brothers, and she was well aware of the time involved in striving to win an argument with them, so she graciously accepted her defeat, but decided one last rally was in order. "As there are two chairs, I don't see why we can't share the table."

He narrowed his eyes slightly, in what appeared to be disapproval, as though she'd suggested they strip off their clothes and dart about through the establishment. "You're an unaccompanied woman."

"Which is the reason the other chair is available." She kept her tone amiable and pleasant, rather than pointing out she knew exactly what she was. For the span of a heartbeat, she thought he was going to smile, but he seemed to be fighting his inclination to do so. "Please. You can read your book and I'll read mine. We needn't speak. It'll be as though we're dining alone."

"You have a book?"

"A miniature. In the pocket of my skirt. Please join me. Otherwise, guilt shall gnaw at me for delaying your dinner, and I won't enjoy mine." She didn't know why she was insisting when he seemed so uninterested in her company, but she never had liked the thought of inconveniencing another.

With a slight bowing of his head, he pulled out a chair and indicated it was for her. Gracefully, because she'd mastered the lessons that had taught her it was the only way a lady sat, she eased down to the wooden seat, grateful when he took the one opposite her, yet surprised he exhibited almost as much grace. She'd watched countless men drop into their chairs within these walls. Few did it with such deliberate care, as though every muscle, bone, and bit of sinew had been trained to respond with an elegance of motion, as if their owner were accustomed to being observed and intended to ensure none found fault with him. He tugged off his gloves and set them aside, while she placed hers across her lap.

"Evenin', Miss Trewlove."

She glanced up at the young woman whose face was flushed with her efforts and her bosom in danger of breaking free of her black bodice's restraints. "Hello, Becky."

"Wot ye be havin' this evenin'?"

"What has Hannah prepared?"

"A lovely shepherd's pie 'n' mutton stew."

"I'll have the pie and half a pint of light beer."

"Yes, miss. And ye, sir?"

"I'll have the pie as well, along with a pint of Guinness."

"Very good, sir. I'll be back in a tick."

Fancy watched as Becky hurried off, grabbing empty tankards and glasses as she went, nodding toward those asking for another pint or beverage. The woman was like a juggler, tossing far too many balls in the air, yet effectively keeping each one from landing on the ground.

"Miss *Trewlove*."

The quietly spoken name, drawn-out almost like it was a bit of confection to be savored, caused her attention to swing back to her table companion. "You say that as though you didn't know who I was."

"I didn't. I assume you're related to Mick Trewlove."

She couldn't stop her pride in her brother's accomplishments from beaming forth. "I'm his younger sister. And you're not to blame. We never introduced ourselves. I'm Fancy Trewlove."

"The Fancy Book Emporium." He mulled it over. "The name of your shop is lacking an apostrophe and an *S*."

Trust a man to point out the obvious or seek to correct what needed no correction. "Their omission was intentional. It's a play on my name you see. A bit of fun. You've yet to tell me who you are."

A hesitation as though he weren't quite sure of himself. "Matthew Sommersby. Two *M*s."

She held out her hand. "It's very nice to meet you, Matthew Sommersby, two *M*s."

The smile he bestowed upon her fairly stole her breath. She'd seen hints of it, a twitch here, a small curl of a corner there, but when he spread his lips into a full smile that revealed perfect straight teeth, when his eyes sparkled as though he was truly pleased, she found herself astounded by the seeming swiftness with which he'd been transformed from a man of such seriousness to one who projected an image more welcoming, more inviting, more sensual, more . . . everything.

"A pleasure, Miss Trewlove." His palm, hinting at the slightest roughness like the finest grains of sand on a beach beneath her soles, came to rest against hers. For some reason she envisioned him kissing the tips of her fingers. He possessed an elegance and refinement that reminded her of courtly gestures. But he merely released his hold, then opened and closed his hand as though wanting to hoard the sensation he'd experienced while touching her.

"I assume you live in the area," she said.

"The next street over. 86 Ettie Lane. I can see the back of your shop from my upstairs window."

Which meant he had a view of her bedchamber, or at least the light from it before she closed the draperies. She doubted he could actually see inside to make note of the furnishings, although she might be visible walking about. "Mick named the street after our mother. Have you lived there long?"

"A little over a fortnight now."

"How are you finding it?"

"To my liking thus far."

"My brother has worked hard to make the area welcom—"

"Here you are, loves," Becky said, setting the pewter tankards on the table. "Drink up 'n' enjoy. Food'll be here shortly."

After the girl wandered off, Fancy continued, "Welcoming, I was going to say." She lifted her tankard. "Cheers."

While he lifted his pint, she took a sip, enjoying the crisp flavor. Gillie served only the best. Watching as he turned back the cover on his recent purchase, she removed the miniature book from her pocket, taking satisfaction from his gaze darting over to capture her movements, unsure why she wanted to bask in his attention. Perhaps because she'd never garnered a man's full interest before. It was no secret in the area where she'd grown up that her family considered her destined for greater things, so most of the boys had kept their distance, none of them wanting to face her irritatingly intimidating brothers.

"What are you reading?" he asked.

"Aesop's Fables."

"Have you a favorite?"

"The Ant and the Grasshopper, I think. It applies to my family. They've always worked hard, seldom taken time for play. Have you one you favor, one to which you can relate, perhaps?"

"The Fox and the Crow. Be wary of flatterers, or something to that effect."

She could have sworn a tinge of bitterness laced his voice and wondered at the cause. Yet she didn't know him well enough to ask for the reasons behind his selection. Although his choice of fable was certainly one she should take to heart when she began making the social rounds. Although as she understood it, the entire Season revolved around flattery. "Have you any advice on how to differentiate between flattery and honest compliments?"

"Unfortunately, no."

Chapter 3

*N*ot that Matthew Sommersby wasn't presently tempted to let loose with a foray into flattery that would have his dinner companion blushing with pleasure. It had been a good long while since he'd been drawn to a woman.

He wasn't certain he'd ever met anyone as small of stature as she was who still managed to project such a large presence. The Queen perhaps. The moment he'd walked into the shop, Miss Trewlove had caught his attention without artifice or fawning or inuendo. She'd merely welcomed him with a warm smile and a sultry voice that had caused him to recheck his surroundings to ensure he'd entered a bookshop and not a brothel. His mind had filled with images of that voice lowered into a rasp as she whispered wicked suggestions in his ear. He had no idea why he'd reacted to her as he had. Most certainly she was a beautiful woman with her high cheekbones, delicate square jaw, and inviting brown eyes, but her attraction had more to do with her confidence and bearing.

He shouldn't have been surprised, at least not once he realized she was a Trewlove. In spite of their humble origins, they were making their mark on Society—Mick Trewlove especially with his tearing down of what had been left to rot and replacing it with buildings in which merchants and residents could take pride. It was one of the reasons Matthew had decided to lease a terrace house here. It was modern and clean, while the area itself provided a good many amenities.

"Why a bookshop?" he asked.

The smile she bestowed upon him seemed to encompass every aspect of her, to reveal her very soul. "The simple answer is that I love stories, but there's more to it than that. My siblings are all quite a bit older than I am. My mother sent them to a nearby ragged school. It cost her nothing as the schools are free, funded by the generosity of others. Lessons were only given in the morning, and they were only allowed to attend until they were eleven, so all that was over by the time I came around. But they learned to read, you see, and after that there was no stopping them."

The fire in her voice, her expression, held him captivated. He couldn't recall the last time he'd felt passionate about anything.

"They continued to educate themselves. Informally. They pooled their earnings together and paid a guinea a year to a lending library. They could only borrow one book at a time, and they took turns deciding who would choose the book to be borrowed, but it opened up worlds to them—and to me. My fondest memories are of each of them reading to me, when I was quite small. It was magical. So, I wanted to open a bookshop in order to surround myself with the stories that my brothers and sister had loved enough to share with me. When I see the spines lined up on a shelf, it makes me happy. I'm happier still when someone takes a book home with them. Tales of adventure or romance or mystery bring undeniable and unending joy. Biographies, history, geography expand our knowledge of what surrounds us. Even if I don't necessarily agree with all the sentiments expressed, I find value in every word written, every word read. That's the reason I have a bookshop."

As though she'd not just upended his world with her impassioned diatribe, she settled back and took a long, slow sip of her beer. When she was done, she licked her lips before lifting her gaze back to his, and he couldn't help but believe he'd never been so enthralled by a person in his entire life, nor would he ever again be so. Her love of books was genuine, *she* was genuine.

"Did you attend the ragged schools?" Knowing the moniker

had come about because so many of the children who attended wore rags, he hated the thought of her in worn and tattered frocks, possibly without shoes. Although he was aware people grew up in poverty, he'd never before carried on a conversation with one who had. He routinely made donations to one charity or another but didn't have an active role in doing good works. He was suddenly feeling quite ashamed that his lack of action might have resulted in a harsher life for her or others.

"Oh no. By the time I was old enough to be schooled, my siblings were all working, and they again pooled their coins, this time to ensure I went to a private school and later to a finishing school. In both cases, the students' parents were merchants, bankers, tradesmen, or some other occupation that saw them with a decent income, but still I wasn't fully embraced. Unfortunately, the circumstances of my birth carry a stigma." She didn't elaborate regarding the circumstances, but then she didn't need to. It was common knowledge that the Trewloves wore their bastardy like a badge of honor. "I found my years at school quite lonely, not that I ever told my siblings that. I don't know why I confessed it to you or rambled on about it. I do hope you'll forgive my dip into self-pity."

"It was hardly self-pity, Miss Trewlove." He didn't want to envision her sitting alone during meals, standing at the edge of a garden, not invited into a game of tag. Although perhaps whatever she'd endured had motivated her to invite him to join her tonight. He was beginning to feel grateful she had. She was without guile and he found it refreshing.

EMBARRASSED TO HAVE shared such intimate and personal memories and thoughts with a stranger, Fancy nodded toward the book he'd placed on the table. "I'd promised you could read if you took the chair."

"So you did."

Striving to make sense of the words in her book was proving to be an exercise in futility. Generally, she had no trouble at all blocking out any distractions when she became lost in a book, but her attention wasn't usually snagged by a gentleman whose stories she wished to learn—for surely, he had stories to tell. He looked to be on the younger side of thirty. Where had he come from before landing here? How did he earn wages?

With her return, Becky set a bowl of shepherd's pie, a piece of linen, and a spoon in front of each of them before rushing off to see to other customers. Mr. Sommersby set his book aside and, in unison, they draped their linen napkins across their laps. He gathered up some pie, and she fought against watching his mouth close over the spoon, but it was a battle she lost, imagining those lips closing over hers. Whatever was wrong with her to allow such naughty thoughts to travel through her mind? Averting her gaze, she concentrated on her own meal.

"Difficult to read whilst eating," he said quietly.

She usually managed it quite well, especially in her youth, much to her mum's dismay since it wasn't the way that proper ladies were to occupy their time at the table. With conversation, they were to involve themselves in other people's lives, listen attentively, gleaning bits of information in order to gain an understanding of the person, build an image of his or her character. With Mr. Sommersby she was failing miserably, which didn't bode well for her entrée into Society and judging the man who might ask for her hand.

"I'm a bit surprised," he continued, "Mick Trewlove's sister would take her meal here and not dine with him in his lodgings at the hotel."

Her brother had an office where he conducted business and a suite of private rooms on the top floor. Mr. Sommersby would have become aware of those facts when he let his residence, since he'd have had to visit the office to sign his lease agreement. "I wasn't in the mood to be put through my paces," she answered honestly.

He arched a dark brow in question.

"Wednesday next, I'll be formally introduced into Society at a ball that my sister, Gillie—the Duchess of Thornley—is hosting in my honor."

All her family members were a bit nervous, not quite sure whether people would attend out of curiosity about the commoner who had caught the attention of one of the most powerful dukes in Britain or if no one would show at all, signaling the *ton's* displeasure that the Duke of Thornley had married beneath him.

Noting the speculation in his gaze, she continued, "As for how I have a sister who is a duchess—"

"I doubt a soul in London exists who hasn't heard tales regarding the Trewloves and their various marriages among the nobility."

Mick had married Lady Aslyn, daughter to the deceased Earl of Eames and ward of the Duke of Hedley—Mick's father, as it turned out, not that the man had ever publicly acknowledged Mick as his son, although they had developed a close relationship of late and were often seen together. Finn had taken to wife Lady Lavinia while Aiden had wed Selena, a widowed duchess. Then, of course, there was Gillie with her duke. Her siblings' marriages should have given them all the social acceptance they craved, but it seemed the aristocracy was reticent when it came to welcoming newcomers into their midst.

"I suppose there is some truth in that. They are all the talk from what I understand. They've set rather high standards and expectations for me, even before they began collecting aristocratic spouses. So, when I have dinner with Mick, he and his wife, bless them, are insistent we follow proper etiquette while dining—selecting the correct utensil from among the ridiculous number set out on the table—and discuss only topics appropriate for dining with the nobs. When I marry a lord, my life will become naught but nights of formal dining and quiet discussions about boring subjects." She looked around her. "I doubt there will be robust laughter or claps on the back or such astonishing joy at reaching the end of a hard day and having a bit of time to relax with friends. So I came here tonight to avoid having to face any faults with my behavior and to enjoy the revelry surrounding me."

"Then why seek to a marry a lord?" His tone was flat, tinged

with a bit of disapproval, as though he had the right to be offended by her plans.

She wasn't keen to have him sitting in judgment of her. "My
family expects it. I grew up expecting it. To be honest, there are
few ways for a woman to better herself except through marriage.
Business ownership or hard work might gain her more success
than a man but it doesn't garner the same amount of respect. It's
rather irritating really, but that is the way of the world. You can't
disagree with my assessment, surely."

"I don't suppose I gave it a great deal of thought, one way or
another. It depends on the lengths you'll go to in order to acquire
what you want."

"All the lengths that are necessary. Would you not do the
same?"

"I'm not certain I would."

"Then I assume you are fortunate, and life has offered you few
challenges."

"You would assume incorrectly." As though embarrassed by
his words, he dropped his gaze to his bowl and began stabbing
the fluffy potatoes on top into the meat filling.

God. How was it that they'd become so short with each other?
A change in subject was needed. "If I may be so bold, you don't
sound as though you come from the streets. I'd wager you've had
some education."

"My father insisted."

"You strike me as being a solicitor. Or a banker, perhaps." Someone with a position of authority and influence. It was simply the
way he held himself, the confidence that rolled off him in waves.

"Nothing quite so interesting, I assure you."

His tone indicated that line of conversation was at an end, but
she wasn't yet ready to let it go. "Now you've piqued my curiosity,
Mr. Sommersby. How do you earn your way?"

He studied her for a long moment, as though torn between telling her to go to the devil or answering with honesty. Finally, she
said, "I am a gentleman with means."

Which told her nothing at all. Had an inheritance fallen into his hands? Had he achieved success at business, investment, with the horses, or gambling? "How do you spend your day?"

"Doing whatever I please."

"Yet you claimed not to be fortunate."

"Everything comes with a price, Miss Trewlove."

What price had he paid? Not that it was any of her business, not that she was rude enough to inquire. She'd already skirted the edge of good manners. Yet, she couldn't deny being curious about him. It was odd how he drew her interest when no other man had—not in this way at least.

She'd found numerous men attractive certainly but had never had her heart fluttering because of the beauty of one of them. She'd never wanted to delve into every aspect of one of their lives, didn't know why she wanted to know all the details of his. Perhaps it was simply that she'd begun preparing herself for analyzing the men she would meet next week as potential husbands, and her mind had decided to practice her skills in order to hone them. Or perhaps he piqued her interest simply because he seemed so determined not to be known.

While they'd been conversing, they'd managed to finish off their meal. Becky hurried over. "Will there be anythin' else, loves?"

"Nothing for me," Fancy said.

"Nor for me," he responded.

"Is 'e with ye, Miss Trewlove?"

She glanced over to see his brow deeply furrowed, and confusion mirrored in his eyes. It was time to repay his earlier generosity in offering her the table. "Yes."

Becky smiled brightly. "Meal is on the house, then."

"No," he said quickly, brusquely. "I'll pay for my meal."

"But yer with Miss Trewlove 'n' Trewloves don't pay in a Trewlove establishment."

"This is a Trewlove pub?"

"My sister Gillie's," Fancy told him.

"The duchess."

She smiled because keeping up with her family members was a task, and it seemed he'd already mastered it. "Yes."

Coming to her feet, aware of him quickly following suit, she reached into her pocket and pulled out a crown. Unfortunately, the newspaper clipping came out with it and fluttered down to land near the toe of his polished boot. Before she could react, he was reaching down to gather it up. She pressed the coin into the serving girl's hand. "This is for you, Becky."

"Ah, Miss Trewlove, ye don't 'ave—"

"You took such good care of us. Thank you."

The girl gave a quick bob of her knees. "Appreciate it, miss, sir." Then someone was calling for her, and she was racing off to see to another's needs.

When Fancy looked at Mr. Sommersby, it was to discover him staring at the embarrassing clipping that had the audacity to open itself up as it made its way down to the floor. She held out her hand. "I'll relieve you of that now."

"Why would you carry this about with you?"

"Because I find the letter terribly romantic and enjoy reading it. And if I may be honest"—she didn't know why she felt a need to confess to him, perhaps because she feared without further justification, he would think her a silly chit—"I hope to meet Lord Rosemont at the ball next week and have the opportunity to spend time in his company." To offer her condolences, to come to know better a man who had given his wife so much of his heart.

Mr. Sommersby hesitated several heartbeats before carefully folding the letter and placing it in her waiting palm. "It is a dangerous thing, indeed, Miss Trewlove, to fall in love with a man before ever having met him."

Chapter 4

*I*f the mutinous glimmer in her eyes was any indication, Miss Trewlove had not taken kindly to his remark. He didn't know why he'd made it. What did he care if she went around snipping poppycock from newspapers and carrying it about in her pocket?

Perhaps because he realized, much to his mortification, that he'd misjudged her. He'd viewed her as open and honest, had begun to take more than a casual interest in her, only to learn that a devious mind possibly lurked behind those deep brown eyes that reminded him of a doe he'd adopted as a pet when he was a lad and spent most of his time in the countryside.

It irked, irked that she was planning to land a lord and would use any means necessary to obtain him. He found it more irritating that because of a daft letter, she might possibly be setting her sights on the Earl of Rosemont.

"I'm not in love with him," she finally snapped, stuffing the clipping back into her skirt pocket. "His wife adored him, and I find it commendable that he should inspire such devotion. But more, her entreaty to bring him out of his sorrow touched my heart. Not that it's any of your concern nor should I have to justify myself." She heaved an impatient sigh. "Thank you for providing conversation during dinner. It's late. I must be off."

It had grown dark. He couldn't remember the last time he'd eaten a leisurely meal. Generally, he wolfed down his food so the task of providing his body with sustenance was done, and he could move on to drink. "I'll escort you back to your shop."

"I'm fine on my own. No one would dare accost me. They know my brothers would see them dead."

"You're assuming everyone hereabouts knows you're a Trewlove. I didn't."

She opened her mouth to protest, and quickly shut it, obviously coming to the realization he'd already won the argument. "I can't stop you if you've a mind to accompany me."

However, she was certainly determined to give it a go, because she turned on her heel and marched briskly for the door, a couple of lads jumping out of her way, obviously realizing they were in danger of being mowed down. Just as she neared the door, he easily caught up to her, reached around her, grabbed the handle, and pulled. She passed over the threshold with a muttered "thank you" that, for some inexplicable reason, made him smile for the second time that evening. He'd grown accustomed to happiness being absent for some time and it was a strange thing to feel it tapping on his shoulder.

In silence, guided by the lit streetlamps, they crossed the street and strolled along the bricked pavement until they arrived at her shop. She reached into her pocket and withdrew a key. This time no paper fluttered to the ground. After unlocking the door, she went still a heartbeat before looking over her shoulder. "I hope you won't be a stranger to the shop, Mr. Sommersby."

She was protecting her business. In spite of her ambitions. Or perhaps because of them. She didn't strike him as a woman who would accept failure of any kind, including when it came to securing her lord. "I'm certain I'll be in want of another book before long, Miss Trewlove. Sleep well."

Pushing open the door, she slipped through and closed it in her wake. He heard the turn of the lock. She'd left a gaslight burning, and he waited until the main part of her shop went dark. Although the windows sporting little shelves for books and knickknacks prevented him from having a clear view inside, he still managed to follow the journey of a lamp's glow as it rose higher—no doubt her climbing the stairs—until it disappeared from his sight, assuring him that she would soon be safely tucked into her rooms. Glancing around, he considered returning to the pub for another brew but as she was no longer there, the din within those walls that usually drowned out his thoughts didn't hold much appeal.

He headed down the street and turned the corner. Looking up at the brick building, he could see pale light spilling out of a window on the top floor. She was in her rooms now, undoubtedly preparing for bed, removing the pins from her midnight-black hair, dragging the brush through the long strands. Braiding it. Then she would slowly unbutton the bodice of her navy frock—

His thoughts came to an abrupt halt. He was not going to be enticed into falling into her web of deceit by her passion for books or her ability to create a shop that invited one in and offered comfort as welcoming as a warm blanket on a chilly evening. Or her large eyes or her pretty face or her kindness to a pub serving girl or her welcoming of a stranger.

He passed the mews that ran between her shop and his residence. Continuing on, he took a right at the street, turned up the path to his terrace house, jogged up the steps, and let himself in. Reaching for the gaslight, he turned up the flame until the soft yellow glow illuminated the front parlor. He went straight ahead through the tiny hallway, ignoring the narrow stairs that led to the floor where he slept, and entered the small room where he ate the meals prepared by the woman he'd hired to come in daily to cook in the small kitchen beyond and keep things tidy. A stuffed chair rested near the fireplace, and he'd spent many an evening reading there. He went over to the plain table that housed a solitary decanter and poured himself a tumbler of scotch.

With comfort in hand, he climbed the stairs. At the top, the narrow landing branched off into a door on either side. He went through the one on his right, into his bedchamber, simply furnished with a fourposter bed, a table beside it, an armoire across from it, and a high-backed brocade chair in the corner. He carried on until he reached the window.

Taking a sip of his scotch, he leaned a shoulder against the window casing. When he was in a contemplative mood, he preferred to become lost in whatever lay beyond his own window. In the early mornings, he'd watched drays pulled by large horses make their way through the mews. Late at night, he'd often witnessed drunkards stumbling around. He'd seen a number of cats, a few dogs, and the occasional child. And sometimes, like tonight, his gaze would drift upward to the faint glow from her window spilling into the darkness and defeating a small part of it. Often he wished it would reach into his soul and conquer the black void that resided there.

Because it was a terrible abyss of emptiness and despair, craving that which he'd never possessed and never would: love. Having put his heart at risk once, he was determined to never do so again.

Watching shadows moving behind the drawn curtains on the top floor of the bookshop, he wondered if the window looked into her bedchamber, if he was observing his neighbor preparing for sleep. He wondered if Fancy Trewlove took the Earl of Rosemont into her dreams.

The poor girl was going to be disappointed when she attended her first ball because her hopes of being introduced to Rosemont would be dashed. He would not bow before her, take her hand, and kiss it. He would not ask her for a dance, hold her in his arms, and sweep her over a polished parquet floor. He wouldn't tell her that she had the most expressive brown eyes he'd ever seen. He wouldn't confess that more than once during dinner, he'd decided that her mouth had been perfectly designed for kissing.

No, the Earl of Rosemont would do none of those things.

Because now he knew her plans, and he wanted no part of them or her.

Chapter 5

At half seven the following morning, Fancy rapped her knuckles on the door to her brother's suite of rooms in the hotel. It was quickly opened by a tall footman who bowed deferentially. "Good morning, Miss Trewlove."

"How are you this fine morning, James?" She skirted around him, removed her hat and gloves, and handed them over to him.

"Very fine, miss. It's kind of you to inquire."

Hardly. It was simply good manners, although she was given to understand the nobility never thanked their servants or engaged them in idle conversation. "I'll see myself to breakfast."

"Very good, miss."

As she made her way down the corridor, she couldn't help but reflect at how comfortable she felt within her brother's lodgings. As she stepped into the smaller dining room, Mick set his newspaper aside and came to his feet. Not that he'd been reading it. Rather he'd been leaning toward his wife seated beside him and telling her something that caused her cheeks to turn a pinkish hue. Fancy wanted that, a man who, long after they'd been married, would whisper wicked things in her ear.

"Good morning, little sister," Mick said, the normal teasing tinging his tone because she was not only the youngest but the smallest of Ettie Trewlove's children. Even Gillie was nearly as tall as her brothers. "How are you this morning?"

A bit tired. Thanks to Mr. Sommersby, she'd not slept well.

Surreptitiously parting the drapes just enough to peer through them, she'd seen him standing in the window of his bedchamber, looking out. Because he was too far away for her to see his features clearly, she couldn't be sure if he was staring at the mews or the sky or even had his eyes closed. His movements, however, were more discernible. He'd leaned against the window casing and sipped something. Scotch most likely. Lazily, languidly. As though the view were arresting and deserving of his utmost attention.

She'd taken those damned green eyes into her slumber and dreamed of a man who enjoyed reading penny dreadfuls, whispering the words provocatively in her ear as his hands stroked places that had never been stroked by a man. She'd grown warm, writhing with need, only to awaken to find her blankets and sheet on the floor, Dickens peering out from beneath the mound with a narrowed glare, leaving her to wonder if perhaps she'd kicked him out of the bed as well. Not that she would confess all that to her brother.

"Doing very well, thank you. And you?" She headed for the sideboard where his personal cook had prepared a virtual feast, not that any of it would go to waste. Aslyn always distributed any remaining food to area shelters tasked with feeding the hungry.

"Couldn't be better."

She walked to the table where a footman pulled out a chair for her. After sitting, she looked at Aslyn. "And you?"

"Perfect."

"In every way," Mick added as he took his seat.

Of all her brothers, Mick was the last one she'd ever expected to be so frightfully besotted. Another reason she didn't often take her dinners here. While she was ecstatic that the couple had fallen so madly in love, it was difficult to watch when she had yet to acquire the same level of devotion. Besides, she often felt like an intruder, knowing if she weren't present a good deal more touching, stroking, and kissing would go on.

"How did you spend your evening?" Mick asked.

"I had dinner at the Jolly Roger. When I returned to the shop, I stacked five books on my head and walked up the stairs balancing them—"

"Did you really?" Aslyn asked. "Five?"

Fancy smiled softly, imagining her sister-by-marriage had spent a good deal of time balancing books atop her head because she possessed one of the finest postures around. "No, I was only jesting. I think I have my walk down pat. I didn't practice anything at all. I simply read." She thought about mentioning Mr. Sommersby, finding out if Mick knew anything at all about his tenant, but she wanted to hold the gentleman close, keep him just for herself. She also wanted to avoid an inquisition. How had she met him? How well did she know him? Was he trustworthy? How did she know? And it wouldn't do at all for it to be known she'd spent time in his company without a chaperone, although she could effectively argue she'd been watched over by the staff at the Jolly Roger. He might even take it upon himself to send Mr. Sommersby packing if he thought the man would distract Fancy from reaching the goal her family had set for her.

"You will have little time for reading once your Season gets underway," Aslyn said. "I've been making a list of the women on whom we'll make morning calls after your introduction into Society. And I've no doubt some will make calls upon you. I'm wondering if it might be better if you spent your days here, since we'll let it be known that ours is the residence where you will take callers. We'll certainly want the gentlemen to visit you here, so you can be properly chaperoned."

"You're optimistic. I think it'll work exceedingly well if you simply send a servant over to fetch me when I'm needed." She didn't want to give up any more time in her shop than she had to because a day would arrive when she'd have to give it up altogether. "Perhaps I'll even entertain a few in the shop. I could serve tea in the reading parlor." It was a room above the shop set aside for people to lounge about in comfortable chairs and read to their heart's content. "It would only require having one of your maids come over to prepare tea in the kitchen in my lodgings."

"I suppose that's an option. Shall we see how it goes?" Which meant Aslyn didn't much like the option. "And, of course, there are always the gardens here."

Behind the hotel, away from the street, Mick had created an oasis of greenery where his guests could take tea, read, or stroll about. It might be more relaxing, less taxing, to take her callers there. If she had callers. She was striving to keep her expectations modest and realistic so as not to be frightfully disappointed when her entrée into Society happened at a snail's pace.

With her fork, she poked at her buttered eggs. Suddenly nothing before her seemed appetizing. Perhaps because the thought of gentlemen calling on her reminded her of Mr. Sommersby's admonishment. *It is a dangerous thing, indeed, to fall in love with a man before ever having met him.*

Mr. Sommersby's reaction had taken her aback. He'd sounded almost jealous, although certainly she'd misread that. They'd only just met, and he hadn't given any indication he had anything other than a friendly interest in her—if even that. Perhaps it was simply that he held a disdain for the aristocracy. He might be a gentleman of means, but if he was living in this area of London and not Mayfair, then his means were no doubt quite modest.

As she'd told him, she was not in love with the Earl of Rosemont. The letter merely served as an example of what Fancy hoped to acquire. Still it had been embarrassing to be caught with it in her pocket. "Aslyn, are you acquainted with Lord Rosemont?"

The widening of her eyes indicated she was surprised by the question. It was one Fancy should have thought to ask sooner since Aslyn had once inhabited the same world as the earl.

"We were introduced, yes, but only in passing. We never spoke at length. I suppose you're thinking of the letter his wife arranged to be printed in the *Times.*"

"I know it's silly to place such stock in a letter a woman wrote on her deathbed, but that's the very reason I find it so compelling, so persuasive—that she would go to such bother before leaving this world. He must be an extraordinary man."

"One would think. However, knowing he would never be a suitor, I paid very little attention to him." She gave a light laugh. "Although to be honest, I saw most men as only a potential dance partner and little else because I always expected to marry Kipwick." The Duke of Hedley's son and heir. Mick had stolen her away from him, originally with the intention of ruining her, but then she'd conquered his heart.

Fancy watched as Aslyn reached over and threaded her fingers through Mick's. He brought them to his lips and simply held them there, meeting her gaze, his warming. "The best laid plans and all that."

Aslyn arched a delicate brow. "Are you referring to yours or mine?"

He chuckled low. "Both."

Fancy knew any further conversation on Lord Rosemont would not be had now as the couple were becoming lost in each other. She folded her linen napkin and set it beside her plate. "I should be off."

Guiltily, Aslyn looked at her. "But you hardly ate."

"I had more than enough. Thank you for inviting me to breakfast. Don't bother getting up, Mick." She pushed back her chair and stood. "I'll see myself out."

As she was walking from the room, she heard soft murmuring, a sigh.

Once she left Mick's apartments and was out in the hallway, she glanced over at the glass double doors with "Trewlove" etched in them. She could see Mr. Tittlefitz, Mick's secretary, already at his desk. She wandered over, pushed open one of the doors, and stepped in. He immediately jumped to his feet.

"Miss Trewlove. What a delightful surprise."

He was one of the most positive people she'd ever met. Having been born a bastard and raised in the rookeries, he had every right to be bitter, but instead always reflected an optimism that made him a pleasure to be around. "I was just visiting with my brother. Based on the whispering I heard as I was leaving, I think he might be a while before coming in."

Mr. Tittlefitz blushed profusely, so much so his freckles were fairly obliterated. "He has nothing pressing on the schedule this morning."

She suspected it wouldn't matter what he had on his schedule. Pleasing his wife would always come first. She could only hope her own husband would be as attentive.

"I've had no luck finding someone to help you with the lessons on the nights I can't be there." She and Mr. Tittlefitz volunteered their time two nights a week in order to offer free reading classes to adults who'd had no or very little schooling. She felt guilty that he would have to carry the brunt of the workload once her Season was fully underway. She'd approached some people about filling in for her, but few had the time to spare when it didn't put coins in their pockets. She couldn't ask her married siblings as they would be at the balls. Her brother Beast was making himself scarce of late.

"Do not worry yourself overmuch. I shall have no trouble at all seeing to matters by myself. Although your presence will be sorely missed."

"I fear, Mr. Tittlefitz, I'm going to wish I was helping with lessons rather than being the center of attention at a ball filled with toffs."

"You shall easily win them over, Miss Trewlove. I've no doubt on that score."

"You say the kindest things."

"I would not say them if I did not believe them to be true."

One of the reasons he was such an effective teacher was because he was so very skilled at offering heartfelt encouragement. "I won't keep you but will continue to give thought as to whom I might entice into helping you when I'm unavailable. It's just a bit of a challenge when most people in the area lead such busy lives, working long hours with little time for leisure—"

Her thoughts leapt to last evening's dinner companion. Would she be able to entice him into helping? Things between them had been awkward at the end, but she could set that aside for a greater good. The question was: Would he?

"Are you all right, miss?"

She gave her head a little shake. "Yes. I just had a thought. A possible solution to our dilemma. I'll have to ponder it a bit more. Have a good day, Mr. Tittlefitz."

"You as well, Miss Trewlove."

Before leaving the hotel, she stopped in the kitchen where one of the staff members gave her a small pitcher of cream. When she returned to her shop, she went upstairs and poured it into a saucer. Dickens immediately arrived to begin lapping it up. He seemed to care little about anything but did love his cream. After putting away her hat and gloves, she returned downstairs.

As always, she simply stood there for a moment, taking in what she had built with help from her family. Every member of her family and Mr. Tittlefitz had been kind enough to help her place the books on the shelves. Everywhere she looked were memories of them assisting her in one way or another, never complaining, doing it all out of the goodness of their hearts. She hadn't expected to find incredible satisfaction in working here. Originally, she'd simply seen it as a way to surround herself with books while filling her days waiting for her first Season. Now it all meant so very much that it would be difficult to walk away from it.

At nine, she unlocked the front door, ready for business. She halfway hoped Mr. Sommersby would have finished his book by now and might drop by to purchase another. She wondered how long he might have stood at that window, how long before he turned away to retire or become lost in the adventures of Dick Turpin. Strange how they'd made a heroic character out of a criminal, but for some reason people expressed a fondness for scoundrels. When it came to the ladies, her brothers had certainly benefited from that attitude.

Matthew Sommersby seemed more gentleman than rogue. As such, perhaps he'd be willing to assist with the classes. If she could reestablish the rapport they'd shared before the clipping had escaped her pocket and caught his attention.

To that end, once Marianne arrived in the late morning to assist her in the shop, she decided to pay the gent around the corner a visit.

The streets and pavements were bustling with activity as people went about their daily chores and business. She greeted by name those she knew, gave a smile and nod to those she didn't. As she made her way past the mews, glancing up at the window in which he'd been standing the night before, she couldn't help but wonder how often he stood there, gazing out.

Turning onto Ettie Lane, her heart picked up its tempo while her feet slowed theirs. The residence was neither large nor intimidating, so the apprehension taking hold surprised her. She was intimately familiar with the layout of these terrace houses for they were all the same and Mick had shared the design with her, had even asked for her opinion on the matter. And then she'd watched them being built. It had been exciting to see her brother create so much from nothing.

So it wasn't the building causing her heart to thump wildly, her palms to grow damp within her gloves, but the gentleman who made his lair within those walls. To approach him for a favor when she barely knew him seemed the height of foolishness, but surely he couldn't object to her request when it would serve such a useful purpose.

Gathering her resolve around her like a finely sewn velvet pelisse, she marched up the steps, banged the knocker, and waited impatiently, practically bouncing on the balls of her feet, hoping whatever fault he'd found with her last night had melted away and he'd deliver a warm welcome.

When the door finally opened, she was surprised to find herself staring at a dark-haired woman whose spectacles made her blue eyes seem far too large for her face. "Mrs. Bennett."

"Miss Trewlove, is something amiss?"

"No, I'm simply surprised to see you here." Knowing the man who ran Mick's construction crew and his wife lived on this street, she glanced around. Had she gotten the wrong house? "I was looking for Mr. Sommersby."

"Ah. He's gone out. Said he'd be awhile, that I wasn't to bother with preparing a midday meal for him."

She brought her attention back to Mrs. Bennett. "You cook for him?"

The dear woman bobbed her head. "Aye. He has me come in each morning to tidy up, not that there's ever much to tidy. He has very little furniture, our Mr. Sommersby. Nothing personal like. Mr. Bennett says I'm not to worry myself over it as long as he pays me every day—which he does. But still, there's a loneliness to the place, you know?"

She'd deduced he was a bachelor. Still, it saddened her to think he might be all alone in the world. "He's not been here that long. Perhaps he's just not settled in fully yet."

"Mayhaps. He's never had a visitor as far as I can tell. Always just the one glass that needs washing. Still, I polish everything up, scrub his floors. Won't find a speck of dust when I'm done."

"That's very commendable on your part. Will you let him know I came by and wanted to have a word?"

"Of course, Miss Trewlove. Don't know when he'll be returning, though."

"It's not urgent. Just at his convenience, I'd like to speak with him."

"I'll pass it on."

"Thank you. And give my best to Mr. Bennett."

"I will, miss."

Darting down the steps, she heard the door close. When she reached the pavement, she glanced back, noting now the absence of draperies at the windows, something she'd overlooked watching him the night before. Although perhaps even now he was out seeing about having some sewn. He had Mrs. Bennett to worry over him. She didn't need to do it. Still, she was more convinced than ever that he would welcome the opportunity to assist others in learning to read. What better way to become part and parcel of the whole of the community and to ease one's loneliness?

MISS TREWLOVE HAD occupied Matthew's thoughts through the night and into the following morning, which was deuced irritating, so he'd decided a day seeing to business was called for. After meeting with his man of affairs and then enjoying a leisurely meal at Dodger's, his favorite club, he'd hailed a hansom cab and had instructed the driver to deliver him to the outskirts of Trewlove's domain, because he was in the mood for a stroll before returning to his residence. He stood for a moment taking in the construction that was expanding the area. The pounding of hammers, the grunting of men, the occasional shouted order, and the creaking of wheels beneath a wheelbarrow's weight created a symphony of sounds that hinted at increased wealth and power.

He'd heard similar sounds when he was a lad and went to the coal mines with his father, in order to better understand the workings of the Yorkshire legacy that would be left to him. He'd gone down into the labyrinth of tunnels, even wielded a pickax a time or two, enjoying the stretch of his muscles, the toil, and the concentration his labors required to avoid creating a mishap. All the worries of living up to his father's expectations had dwindled as the target at which he needed to strike had become his sole focus.

He'd applied the same attention to gaining a wife, falling too hard and too fast. He'd actually been grateful his father hadn't been around to witness the cock-up he'd made of that enterprise.

"Where women are concerned, always think with your big head, not your little one," his father had often instructed him. "Females can be manipulative wenches."

His mother had been responsible for teaching his father that lesson. The old man had held no qualms about revealing that tidbit of information. They'd been married a little over six months when Matthew's sister—now the Marchioness of Fairhaven—made her appearance, so evidence existed his father had been caught by deception as well. He'd never heard one kind word spoken between his parents. Their home had been chilled by their disdain for each other. Matthew suspected his father had breathed a sigh of relief when he was born because it gave the earl an excuse for avoiding the countess's bed.

He should have paid more attention, learned from their example. Perhaps then he would have foreseen he was destined to repeat his father's mistake when it came to acquiring a wife. Eventually he would have to marry again in order to secure the lineage, but intended to go about it like a business arrangement, listing out the required qualifications. No brown doe-like eyes, no warm, welcoming smile. Nothing to lure his heart from its guarded state.

Like a dog coming out of a lake ready to rid itself of the water clinging to its fur, he shook off the morose thoughts as he realized he'd reached his residence. The walk hadn't served to maintain the good spirits he'd achieved that morning. It was always a difficult journey down the path of regret.

Unlocking and opening the door to his residence, he staggered to a stop as Mrs. Bennett came hustling out of the room that served as his main living area. He hadn't expected her to be about. She generally left once she'd finished cleaning up after his midday meal. As she hadn't needed to prepare anything for him, she should have been gone by now. "Is something amiss, Mrs. Bennett?"

"Ah, no, sir. But I wanted to let you know Miss Trewlove stopped by. She'd like to have a word."

He furrowed his brow, not certain he'd heard correctly for surely she had no reason to call upon him, not after they'd left matters between them a bit terse. "Miss Trewlove?"

"Aye, sir. She has the bookshop on the high street?"

"I know who she is."

"Well, then, sir, she come by earlier, as I was finishing up."

What the deuce could she possibly want? "It would have been perfectly acceptable to have left me a note, Mrs. Bennett."

"I thought it too important. I wanted to tell you myself, in person."

"While I certainly appreciate your dedication, in the future, a note will suffice. No need to wait about for my arrival. I could have been out until all hours of the night." Not that he'd done that in ages. Reaching into his pocket, he withdrew a coin for her.

"Oh no, sir."

"Please. Your dedication deserves an additional token of appreciation." He'd paid for her daily services before he left.

After she finally took his offering, he saw her to the door and bid her a good day.

Curiosity getting the better of him, he shortly followed suit and left the residence. When he reached the shop, he opened the door, stepped over the threshold, and didn't much like the ferocity with which disappointment slammed into him because a young woman with wheat-colored hair was standing behind the counter. Not the one he expected, not the one he wanted. No, he didn't *want*. Want implied desire, and he most certainly didn't have yearnings when it came to Miss Trewlove.

The young woman bestowed upon him a dazzling smile. "May I help you, sir?"

It hadn't occurred to him that Miss Trewlove wouldn't be about. Yet, still among the musty aroma of all the books she'd gathered to lovingly arrange on shelves and in various places around the room, he detected her scent, a mixture of oranges and a fragrance uniquely her. "If you'd be so good as to let Miss Trewlove know when she returns that Mr. Sommersby stopped by."

Her face brightened further, her eyes widening with pleasure as though she sought nothing more than bringing him joy. "Oh, she's here. Upstairs in the reading parlor."

Unsurprised she'd have such a thing in her shop, he imagined her curled up in an extremely large overstuffed chair.

The clerk was still smiling with exuberance. "You may go up, if you like."

May not *can*. He suspected Miss Trewlove had had a hand in educating the shopgirl, generously sharing what she might have learned in order to better others' lives. "Thank you."

He made short work of ascending the stairs, taking the steps two at time, certainly not because he was anxious to see Miss Trewlove, but he was curious to know why she'd bothered to stop by.

At the landing was a small hallway. Another set of stairs stood at the far end. He assumed they led up to her lodgings, to the window where light often spilled out late into the night.

Bringing his mind back to his purpose in even being here, he noted the open doorway to his right, strode over to it, and came to an abrupt halt. She was indeed sitting in a large overstuffed chair but wasn't curled up. Her posture was erect, graceful, perfect. A dozen or so children in an assortment of poses—sitting cross-legged, on their knees, stretched out on their bellies—were gathered at her feet, all as enthralled as he was. She was reading *Alice's Adventures in Wonderland,* her voice animated as she took on the role of various characters. He was familiar with the tale as he'd given a copy to his niece at Christmas and she'd pleaded with him to read it to her, which of course he had. He had very little resistance when it came to the pleadings of the females ensconced in his life.

Which was no doubt the reason he was here—even if Miss Trewlove wasn't exactly entrenched in his life, she was certainly some part of it. Otherwise, he'd be able to stop thinking about her, from wondering what precisely she was doing every minute she wasn't visible to him. Entertaining children, it seemed.

She lifted her gaze from the words, and it landed on him as solid as a punch. Her mouth curled up at the corners, spreading her lips into a radiant smile as though she'd spied her salvation, the deliverer of whatever she desired. He should turn on his heel and leave at once. Instead, he remained rooted to the spot, held in place by some invisible force—by her and the joy wreathing her face at his arrival.

"Mrs. Byng, will you be so kind as to take over the reading for me, please?" she asked, not taking her gaze from him, as though fearing he might disappear if she should. He wondered if she sensed his reluctance to remain.

A young woman with red hair seemed startled by the request. "Ah, Miss Trewlove, I don't read nearly as good as you."

"You read perfectly well, Mrs. Byng, and I'm certain the children would welcome a respite from my voice for a while. I would be forever in your debt."

"Nonsense," the young woman said, getting up out of her chair. "'Tis me wot owes you."

He wondered exactly what her debt was. Probably a book she'd purchased on credit.

Miss Trewlove rose with such exquisite grace that she'd be putting a good number of Society's ladies to shame the following week. Few matched her poise. After handing the book off to Mrs. Byng, she skirted around the children, patting a head here and there, before strolling elegantly toward him. It had been a long time indeed since he'd felt the pull of a woman. As much as he wanted to be nearer to her, he stayed as he was.

"Mr. Sommersby, I take it you received my message." She sounded breathless, as though she'd run to him, and he envisioned how rushed her breaths might become as passion arced through her beneath his hand, his body. He resented that he felt a spark of envy toward the man who would introduce her to the pleasures to be found when bodies were joined.

"I did."

"May we?" She indicated the hallway.

With a slight bowing of his head, he stepped back into it. She followed. It was more shadowed here, and he imagined the satisfaction to be found in luring her into the darkened corner and taking possession of that mouth that still harbored a slight smile. Not where his mind needed to travel. He nodded toward the doorway. "You have a way of bringing the story to life."

She arched a brow, her smile turning teasing. "A compliment? The next thing I know you'll confess to liking me."

"I don't dislike you, Miss Trewlove."

"No? I wasn't quite certain after things ended as they did last night."

"I simply take exception to your hunt to marry a lord."

"Would you take exception if I was born on the right side of the blanket?"

"The circumstances of your birth don't signify. You're chasing a title, and behind that title is a man."

"Who will no doubt be chasing my dowry." She crossed her arms over her chest, tucking them beneath her breasts, which served to bring them to the fore. His eyes should not have dipped in order to fully appreciate the lovely display, but they did, damn them. "Why do you care—"

Because they're perfect, sized to fill a man's palms without leaving him wanting for more.

"—whom I should marry?"

Right. They were discussing something else entirely. "I have respect for the aristocracy and for men in particular. I don't like to see the male of the species tricked into marriage, no matter how comely the trickster."

Now, she balled her fists and sent them to her hips, narrow hips if the way her skirts fell were a true indication. Miss Trewlove curved in and out in a most delectable manner.

"Whatever gave you the impression I would use deceit to gain a husband?" She sounded truly insulted, then rolled her eyes. "The letter? I can admire a man, a relationship, without using what I know of it for duplicity. Have you an encounter in your past that causes you not to trust women?" She gave him a long, slow, thorough once-over that made him feel as though she were skimming her fingers over every inch of his skin. Sympathy filled those eyes that reminded him of the finest chocolate. "Did she break your heart?"

What Elise had done, how naïve he'd been, was none of her concern. "If I'd realized it was your wish to spar and pry, I'd have not ventured from my residence."

With a grimace, she squeezed her eyes shut. "My apologies. I wanted to ask a favor of you, and I've probably mucked things up to such an extent you'll refuse me." When she opened those large eyes of hers, they reflected such sincerity that it might be impossible to find the words to refuse her, whatever she asked. "I hope you won't think me overly familiar, but I noticed last night, during the few minutes when you were actually paying attention to your book, that you seemed to excel at reading as you were turning the pages quite quickly."

"As I said, I was educated. Oxford."

Her eyes widened slightly. "I see."

He didn't know why he'd felt a need to impress her. Unwilling to elaborate further, he felt a fool for mentioning it in the first place.

"Then you're perfect," she said.

He scoffed. "I don't believe that term has ever been applied to me." Certainly not by Elise, at least not after they married. Before that, she had him strutting about like a bloody peacock, thinking every aspect of him pleased her, when it was only his title that held any significance for her.

"Well, for what I have in mind you're perfect. My brother's secretary, Mr. Tittlefitz—you might have met him when you leased your residence as he sees to those matters—and I hold a class for adults every Monday and Wednesday. We focus on teaching reading. As my nights are going to become quite busy once I am introduced into Society, I wondered if you might be willing to take over for me when I'm not available."

Not if his life depended on it. Why would he want to spend any more time in the company of a title chaser than he had to? Even if she wouldn't be there, their paths would surely cross to some extent. The only favor he intended to do was for himself, and that involved keeping his distance. "I'm sorry. I fear I haven't the patience for such a task."

"But it is so rewarding."

"Do I look to be a man in need of rewards?"

She couldn't have appeared more stricken if she'd just witnessed him kicking a puppy. Damn her for making him regret the harshness of his tone.

"To be quite honest, you struck me as a man of leisure who might be in want of a way to fill his hours and wouldn't need recompense for the task."

Her mien reflected that of a woman challenging a man— damned if he didn't want to give in to her, to allow her to have the victory, but that way lay madness. "I may be a man of leisure but that does not mean I haven't responsibilities and duties that take up a good measure of my time."

"Excuse us, Miss Trewlove."

Without hesitation, she moved nearer to him, out of the path of the women and children exiting her parlor, bringing with her the tantalizing scent of oranges.

"Goodbye, Mrs. Byng. See you next Friday." She patted the heads of the children, bid farewell to the mothers, giving attention to each person, large and small, young and old, who walked by. Or were carried. Even the babes in arms received a touch on the cheek or tip of the nose.

When everyone had departed, she looked up at him, and he realized he'd not taken a step back, not one iota, that he'd remained inappropriately near, so close he could feel the warmth radiating from her. His hand flexed, twitched, as though it desperately wanted to reach up and cradle her cheek, determine if it was as silky soft as it appeared.

"My apologies, Mr. Sommersby." Her low voice was the rasp of whispered secrets. "Of course, you have important matters that require your attention. I do hope you'll forgive my impertinence."

At that moment, he had the absurd thought that he'd forgive her anything, and understood with absolute surety that she was a danger. She wouldn't use the letter as a means to her end. She would use her brown eyes, her luscious mouth, her pert breasts, her narrow waist, her kindness. In the end, some gentleman would fall without ever realizing he'd been felled. Such was her power.

He stepped back. "Good day to you, Miss Trewlove." Then he strode down the hallway to the stairs and descended them as though hellhounds were nipping at his heels.

Chapter 6

That evening, Fancy slipped out of her shop, closed the door, inserted the key—

"Miss Trewlove."

With a tiny screech, pressing her hand to her chest in order to keep her heart behind her ribs, she swung around. "Mr. Sommersby."

He'd not been waiting for her, surely. Granted, she'd been preoccupied with locking up but certainly would have noticed had he been there. He'd merely come around the corner at the precise moment she was striving to sneak away, and her guilt was attributing nefarious purposes to his arrival. People were still out and about, going to the pub, going home. Wagons, carts, and buggies traversed on the street. Children ran hither and yon. Amidst all that, it was merely coincidence that their paths crossed. Besides, after their encounter that afternoon, it was unlikely he'd search for any excuse to be near her. She certainly had no desire to be near him. "If you're in want of a book, you'll need to return tomorrow as I'm in the process of closing up."

"Yesterday, it seemed nothing would prevent you from matching a person with reading material."

"Yesterday I didn't have plans."

"I'm intrigued. You're not by any chance going to the Jolly Roger for dinner?"

Was that interest in his tone, hope that they might again share a table? The man confounded her. Earlier it had been as though he couldn't escape her presence fast enough. She owed him no explanation, but found a sort of perverse pleasure in revealing that her life also included things that took up a good portion of her time. "Actually, I'm off on an adventure."

She peered up at the windows leading into Mick's office, grateful not to see him standing there. After telling him that she'd be dining in tonight, she didn't need him to catch sight of her up to no good. She couldn't remember a time when she was allowed to do anything that wouldn't better her marriage prospects. She'd been restricted from exploring areas far from home because her mum had worried someone might lead her astray, might introduce her to spirits, cigars, gambling, or profanity. Her siblings had all been able to do as they pleased, whereas she'd been watched like a hawk. Surely a bit of rebelliousness was in order.

"What sort of adventure?"

"I really don't see that it's any of your concern."

He released a long, drawn-out suffering sigh. "I realize you are no doubt miffed about my response earlier—"

"No, not at all." A lie. She was greatly disappointed his answer would result in them having fewer opportunities to become fast friends and would place an additional burden on Mr. Tittlefitz. "Your time is yours to do with as you please. As is mine." Then as a bit of obstinacy hit her, she decided she really didn't care if he knew her plans. As a matter of fact, she took satisfaction from the thought of possibly shocking him. "Now, if you'll excuse me, a penny gaff awaits."

His eyes narrowed slightly, his gaze becoming more intense, as though she'd suddenly grown a second head. "Why in God's name would you go to a penny gaff?"

Again, she owed him no explanation but where was the harm in giving one? While Aiden owned a club catering to women's fantasies, she was forbidden from going there and had to make do finding her own entertainments. With a sigh, she turned the lock before slipping the key into a hidden pocket at the waist of her skirt, very much aware that light fingers would be about where she was going, so anything of import that might be nicked was hidden away. "When I have my entrée into Society, I will be expected to behave with utmost decorum and places such as this will be forbidden to me."

"They should be forbidden to you now."

She rolled her eyes at his admonishment. What should it matter to him how she spent her evening? "They have been, which is why I'm going tonight. It might be my last chance to actually experience one."

"Alone? Without a chaperone? Have you gone mad?"

"It is not the sort of place where one takes a chaperone. Besides, she might tell Mick, and he'd be none too pleased."

"As well he shouldn't be. I forbid it."

She barked out a laugh. "You are not in a position to forbid me to do anything, Mr. Sommersby. Good evening, sir."

With a slight turning of her shoulders, she edged past him and strolled up the walk. His footsteps, loud and with purpose, echoed around her.

"How are you going to get there?"

"I'm hiring a hansom a few streets over." When she was well beyond Mick's keen eyesight.

"You can't go alone. There are dangers, Miss Trewlove."

"I'm prepared for them."

"Pickpockets, brigands, thugs. All manner of men with ill intentions who will not hesitate to take advantage of a woman alone."

"I appreciate your concern, Mr.—"

He grabbed her arm. Fortunately, it wasn't the one holding her reticule. She swung it with all her might. It *thunked* against his head and sent him staggering back, his hat flying into the street. Catching his balance, he pressed his hand to his head. "What the devil is in that thing?"

"Books." Darting forward, she rescued his hat before it was crushed beneath the wheels of a passing carriage. Back on the pavement, she extended it toward him. "I'm so sorry. I reacted without thought, although I also suspect you were striving to demonstrate how a blackguard might attempt to take advantage."

He failed to respond to her assessment but had an air of guilt about him. "Why would you take books to a penny gaff?"

She lifted her reticule. "Because they provide weight in case I'm accosted. I have a small dagger hidden away behind the waistband of my skirt and a knife tucked into my boot."

"Do you know how to use them?"

"Quite effectively, actually. While my siblings have always sought to protect me, they also knew I lived in the rookeries and they couldn't watch over me every hour of every day. So they taught me how to look after myself. I do hope I didn't damage your skull. You have a rather nicely shaped head, and I'd hate knowing I made you lopsided."

He laughed, the sound deep and rich, echoing around her, through her, taking up residence in her soul.

"Miss Trewlove, you are . . . I am beyond words. Still, I can't allow you to traipse off into an unsavory part of London."

Penny gaffs were generally found in the poorer sections of London. "Again, Mr. Sommersby, you are not in a position to *allow* me to do anything."

He shrugged. "I suppose I shall have to pop into the hotel to let your brother know."

A fissure of fury swept through her. "You wouldn't dare."

"I can't help but believe that if something unpleasant were to happen to you and he found out I let you go off unaccompanied that he'd have my head."

"Don't be daft. He's not going to find out."

"People are wandering about. I'm certain one or two have made note of our conversing. Word is likely to get back to your brother, and I will have no defense for allowing you to go off alone."

Why was he insisting upon accompanying her? After this afternoon, she'd fully expected him to avoid her at all costs. She was on the verge of screaming like a shrew. "Mr. Sommersby, it would be inappropriate for me to be seen with a man without benefit of a chaperone."

"What are the odds you'll run into anyone you know?"

"Oh, one in a thousand, I should think, but—"

"Thus we're unlikely to be seen or recognized by anyone of importance."

"True, but—"

"You've also had dinner with a gentleman without benefit of chaperone."

He had her there, but still she felt a need to argue. "I was not having dinner with a gentleman. He was merely making use of the chair at my table."

He flashed a grin, so devastatingly perfect that she would be content to spend the rest of her life saying things that would bring forth that smile. "Semantics."

"I would further argue that Becky, nay the entire staff, served to chaperone that dinner."

"I'll give you that. I felt their eyes on me the entire night." He took a step toward her. "How's this, then? You are going to the penny gaff alone. I, however, have decided I'm in the mood for some entertainment this evening and am going as well. Not with you, of course. But as we're heading in the same direction, I daresay space will be available on the seat in your cab, so where is the harm in our sharing the ride?"

THERE WAS HARM aplenty within the small confines of the hansom cab, he realized when her thigh was pressed up against his, when the rocking motion of the conveyance occasionally caused the side of her breast to rub up against his arm. She seemed unaware of the touch whereas his body reacted as though she'd climbed into his lap.

Leaving her shop earlier, he'd felt rather like an arse for not accommodating her request, even as he justified his reasons for avoiding her. Then on his way to the pub, he'd been taken aback by the joy that had spiraled through him when he'd rounded the corner and caught sight of her in a modest deep buttery shaded frock with a square neckline that revealed the hollow at the base of her throat and an inch or so of skin below it. He'd been dazzled and unable not to think about dipping his tongue in that provocative spot in the center of her collarbone. Which was no doubt the reason he'd been so damned reluctant to part ways and was now accompanying her on her adventure. Lust was once again driving him to make stupid decisions, and yet he couldn't seem to find it within himself to regret the choice he'd made.

She'd instructed the driver to take them to the Devil's Door. He wasn't familiar with that particular establishment but was rather confident as to what he would find there since he'd visited other gaffs in his youth when he and his friends had been in the mood for ribald entertainment. "How did you even hear of this place?"

"When I was twelve or so, a lad who lived near us invited me to go with him. I asked Gillie what I should wear"—she slid her gaze over to him—"and that put an end to that. She explained that it wasn't the sort of place a proper lady would ever frequent. But I've thought about it over the years and decided before I truly become proper, I should have a night of being improper. So here we are."

"What became of the lad?" He wondered if she'd loved him, retained a tender spot for him in her heart.

"Six months later, he married another lass who lived in the area."

"Good Lord! How old was he when he asked you to go with him?" He suspected it was more the fellow's age than where he was taking her that has resulted in her sister squashing things.

"Fifteen. They marry young in the rookeries. His bride was all of fourteen, although I doubt she was actually ever a bride. I suspect they had no ceremony. They might not have even had a license. Often couples simply move in together, declare themselves married, and who is to know different? My siblings will pay for the license of any of their employees who wish to marry. As you can well imagine, they are keen to ensure the children are legitimate."

"Was it difficult growing up not being so?" He abhorred the thought of her being made to feel less.

"My family made it not matter. Still I was aware that it did. My children will be legitimate, and that's important to me. As will be their father, a right and proper lord, who can trace his lineage back generations. The wonder of that, to know who came before him."

He'd always taken it for granted, had actually seen it as a burden, not only to live up to his parents' expectations, but to the expectations of those long dead.

"Anyway, that's how I know about this particular theater. Have you ever been to a gaff?"

"I have."

"Did you enjoy the shows you saw?"

"To be honest, I can barely recall them. But if you enjoy the din in the pub, the rowdiness of a penny gaff should absolutely delight you."

Her profile was to him, but he saw the slow upward curl of her mouth. Would any lord be able to resist that innocent yet seductive movement? Could he?

"I'm counting on it."

"If I may be honest, I'm a bit surprised your family doesn't keep a closer watch over you. Young, unmarried, living alone."

"They don't imagine me misbehaving, doing what I ought not because I was ever so good while I was growing up, never got into trouble. I also think they believe having Mick living across the street, able to drop in on me at any time, serves as a deterrent to misguided actions." That slow upward curl again. "But he is very much preoccupied with his wife. He's mad about her, you know."

"I assume you're hoping for the same level of devotion."

"It would please me immensely to be so adored, but I am realistic enough to know my dowry will no doubt play a large role in determining my future. I'm trying very hard not to feel as though I'm being sold off."

He'd never thought of it in those precise terms. "Women have come with dowries for centuries. It's not an insult to have one."

"I know. I'm very fortunate. I simply hope it's not the only thing he likes about me."

He wanted to remove his gloves and skim his fingers over her cheek in reassurance. Instead he kept them balled into a fist on his thigh. If he had not left Society, would he have met her at a ball? Would he be as intrigued? Would he willingly walk into a trap to have her?

"It's probably very unwise of me to be alone with a man about whom I know so little." Within the confines, her voice was a low hush as though she wasn't quite certain she wanted the words to be heard. "In which area of London did you grow up?"

"I didn't. I grew up in Yorkshire."

"A country lad. I hadn't envisioned that for you."

"What had you envisioned?"

"I'm not really certain. A father who was a success at some business. A solicitor perhaps."

"A curmudgeon mostly, but he was skilled at investing and managing his income. I've benefited from his attention to details."

"Is he no longer here?"

"No, he passed some years back."

"Do you miss him?"

"I miss having his counsel."

"I believe that's the most you've ever shared with me, Mr. Sommersby. I feel considerably safer."

"I would never take advantage, Miss Trewlove."

"I should hope not. My brothers would kill you if you did, and your body would never be found."

He grinned broadly in the encroaching darkness. "Such a tragic end. Perhaps you could write a penny dreadful about it. Although I'd prefer you make me the hero, as the hero never dies."

"Regretfully that is not always the case. My father was a hero. He died in a war on foreign shores before I was born. But my mum told me all about him."

"You know who your mother is?"

Her light laughter floated around him. "Ettie Trewlove is my mum."

"I'm confused. I was under the impression she only took in by-blows."

"The others, yes, but not me. She gave birth to me."

Which further explained why her siblings were so protective of her. Not only because of the age difference, but because she was the child of the woman who had raised them. "She must have been remarkably young when she began taking them in."

"Barely twenty. Her husband had died, and she needed a way to earn some coins. She lacked an education, you see, so her options were limited."

He wondered if that was part of the reason that she was teaching others to read. His reason for not helping her suddenly seemed petty and selfish, especially as his resolve to avoid being in her presence had lasted only a few hours. He didn't want to be drawn to her, and yet he was.

She leaned forward slightly. "Ah, here we are."

The cab came to a stop. Matthew passed up the fare through a small opening in the roof and the doors quickly flipped open. After climbing out, he handed Miss Trewlove down and glanced at the building before them where people were streaming in. "It looks to be a church."

"A converted one from what I understand. Quite appropriate, don't you think, as I'm certain it's filled with sinners."

He'd wager no truer statement had ever been spoken. After he paid their admittance fee at the door, they climbed the stairs to a balcony and made their way to the benches at the front, which provided a clear view of the stage and the rows of pews lined up before it. A good deal more pandemonium was visible in the front. Young lads, many appearing to be in need of a bath, were jumping around, running hither and yon. Women were jostling bawling babes, no doubt trying to soothe them into silence. Some men were shouting and shoving on each other, while a few were sitting back puffing on their pipes.

She looked over at him and smiled. "So much mayhem. It's marvelous, isn't it?"

He thought of dinners, plays on Drury Lane, recitals, and garden parties he'd attended. Much more civilized, much less chaotic. "I think I would tire of it night after night."

She nodded. "I agree. It should be saved for special occasions. Although for some of these people, I suspect it offers an escape, especially for those who can't escape into books."

"Are you always thinking about books?"

Her gaze lit upon his lips. "Not always." When she looked away, her cheeks were lightly flushed, and he wondered how much more they might darken if he gave in to temptation and kissed her.

But before he did something he shouldn't, a gentleman in an ill-fitting jacket strode onto the stage and began offering what Matthew was certain he believed to be witty comments about Americans. The crowd laughing uproariously spurred him on. Miss Trewlove, seeming less than entertained, leaned toward him, her mouth near his ear, bringing with her the scent of oranges. He was rather certain her actions were the result of the loud clamoring that made it difficult to hear anything, that she didn't mean to be provocative, yet provocative she was. How simple it would be to turn his head and capture her mouth.

"Why do people find it humorous to make sport of others?"

"To distract others from making sport of them."

As far as Matthew was concerned, the gent couldn't leave the stage soon enough. He was followed by a lady who couldn't have been any older than Miss Trewlove. She was far too thin, her skirt and petticoats too short, revealing her slender ankles and bare feet. But she belted out a song about two lovers whose parents sought to keep them apart. It ended with their deaths at their own hands with the aid of a silver dagger in order to be together for eternity. Glancing over, he saw Miss Trewlove discreetly wiping tears from her cheeks. Pulling a handkerchief from his pocket, he slipped his finger beneath her chin and turned her head toward him. Very gently, slowly, he gathered up her tears. "It's only a song."

"But such a tragic one." Her brown eyes held so much sadness he wished he had a talent that would bring her a measure of cheer, chase away the sorrow.

"That is the way of love sometimes."

"Still, I can't imagine it's better not to have it, even if only for a little while."

"But having had it, could you give it up?"

"I don't know. And who is to say that we cannot love more than once?"

Having collected all her tears, he stuffed his linen back into his pocket, touched by her tenderheartedness. A flurry of coins was tossed on the stage. The girl gave a series of quick bows and curtsies as she scurried around, gathering up her loot, and then she was gone. Leaning in, he whispered, "I'll find out who she is and send money round to her tomorrow."

Dear Lord, but he'd empty out his coffers for the smile she bestowed upon him. "That's so generous of you, Mr. Sommersby."

Hardly, not when he could easily afford it. "You enjoyed her performance, did you not?"

"I did. Do you think she really has no shoes?"

"I suspect the absence of them is part of her costume."

She shook her head. "I forget these people are performers."

"The really good ones manage to do that, to make you forget it's all an act."

His wife had certainly fallen into that category, laughing at his jests, bestowing upon him long, lingering gazes whenever he was walking toward her. She'd always smiled brightly upon first catching a glimpse of him, causing his heart to ratchet up its beat a notch in anticipation of his being nearer to her. Until he realized all her actions had been merely a ploy to achieve a certain end: his standing beside her at the altar.

FANCY DIDN'T ENJOY most of the performances, especially the lewd ones, where people pretended to fornicate. Children were in the audience for goodness' sake.

Still, she was glad she'd come, had the experience of it so if anyone spoke of penny gaffs, she'd at least have an idea of what they might have seen. She was especially glad Mr. Sommersby had accompanied her.

When they stepped out of the theater, she spied a woman selling meat pies. "Oh, I'm famished. Would you like one?"

"You don't know what's in it."

"Well, it's a meat pie."

"What sort of meat? Dog? Cat? Rat?"

"Honestly. Just because this is a poorer area of London does not mean the food suffers." She stepped up to the cart. "A meat pie, please."

"Make it two," he grumbled, before handing over the required coins.

"It wasn't my intention for you to pay for everything tonight."

"It's no hardship, Miss Trewlove."

"That's not the point. I don't want to be beholden."

"It's the least I can do after inserting myself into your night."

Not about to confess that she was glad he had, Fancy glanced around. The crowd who'd left the theater had dispersed, and those who'd been waiting for the next show had made their way inside. "We'll sit on the steps, shall we?"

She didn't wait for him but settled herself halfway up the stairway that led into the theater. He dropped down near her, his long legs stretching out before him. He wasn't as near to her as he'd been in the cab, and she rather regretted that no portion of him was touching her. It had been quite lovely to brush up against him as they'd traversed through the streets.

"It's surprisingly good," he muttered.

"I noticed a queue earlier when we arrived. If you set up a stall outside a theater, you need to establish a reputation for dependable fare if you hope to have any success at all."

He gave her a sideways glance. "Your brother teach you that?"

"No, I figured it out on my own, not to mention that it makes a great deal of sense. People don't return if they're dissatisfied with the results of a purchase." She shrugged. "Well, around here they might return in order to introduce you to their fists."

She bit into the tasty crust, laughing lightly as the thick filling dribbled down her chin. With her gloved hand, she wiped it away. So unladylike. But it was rather delicious.

When he didn't respond, she looked over to find him studying her with a hunger in his eyes as though he wished to lick the broth from her skin—or perhaps she was merely projecting her own desires onto him.

"I have a linen in my pocket." His voice sounded rough and raw.

"The one with my tears?"

He nodded. She'd been deeply touched when he'd gently wiped away the dampness, and for some reason she didn't want to soil the cloth, having an irrational thought that perhaps he would never again wash it but would keep her tears for eternity.

She shook her head. "It's really too late now. I'll continue to use my gloves and simply remove them when I'm done."

"They'll be ruined."

They were already ruined. She noted he'd had the wisdom to remove his before they began eating. "I've another pair."

Abruptly, he returned his attention to his meat pie, and she took another bite of hers. Then she felt a need to confess, "I've peered through a part in my draperies and caught you lurking at your window late at night."

"I'm hardly lurking, simply looking out over the mews."

"Not at my window?"

"Sometimes my gaze might pass over it, but it is not my intention to spy on you, Miss Trewlove."

She didn't know why his words disappointed her. Perhaps because she wanted him to be as intrigued by her as she was by him. "From your window across the way, you can see my bedchamber but not the perfection of what rests on the other side."

"Are you referring to yourself?"

Her light laughter floated around them. "I'm not so arrogant as all that. Beneath my window is a small reading nook. My brothers built a bench into the wall. My mum sewed a thick stuffed cushion and embroidered pillows for it. Sometimes I sit there and read until the world falls away."

"Don't let my looking out prevent you from doing what you enjoy."

"Now who's being arrogant, to think you could stop me from doing something I wished to do? I simply wanted you to be aware that if you should see me sitting there, it's not because I seek to garner your attention, but rather it is my habit to do so."

"I shall keep that in mind. What will become of your shop when you marry? Will you continue to manage it?"

"I won't have time, will I? Not with all my social and wifely obligations. Morning calls, dinners, plays—being seen everywhere. Mick still owns the building." He'd been unwilling to give it to her because the law wouldn't allow her to keep control of it once she married. Her husband would be able to do with it as he pleased. "He has promised to let me have a say in how it's managed, but I won't be working there, certainly not living there. No, Marianne will take over the running of things, although I hope to still have a hand in the teaching. Ladies married to lords do good works, you know. That shall be mine."

It would be a very different life, but she was excited about the possibilities of it. The challenge was in finding a man who also saw the potential and embraced it. She took the last bite of her pie, wiped her gloved hand over her mouth, and began tugging it off.

"You missed a spot."

Turning, she found him studying her so intently she feared she looked an absolute mess. She lifted a hand, the glove dangling halfway off it. His fingers closed gently around her wrist. "May I?"

His voice held such sincerity she might have nodded had he asked to ravish her, but all he wanted was to remove a tiny bit of food that she'd overlooked. In amazement, she watched as he touched his tongue to his thumb—quite possibly the most sensual thing she'd ever seen a man do.

"Just there," he said, pressing his thumb near the corner of her mouth.

Then he licked off whatever he'd gathered, and she grew so warm that it was possible the moon had morphed into the sun.

"And there." He touched the other corner.

"And here." Her chin.

"And there." The space between her brows, where his thumb lingered.

People strolled by, and she wondered what they thought of this couple on the steps barely moving.

"And there." Her left temple.

"I daresay, I wasn't that messy."

"Your face is perfect, Miss Trewlove."

"From your mouth to the lords' ears. And I don't mean God's. I mean the viscounts, and earls . . . I hope they find me comely."

"I don't see how they can't." His tone was terse, rife with disapproval. As though she'd suddenly ignited, he'd moved his hand away, and she found herself aching once more for his caress.

"May I be honest with you, Mr. Sommersby?"

"I daresay, I hope you always are, Miss Trewlove."

She took a deep breath, not at all certain her words would ease whatever tension had abruptly risen within him. "You confound me, sir."

"And how is that?"

How to explain so it didn't appear that she truly cared, when in fact she cared a great deal, more than was wise for a woman who was on the cusp of going on a husband hunt. "You don't seem to know your own mind."

He arched a heavy dark brow. "Indeed."

"It's as though you can't decide whether or not you find me to your liking. This afternoon, for example, I was left with the impression you couldn't wait to be rid of me. Now, here you are, having inserted yourself into my adventure, making it a much more pleasant experience than it would have been had I come alone as planned. You saw to my tears and tidied my face, and yet, I can't help but believe that just now I've offended you."

He released a long sigh before shifting away from her, planting his elbows on his thighs, clasping his hands, and staring into the street where the first wisps of fog were making their presence known. "I was once married. It was not a happy arrangement."

Her heart lurched at the confession he'd made and the somberness of his tone. "Did you get divorced?"

"No, she passed away. But our marriage came about because she arranged for us to be caught in a compromising situation. I had no choice but to marry her. So when you told me you were willing to do all that is necessary to acquire your dream of landing a peer—"

"It's not my dream."

He jerked his head around to stare at her.

"It's my mum's." She felt rather silly saying that. "I'd be content to spend my life as a spinster working in my shop."

"Then why not simply do that?"

She looked up, wishing the stars were visible. "Because they have all worked so hard and sacrificed so much to see me well situated that I have to at least give it my best. I fully realize that a woman of my scandalous background will not be any lord's ideal, but I doubt a one of them will find any lady more prepared to manage a household than I. I can exhibit grace and confidence and be an asset. If you will not think me too obnoxious, I must admit I will be quite the catch."

He gave a short chuckle, a small grin. "It seems you can add a lack of modesty to your list of attributes."

"Mick says we must project what we want the world to believe." Growing somber, she dared to place her hand over his forearm. "I'm sorry about your wife, your marriage. Have you been a widower long?"

"During some moments it feels like forever; during others as though no time at all has passed. I mourn her death, did not wish it upon her."

"But you have scars from her deception."

He studied her a full minute before confessing, "I do find it a challenge to trust women's motives."

"Rest assured, I have no plans to trick any lord into marriage. My siblings have all married for love. I'd rather like to follow that custom. So I'm in no rush to tie the knot. I intend to take my time and find the right fellow."

"And if that means no more penny gaffs?"

She smiled. "One was more than enough. Besides, I'll have theater and operas."

"No more meat pies eaten on steps."

"I'll have the memory."

He trailed his fingers down her cheek, along her jaw. "Will you?"

"I shan't forget tonight. I'm glad the seat in the hansom cab had room for you."

His hand dropped from her face, and he began tugging on his gloves. "It's late. We should probably be off."

Just like that, whatever magic spell they'd woven around each other was broken. Probably for the best.

He stood, reached down for her hand, and tugged her to her feet. They carried on as though the night had been nothing more than an outing between friends. But at least it seemed they were at last friends.

Without much bother, they found a hansom cab. Sitting practically snuggled against him seemed the most natural thing in the world.

When they arrived at her shop, she unlocked the door and smiled up at him. "Thank you for sharing my adventure, Mr. Sommersby."

"It was my pleasure, Miss Trewlove."

Once inside, she locked the door, leaned against it, and waited for the echo of his retreating footsteps. It seemed to take forever for them to sound. When they finally did, she rather wished that instead she'd heard a knock. For a chance to visit with him some more, she would have welcomed him in, even as she knew it would serve no good purpose.

Chapter 7

It was nearly two in the morning when Matthew let himself into his massive London residence. Having left the heavy mahogany door open so the light from the lamps lining the drive could at least chase back the shadows a bit so he could make out the shapes, he crossed over to a table, struck a match, and lit the waiting oil lamp. The residence had been built nearly a century and half earlier, so it didn't have the convenience of gas lighting, which his terrace on Ettie Lane did. However, his terrace could easily fit into the foyer and front parlor while still leaving space for walking around their edges.

After closing the door, he lifted the lamp higher and glanced into the parlor. All the furniture, portraits, paintings, and statuettes were shrouded in white, giving the residence a ghostly feel that suited his mood. He didn't want to see the portrait of Elise hanging over the fireplace or his ancestors looking judgmentally down on him as he began his journey along the hallway.

Ever since Elise had taken ill, sleep had been an elusive mistress, seldom on hand to give a man satisfaction. This night was no exception, but it was made worse by the fact that when it came to Miss Trewlove, he'd begun to feel like a royal arse. It was quite possible he'd misjudged her when it came to how she might endeavor to gain a husband. The more time he spent with her, the more she contradicted his notions about her.

He didn't know why he'd been so insistent on joining her tonight. She obviously hadn't wanted his company, not that he could blame her for that. She had the right of it. Where she was concerned, he didn't seem to know his own mind. He wanted to avoid her, and yet when the opportunity presented itself to be in her company, he'd leapt on it like a ravenous hound being tossed a bone. She intrigued him, damn it all. With her mixture of innocence and worldliness, she was a puzzle box he wanted to figure out how to open.

And she made him feel guilty about his treatment of her from the moment the letter had fallen out of her pocket. He'd assumed she was as conniving as Elise and, as a result, had treated Miss Trewlove abominably and unfairly.

When he reached the library, he merely stood in the doorway and took a moment to appreciate what had always been his favorite chamber in the residence. He had a keen desire to bring Miss Trewlove here. He imagined her sighing in wonder, gasping in delight at the two floors of bookcases, the upper one accessible by a wrought-iron spiral staircase in the corner. He had no idea how many books lined the shelves. A couple of thousand at least. Not that any of them were visible at present. The staff had suspended sheets of white cloth over the shelves to protect the treasures stored there. Including the one he'd come to find.

He strode over to a far corner of the room, near the spiral staircase, carefully set the lamp on a low table draped in white, reached up, and yanked down a sheet to reveal a section of books. He was relatively certain he'd last seen the one he was looking for in this area.

He couldn't decide if Miss Trewlove would be appalled that the books within these walls were shelved with no rhyme or reason or if she'd find the chaos delightful. Although he had a feeling she'd roll up her sleeves and pull every book off the shelf in order to arrange them in categories, no doubt taking pleasure in touching each and every one. When he'd first stepped into her shop, he'd been cocooned in wonder. Nothing within her walls was left to chance. It all reflected a celebration of the written word. She'd gone to a great deal of bother to arrange everything just so. She'd not told him that, of course, but it was evident in the way every aspect came together in such a pleasing manner to reveal her absolute love of books.

And so it was that he wanted to gift her with something that would make him feel less of a disappointment, less of a cad, less judgmental. Therefore, he'd come here in the dead of night to—

"My lord?"

He swung around to face the butler, who had served this household longer than Matthew had memory, standing in the doorway with an untied dressing gown hanging off his lanky form, a lamp held aloft in one hand, and a . . . no, it could not possibly be.

"Jenkins, is that a pistol you're holding in your trembling hand?"

"Aye."

"Pray, tell me it is not loaded."

"What good is it unloaded, I ask you?"

"Then please point it at the floor and not at my person."

The elderly gent did as ordered. "I heard a commotion, my lord, and came to investigate. Not knowing what to expect I came armed for trouble."

"I did not create a commotion. I was as quiet as death."

"Still, I heard you. What are you doing here, sir? Are you moving back in? Should I rouse the servants to start setting everything back to rights?"

"Don't rouse anyone. I'm simply looking for the copy of *Mr. William Shakespeares Comedies, Histories, & Tragedies.*" He found some irony in the original title lacking the apostrophe that he'd accused the name of Miss Trewlove's shop of not having. Published in the early part of the seventeenth century, the leather-bound book contained the original versions of his plays. One of Matthew's ancestors had managed to purchase one of the only seven hundred and fifty copies printed. "Any notion as to where I might find it?"

Jenkins craned his neck, looking around the library, his eyes wide as though a horde of invaders had suddenly made an appearance. "No, my lord. Although I believe the rarest books are up there." He nodded toward the shelves at the top of the staircase.

"You might be correct on that score." He walked over to the desk, the only piece of furniture not shrouded. A large silver bowl was filled to overflowing with bits of vellum.

"The invitations you've received, sir." Jenkins approached. Even in slippers, he made not a sound. The man had long ago mastered the art of not being heard or being seen as an intrusion when he entered a room. Often he left with no one the wiser. "As they weren't on the list of items to be sent round to you, I wasn't quite certain what to do with them."

Toss them in the fire would no doubt give the butler an apoplectic fit. Matthew was relatively certain that for some of the events, the time for attending was past. Still a modicum of civility remained in him, and he knew he should at least send acknowledgment of having received them. "I'll take them with me."

"Very good, my lord." Jenkins seemed far too relieved by that answer.

"In the future, include them with the letters that arrive in the post that you have brought to me every few days." If something appeared urgent, it was brought to him immediately. Otherwise, he saw no point in constantly sending a footman out.

"As you wish, sir."

Then he could toss them in the fire and save Jenkins the worry over them.

"Another matter I need you to take care of for me. When I find the book, I'll leave it here on the desk with a note." He took a piece of foolscap out of a drawer, dipped his pen in the inkwell, and scrawled Fancy Trewlove's name and the address of the bookshop across the paper. "I want you to wrap up the book with the note and have it sent to this address. Don't use the post." The postmark would indicate the post office from which it had begun its journey, and he didn't want her to know it came from Mayfair. "It is to have no markings on it to indicate from whom or from where it originated. Have a footman deliver it, but he is not to be dressed in livery and is not to use one of my marked carriages. It is a gift, but it is to be an anonymous one."

"It will be delivered with the utmost discretion. Shall I help you search for the book, my lord?"

"No. I've disturbed your slumber long enough as it is. Good night, Jenkins."

"I'll have the servants put matters back to rights in the morning, sir." He glanced over at the one exposed bookcase before once again meeting Matthew's gaze. "Good night, my lord."

After his butler silently shuffled out, Matthew returned to the shelves where he thought he'd last seen the book. The tome was taller than most, which should have made it easier to find but his relations had collected a goodly number of tall books. The one for which he searched should probably be stored under glass. He had little doubt Miss Trewlove would give it the care it needed.

It was an expensive gift he was going to bestow upon her, but knew of no one who would appreciate it more.

Three hours later, he found the tome exactly where Jenkins had predicted it would be: on the upper floor. With a great deal of care, he set it on the desk, pulled out another bit of foolscap, and considered the message that should accompany it. Finally, with his expert penmanship, he scrawled out the words.

It is in want of someone who will appreciate, love, and cherish it.

As he strode from the room, he had the uncomfortable sensation that he'd been referring to himself more than the book.

Chapter 8

"*I* think you're going to enjoy *The Moonstone* very much indeed, Mr. Harper." Fancy couldn't help but believe that Mr. Sommersby would also enjoy the mystery and wondered if he'd read it.

"I'm looking forward to reading it, Miss Trewlove, which isn't something I ever said before you taught me my letters."

"You were a fast learner. I'm ever so glad you found the effort worth your while."

Once the transaction was completed and Mr. Harper took his leave, she gave the shop a quick perusal. Two ladies had come in together and were browsing the area where they were most likely to find a story that involved a grand love, while a gentleman was searching through her travel books. She'd already offered to help each of them, but they preferred looking on their own. She certainly understood that. Before she had her own shop, she'd spent hours in bookshops or combing through bookstalls searching for the perfect story to take home with her.

Saturday was usually her favorite day of the week because she generally had a few more customers. Several people, including a mother with her three children, were upstairs in the reading parlor. Marianne was keeping a watch on things up there. Fancy needed to hire someone to assist her clerk during the hours when she, herself, might not be available. The notion of asking Mr. Sommersby if he'd like to take on the job flashed through her mind, but she quickly squelched it. She didn't know why she was intent on making opportunities to have him about. Perhaps because, like the book she'd just sold, he was a mystery.

The bell above the door tinkled and an elderly gentleman carrying a large brown wrapped package secured with string wandered in, stopped, and glanced around to take in every nook and cranny. It always amazed her that people resided in this area whom she had yet to meet, but then as it was growing and expanding more were moving in. "Good morning, sir. How may I help you?"

Swinging his gaze back to her, he removed his hat to reveal pale gray eyes. "Miss Fancy Trewlove?"

"Yes."

He walked toward her with smooth, lithe motions, seeming to move quickly while giving the impression of not moving at all, his steps eerily quiet as though he loathed causing any sort of disturbance. When he reached the counter, he set his package upon it in the same respectful manner that one might place a present before the Queen. "A gift for you."

As his hat began its journey back to his head, he turned on his heel and walked silently toward the door.

"Who is it from?"

He didn't stop, didn't hesitate.

"Who are you?"

Without a word, he opened the door and exited her shop. She rushed after him, but by the time she'd made it out onto the pavement, he'd disappeared, leaving her to wonder if he hadn't been a mirage. But when she returned to the counter, the package was still there. Tugging on the bow, she loosened the string and parted it, then carefully removed the paper to reveal an oversize leather book, well preserved but obviously quite old. She lifted the note resting on it, deeply touched by the inscribed words written by a meticulous hand.

"Well, you've certainly been brought to the right place," she whispered, gingerly turning back the cover. As her gaze fell on the title, she released an audible gasp and pressed her hand to her mouth. This rare edition had to be worth a fortune.

"Are you well, Miss Trewlove?"

She lifted her gaze to the two young women who'd been browsing. They looked enough alike to be sisters. One was a frequent visitor. The other had never been in her shop before. "Yes, I'm quite well. Thank you for inquiring. Have you found something to your liking, Miss Sear?"

"Indeed. My sister and I are going to take *Lorna Doone*." She placed the book on the counter. Originally the story had come out in three volumes, but its popularity had grown after it was released in a single, fairly inexpensive edition.

"I think you'll enjoy it very much."

"I don't see how we can't, not if it's as romantic as claimed."

"We so enjoy romance," the second Miss Sear said.

"They're my favorite as well."

Once they'd completed the transaction and left the store, Fancy turned her attention back to Shakespeare. She couldn't fathom who would send her such a treasure. With a great deal of care, she carried it into her office and set it on the desk.

Strange how her first thought was to find Mr. Sommersby and tell him about it. She had no doubt he would be as in awe of it as she was.

Throughout the day, she periodically popped into her office just to look at it, touch her fingers to the nearly pristine leather of the cover. Had it ever been read, or had it simply served as a prize, something to possess in order to boast about having? Now it was hers, but for what purpose?

All afternoon she pondered its arrival. After locking up, she carried thoughts of it to the pub with her, anxious to share the news of it with Mr. Sommersby. When she didn't see hide nor hair of him, she sat at a table near the window, positioning herself so she had a clear view of the door, intent on catching his attention when he walked in.

Only he never did.

"As you can well imagine, I'm the most popular lady in London at the moment."

Lounging in a thickly padded armchair in the Marquess of Fairhaven's library, sipping his excellent scotch, Matthew could well imagine it, but then his sister had always garnered attention. Her dark hair and green eyes that matched his guaranteed it.

"All the ladies are calling on me, seeking information about you." She gave him a pointed look. "And what am I to tell them, I ask you?"

It was the same question she posed each time he visited. "I'm still in mourning. I've taken a sabbatical from Society. I've flown to the moon. I don't care, Sylvie. Tell them whatever you like."

She downed her sherry like a sailor hitting his first pub after arriving in port following years at sea. A footman hurried over and refilled her glass. "You're not taking this seriously. I don't even know where you're presently residing. Are you living on the streets?"

"Don't be dramatic, darling," Fairhaven said, his tone offering comfort and reassurance. He had to give his sister credit. Following their mother's example, she'd gone after her husband's title. He recalled once overhearing his mother chastising his sister shortly after she had her coming out. "You've fine cleavage, my dear girl. Use it to your advantage to lure in the gent of your choosing."

Apparently, she had done just that. But unlike their mother, Sylvie had managed to win her husband's heart.

"His appearance should reassure you that he is taking care of himself, even if it does appear he's misplaced his razor."

He almost smiled at that. He'd always liked Fairhaven.

"Have you a valet?" she asked.

"No."

Her face crumpled as though he'd admitted to using opium.

"I'm enjoying the independence, the solitude." Besides, his terrace was too small to house live-in staff. It was working out quite well to have Mrs. Bennett pop by each morning to tidy up after him.

"I daresay, darling, he looks healthier now than he did when he came to London two months ago. He was so pale and wan then."

"And thin. Yes, I know. You do look as though you've filled out a bit. You were wasting away, and I was so worried. I know Elise's passing was difficult, but then so was your marriage. I wish you'd been able to find it within your heart to forgive her for placing you in a position of having to marry her."

He had to an extent, although he'd told Elise he had forgiven her completely, in hopes of easing her journey from this world into the next. While he no longer harbored the anger at her betrayal, neither could he forget how easily he'd been manipulated. Elise had sworn she'd not planned to trick him, but then a guilty person once caught always claimed innocence.

When the ladies had begun calling after the letter appeared, he'd studied each one, wondering how she planned to entrap him. They'd each been so eager to gain his attention. With so many vying for the role of his countess, the competition was fierce. How many would decide drastic measures were required to gain what they wanted? He knew full well it wasn't him personally but his title that called to them.

"Speaking of forgiveness, have you forgiven me for carrying out Elise's wishes?" It was his sister Elise had entrusted with her letter.

"I don't hold you responsible. You didn't know the trouble it would cause."

"Honestly, I don't understand why you can't see that she did it with your best interest at heart."

"May we speak of something else? Are you making the most of the Season, attending balls?"

She brightened. She thrived in a social environment. He suspected Miss Trewlove would as well. He wondered if she'd been pleased by his package when it arrived and had no doubt that it had been delivered because Jenkins was dependable and would see to the task. He wished he'd been in the store browsing when she'd opened it so he could have seen her reaction. Even knowing it was an incredibly valuable item, far too costly for a gentleman to give a lady, he had no regrets for sending it to her. He had little doubt if she knew from whence it came, she'd have not accepted it. Anonymity had been his only course of action.

"Oh yes," Sylvie enthused, bringing him from his thoughts. "Of course, I'm accosted at every event, mostly by mamas wanting to ensure I alert you that their daughters are available. You could have your pick of the lot, you know."

Because of the damned letter. He could even have Fancy Trewlove, if he wanted. All he had to do was confess his identity, and she would fall at his feet like all the others. Only he didn't want her to want him because of the letter or his title or the fact that he could place her on a pedestal within Society. He longed to be wanted for who he was without all the paraphernalia that came with being *what* he was.

He wanted to feel again the way he'd felt last night. His time with her had been refreshing. No insincere flirtation, no seeking of attention. Simply an enjoyment of each other's company, an easing into a friendship, without pressure or expectations.

"Will you be attending the Duke and Duchess of Thornley's ball?" He'd found an invitation to it in the stack he'd taken from his residence in the early hours of the morning. He imagined Fancy clutching the clipping from the *Times* to her breast. *Do, please, invite the Earl of Rosemont.*

"Absolutely. That affair is all the talk. I wouldn't dare not go. You no doubt received an invitation. You should attend."

"I'm not in the mood to be accosted by every mama in attendance."

"You will never find happiness if you keep yourself cloistered away. Honestly, Matthew, you must get on with things. You're all of twenty-seven and our family has a tendency to have difficulty breeding—if you delay much longer, you might not get your heir."

"I'm not in want of a brood mare, Sylvie."

"I didn't mean to imply you were, but surely with a bit of effort, you could find a woman well suited to you, more suited than Elise, say."

Saved from having to comment on his sister's assertions when the butler arrived to announce that dinner was served, he followed the couple to the formal dining room with every bit of silver perfectly aligned. Suddenly he had an intense urge to be sitting on steps outside a raunchy theater, eating a meat pie, and wiping crumbs from an incredibly delectable mouth.

FANCY DIDN'T OPEN her shop on Sundays. It was a day of rest, although she seldom rested. That morning she'd attended church with her mother and then helped prepare a lovely meal. All her siblings, except for Beast, and their spouses were gathered elbow to elbow at the long oak table that dominated the room in the small dwelling in which they'd all been raised. As the family had increased in size, so her siblings had replaced the table, but it was time for a bigger one, especially as soon, with luck, Fancy's husband would be joining them for the monthly Sunday luncheon when they gathered to catch up. It seemed of late, their lives were all going in different directions and so they made a point of not losing touch with each other.

"Two more nights, my love, and then you step from this drab world into a fancy one. Are you nervous?"

Fancy gave a light, staccato laugh. "I wasn't until you mentioned it, Mum." She'd been striving very hard not to think about the upcoming ball, about how everything would change. Although yesterday morning's delivery had gone a long way to keeping her thoughts occupied.

"Are you going to wear the white frock with all the pearls?"

While her sisters-by-marriage had suggested she go to Paris to have her ball gowns made, and had even offered to accompany her, she'd decided to use Gillie's seamstress instead. The young woman, extremely skilled with a needle, was striving to build her business, an endeavor aided by the fact that one of her clients was now a duchess. Fancy had also liked the notion of staying in London so her mum could accompany her, and help her select the fabric and styles. Knowing her mum wouldn't attend any of the balls, she'd wanted to include her in as many aspects of her Season as possible. "Most certainly. It's my favorite of the lot."

"How will you wear your hair?"

"We'll bring her by on the way to the ball, Mum, so you can see her in all her splendor," Mick said.

"That would be lovely, Mick." Reaching out, Mum placed her hand over Fancy's where it rested on the table. Fancy always sat to her left, near her mum's heart—or so her mother would say when Fancy was younger and she was telling her where to sit. Tears pooled in her eyes. "You're going to have your fancy life."

"I have a fancy life now, Mum. I'm happy, more than happy actually."

"But it'll get even fancier. I've wanted this for you for so long. It's a dream come true, you know? To see my gel treated like royalty."

She was a long way from that, although she'd certainly felt special the last time that she was in Mr. Sommersby's company. She was rather glad they'd sorted things between them. "I know, Mum."

"You'll win them all over."

"I shall certainly try." Then because she didn't want to think about her upcoming introduction into Society, she turned to Aiden's wife, Selena. "How are your sisters enjoying Europe?"

Selena had three sisters. Constance and Florence were twins, the same age as Fancy. Alice was seventeen. Her brother was the Earl of Camberley.

Selena smiled softly. "Based on the letters I've received, they are having a marvelous time. The twins are worried they'll be a bit long in the tooth to make a good match when they have their coming out next year, but they understand the wisdom in waiting. They'll have a more successful Season once Camberley has put himself and his estates to rights." Reaching over, she rubbed her husband's hand, bestowing upon him an expression of warmth, love, and gratitude because he was responsible for ensuring her brother got his financial affairs in order so he could regain his standing among the *ton*.

"I do hope you'll give them my best when you write them. And who knows? If all goes well for me this year, I'll host a ball in their honor upon their return." The twins were to have had their coming out the year before but when Selena's husband had passed, they'd all observed a proper mourning period. While Selena's morals were now questioned since she'd married within a few months of her husband's death, having been a duchess for years, she knew how to project power. Her sisters weren't going to suffer overly much because of her scandal. What was one scandal in a family that hadn't any? Whereas Fancy's family was one of naught but scandal—whether it revolved around the circumstances of their birth or the roads they'd traveled in life. Each had then brought scandal to the one they'd chosen to marry. Born in sin, raised in sin, it seemed they were all destined to die in sin. Every season marked them as sinners.

No matter that their mother read her Bible every day. Several times they'd tried to convince her to take on a maid-for-all-work at least, possibly a cook. But she refused anything that would make her life easier. Sometimes, Fancy wondered if her mum was punishing herself for some reason.

She'd been unable to object, however, when the lads had gutted the residence and rebuilt a warm and comforting abode within. Nor could she stop them from having coal delivered on a regular basis. Shop owners extended her mum all the credit she required because they knew the Trewlove siblings would make good on any debts owed. Fancy wasn't yet in a position to make much difference, but when she married, she could carry a greater portion of her share. Perhaps she could even convince her mum to move in with her so she could spoil her, if she married a man who would be so generous. That was her goal, to find a man who would not only accept her but accept her family.

After the meal, when her siblings' children had awakened from their nap, Fancy played with them, imagining it was likely she'd have her own child within the year. Lords were keen to gain their heir as soon as possible, and she was determined to be a good and dutiful wife. But when she thought of the boy she might deliver to her husband, she imagined him with dark hair and striking green eyes.

WALKING INTO HER shop later in the afternoon, Fancy couldn't help but think of Mr. Sommersby and how a misunderstanding had nearly led to them not becoming friends. Although perhaps she was being overly optimistic there, and they were more acquaintances than friends. She rather wished he'd be at the ball—a familiar face among the crowd. A gentleman of leisure, he might be welcomed. Although as he was residing here and not in a more exclusive fashionable area, it was doubtful he associated with the aristocracy.

No, if she was to spend any more time with him, it would have to be here. Although perhaps she'd enjoyed their evening together far more than he had. At one point, as his thumb had traveled over her face, she'd thought he was on the verge of kissing her. Had wanted him to. Out of desire more than anything, but also curiosity. She didn't want to be a complete innocent when she made her debut. She was well aware the men who would dance with her had no doubt kissed a staggering number of women. They wouldn't be judged as immoral. But women, women were supposed to remain pure, untouched, pristine. But sometimes she had an urge to get a little dirty.

However as a by-blow, she'd never be seen as pure. She might as well do a little something to earn the judgment. Perhaps she should have kissed him, rebelled just a little.

But she wanted to do nothing to put her own dream at risk, her dream of finding a man who would love her, in spite of her beginnings. Her only fear was that a time might come when she would have to choose between fulfilling her mother's dream or her own. It caused a roiling in her stomach to even contemplate marrying a man she didn't love. Taking into her body a man who stirred nothing in her heart would in all likelihood destroy her.

As though sensing her morose thoughts, Dickens rubbed up

against her leg. Bending down, she lifted him into her arms. "I'm being a silly chit, worrying about things that might never be. I must make the most of my freedom while I have it. And it's a glorious day outside."

She climbed the stairs to her lodgings, set Dickens on the bed, and proceeded to change out of the elegant frock she'd worn to church into something with fewer flounces. She pinned a smaller hat into place. The wind had nearly ripped the broad-brimmed one from her head as she and her mum had walked home from church. A smaller one would serve better.

Taking her key from her reticule, she slipped the brass into her pocket. Strolling over to the corner, she picked up her kite. Dickens mewled. Meandering by him, she gave his head a quick scratch. "Yes, I'm going out for a while."

Once outside, she walked past the mews and the street upon which Mr. Sommersby lived, carrying on past other streets and residences until she reached the park. Mick had set aside several acres of land where people could take a leisurely stroll or children could play without worrying about being trampled. A pond had been created in the center of it, saplings planted here and there that would eventually provide shade.

She sought the open area where already kites were soaring. Lifting hers, she tested the wind before taking a quick jaunt, hearing the snap of the breeze catching her kite, feeling the tug. Reeling out the spool of string, she slowed, finally stopped, and watched as the kite took flight, wishing she could be up there soaring with it. As excited as she was about the coming ball, she dreaded it as well, feared disappointing her family, disappointing herself. What if no lord—

"Are those books on your kite?"

Swinging her head around, she was taken aback by the joy that spiraled through her at the sight of Matthew Sommersby standing beside her, gazing on her almost affectionately. The thick carpet of grass had muted his approach. "My brother Aiden painted them on the paper for me. He's terribly skilled, created all the framed artwork in my shop." And she was babbling. "You didn't dine at the Jolly Roger last night."

"No. I dined at my sister's."

"You have a sister?" For some reason, she'd had the impression of him being all alone in the world.

"I do. She's older. Can be a bit dictatorial and interfering at times."

As the youngest in her family, she could certainly relate. "Was she so last night?"

He chuckled low, and it was a sound that reached deep within her to warm her soul. "She was, as a matter of fact. Took me to task on a number of matters."

"Will you avoid her, then?"

"No. It's only the two of us now, as our mother has also passed. My sister is married to a good man. Has a daughter. A rambunctious little thing. It occurred to me too late that I should have stopped in your shop and purchased her a book. I shall remedy that the next time I go to visit."

"I look forward to helping you select the most perfect book." But then she was beginning to realize she looked forward to any excuse to be in his company. Not wanting to give him a reason to move on, she asked, "Do you not have a kite?"

"No."

"Would you like to fly mine for a bit?"

"I'd not deny you the pleasure you're obviously enjoying from your own efforts."

"My pleasure would only increase if you were enjoying yourself."

Although his hat shaded his face, something dark, like yearning, flashed across his eyes before he averted his gaze. "Your brother was wise to set aside land for a park. It'll increase the value of his residences, make them more appealing to his tenants."

"He let me help plant the saplings. I look at the children playing today and imagine them years from now with their own children rollicking about in the shade the trees will provide."

His gaze came back to her. "You like giving to people, even if you're not there to see them receiving your gifts."

The sun had either come closer or she was embarrassed by his words because her cheeks felt as though they were suddenly aflame. "It's a fault of mine I suppose."

"I've yet to find any fault with you, Miss Trewlove." His attention swung up to the sky, to the kites floating toward the heavens, and she was relatively certain *he* was now embarrassed as his cheeks sported a reddish hue.

"That's not quite true." She knew he found fault with her hunt for a lord.

He glanced down at her. "No, it's not."

"I prefer honesty between us, Mr. Sommersby."

"Then I find no fault with your company. How's that?"

It made it her feel as though her entire body was smiling. "I'll accept it as a compliment."

With a nod, he turned his attention back to the sky.

"What is your favorite memory of flying a kite?" she asked.

"I've never flown one."

"Never?"

"My parents didn't allow for such frivolities."

"It's not frivolous if it brings joy, helps one relax. You must give it a go."

"I will either lose hold of it and it will go flying too close to the sun and burn or I shall send it plummeting to the earth where it will crash into a thousand pieces. In either case, it will be of no future use to you."

"Nonsense. But if it should happen, I can always build another. The wind will fight you and try to steal the kite, but you are lord and master here. I'll guide you." Without thought, she stepped in front of him. "Place your hands over mine where they rest on the spindles."

"Miss Trewlove, I'm not certain this is wise."

"It's only a kite, Mr. Sommersby. Come along, don't be shy." It seemed an eternity passed before his arms circled her and his hands came to rest on hers as they clutched the wooden spindles of the reel that Beast had carved for her so it was easier to control the length of string that kept the kite tethered to her—in much the same manner that Mr. Sommersby was now tethered to her. She'd not considered how his strong, muscled arms would bracket each side of her, how his chest would press lightly against her back. She felt like a caterpillar in a cocoon going through a transformation, although she wasn't quite certain what would emerge at the end of it. Never before had she been so aware of a man. In spite of the fact that he was layered in clothing—shirt, waistcoat, coat—the heat from his skin still managed to mingle with hers. So much heat that she felt as though she were candlewax and melting. Her knees threatened to give way at any moment. She was at once grateful they both wore gloves and tempted to jerk them off so the silkiness of her hands could brush against the roughness of his palms.

Her mind was devoid of thought, as the acute awareness of his nearness overwhelmed her in a most pleasant manner. "Are you enjoying Dick Turpin's adventures?" she heard herself ask.

"Very much so."

He'd dipped his head, his mouth near her ear, his low voice causing distant areas of her body to react as though he'd pressed his lips there, his warm breath skimming over her ear, across her cheek, sending pleasure spiraling through her. She had to get a hold of herself, was giving a lesson here. "I'm going to slowly slide my hands out from under yours—"

"I rather wish you wouldn't."

How very much she wished the same but being held in his arms like this was so terribly inappropriate. "I thought you might like to grip the spindles, so you can have a keener experience."

She felt his hands close more securely around hers. "I'm perfectly content with the experience."

Oh, that voice. Rough and raspy. She thought no orchestra in the world could play a tune that would rival it in creating a deeply enamored response within her breast. If she carried on with these unsuitable thoughts, she feared she might swoon, when she'd never swooned in her life—although the finishing school she'd attended had held a lesson on how to do it gracefully. She'd considered it a silly waste of time, but how was she to have known then that a man's nearness could make it feel like one's stays were slowly shrinking, making it difficult to breathe? Time to concentrate on the reason she was now locked within his arms. "Can you feel the breeze buffeting the kite?"

"I can."

"Can you imagine how lonely the wind must be up there with only the birds for company?"

"It'll have your leaves to toy with once the trees grow."

She smiled with pleasure at the acknowledgment her meager efforts would have far-reaching consequences, just as the reading lessons she taught did. It was impossible to know how the smallest of actions might eventually make an incredible difference. "Yes, it will, but that is years from now. Shall we take the kite a bit higher, give it more freedom?"

"If you like."

"We'll slowly turn the reel, letting out more string but carefully. We must pay attention to ensure we don't lose the interest of the wind. Otherwise our kite will fall."

"Did your siblings teach you that?"

"They taught me everything of importance. They also made sure I had everything they didn't: dolls, tops, kites. My mum says they lived their childhood through me. They never really had one of their own, you see. It wasn't Mum's fault. It's just the way it is in the rookeries. I think we've given it enough lead."

Glancing back over her shoulder in order to glimpse his joy, she discovered his intense gaze focused on her and was left with the impression he'd been studying her profile for some time. "You're not watching your kite."

"I've found something far more interesting."

"Wouldn't you rather be up there with it?"

"I'd rather be down here . . . with you." His sun-weathered skin growing darker as though he was quite possibly blushing, he gave his attention back to the kite. "I rode in a hot air balloon once."

"Really? I'd love to do that. It must have been grand to see the world from up there."

"It was like stepping into the pages of a book, visiting an entirely different realm. At the time I wanted to stay up there. Now I'm glad I didn't. Otherwise I'd have never learned how to fly a kite." He slid his hands from hers and quickly stepped back, leaving her feeling somewhat abandoned and forlorn. "Thank you, Miss Trewlove, for sharing your kite with me."

Turning around partially, she faced him as much as possible while still maintaining control of the kite. "You're welcome to borrow it anytime you like."

"You're far too gracious, Miss Trewlove. I'll see you Monday night."

It felt as though her heart was about to follow the way of the kite and go soaring. "You're willing to teach now?"

"I'm willing to see what it's all about. Seven, correct?"

"Come a little early, so I can explain a few things before people arrive."

He doffed his hat. "Monday."

As he strode off, she realized she didn't need to travel in the wicker basket of a balloon to know what it felt like to float on air.

Chapter 9

Glancing around at the reading parlor of Miss Trewlove's shop, Matthew remembered one of Aesop's fables warned that when a man faced temptation, he was likely to give in to it. That had certainly been the case yesterday afternoon. He never should have approached Fancy Trewlove, and he most certainly should not have stepped forward and wrapped his arms around her. Even now, if he had pen in hand, he would be able to outline exactly where her body had nestled against his.

With her in his embrace, his sister's remark regarding finding a woman well suited to him had bounced around his mind like tumblers at a circus.

Her hunt for a title aside, what if Fancy Trewlove was well suited to him? Where was the harm in exploring the possibility? He couldn't deny being intrigued by her and enjoying her company. It was unlikely she would attempt to trap him into marriage, because she was unaware he possessed that which she yearned so desperately to acquire.

Or what her family wished her to acquire, if she'd spoken true about her own dreams.

He was fascinated by her makeshift classroom. And it was makeshift. No desks. No proper tables. A few low ones designed as a place to set a cup and saucer or a glass. Or a pair of feet if a rude person took up position on one of the nearby settees, sofas, or chairs.

Yet a coziness enveloped the room, very much like that found in a library. In the corner rested a mound of pillows that he knew children sat upon while listening to Miss Trewlove read. On the walls throughout were the paintings her brother had created. Whimsical forest animals and mythical creatures reading. Although he was most intrigued by the hanging over the mantelpiece. It reflected Miss Trewlove lounging on a sofa with books scattered on the floor around her.

When he'd peered into the room a few days earlier—was it only a few days?—he'd not noticed the artwork or the shelves lined with books on either side of the fireplace. He'd been arrested by her, all his attention devoted to her. It was always that way with her.

Even at the park, after he'd noticed her, he was lost. He'd intended just to take a late-afternoon stroll through the green, and instead he'd received a lesson on kite flying. Even if their relationship didn't develop into anything permanent, he wanted to become one of the memories she spoke of in later years, wanted to be more than on the periphery of her life.

"I'm truly glad you're here, to get a feel for all we accomplish with the lessons we offer," she said, coming up alongside him.

She hadn't been in the room when he'd first walked into it. Based on the strength of the orange scent surrounding her, he assumed she'd been finishing up her bath in her lodgings above. That thought had him imagining her sinking into the tub of steaming water, dew forming on her skin, gathering in the little notch at her throat that had so enthralled him during their adventure. "Your girl downstairs told me to come up."

"Yes, Marianne watches the door, keeping potential customers out, allowing only students in, as the shop is closed for the evening. You seem to be giving everything a thorough study. Do you find it all to your liking?"

He found her to his liking. Would she give up her quest for a title in order to be with him? Although in the end, through him, she'd acquire what she sought. "I've yet to discern any rhyme or reason to these books, am unable to determine their category." Most appeared to be fiction, but he also noted some biographies and histories as well as a few on travel.

"For the most part, they're stories or subjects I've enjoyed reading."

"It seems an odd thing, though, to send your customers up here, searching for something, rather than having the books downstairs."

"Oh, these are for reading within this room or borrowing."

He faced her. She wore a prim and proper dark burgundy frock that buttoned all the way to her throat, hiding that enticing little hollow, for which he was grateful. He didn't need the distraction or to have his body rebelling as want gave way to desire. "A lending library?"

"Precisely. Except I don't charge a yearly subscription fee. Anyone may take any book home."

"What induces them to bring back the books?"

"Well, hopefully good manners. If, however, they don't return the book, I assume it's because it found a place in their heart—and I don't penalize them for it."

"How can you afford that?"

"Donations. Mostly from my family members, a few of their spouses' relations or friends. Even the lessons we teach are based on the generosity of others. On this shelf here"—she swept her arm to the side—"we have primers. Each new student receives one to take home with him or her, to keep, so they can study it at their leisure. One of the challenges we face is that people have differing levels of knowledge when they arrive and then some are faster learners than others."

"It seems as though it would be less confusing to have terms, as in schools."

"I agree but haven't it in me to turn someone away after they've found the courage to walk through the door to ask for help."

"How many students have you?"

She shrugged. "Probably a dozen or so at any one time, although often fewer show up. Work, family, or life sometimes interferes. Another challenge, remembering what a person has learned and coaxing them along in the right direction."

"It seems it would be a lot less work if you had a more formal schedule."

"Eventually perhaps I will. I hope someday to have a proper school that will focus on the needs of illiterate adults."

A sound at the door caught his attention. She turned and beamed a radiant smile at the tall, slender gent with striking red hair tamed into a modern fashion. "Mr. Tittlefitz."

He approached cautiously, his suspicious gaze flickering between Matthew and Fancy. "Miss Trewlove."

"I'm rather certain you've probably already met Mr. Sommersby. He's leasing—"

"86 Ettie Lane."

"You've quite the memory," Matthew said, reluctantly impressed by the young man's skills.

"Mr. Trewlove expects me to know the tenants, and to quickly see to whatever needs might arise. It helps to recall where they reside."

"I'm certain you've exceeded his expectations, Mr. Tittlefitz," Miss Trewlove said.

The man looked at her with such an adoring manner, she might as well have proclaimed him King. Anyone who drew breath could discern the secretary had a tender regard for his boss's sister, which Matthew was selfishly grateful didn't appear to be returned in kind. She favored him as no more than a friend.

"Mr. Sommersby is considering assisting with the teaching on the nights when I'm not available."

The falling of the young man's joy was subtle. "I could handle it without help." Obviously, his pride had been nicked.

"That's too much to ask of you."

"You may ask anything of me, Miss Trewlove."

Reaching out, she rubbed his shoulder. "I won't take advantage of your generosity and kindness, Mr. Tittlefitz." Looking past him, the smile she gave to the tall, broad man escorting two women through the door was ten times what she'd given Tittlefitz, and Matthew knew a sharp tightening in his chest. Not jealousy, surely.

"Beast!" She rushed across the room and flung herself at him, her arms circling his neck as he caught her easily and held her close. The smoothness of their actions indicated they'd engaged in them a thousand times.

"Her brother," Tittlefitz explained quietly beside him. "He doesn't come around much."

"Doesn't like books?"

Tittlefitz chuckled low. "Too busy terrorizing the darker parts of London from what I understand."

Beast finally released his sister. Matthew could see where the man might have acquired that moniker. His presence fairly swallowed the room, made it seem too small. He possessed a confidence that indicated he was not one to be toyed with.

"I've not seen you in ages," Miss Trewlove said.

"I've been busy, but the lasses here were wanting to learn to read, so I decided to bring them to you."

Matthew watched as she turned to the girls—girls who, to his eye, were women, probably younger than twenty-five although they had a worn, frayed look about them like clothing that had been washed far too many times—and gave them an enthusiastic greeting. "We're so pleased to have you here."

She waved him and the secretary over. "Allow me to introduce Mr. Tittlefitz, one of the tutors. And Mr. Sommersby, who is considering taking on the task of instructing as well. And you are?"

One of the girls—short of stature and quite buxom—homed her gaze in on him and stepped forward. Although she was buttoned up to her chin and down to her wrists, she still managed to bring attention to her well-endowed attributes by moving in a sinewy, lithe motion, like a snake on the verge of striking. "I'm Lottie, I am, and I'm 'appy to do some instructin', 'andsome."

"That's not the reason you're here, Lottie," Beast said, a firmness in his tone that would brook no argument.

"Right." She winked at Matthew. "Maybe after lessons."

"I'm Lily," the other girl said, a bit shyly, not nearly as bold as Lottie. "I know some of me letters, enough to spell me name. I just don't know how to put the rest of 'em to use, so they mean somethin'."

"When we're finished with you, Miss Lily, you'll be able to read and write anything you like," Miss Trewlove said with confidence that would transfer to the doubtful. "Go with Mr. Tittlefitz. He'll get you primers."

"I'll be leaving now," Beast said. "You girls take a hansom back to the lodgings."

"Thanks, Beast," they said in unison, before traipsing after Tittlefitz.

Matthew felt a pat on his backside as Lottie walked by him. Ah, yes, these were well-worn ladies who thrived in the night.

Beast heaved a heavy sigh. "If they give you any trouble, let me know. Sometimes they like to be a bit mischievous, especially Lottie."

"They'll both be fine. Once lessons get started, they'll become enthralled by the learning." She rubbed his arm. "Don't you worry."

After giving his sister another hug, he left. She turned to Matthew. "Mr. Tittlefitz handles the newer students, teaching them their letters and some of the basic words. Miss Lottie might be disappointed when she realizes that. Although you're more than welcome to sit in their circle and observe how he gets on with them if you like."

He couldn't stop himself from smiling. "Is that jealousy in your tone, Miss Trewlove?"

"Certainly not. It's just that she seems to have taken an interest in you."

"I suspect she takes a keen notice of all men. How do you suppose she came to be in your brother's company?"

"Beast has a heart of gold. He's always finding strays or those suffering through hard times and doing what he can to better their lives." She leaned conspiratorially toward him. "I suspect she's a fallen woman—both of them actually—and Beast is striving to reform them. Learning to read is the first step."

"You're not put off by them?"

"If not for my family, it's quite possible I might have traveled the same road they did. I don't sit in judgment, Mr. Sommersby. If you do, then I mistook you for the caring sort, and you are probably not the one to help us out when I'm occupied."

Her eyes reflected her disappointment in him, and it irked that he may have given her reason to find fault with him. "I'm not judging them." He'd be hypocritical if he did. He'd turned to prostitutes in his youth. High-priced ones, to be sure, but they still plied their wares like the poorest of girls who catered to those who lived in the rookeries. "Many women I know wouldn't be as accepting as you. You're quite remarkable."

Lowering her head slightly as though embarrassed, she looked up at him through her long sooty lashes. "Hardly."

He couldn't help but think that suffering through a lack of acceptance in her youth made her more tolerant of others now. "If I'm to replace you, it seems I'd benefit most from sitting in your circle."

Before she could respond, footsteps caught their attention. A woman crossed the threshold and staggered to a stop at the sight of him. Her cheeks flamed such an intense red that he was surprised they didn't ignite.

"Good evening, Mrs. Bennett," Miss Trewlove said. "I believe you know Mr. Sommersby. He's considering assisting Mr. Tittlefitz on the evenings when I'm not available."

His maid-of-all-work gave a little bob of a curtsy. "Mr. Sommersby, sir."

"Mrs. Bennett, it's a pleasure to see you."

"She's one of our best students," Miss Trewlove said.

He'd thought it impossible for her face to flare any redder, but it did, and with slowly dawning awareness, he realized she was mortified he knew she came here. He also now understood why she hadn't left him a note to alert him that Miss Trewlove had paid a call. She couldn't write. "I've no doubt of that whatsoever."

Mrs. Bennett held up her primer, a bit frayed at the corners, the spine bent. "'Tis a gift to be able to read."

"One that is easily shared," Miss Trewlove assured her. "I daresay, Mrs. Bennett, you'll be teaching before too long."

"Ah, I'm not there yet. But soon, hopefully. My husband can read but hasn't the patience to teach me."

"I suspect he's worn-out at the end of the day after giving most of his patience to his workers at the construction site," he said. "But your efforts are commendable, Mrs. Bennett. Learning a new skill, any skill, is always a challenge."

The blush in her cheeks began fading. She seemed truly grateful for his words. He'd complimented numerous ladies, but the praise had always been flirtatious, light and teasing, and women had taken the admiration as their due.

"Get settled and we'll begin work shortly," Miss Trewlove said.

With a duck of her head, Mrs. Bennett scuttled past Matthew. How did she follow a recipe book? She couldn't. Her only choice was to cook whatever her mother or a relation or a friend had taught her, remembering every ingredient, every measurement. He couldn't help but be impressed that she managed not only her household but his. "She was embarrassed by my presence," he said quietly.

"People fear being mocked, berated, or belittled for not possessing skills that others take for granted."

"You give them pride."

"We give them the ability to read. Within these walls we provide a place where they are not judged. Some people learn quickly, others not so fast. We make sure they never feel ashamed—even if they don't master the skill."

"And if I'm like her husband and haven't the patience for it?"

She smiled softly. "Then I'll have misjudged you."

SHE HADN'T. NOT if his enthralled attention was any indication.

Another new student arrived. Based on his wariness as he studied his surroundings like a trapped animal searching for an escape, she suspected he was recently released from prison. In which case, her brother Finn had sent him. Although it had been years since he'd been incarcerated, he tended to offer help to those who needed it when they were set free. He joined Mr. Tittlefitz's group.

Three more current students—two men and a woman—joined her circle. They took turns reading aloud, the others following the story along in their primers. When one of them blundered, she'd gently nudge the lady or gent toward the correct word, helping to sound it out. Although on a couple of occasions, she'd lost her place and stumbled, and Mr. Sommersby had been the one to assist her. It was disconcerting having him so near, sitting beside her, facing the students.

Her lungs were filled with his scent of bay rum. He looked so splendidly handsome in a navy jacket and trousers, gray waistcoat, snowy white shirt, and perfectly knotted cravat. Her gaze kept wandering over to him, and every so often, his would glide over to clash against hers. Her cheeks would warm as she turned her attention back to the task at hand. She couldn't help but believe that something was shifting between them and could only hope it wasn't unwise to find excuses to have him near.

An hour in, several footmen from the hotel dining room paraded in, carrying small cakes, biscuits, and tea. She stood and clapped her hands. "Refreshments have arrived. We'll take a short break now."

As people scattered, the footmen set their items on a table near the door and began serving.

"Your brother provides the food and drink, I assume," Mr. Sommersby said quietly just over her shoulder, creating a tingle of pleasure that traversed along her spine with his nearness. It took every morsel of dignity she possessed not to back into him so his arms could encircle her as they had yesterday afternoon.

"Yes. I suspect the offering entices at least one of our students to return." She faced him. "May I prepare you some tea?"

"No, thank you. After this, I'll be headed for a glass of scotch."

"Is it so awful?"

He slowly shook his head. "No, but it is humbling to realize how often I've taken reading for granted. It's a remarkable thing you're striving to accomplish here, Miss Trewlove."

"It's a small thing really. I appreciate how you helped me earlier when I stumbled."

His gaze roamed slowly over her face as though he were searching for something. "Why did you stumble?"

Because I find myself drawn to you and in two nights, I'll be at a ball hoping to garner the favor of some lord—

"Whew, it's 'ot in 'ere, id'n it?" Lottie asked as she wedged herself between Fancy and Mr. Sommersby, who was forced to take a step back to avoid having the woman pressed up against him.

Fancy watched in fascination as Lottie gave freedom to three buttons on her bodice and then trailed her finger over the exposed flesh. "Would ye loike to go outside, 'ansome, where it's a bit cooler?"

"No, thank you."

She shifted her gaze to the side, to Fancy. "She's a proper lady, she is. She won't even give ye a kiss."

Fancy nearly shoved the woman aside in order to prove her wrong by latching her mouth on to Mr. Sommersby's. That thought brought her up short. Whatever was wrong with her? Was she truly thinking of kissing him? She couldn't deny wondering what it might be like to have his mouth pressed up against hers. "I would very much hate to have to report your inappropriate behavior to Beast. You might want to do yourself a favor by returning to your studies."

Lottie winked at Mr. Sommersby. "Ye might get that kiss ye be wantin' after all."

She sauntered away, her hips swaying in such an exaggerated fashion that Fancy was surprised the woman didn't harm herself. Her parting words made it difficult to meet Mr. Sommersby's eyes. Instead she settled on studying his chin. It was one of the finer examples of nature doing its best work. It jutted out, not too much, but enough so it didn't become lost in the muscles of his throat. It fanned out into a strong, square jaw, well-defined but then everything about him was.

"We should probably return to our lessons now." She despised how her voice sounded almost meek, a tiny bit breathless.

"She wasn't half-wrong, you know."

Her gaze did jump to his then. "About it being hot in here?"

"About my wanting to kiss you."

Chapter 10

$\mathcal{H}$e shouldn't have said it, but hell, it was hard not to want to devour her mouth when the woman was passionate about every damn thing in her life. He watched her turn red and nod jerkily, before she mumbled something about getting back to work. Then she gathered her students around her like a goose her goslings—or perhaps a knight his armor. He'd unnerved her, which hadn't been his intention. Yet, he'd felt a need to at least confirm he was drawn to her.

Did she truly think that men attending the ball weren't going to want a taste of that luscious mouth? That any gent in her company wasn't wondering what it might be like to press his lips to hers, urge them to part, and slide his tongue inside in order to know fully the velvety confines within and the taste of her?

If his thoughts continued on this path, he was going to grow hard and embarrass himself. The doxy would certainly notice and no doubt call attention to him or at least tease him unmercifully later. So he focused on her hair, the silkiness of it, and how the heavy black strands would flow over his hands if he removed the pins holding them in place. He shifted uncomfortably in his chair. That foray certainly hadn't helped matters.

So he concentrated on the fact that her attention wasn't on him, was on the others as they struggled to make sense of the words that told the story of a young girl who dreamed of attending a ball and capturing the attention of a prince—very much as Miss

Trewlove dreamed of capturing the attention of a lord at her up-coming ball. He imagined her being whisked over the dance floor, the joy that would light her eyes, the smile she would bestow on her partner. She would meet more than a handful of other gents, become enamored of them, and perhaps one would take her for a ride in a hot air balloon—if he cared enough to learn about the things she might enjoy. If she wasn't merely a dowry to fill empty coffers. If they would look beyond her birth in order to appreciate the remarkable woman she was.

She had the skills and intelligence to successfully manage a bookshop. She had the generosity of spirit to make books available to those who couldn't afford them. She sought to better the lives of the overlooked by giving them the gift of reading. She didn't sit in judgment of people, not even women who earned their keep upon their backs. She was goodness, and kindness, and saw the best in those around her.

Becoming aware of the echo of books closing, he realized he'd lost his way in the narrative, hadn't been listening as passages were read. Not that it mattered, not tonight. He wasn't a tutor, merely an observer.

People stood. Offering words of encouragement, she hugged each one before they began wandering toward the door. She even had something reassuring to say to the pupils Mr. Tittlefitz had worked with. While the secretary began tidying up, spread-ing chairs throughout the room, not having to bother with the refreshments because the footmen had cleared all that away be-fore taking their leave, she turned to Matthew. "What do you think?"

"It's a commendable endeavor."

"Will you be part of it?"

He gave a brisk nod. "On the nights when you're not available."

Her beatific smile nearly dropped him to his knees. Did she have to be so bloody grateful?

"He's going to assist you, Mr. Tittlefitz."

"Jolly good." The man's tone lacked enthusiasm, and Matthew

was left with the impression the fellow didn't think it was good at all. "I'll see you Wednesday, then. Good night, Miss Trewlove, Mr. Sommersby."

"Enjoy the remainder of your evening," she encouraged him.

With a brusque nod, the young man made toward the exit, surprising Matthew by his willingness to leave him alone with Miss Trewlove, although he supposed her young clerk was about somewhere.

"Oh, Mr. Tittlefitz?" she called out as he reached the door. Abruptly, he stopped to face her. "Would you be so kind as to walk Marianne home? She doesn't live far from here, and while I know Mick works hard to keep the streets safe, it is dark."

"I'll be happy to escort her, Miss Trewlove."

When Matthew could no longer hear the man's steps on the stairs, he spoke. "He is enamored of you, you know?"

Her cheeks blossomed like the pinkest rose unfurling. "I'm aware, but I've never viewed him as anything other than a friend." Pressing her lips together, she looked somewhat guilty. "However, Marianne has a tender regard for him."

He tilted his head to the side, giving her what he knew was an admonishing stare. In his youth, he'd spent hours before a looking glass practicing a series of expressions designed to put people in their place or cause them to move more quickly. "Are you playing matchmaker, Miss Trewlove?"

With a grin, she held up her thumb and forefinger with only a tiny bit of space between them. "Perhaps a little. They're really quite perfect for each other, if he would only notice her."

"When one's head is turned by another, it's difficult to notice anyone else."

"Do you speak from experience?"

"Unfortunately. I suppose the lessons are at the same time on Wednesday."

"Yes, although the students will be different. One class a week is all most of the students have time for."

"You won't be here at all?" Her absence made him fear the

evening would be rather bleak. Still, he would endure it if for no other reason than to please her.

"I'll pop in before I head to the ball."

"Are you nervous?"

"No, I have complete faith in your ability to guide the students in their reading."

He had little doubt she'd purposely misunderstood his question, and perhaps her doing so provided the answer and yet he yearned to hear it from her. "About the ball."

She nodded. "Rather. I'm not certain that even having relations who are part of the aristocracy is enough to see me accepted."

"Simply be yourself, Miss Trewlove. You'll win them over."

Her light laughter echoed around them, through him as though the center of his chest served as its North Star. "As though you know what the nobility will welcome." She turned on her heel. "Come along."

He followed her down the stairs. Her hips didn't sway as much as Lottie's and yet they were all the more provocative because of it. She was all the more provocative. She was small of stature and yet there was a mightiness to her that filled the space as adeptly as her brother had earlier. Something about her made it impossible to ignore her, not to notice her, not to want to map out every aspect of her from the tips of her toes to the top of her head, as well as her heart and her soul and her thoughts, beliefs, and dreams. Never before had he found a woman so compelling, had he yearned to fully understand everything about her, every aspect that encompassed her and made her who she was. He'd like very much to have her arms around him, to have her pressed up against the length of him, to have his hands skimming over the silkiness of her cheek.

The shop was quiet, in a comforting sort of way. Somewhere a clock was ticking. He stood at the door, waiting to depart, while light from a distant streetlamp spilled through the window to flow over her, creating a mesmerizing array of light and dark shadows, deep curves, enticing lines. She was temptation itself, and he had the unconscionable image of her suddenly reaching up, loosening the three buttons that followed the line from her throat, and slowly trailing a finger along the narrow length of exposed skin.

"May I show you something?"

Please do. Even one loosened button—

He gave his mind a mental shake. His thoughts were traipsing toward the gutter, and she deserved much better than that. "What did you have in mind?"

"Over here. I've placed it against the far wall so the sun can't reach it."

He followed her across the room to where a large clock stood. Beside it was a glass case perched on a wooden pedestal. Beneath the glass, open and spread beautifully like a butterfly's wings, was the book he'd sent to her.

"It contains the original versions of Shakespeare's plays," she whispered reverently. Gingerly she touched her fingers to the edge of the case, and he imagined the prince approaching Sleeping Beauty with the same caution. "It was printed more than two hundred years ago. After all these years there can't be that many copies left. Do you have any idea what a rare find this is?"

He'd known she'd appreciate it, far more than any of his ancestors had, far more than any future generations would. "How did you come to have it?"

With her brow deeply furrowed, she looked up at him. "That's just it. I don't really know. An elderly gentleman brought it in and left it with no explanation."

Jenkins. He should have known the man wouldn't leave the chore to anyone else.

She sighed, waved her hand. "A few bookshop owners and a couple of antiquities dealers know I'm always in the market for the unusual but this . . . it's worth a fortune."

"You could sell it to finance your lessons."

She glared at him as though he'd sprouted horns and a tail. "It's not the sort of thing one sells. If anything, I should donate it to a museum. But it seems rather at home here, and I'm reluctant to part with it."

"Especially as you already had a way to display it."

"Oh no. I designed what I wanted, and then took it to Mr. Bennett before going to church yesterday. He was kind enough to put it together for me using leftover bits from all the construction Mick is doing and brought it to me this morning. I just wish I knew who sent it."

"Someone who wanted you to have it, I should think."

"But why?"

"I wouldn't look a gift horse in the mouth, Miss Trewlove. I doubt any other person alive would give it as much care."

She smiled softly. "You may have the right of it there. Of all the people I know, I thought you would appreciate it the most."

What he appreciated was that he'd accurately judged the joy it would bring her. Looking up at him, she held his gaze for the longest moment, as though she were waiting for something, for something more than words about a book. He was incredibly tempted to take her face between his hands and tell her that she was as rare a find as the original version of Shakespeare's plays. "I should be off."

The forced words sounded almost strangled. He wondered how she would react if he leaned in and kissed her. Would she stop him? Was she saving those lips for her lord—or would she be willing to experience a taste of passion and pleasure?

"You're welcome to take a book with you. Not to borrow, but to keep. It's how I thank those who assist me in my endeavors to educate."

"It's a wonder, Miss Trewlove, that you make any profit at all with your penchant for giving people books without taking coins in return."

"I wouldn't object to your calling me Fancy."

A courtesy she'd obviously not bestowed upon Mr. Tittlefitz, a courtesy he would be a fool to accept as viewing her in an informal light could have him lowering his guard, allowing her to skirt past his defenses when she was already battering at the wall. How easy it would be to simply allow it to crumble, to open himself up to the possibility of having her in his life on a more permanent basis. But he needed to test the waters with her first. He'd lived the old adage about marrying in haste and repenting in leisure. He wasn't going to make that mistake again. "Good night, Miss Trewlove."

She offered up a tentative smile, and he regretted that he might have hurt her with his rebuff of her offer to call her by her Christian name. "Good night, Mr. Sommersby."

He didn't go straight home, but instead wandered through the streets, his mind a chaotic swirl as he debated the wisdom of pursuing her without telling her who he was. But how else was he to be sure her feelings toward him weren't influenced by his position? When he finally returned to his residence, he followed his usual routine of pouring himself a glass of scotch, walking upstairs to his bedchamber, and gazing out the window.

Only tonight he was met with a lovely view. Fancy Trewlove sitting in the reading nook she'd told him about. Her profile to him, her back against a wall. He could see only a portion of her: chest, shoulders, head, bent knees upon which a book rested. Then she twisted slightly, lifted a hand, and waved. So simple an action that seemed to reach down and touch something deep inside him.

Without much thought, he set his glass aside, shoved a chair in front of his own window, grabbed a book, and sat. With any luck, he'd give the appearance of reading, while in truth he was simply watching her, wondering how the mere sight of her could bring such calm to his soul, knowing when he finally retired for the evening, he would dream of making love to a shopgirl.

Chapter 11

*T*he following afternoon, inside the sweet shop unimaginatively named "Sweet Shop," Matthew studied the selections within the glass case. In the mood for some sugar, but without even a hint of lemon, he'd already perused the jars on the shelves and found nothing of interest. When the bell above the door jangled, he didn't bother to look, his focus narrowing to some red hard candies.

"Good afternoon, Miss Trewlove," the silver-haired lady behind the counter said with enthusiasm.

He couldn't stop himself from turning then. Did the woman always wear a smile? Was she always glad to see people?

"Hello, Mrs. Flowers." Her eyes warmed. "Mr. Sommersby."

"Miss Trewlove." Her yellow frock reminded him of the sun cascading over a field of clover. With so little effort, she seemed able to brighten the dullest day.

Moving up to the counter, she set a piece of paper on top of it. "These are the sweets I'd like to have on hand for Friday's reading time."

Mrs. Flowers—he now knew the woman's name thanks to Miss Trewlove and regretted that he'd been remiss in introducing himself. It was such a small thing to call someone by name, but he'd seen an immediate change in the clerk as though she'd been greeted by royalty—took the paper and read it over. "Ooh, strawberry bonbons. They'll delight the little tykes."

"I thought they might."

"They'll make a mess with them, though."

"I'll have damp linens on hand for cleaning sticky fingers."

"But if they get your books dirty—"

"I'd rather they look at them with dirty fingers than not look at them at all."

He couldn't imagine his own mother having that attitude. As a lad, he'd been bathed and placed in fresh clothes anytime he came in from outside or just before he was presented to her in the afternoon, so she could ask him how he'd occupied his time. He suspected Miss Trewlove would give her children more than half an hour a day, that she wouldn't have to ask how they'd spent their day because she would be involved in their play, their studies, their lives. She would embrace them, never causing them to doubt they were loved.

"Then I'll have this order filled and delivered to you before noon on Friday. Is there anything else I can get for you?"

"Think I'll just have a look." She eased over until she was standing near enough that he could smell the fragrance of oranges. "Have you a sweet tooth, Mr. Sommersby?"

"On occasion. I'm not really certain what I'm in the mood for, however."

"I favor toffee myself."

"Hmm. I haven't had that since I was lad. I'll take a dozen toffees, Mrs. Flowers."

"Very good, sir."

"I'll have the same," Miss Trewlove said.

"Put them on my tab, Mrs. Flowers."

"Please don't. You're going to start rumors flying about."

Rumors that perhaps he had an interest in her. Based on the way Mrs. Flowers was watching them, he doubted a penny purchase was going to make any difference. She was going to tattle one way or the other. As he'd long been fodder for gossip, he wasn't bothered by the notion of a bit more, especially when it would be harmless nattering. "It's a small way to thank you for welcoming me into the area. Besides, when you have your coming out, you're going to discover nothing prevents the spread of sensationalized tales. You might as well embrace it."

After he paid for the purchases, he handed her the sack and followed her out onto the pavement. She immediately popped a toffee into her mouth. He watched the twisting of her lips as she stroked her tongue over the hard candy. He didn't know if anything had ever been more sensual than the movements he couldn't see, could only imagine as he envisioned her sucking, stroking, working her tongue over another hard surface. Christ, he needed to regain control of his errant thoughts.

She stood there as though reluctant to leave him as much as he was to bid her farewell. "Have you plans for your last evening before your Season officially begins?"

A bit of wickedness sparked in her eyes. "I hear the Fire King will be performing in Whitechapel. I intend to go see him. I'm rather certain there will be room in the hansom if you've a mind to spend your night enjoying street entertainments."

"DID YOU GROW up in Whitechapel?" he asked her several hours later as they strolled along the crowded street where people jostled each other to get a view of the tumblers or the jugglers or the men walking about on stilts.

"No, but near here."

Matthew had been to fetes, fairs, carnivals, even a circus. What he was observing now reminded him of a carnival, but it was in the city, in the streets, rather than in the country, on a lawn with lots of space around it. He suspected a good many of these people hadn't the means to take the railway out into the country, and so the performers had brought their talents here and created a festival with a joyous atmosphere.

But in spite of all the frivolity and the attention-seekers, his gaze kept drifting over to Miss Trewlove, her enthusiasm and excitement intoxicating. She appreciated her surroundings in a way few did. She understood the need for the poor to escape into fantasy, the need for the performers to be valued. She took in everything with the same intensity that he imagined she took in the pages of a novel, wondrously transported into another realm. She didn't judge, found no fault. She merely immersed herself in the ambiance.

He couldn't imagine any woman of his acquaintance walking boldly among those who appeared they'd not bathed in a while or whose clothing was frayed and tattered while smiling at them, greeting them as though they were long-lost friends.

"Do you know these people?" he finally asked.

"I've never seen them before, but they aren't so different from all the people I do know. Struggling to make ends meet, doing the best they can with what they have, hoping for something better for their children, enjoying a night without cares." Earlier, she'd entwined her arm around his to ensure they weren't separated, and now she gave it a squeeze. "Don't you love how much fun everyone is having?"

He loved how much fun she seemed to be having, completely free of cares, giving no thought to what she might be facing tomorrow night. As the wife of a lord, she would host affairs, and he couldn't imagine that anything under her command would be staid or dull. She would find a way to make everything interesting and exciting.

"Oh, look, there he is! Come on!" She grabbed his hand, and while they both wore gloves, it seemed far more intimate a joining than her arm intertwined with his.

He found himself closing his much larger hand around her smaller one. So tiny. He was beginning to understand why her family was taking such extreme measures to see her well situated—whether within the nobility or not. They felt a need to protect her, to ensure no harm ever came to her. Yet, he wasn't certain she was deserving of their worry. Here she was wending her way between people, causing others to step aside as though the Queen were barreling through them. No one took offense, no one reacted in anger. She had the ability to be soothing even as she made people feel guilty for being a barrier to her destination.

With a great deal of poise and confidence, she worked her way to the front, tugging him along behind her. It was packed here, people scrunched up together, stretching their necks, striving to get a better view of what was happening within the circle they'd created. He slid in behind her, putting his arms around her, much as he had when they'd flown the kite, but there was no spindle to hold so he simply folded his hands over her stomach. He had little doubt that if she objected, she'd have elbowed him in the gut or stomped on his foot. Instead, she merely settled against him as though she belonged there.

And damn if he didn't feel that she did.

Turning her head slightly, she fairly yelled in order to be heard above the cacophony. "Isn't he marvelous?"

Finally, he turned his attention to the reason they'd undertaken this adventure. The gentleman strutting around the empty space that had been made available to him was well over six feet, possibly falling just shy of six and half. He was broad, muscle upon muscle visible because he wore naught but breeches and boots. His dark skin glistened in the light of the flaming torch he held.

"Behold!" he called out in a booming voice. "The wonder that was once dragons!"

He took a sip from the pewter tankard he held, strode around the edge of the makeshift circle, before taking up position in its center. He held up the torch, puckered his mouth slightly as though to whistle, spewed liquid, and when he drew the torch away, a stream of fire arced upward into the darkness above. When the fire vanished, he spread his arms wide and smiled broadly. "Are you entertained?"

The crowd was deafening with their cheers, and once again, he strode around the perimeter, before moving to the center and giving those watching another display of his control over fire. Once. Twice. Three times.

Matthew could fairly feel Miss Trewlove shimmering with excitement in his arms, and he rather wished he'd been the one responsible for her trembling, her exhilaration. Yet he couldn't deny the Fire King deserved the adulation showered on him, as his minions gathered up the coins tossed at his feet.

He handed his torch and tankard off to someone and gave a sweeping bow before raising his arms high. "Thank you, my friends. Please be gracious enough to move on and allow others in before the next performance in fifteen minutes."

Matthew lowered his mouth to the delicate shell of her ear, so he wouldn't have to shout. "I suppose we should be moving on."

"Not yet."

Glancing in the direction she was looking, he realized the Fire King was striding purposely in a direct path toward her. As though anticipating his arrival, she moved out of Matthew's arms, which caused him to have an instant dislike for the man.

"Hello, Fancy." Leaning down, he bussed a quick kiss over her cheek—which she'd turned up to him—and it took everything within Matthew not to punch the bloke's perfect nose.

"The last time I saw you, you were swallowing fire."

"Got bored with that. Decided breathing it was more exciting."

"How do you do it?"

"Tricks of the trade, my sweet."

My sweet? A bloodied nose was becoming more a probability.

Fancy—damn it, if this man could address her as such, Matthew could certainly think of her with less formality—turned slightly. "Fire King, meet Mr. Sommersby."

"Mister?" The Fire King—what a ridiculous name—repeated. "Thought you were destined for a duke, my girl."

My girl? A bloodied nose and a blackened eye, perhaps, were in order. And did every person in Christendom know she was on the hunt for a lord?

"We're not married," she said. "We're simply friends enjoying a night of entertainment."

"Your brothers don't know about him, I suspect."

"No, and you're not going to tell them."

"When would I have the opportunity? I haven't seen them in ages." He gave Matthew a long once-over. "Take care of her, mate."

Then he was striding off with his torch and tankard bearer striving to catch up.

"You didn't mention you knew him." Matthew modulated his tone, striving not to sound jealous.

"I met him shortly after he began performing. The Fire King. What young girl wouldn't be captivated? He has quite a following."

"I imagine he does."

She angled her head slightly. "You sound jealous."

"Don't be absurd." He was being absurd enough for both of them.

She slipped her arm around his. "Shall we see what other entertainments await us?"

GROWING UP, FANCY had always enjoyed the nights when the streets transformed into a festival. Some of these people made their living performing while others brought out their talents only on those occasions when they could share the attention. She suspected it wasn't an easy life, but then very little in the rookeries was.

But on nights like this it was so lively, so energetic. And she certainly enjoyed sharing it with Mr. Sommersby. He seemed at once enthralled and wary, as though expecting to be attacked at any moment. Although she knew all she had to do was say, "I'm Fancy Trewlove," and any bad characters would skitter away. Such was her brothers' reputation and power in this area of London. While Mick, Aiden, and Finn were no longer a part of the rookeries, like Beast now, they had at one time ruled them. Anyone with any sense at all avoided getting on the wrong side of a Trewlove. It always ended badly, and not for the Trewloves.

She very much liked having her arm wrapped around Mr. Sommersby's. She liked even more the way he would shift his body slightly to protect her if it appeared that anyone with too much drink in him might stagger into her. His movements were subtle, but she noted them all the same. Although it seemed she noted the smallest of things about him. His alertness and the way his head swiveled as though he were constantly watching for any sign of danger. His hands fisting as she'd spoken with the Fire King as though he were jealous. The subtle way he removed coins from his pocket and handed one at a time off to the barefoot children they passed. So many coins, leading her to believe it was a habit he engaged in when he wandered through the poorer sections of London. He'd known what to expect here, and he'd come prepared.

It was chaotic in this area tonight. Food carts. Drink carts. Shell games. A sword swallower. A few small tents rested along the walls. Inside were all manner of things to be seen for a penny. A female contortionist advertised as being a human puzzle box. "It's impossible to tell where she starts and where she ends!" the barker shouted.

But Fancy was drawn to the rotund man with the balding pate shouting about debauchery and wickedness. "Come one, come all to decadence in all its glory!" Then he caught her eye and began waving her over with exaggerated sweeps of his arm. "Come, lady. Come and behold what your eyes have never seen!"

"What do you suppose that's about?" Fancy asked Mr. Sommersby.

"If it's something you've never seen then it's probably something you shouldn't see."

His words only served to ignite her curiosity more. "I'm going to have a look."

"Miss Trewlove, I'm not certain that's wise."

"It's not as though I'm swallowing fire. You can come with me if you like."

Boldly, she approached the gent and handed him a penny. With a flourish he held back the tent flap, and she was a bit relieved when Mr. Sommersby followed her inside the confining space. A lit lantern rested beside a stereoscope on a small table. She glanced around. "Do you believe that's it?"

"Appears so. I'll have a look—"

"No, I'm going first." Taking a deep breath, she picked up the stereoscope and peered through the two glass circles at the image that seemed almost real enough to touch. She was very much aware of Mr. Sommersby's chest brushing up against her shoulder blade, and that touch was no doubt responsible for the heat cascading through her—not the disappointing photograph at which she was looking.

"Well?" His voice was a rasp near her ear, his warm breath skimming along her cheek.

"It's a woman . . . lounging on a settee . . . in her unmentionables." Except they were barely on. The swell of one breast was clearly visible, her nipple hidden, although it appeared the cloth was in danger of slipping away completely.

"My turn."

"Absolutely not." She jerked the contraption away from her eyes and hugged it to her midsection. "You don't need to view a woman in her disarray."

He'd not moved, was still incredibly close. "I've seen women in their unmentionables, Miss Trewlove. In fact, I have taken great pleasure in removing said unmentionables."

His voice had gone deeper, lower, to a depth where secrets were best shared, and she quite suddenly found it difficult to breathe, imagining his finger gliding along lace and slipping silk down, down, down until nothing was covered. She was trembling with desire as the images bombarded her. "It's not fair."

"Pardon?"

She glanced back at him, not having to look far, realizing his mouth was now incredibly close to hers. The heat, the desire, the yearning increased. It was wrong, so wrong, not at all proper. "Where's the photograph of a man in his smalls?"

His eyes grew large. "You want to see a man in his smalls?"

"Why not? The barker claimed I'd see what I'd never beheld. I've seen myself in my unmentionables, standing before the cheval glass." When his eyes darkened, and his gaze intensified as though he was now having the improper thoughts that his earlier words had elicited within her, she suddenly had a need to torture him as much as he had her. "In fact, I have seen myself in nothing at all."

He went still, so very still, as though he might shatter if he moved. His eyes smoldered to such a degree, she thought she might very well ignite. She wasn't particularly learned when it came to men but had no doubt that she was witnessing the birth of desire. "You're playing a dangerous game, Miss Trewlove."

"Am I?"

Slowly, he lowered his head, not to her mouth as she'd expected, but to her neck, just below her ear where the skin was more sensitive than she'd ever realized. He kissed, nipped, stroked his tongue over the delicate flesh, and the incredible sensations traveled clear down to her toes. When he took her lobe between his teeth, she nearly cried out from the pleasure of it. Her knees weakened. The stereoscope slipped from her hands and fell to the ground. She didn't care, didn't care about anything other than the journey of his mouth along the underside of her jaw. All the din and commotion outside fell away. All she heard was his breathing and low moans.

When he pulled away, she nearly begged him to come back. "You're the one playing a dangerous game." She did wish she hadn't sounded breathless, had given the impression of being more in control.

His grin was devilishly wicked. "But I understand the rules. Don't think for a moment I'm not tempted to set you on that table and take you here and now. But I would ruin you for anyone else."

Ruin me. Had she really just had that thought?

"I don't think you're ready to pay that price," he continued.

She was not going to be disappointed he was a gentleman and not a scoundrel. He had the right of things. Being ruined would not fit at all into her plans. Although she had the impression that he wasn't referring to ruining her precisely but rather that she would never find with any other man the satisfaction she would find with him. She might label him as arrogant if she wasn't convinced that he was no doubt speaking the truth.

Seeming to comprehend that she had no witty response to his

claims, he bent down, picked up the stereoscope, and placed it back on the table.

"Aren't you going to look?" she asked. "You paid your penny."

"Oh, I've gotten more than my money's worth." Then he offered her his arm, and she wrapped hers around it.

"Took ye long enough," the barker said when they finally exited the tent. "Gonna have to ask for another penny."

Mr. Sommersby handed it over, and they strolled on. She had come here to distract herself from thinking about what tomorrow night would bring. But now she had to wonder if it would be possible to meet any lord whom she would desire as much as she did this man.

Chapter 12

"*O*nce . . . up . . . on a . . . ti . . . time . . . theer . . ."

"There," Matthew correctly gently.

The reader, a woman who appeared worn by life, her blond hair pulled back in an untidy bun, looked up at him with large pale blue eyes. "But I thought the *e* at the end made the vowel sound different. Like in time. The *i* don't sound like the *i* in Tim and that's 'cuz of the *e* at the end."

"Yes, well, there are exceptions. Some words you have to memorize rather than sounding them out."

She scowled. "Readin's 'ard."

"At first. But it does get easier, and it's rather worth the challenge of it."

She returned her attention to the primer, having more luck with the words that followed. The book was the sort used in schools. The alphabet was listed in the beginning, then two stories followed. She'd apparently already made her way through *Cinderilla* with Fancy and was now eagerly tackling *Little Red Riding Hood*. He suspected for many the primer Fancy gave them was the first book they'd ever owned. For some it was no doubt the first they'd ever held.

Four others sat in the circle with him, following along in their primers, awaiting their turn to read the words aloud. He strove very hard not to make those gathered around him feel embarrassed when they stumbled. Even if one didn't read perfectly, one was trying and that was the true accomplishment—seeking to better oneself, doing what was necessary to reach that end.

Just as Fancy was seeking to better her lot in life by attending a ball tonight and snagging the attention of some lord. He was tempted to give her a list of swells to avoid, but then she'd wonder how he knew them, and he'd have to confess he was the one about whom the letter had been penned and published for all the world to see. The suddenly heralded Earl of Rosemont. She'd view him differently then, and he didn't want to be looked upon like he was a prize to be won.

He was continually distracted by the bumps, taps, and scrapes coming from the floor above him. An hour earlier, a veritable phalanx of maids had paraded past the doorway and taken the stairs up to Fancy's lodgings. He suspected the servants had been sent over by Lady Aslyn. His mind kept envisioning what was happening up there as they prepared her for this auspicious night that could very well set her on a course that would take her away from her little shop.

It didn't help at all that the night before she'd put in his head the image of her standing before a mirror sans clothing. A bath would have been prepared. She would have lowered her nude form into it. The steam would float up to caress and coat her skin in dew, some gathering in that enticing notch at her throat. The water, if not the soap, would be perfumed, and she would arise from the tub like a nymph from a lake, carrying the scent of flowers in a meadow.

Someone would use soft linen to remove the water droplets from her flesh. Another would brush the long silky length of her black hair. He imagined how marvelous it would feel to sink his fingers into the glorious strands or gather up the thick tresses and drape them over her shoulder in order to leave her nape unobstructed so he could place a warm kiss on either side of her ridged spine. The last thought caused a reaction in the lower half of his body that had him shifting uncomfortably in his chair, a reaction he should have grown accustomed to by now because it happened each time he thought of touching his lips to any aspect of her body. Her mouth, her fingers, her toes, her breasts—

Christ, he needed to get hold of himself. Thank goodness, the noises above had quieted. Suddenly light footsteps began echoing from the direction of the stairs. In perfect alignment signaling pride as though they'd just achieved victory in a crucial military campaign, the maids marched by the open doorway.

The room went quiet. No stammering of words or encouragement uttered, the girl in the red hooded cloak abandoned, her story no match for the suspense that had captured everyone's attention, their gazes going to the empty portal where the servants were last seen. Because if they were done with their task and taken their leave, then could *she* be far behind? So like the others, he gave his full attention to the doorway and waited, as an anticipation he'd not known in years took hold and blossomed. An itch took up residence on the tip of his nose, but it went undisturbed as none of his muscles seemed wont to move.

Then she appeared and stole his breath.

Her white gown, what she might have worn had she been presented to the Queen, lovingly caressed her form, outlining the gentle swell of her breasts, the tuck at her waist, the rounding of her hips. Pearls adorned her throat. Miniature ones sewn in intricate patterns over the bodice caught the gaslight and winked as she strode into the room. A fan dangled from her wrist. Long white silk gloves traveled from her fingertips to just past her elbow, and he imagined a gentleman taking her for a stroll about the garden searching for a dark corner where he could roll them off and kiss the suddenly revealed flesh.

Her dark hair had been gathered into an elaborate coiffure, held in place with pearl combs that stood out in stark relief against the black background of her tresses. Her brown eyes seemed larger, more luminous. Her cheeks sported a bright pink, no doubt a result of her excitement for the evening ahead. She smiled warmly, softly. "I simply wanted to wish you all a good evening before I leave."

"You . . . you look . . . uh, gorgeous, Miss Trewlove," Mr. Tittlefitz stammered.

"Thank you, Mr. Tittlefitz. You're most kind to say so. I do rather feel like Cinderilla after all the attention the kind maids gave me."

She slid her gaze over to Matthew. Only then did he realize that at some point her arrival had stirred him to come to his feet. She was waiting for him to speak. He was rather certain of it, and yet no words he uttered would do her justice. Still he could not allow her to leave with even a pinch of her confidence shaken. "No woman there shall outshine you."

Her cheeks turned a deeper hue. Her eyelashes fluttered, not in a teasing manner, but as though she were touched by his paltry compliment. Or perhaps embarrassed he should say such a thing. What had she wanted to hear from him? Whatever it was, he'd have spoken the words she yearned for—if he'd only known what they were.

She looked back at the younger man. "You will lock up when you're done here tonight, Mr. Tittlefitz?"

"Yes, miss. You're not to worry yourself. Mr. Sommersby and I have everything well in hand."

"And you'll see Marianne home?"

"Yes, miss."

He couldn't help but smile. Even on the most important night of her life to date, she was still thinking of others, striving to play matchmaker, and he wondered if she ever selfishly put herself first.

"Good night, then." With poise befitting a princess, she disappeared from sight.

Being introduced into Society was a nerve-racking affair that slowly morphed into a tedious, boring one as Fancy stood beside Gillie, welcoming the guests who descended the wide sweeping staircase into the elaborately decorated grand salon—with its massive sparkling chandeliers, ornate molding, and painted ceiling—after being announced in a deep, booming voice by the majordomo outfitted in a red jacket, heavy with gold braiding, gray knee pants, and white stockings that showed off his lovely calves, which looked to be natural. She was well aware footmen took pride in their calves, some even going so far as to pad themselves with false ones.

Gillie's lavender gown was not as revealing as some, but then her sister never had flaunted her femininity. Her duke was at her side, his eyes reflecting the sort of tenderness and fondness Fancy hoped to inspire in some young lord.

She dearly wished her mum was here to see it all, but she felt out of place around such extravagance. One wall was naught but mirrors, which made it seem that so many more people were here than there were. The room was two floors in height, a balcony circling three sides, cutting it in half. Potted plants, ferns, and fronds lined the walls. Flowers seemed to be everywhere. It was all so glamorous. It was the world her mother had wanted her to step into, and yet the dear woman didn't believe herself deserving of walking into this room tonight.

Oh, she'd visited Gillie's residence, but when only family was about. She shied away from meeting anyone she considered above her. Her mum's refusal to recognize her own worth saddened Fancy.

She had traveled in the coach with Aslyn and Mick. As promised, they'd stopped at their mum's so she could see Fancy decked out in her finery. Her mum had wept at the sight of her—tears of joy, she'd claimed. Fancy desperately wanted tonight to be a success, to bring her one step closer to helping her mum realize her dream of Fancy having a posh life.

On her journey here, Aslyn and Mick had run her through her paces to ensure she knew how to address everyone who was likely to be in attendance. Her family's greatest fear had been that no one would show. It was a fear not realized. The room was practically wall-to-wall people. She wasn't vain enough to think they were there on her account. No, she suspected the majority of them had come to gawk at the Duke of Thornley's wife and measure her worth as she hosted her first ball. Although Gillie seemed far more relaxed than Fancy felt.

It hadn't helped calm her nerves any that when they'd arrived, the Duke of Thornley had casually told her, "Bertie sends his regrets, but affairs of state will prevent him from attending."

Bertie. Prince of Wales. Future king.

Thornley had spoken his name as though he had an intimate friendship with the man, played lawn tennis and polo with him. He probably did. She'd never really given any thought to the fact that her sister's husband spoke to royalty and no doubt did it with the same aplomb he exhibited as he faced the queue of guests waiting to be received. He seemed to know them all. After greeting someone, he'd turn to Gillie and say, "Duchess, I want to present to you Lord Whoever or Lady X or Lord and Lady Z or the Duke of Whatever." Gillie would smile the smile that welcomed everyone into her tavern and made them feel right at home. "A pleasure. My sister, Miss Trewlove."

Each guest curtsied or bowed to Gillie—she was after all a duchess. Fancy received a few curt nods of the head, a good many quick touches of her gloved fingers, a few actual kisses to her fingertips, followed by "My pleasure." Then on they walked to visit with those they knew, to enjoy refreshments, or take a turn about the dance floor while a twenty-piece orchestra seated in the balcony played the most enticing music.

And so it went.

The elaborate dance card shaped like a fan with a tiny pencil attached to it via a string that she'd been given by a young maid when she'd first arrived dangled from her wrist, not a single dance claimed. No waltz, no quadrille, no polka. She told herself it was because the gents didn't know how long she would be receiving, but she fully understood she was expected to stand and greet for two hours, until half ten, unless the guests coming down the stairs dwindled to nothing.

She wished she'd asked Gillie to invite Mr. Sommersby, for surely she would have, even though he wasn't of the nobility, simply as a favor to Fancy. She wished she could look toward the stairs and see him descend them. Of course, then he wouldn't be available to help with the teaching, although he could always arrive here late. People did. It was the reason the queue seemed never-ending.

When she'd walked into the reading parlor, Mr. Sommersby had immediately snagged her attention. The slow way he'd come to his feet, as though entranced. While Mr. Tittlefitz had looked at her like she were a delight to behold, Mr. Sommersby gazed at her as though she were a dollop of clotted cream he would like to slowly lick. It was an absurd thought to have had at the time because the heat in his eyes was melting in its intensity. She'd been surprised he hadn't actually crossed the room to her, had stayed where he was, his fingers clutching the primer, his knuckles turning white. She wondered if he'd left dents in the book.

His reaction more than anything had helped to settle her nerves, had assured her that her gown and elaborately coifed hair didn't make her appear foolish, reaching for something beyond her grasp. The way he had looked at her had convinced her that if he were here, he would claim a dance.

If only some other gentleman would.

It was an odd thing indeed to find herself comparing each gentleman to whom she was introduced to Mr. Sommersby. His hair wasn't dark enough, his eyes not green enough, his shoulders not broad enough. His voice not rich enough. None of the polite words spoken sent delicious shivers along her spine, conjuring up images of forbidden acts and sultry nights.

She'd thought—hoped—he might kiss her the night before after he walked her to her door. But he'd refrained and that was all for the good. She knew ladies of quality did not go about kissing men, and she was striving to be a lady of quality.

Although she was left with the impression that they weren't all above reproach. It seemed not all ladies arrived with their husbands, not all husbands accompanied their wives. It made it a challenge to match up couples, to sort out who was paired with whom when they were introduced a number of people apart. On the other hand, surely, she wasn't expected to remember the name of everyone to whom she was introduced—although most likely she was. She'd been taught little tricks for doing so. Lord Winters of the red-tipped nose, Lady Winters of the ruddy cheeks as though both had just arrived fresh out of a winter storm. She was determined to get all the names right when their paths again crossed, to impress them with her feat. She wanted to be remembered as more than the bastard, wanted something other than her birth to distinguish her from all the others here who were not raised by Ettie Trewlove.

"You're late," Gillie snapped.

Fancy glanced away from the man to whom she'd just been introduced, Lord Brockman of the shiny pate and broad smile—balding, broad, Brockman—and knew a surge of warmth at the sight of her brothers Finn and Aiden, with their lovely wives, Lavinia and Selena, on their arms.

"We purposely delayed our arrival to give you a respite from meeting strangers," Aiden said. "We thought you'd welcome the familiar."

Gillie narrowed her eyes. "You weren't thinking it'd give you less time around the nobs?"

"Well, that, too," Aiden said with a laugh.

"You're here now. I suppose that's all that matters."

"Seriously, Gil," Finn began, "we thought you'd appreciate a friendly face an hour in. Although to be honest, we did get held up with the crush of people arriving. Mum should see this. She'd be delighted."

"Is it only an hour?"

"Afraid so."

Aiden turned to Fancy, gave her a gentle hug and kiss on the cheek. "You look lovely."

"I don't suppose Beast came," she stated more than asked.

"He's not one for affairs such as this," Finn said.

"None of us are," Aiden pointed out. "Yet here we are."

"It is more important for you, with your wives, to be accepted by Society," Gillie said firmly. "Especially if you have any hope at all of seeing your children accepted."

Fancy fought not to feel self-conscious that her origins were plain and humble, that she would be faced with the same challenges of seeing her children accepted. While they knew nothing at all about Gillie's true parents, the three brothers attending tonight did know who had fathered them and that noble blood ran through their veins. Whereas she knew she couldn't claim so much as a drop.

Aiden lifted her wrist. "What's this, then?"

"It's a dance card."

"I know what it is. I had to sit through Mick's lectures." Mick had once had a lover who had taught him a good bit about the nobility and etiquette, and he'd shared all he'd learned with his siblings. When she was old enough, he'd taught her as well—although he hadn't mentioned where he'd learned it. She'd picked up that bit eavesdropping on a conversation. "Why are there no names on it?"

"It's a challenge to know when I'll be available since I'm unsure as to when I'll be done here."

He narrowed his eyes at her lie, heaved a sigh. "How much longer must you stand here?"

"An hour at the most."

Taking the pencil, he scrawled his name beside a waltz, then winked at her.

Selena rubbed his arm. "We're holding up the queue." She bussed a quick kiss over Fancy's cheek. "It'll take a little time, but eventually it'll fill up."

She remained optimistic that her sister-by-marriage spoke the truth.

Finn also claimed a dance after greeting her. Lavinia gave her a hug. "The first one is always the hardest."

She was further encouraged. "It's more promising than I expected."

Not completely true. She'd hoped for more than her brothers' names on her dance card.

Lavinia gave her an understanding smile. "It will get better."

The couples wandered off, and Fancy found herself being introduced to a matronly woman with a very disapproving expression on her face. Better couldn't come soon enough.

Introductions continued. The young, the old, the debutantes thrilled with another opportunity to dance, flirt, and possibly catch the eye of a gentleman. People were polite with her, but distant. But then that was the way of the aristocracy, was it not?

So many people murmured their pleasure at meeting her that she lost track of the number, as well as the names. Even the little game she played for associating names with individuals began to fail her. Simply too many needed to be remembered. Then she realized she wasn't extending her hand to anyone or plastering a smile on her face.

"That's done," Thorne said. "Let's make a break for it before the next round of guests arrives." He held his hand out to his duchess, and hers glided into his so easily, but then Fancy wasn't surprised. She'd seen the closeness between them too many times to count. She longed for that sort of relationship, where so much was communicated with merely a look or a touch. To be known so well.

Gillie waved Mick and Aslyn over. "Mick, you'll dance with Fancy." Her words were a command, not a question. Owning a tavern and a pub, she was accustomed to ordering people about.

"Naturally." He winked at his wife. "You'll have my next dance."

"And each one after that," she replied, a twinkle in her eyes.

The duke raised his arm and signaled the orchestra. The music quieted, went silent, and everyone turned their attention to Thornley. Such was his power, his ability to command an audience with little more than his presence. Then he took Gillie's hand, urging her closer to him, and tucked it within the crook of his arm. "My duchess and I thank you all for joining us this evening. It is our pleasure to have you share her sister's debut into Society. She is an exceptional young woman, and we are wishing her the very best." A look toward the orchestra, another gesture.

"A tune not on the dance sheet," Gillie whispered. "This one is for you, Fancy."

The gentle strains of the violin lilting through the parlor were soon joined by flutes, lutes, the pianoforte, and a host of other instruments creating a lush version of "The Fairy Wedding Waltz."

As one the crowd scattered to the edges of the chalk line that designated the area marked for dancing. The duke led his duchess into its center, took her in his arms, and swept her over the polished parquet. After they circled once, Mick escorted Fancy onto the floor.

"My first official waltz in a ballroom," she said lightly, striving not to reveal her nervousness, concentrating on his beloved face. One of her earliest memories was looking up from her small bed to see him hovering over her as he sang her name over and over to lull her into sleep. Even when she'd been only two or three, and he sixteen or seventeen, he'd taken on the role of her protector, being more of a father to her than a brother.

"It's been a long time coming."

"You made it possible."

Quickly, he jerked his head around. "Gillie did all this."

"But you paid for the schooling that taught me to comport myself as a lady might. You gave me the confidence to not mind that so many eyes are following us at this moment."

Thankfully, the duke again lifted an arm, and soon other couples were swirling about the floor, having to watch their own steps or partners in order to avoid ramming into anyone. But still, she saw the speculative gazes, the curious looks, the occasional dismissive nod. She didn't think anyone would insult her with so much of her family about, but nothing was to prevent people from ignoring her.

"You're as good as any of them," Mick said.

"Unlike you, I carry no noble blood in my veins."

"It's all red, Fancy. Besides, you are not your beginnings. None of us are. We are what we have made ourselves to be. You're a shopkeeper. And you're doing good work with your tutoring in the evening. You've nothing of which to be ashamed."

"I hope some of the gentlemen here feel the same."

"They're fools if they don't. And I won't see you married to a fool."

She laughed lightly. "I suppose if no one should ask me to dance it will because they are terrified of you."

"If they are good men, they shouldn't be."

Through her mind flashed a vision of misters Sommersby and Tittlefitz giving up their evenings in order to help others better themselves. She had an unkind thought that the gentlemen in attendance here were beneath them because they were seeking entertainment, and yet if not for their presence, she wouldn't be here either. "Have you encountered many of these lords at your club?"

The Duke of Hedley had helped Mick get a membership at White's. Most assumed it was because Aslyn was the duke's ward. But the duke was also Mick's father, had been the one to place him in Ettie Trewlove's arms. Mick's thick dark beard hid the dent in his chin that so matched Hedley's, but nothing could disguise the blue eyes they shared.

"A few. They're becoming more accepting of me." He lifted a shoulder. "Or at least my acumen when it comes to business. It's the reason most approach me." His diction was as polished as Mr. Sommersby's.

Why did she continually think of the man? Every gent she'd met seemed paltry beside him. Not only physically but also by the manner in which they projected themselves. He would have been impossible to ignore descending the stairs. If he were on the dance floor at that very moment, he'd be drawing her gaze. She seemed unable to rid herself of thoughts of him. She was here to meet a lord, to become part of the aristocracy. "Are there any for whom you have a high opinion? Anyone in particular you think might make a good husband?" *Who might come to love me? Who would give me no reason to regret giving him my hand in marriage? Who would go to penny gaffs with me or enjoy a night of street entertainments?*

"You should pose that question to Aiden. He knows the ones who are in debt. You would no doubt be wise to avoid those fellows."

It was the same tone he'd used when he'd caught her sharing the rock candy that he'd brought her from Brighton with a lad five years older than she. "You don't want to settle for a lad around here." She was all of six at the time and the thought of "settling" with anyone had yet to enter her mind—until he put it there.

"But what if I like one of those fellows? Do I ignore my heart's longings?"

"The heart is not always wise. Follow it with caution."

"You're such an expert on love." The words were sharp and to the point.

A corner of his mouth curled up. "Have you met my wife?"

She couldn't help it. She laughed lightly. "I think you just got lucky there."

"I was indeed fortunate. I want you to be even more so."

The music drifted into silence. Easing out of his hold, she patted his arm. "I am going to make a remarkably good match and know so much happiness that you'll grow sick of me boasting about it."

AIDEN TREWLOVE ADORED vice and sin. He had a gaming hell known as the Cerberus Club as well as the Elysium Club that catered to fulfilling women's fantasies. For many ladies, one of those fantasies was not being a wallflower. He'd never attended a formal ball before tonight but watching as no gentleman asked his sister for the honor of a dance, he finally understood why women flocked to the ballroom at his establishment. Within those walls, they were guaranteed a dance.

Oh, Fancy had danced. But every gentleman who had taken her upon the floor was related to her in some way. Mick and Finn were her brothers through their mum. Thorne was related to her through Gillie. Lord Kipwick through Aslyn. Lord Collinsworth through Lavinia. Lord Camberley through Selena. But none of the other gents had gone near her, bugger 'em all.

"You're scowling quite fiercely."

He glanced over at his beautiful wife. She'd been a duchess, three days a widow, when he'd first met her. People still referred to her as *Duchess*. He didn't mind. In her heart, she was Mrs. Aiden Trewlove and that was all that had ever mattered between them—what was in their hearts. "No one is dancing with her."

"She's danced several times. I've asked Kit to take her out on the floor."

Viscount Kittridge. One of Selena's dearest friends. "Someone she knows through you. I'm talking about all these mucks she's only just met."

"It's her coming out, her introduction into Society. It takes a while for the gents to warm up to a debutante."

He gave her a pointed look. "How long did it take you, at your first ball, to have your dance card filled?"

She sighed. "Five minutes. But I was raised within Society."

He grinned. "And you were touted as being the most beautiful woman in London. That probably didn't hurt."

Her smile was soft, but bright. "No, I suppose it didn't."

"I should have brought some of my gents from the club."

"Is that who you want her to marry?" She rubbed his arm. "Patience, my love."

He shook his head. "I haven't got it, not where Fancy is concerned. I'll not see her hurt or disappointed. I won't be long."

He made a move to leave her, but her fingers closed around his upper arm, holding him in place. "Don't start trouble."

"I'm only going to have a few words with one gent, and after that, all should fall into place."

"I'll have another dance once you're done."

Grazing his fingers along her cheek, he almost took her mouth then and there. He did love her. "I'll give you three." Then because she was his wife, he pressed a kiss to her forehead. "I love you, Lena."

"Find us a dark alcove somewhere, and I'll show you how much I love you."

His laughter echoed around him as he strode through the grand salon until he reached a circle of three men, chuckling and cackling, as though they hadn't a worry in the world. If he discovered they'd been making sport of his sister, they'd each suffer a drawn-out, painful death. "Dearwood."

They immediately went silent and the two whose name hadn't been spoken skittered away like cockroaches suddenly revealed by light. Did his family really want Fancy to marry one of these fops?

Turning to face him, the earl visibly swallowed. "Trewlove."

"I have your vowels."

The man's eyes widened. "Here? On you?"

He sighed. "No. At my club. Dance with my sister and I'll tear them up. Your debt to me will be considered paid in full."

Dearwood was an unattractive fellow when his jaw was hanging down. "But do close your mouth before taking her upon the dance floor."

His lips snapped together as he gave a brisk nod before turning on his heel.

"Dearwood?"

The man came to an abrupt halt and glanced back, his stricken expression indicating he feared the club owner was on the verge of rescinding the offer. "Discreetly let it be known that this offer is open to any man who owes me blunt."

STROLLING AS UNOBTRUSIVELY as possible among the layers of people away from the dance floor, Fancy refused to go anywhere near the section of chairs, take a seat, and delegate herself a wallflower so early into the process. She hadn't expected immediate acceptance, had known she'd be an object of curiosity. Still, she'd anticipated a few of the gents unknown to her before tonight would at least be interested in satisfying their inquisitiveness by taking her on a turn about the dance floor.

She passed small clusters of two or three people, chatting away, averting their gazes or stepping in to make the circle smaller when they caught sight of her approaching. Not a cut direct precisely, but certainly not an invitation to join them. She wasn't rude enough to intrude. As she walked on by, she would catch snippets of conversation.

Pretty enough. That didn't mean they were discussing her.

Five thousand a year. Probably a reference to her. Each of her siblings were contributing a thousand pounds a year to her dowry.

Scandalous . . .

Seemed pleasant enough . . .

Where's the card room? At that one, she leaned in, smiled, and said, "Up the stairs, to your right, third door down." The gents had stared at her for several seconds as though they'd never before had a question answered by a woman and then scrambled away so fast one might have thought she'd whispered, "I have leprosy."

Ancestry is so important . . .

Rather like her smile . . .

Purchased a new curricle . . .

Fine selection of liquors in the refreshment room.

Well, the duchess is a tavern owner.

Having finished her third trip around the room, she stopped a passing footman and picked up a coupe of the very excellent champagne from the tray he was balancing on his splayed fingers. She rewarded herself with a glass after each turn in order to shore up her resolve for another sweep by the guests. Her sisters-by-marriage had hovered around her at first until she'd convinced them to dance with their husbands, that she was fine on her own. Besides, she didn't want to give any lords the notion she needed to be mollycoddled. They'd want a wife who could look after herself, surely.

Although she had to wonder: If the ladies didn't acknowledge her as belonging, would the gents? She understood the power that a woman held, especially when it came to Society. Gents might make the laws that governed the land, but it was the ladies who created the rules that determined acceptable behavior.

Perhaps she needed to find a way to earn the ladies' favor. Nothing like a mother suggesting to her son that he might want to take a closer look at Miss Trewlove.

"Excuse us, Miss Trewlove."

Turning toward the unexpected feminine voice, she was met by three ladies, who seemed at once nervous but giddy, their smiles flickering like a candle flame on the verge of running out of wick as though they weren't quite certain they should speak to her. She'd never realized flaxen hair came in different shades until she saw these three together. Wheat. Moon. Straw.

She gave them her most welcoming smile. "Ladies Penelope, Victoria, and Alexandria."

Their eyes widened considerably.

"You remembered our names," Lady Penelope said. "There must be at least two hundred people in attendance."

And she'd been introduced to nearly every one of them. "I'm quite skilled at remembering names. It's a little game I play, you see. Lady Penelope, your eyes are an unusual coppery shade that remind me of pennies, hence Penelope. Lady Victoria, you have such a regal bearing and so naturally I thought of the Queen, and since you share her name you were unforgettable in my mind."

"And me?" Lady Alexandria asked eagerly.

"You were a bit more complicated. Your gown is so lovely with all the flounces reminding me of waves rolling upon the shore, which led me to thinking of a city on the ocean. Alexandria."

"That's remarkable, Miss Trewlove," Lady Penelope said, and Fancy decided she was the leader of the group as the other girls nodded enthusiastically.

"As I said, it's just a game I play. It helps me to remember the names of the people who visit my bookshop." She'd long thought it made her customers and students feel special if she could recall their names after one introduction.

"Well, I say it's brilliant. We shall have to give it a go." More nods.

"It's your first Season, isn't it?" They appeared so young, seventeen if they were a day, and made her feel remarkably ancient or at least incredibly worldly.

"It is, indeed."

"How's it going thus far?"

"Quite well, really. I've had three gentlemen call on me. My dear friends have each had two."

"But we've not settled on anyone," Lady Alexandria said hastily.

"It seems far too early for that," Lady Victoria added.

"I quite agree," Fancy said. "You have no idea who you might meet before Season's end."

"Which is actually why we approached you." Lady Penelope grinned, blushed, looked to her friends for encouragement. "Do you know, offhand, if the duchess invited Lord Rosemont?"

It seemed Fancy wasn't the only one who'd been touched by the letter. "She did, yes."

"Do you know if he's about?"

"I did not meet him in the receiving line."

"They say he's quit London." Lady Victoria pouted. "We're so hoping it's not true."

"Although it's also rumored he has taken up residence elsewhere rather than in his usual London abode, because, according to my brother, he does still make an appearance at Parliament when needed," Lady Penelope added. "So we were very much anticipating he'd be in attendance. He promised each of us a dance when we called on him."

"You called on him?"

"Mmm. I don't think there's an unmarried lady in London who didn't."

Which might account for his quitting London. She felt rather uncomfortable that she, too, had been wishing for a moment with him in order to express her condolences.

"I'm not really surprised we've yet to encounter him at a ball.

My older sister told me that in some circles he's known as Rosemont the Recluse. She knew Lady Rosemont, you see, and said she often attended affairs without him. My sister was actually quite taken aback by the devotion expressed in the countess's letter. Did you happen to come across it?"

"I did, yes."

She sighed melodramatically. "I think we all want a man to love us like that."

"Ladies."

At the deep voice, Fancy turned and gave a small curtsy. "Lord Dearwood."

"How did you remember his name?" Lady Penelope asked, and it seemed Lord Rosemont was quite forgotten.

Young buck with a wooden smile. "Stag in the woods," she said instead.

"How clever!" Lady Penelope enthused. "But I would have gone with deer in the forest."

"There's no right or wrong," she assured the young lady. "It's whatever will help you remember."

"What's this, then?" Lord Dearwood asked.

"Miss Trewlove plays a game so she can remember everyone's name."

"Well, not everyone's," she said, heat warming her cheeks. "Sometimes it doesn't work and I forget what I associated with the person and think it would have been simpler to memorize the name."

"I'd like to hear about that game at some point, but for now, Miss Trewlove, I was hoping you'd honor me with a dance."

The three ladies gave a gleeful squeal before skittering away. Definitely younger than she was.

Fancy smiled at Lord Dearwood. He wasn't unattractive, was probably as old as her brothers, and something about him indicated he was a man who enjoyed far too much vice or at least food and wine. Perhaps it was the way the buttons on his waistcoat were straining against the cloth. "I'd be honored, my lord."

Offering his arm, he led her to the edge of the dance floor. "We'll wait for the waltz to end, shall we?"

"Would you mind signing my card whilst we wait? I thought to keep it as a souvenir."

"Certainly."

As she watched him scrawl his name, she couldn't help but think of a man with larger hands, longer fingers, more elegance in his movements. She really needed to rid herself of thoughts of Mr. Sommersby. "Are you enjoying the ball thus far?"

"Oh yes, especially now that you'll be dancing with me."

She felt the heat of a blush rushing up from her décolletage into her hairline at the flattering words that were spoken with such sincerity. "That's exceedingly kind of you to say, my lord."

"Not at all. I owed your brother a bloody fortune."

Everything within her stilled. "I beg your pardon?"

His wide grin reminded her of one she'd seen on a chimpanzee at the zoological gardens. "He's canceling my gambling hell debt."

She couldn't stop her voice from going flat. "If you dance with me."

"Precisely." He nodded toward the floor that was clearing of couples, as others moved into place. "Shall we?"

"With all due haste."

It was an odd thing to be held by someone she'd only just met, and she was grateful the quadrille limited how long and how often he touched her. The other couples who served as partners in this particular square were a somber lot, and she wondered if they wished she wasn't there, although she did catch a few side glances as though they were curious but didn't want anyone to know they were. Although perhaps they knew the truth of the situation and were as uncomfortable as she was with the fact that a bribe was required to get a bloke to dance with her.

Chapter 13

$\mathscr{I}$t was difficult to concentrate on reading when Matthew's gaze kept wandering to the darkened window across the way. He had shoved a chair in front of his and taken up position after returning from the reading lessons. Ever since Fancy had bid them a good night, he'd been tormented envisioning her at the ball dancing with one lord after another.

While the decent part of him hoped her dance card would have a scrawled signature beside every dance, the selfish part hoped she took no pleasure from the attention.

Damn it all to hell, he felt like a rotten cur.

After returning to his terrace, he'd considered going to the ball. He even had evening attire on hand. God alone knew why his valet had decided to pack it. He'd certainly had no plans to attend any formal functions, although it was always possible an obligation he couldn't escape would arise.

Earlier he'd gone to the bother of drawing a bath. Soaking in the steaming water had managed to give him time to put matters into perspective and to debate the disadvantages of attending the ball. At the edge of his mind he recalled promising dances to at least two dozen women, so dance cards would be dangled in front of his nose like carrots to get a horse moving. First and foremost, however, was the matter of explaining himself to Fancy.

"You wanted to meet the Earl of Rosemont. Funny thing. You've already met him. He is I." He imagined delivering the news with a bit of a laugh and a broad smile. Unfortunately, he couldn't envision her receiving it with equal good humor. She would no doubt be hurt, possibly livid. Revealing himself in such a public arena was such a dreadfully bad idea.

However, if she did manage to overlook his failure to elaborate on his identity when they met, he would no longer be able to discern if what was developing between them—friendship or something more—was influenced by his title. Might she seek to lure him into a conservatory?

All the lengths that are necessary.

She had declared those words, and they'd resounded as a promise, a vow. Although she claimed she would draw the line at deception, he'd learned that a woman's words couldn't always be trusted.

He rather liked that she didn't know his full identity, that when she looked at him, she wasn't doing it through the lens of his title. So he'd left his bath resolved to stay in and let her have her night. To flirt and be flirted with, to dance the evening away, to have a debut that was all she hoped for. Even if it didn't include the Earl of Rosemont.

Once more he glanced toward her window. The ball would no doubt go on until two in the morning. For him, the minutes were ticking away into an eternity.

AFTER HER FIFTH dance following the one that she'd shared with Dearwood, she was more than displeased with the additional information she'd gleaned and went in search of her brothers. While they were tall, a good many men were equally so, which made it difficult to spy them in the crush of the crowd. She did wish Beast had attended. He was a good head taller than most, which would have made him easier to spot. Then she caught sight of them on the far side of the room, near one of two fireplaces. Quickening her pace—

"I say, Miss Trewlove."

She came to an abrupt halt as a tall, narrow-shouldered gentleman stepped in front of her. What was his name? Good Lord, with more important matters weighing on her mind she couldn't think.

"Will you honor me with a dance?"

Blond. Broad. Blue Eyes. Viking. Fiords. "Not at this moment, Lord Beresford."

She made to move past him, and he wrapped his gloved fingers around her upper arm. The scathing look she cast his way had him immediately releasing his hold, appearing somewhat contrite.

"But it's simply not done, Miss Trewlove. To rebuff a gentleman's request for a dance."

"I'm not declining altogether. Just not right now." She held up her wrist, the dangling dance card twirling. "I have a few dances left. Select the one you'd like. Just not this one."

With great deliberation and very slowly, he printed out his name as though he anticipated she might like to use it for an embroidery pattern at some point. He beamed at her. "A waltz."

"I look forward to it. Now, if you'll excuse me." Without waiting for his permission, she threaded her way around people, having to stop twice more to impatiently allow gentlemen to sign her dance card. Who would have ever thought she wouldn't take delight in the attention? Finally, she reached her brothers, grateful Gillie was there as well, so she could confront them all in one go. Thankfully no one else was near. It seemed when the Trewloves were gathered en masse, people were wont to keep their distance. Her siblings all seemed to be in good cheer, chatting, laughing, sipping what appeared to be scotch—probably from Gillie's personal stock.

"Have you no faith in me?"

They all swung around so fast at her words that it wouldn't have surprised her to learn they'd each gone dizzy.

"What are you on about?" Gillie asked sincerely. "Of course we have faith in you."

"Then why are you bribing men to dance with me?"

"I beg your pardon?"

"Aiden is canceling any debt owed to his club, Finn is offering breeding or training services, and Mick is offering investment advice. Are you saying you've not offered anything to entice the fellows into dancing with me?"

Gillie's jaw tightened as she glared at their brothers. "You daft dunderheads. You didn't."

"No one was dancing with her." Aiden's voice was clipped, harsh, and she could sense how much it angered him that they'd been ignoring her. He'd always concerned himself with ensuring women were happy. It was one of the reasons his newest club catering to ladies was such a success. While the knowledge lessened her own hurt a bit, it couldn't erase it completely when viewed from a different perspective.

"You didn't believe I could entice them on my own?"

"Eventually, yes. One dance and you'll have them eating out of the palm of your hand. But they weren't moving fast enough to suit me."

"It is not you they have to suit."

"If they want to marry you, it damn well is."

She loved her brothers, but at the moment at least one of them was in need of a smack across his head.

"We were trying to make the night unforgettable for you," Finn said, looking somewhat chastened. He'd always been the more sensitive of her brothers.

"Well, you've certainly managed that." She held her hand out toward Gillie. "May I?"

Her sister glanced down at the tumbler she was holding. "It's scotch."

"I assumed as much."

Gillie handed her the glass, and Fancy took a good healthy swallow, licked her lips.

"You've had it before."

"I'm not as innocent as you all think."

"The quiet ones never are," Finn said softly.

"I am, however, rather mortified."

"We meant well," Mick stated tenderly.

"I know you did. It's the only reason I won't stay cross with you for long. But if gentlemen believe you'll offer them some sort of compensation for showering me with attention, they'll never dance with me on their own volition. They'll be waiting for the payoff, and to be honest, it should be me." She grimaced. "And the dowry you've all so graciously put together."

He scowled. "They should want you without the dowry. But our origins prevent you from being accepted without it. Still, once these nobs get to know you, as Aiden implied, they'll love you as much as we do."

It was impossible to ask for a more loving, supportive family. She took another sip, allowing the heat to relax her. "I appreciate the sentiment. However, after everything you all have done for me over the years to get me here, it's now time to shove me out of the nest and let me fly. I'm fully capable of flying."

"It's hard to realize you've grown up."

"Well, I have." The music drifted into silence. She downed what remained of the scotch before giving the glass back to Gillie. She lifted her wrist. "I have another dance claimed, so I must be away. Please, don't interfere again."

"I think they're duly chastised," Gillie said.

But knowing her brothers, she feared they'd unintentionally clipped her wings.

"I DARESAY YOUR debut was a rousing success," Aslyn announced with enthusiasm as the carriage traveled toward Mick's hotel.

Apparently, Mick had yet to tell his wife how the rousing success had come to be. "Yes, I was quite taken aback by all the attention." After confronting her brothers, she'd stopped prodding her dance partners in order to determine why they'd approached her. She didn't want to know if they had no success at gambling, investing, or horse management. Instead, she'd made inquiries regarding their estates, hobbies, and pleasures. Some seemed taken aback that she had such an interest in them, but all welcomed the opportunity to talk about themselves.

"The next ball should go even better."

It would occur the following Wednesday and would be hosted by Aslyn's former guardians, the Duke and Duchess of Hedley. Again, people would come out of curiosity because the couple never entertained. But they were doing so because Mick had asked. Her family was calling in favors. She didn't want to consider the cost to them or their pride—all so she could have the fairy-tale life they'd envisioned for her. Which made it difficult not to forgive them for tonight's error in judgment.

"I've bought a bit of acreage on the outskirts of London," Mick said. "I'll be adding that to your dowry."

"No." The word came out succinct and to the point. "I appreciate it, but you've given me far too much already. Lessons, allowing me to use your building for my shop, a dowry that is a yearly income, not simply a sum, and now my Season. I can never repay—"

"Family doesn't repay."

"He's stubborn, Fancy," Aslyn said.

"Yes, well, so am I. For most ladies, a five-thousand-pound dowry would be more than enough. But mine is five-thousand-per-year as long as I draw breath, which I am planning to do a very long time. It's as we discussed earlier. You can't continue to entice gentlemen to want me. If they aren't content with my dowry as is, then they aren't worth considering. I'd be happier as a spinster managing my shop. Perhaps then you would let me purchase it from you."

"You know my reason for not putting the building in your name. When you marry, your husband could do anything with it he damned well pleased. Turn it into a bordello. Neither you nor I would have any control over his actions."

"But if I were to not marry—"

"It would break Mum's heart, Fancy."

What of her heart, what of her dreams? What if she found

herself falling for a man who possessed no title? Still, she simply nodded.

"I remember when you were born, how she cradled you in her arms, tears in her eyes. I'd never seen her weep before. She was always so strong. From the very beginning she had dreams for you."

"I know."

"I'd be dead if not for her."

She knew that as well, knew not all baby farmers took such loving care of their charges. "I'm not ungrateful, Mick. But, please . . . don't add anything else to my dowry."

"As you wish, but some lord is going to be very fortunate to have you, sweetheart. I intend to make certain he's worthy of you."

Glancing out the window, she couldn't help but feel that her marriage to a noble would be the crowning achievement of all he'd worked toward. Although she knew a good many young ladies would envy her position, she sometimes found herself wishing she had no dowry at all so no doubts would creep in regarding the reasons a man had asked for her hand. If one ever did. She was truly in no rush to take a husband. If she had two or three Seasons, she wouldn't be disappointed. Her shop sustained her. For now, it was all she really needed.

"I'd like to go see Mum in the morning, let her know how the night went."

"You won't mention—"

"No, I'll not mention how you and the others interfered," she assured him.

"What's this?" Aslyn asked.

"I'll explain later."

She'd like to be a fly on the wall when Mick did that. She suspected her sister-by-marriage would have a reaction similar to Gillie's.

"What time would you like the carriage readied?" Mick asked.

"Seven."

In the dark confines, with only the occasional streetlamp casting light to wash away the shadows, she saw the flash of Mick's smile. "Most ladies would sleep the morning away after attending a ball."

"I want to be back early enough to open the shop on time."

"I think people would understand if it opened later than usual."

"I'm as serious about my business as you are about yours, Mick. I'll be unlocking the door at nine."

When the carriage came to a stop in front of the hotel, Mick leapt out and then handed Aslyn down before reaching back in for Fancy. Once her feet hit the bricked walk, she rose up on her toes to kiss his cheek. "Good night."

"I'll see you safely home."

"Mick, I'm across the street. No one is about." It was after two in the morning and the streets were quiet, every business shut down for the night.

"Still." He escorted her to the shop and waited until she'd closed the door behind her and turned the lock.

When Mr. Tittlefitz had locked up, he'd left a gaslight burning low to welcome her home. Shadows quivered around the bookshelves. With her back against the door, she inhaled the beloved fragrance of ink, paper, leather, and binding that filled shelf upon shelf. If she could find a way to capture the scent, she would dip candles in it and burn them throughout her future residence so she would always be comforted. She did hope her husband had an extensive library, was a reader of books. Could she marry someone who wasn't?

Shoving away from the wood, she headed up the stairs, her steps increasing in tempo as she neared her private rooms.

She didn't know what was driving her, knew only that she wasn't where she wanted to be. Dashing through the front parlor, where low light greeted her, she rushed into her bedchamber and came to a stop at the window, the draperies falling on either side of it.

Warmth, joy, and relief swamped her at the sight of Mr. Sommersby standing with his arms upstretched and spread wide, his hands pressing against the window casings. In spite of the late hour, he was still awake, looking out, the unbuttoned cuffs causing his sleeves to have slipped down to his elbows, his throat visible because of his disheveled state, and she wondered if he'd been waiting for her return. Placing her forehead to the cool glass, she feared he'd think her forward if she were to knock on his door at this late hour. It was ridiculous how much she longed to speak with him, to tell him of her night.

Then he was gone.

But still she stood there, waiting for him to douse the light before crawling into bed. Was any man with whom she'd danced thinking of her at the moment? Did they wonder if she'd gone to her slumber, if she'd carried them into her dreams? She wouldn't. Not a single one. But Mr. Sommersby—

A looming shadow caught her attention, charging through the mews with a purpose to his stride. It sent her heart into a gallop, a pace that only quickened when she heard the pounding on the back door that led into the storeroom. Delivery men used that entrance so as not to disturb any customers. But for a gent who lived around the corner, it was the most direct route to her shop.

She rushed from her rooms and down the stairs, the litany "I'm coming, I'm coming," reverberating through her mind until she reached the wide portal, shoved back the bolt, and swung it open. The light from the streets barely reached here, and she hadn't thought to turn up the gaslights, so he was almost lost to the shadows, and yet still she felt she saw him clearly.

"I wanted to ensure you were all right." His voice came out strained, as though he'd been in fear of her life, as though she'd gone on safari and spent the evening facing wild animals that were intent on devouring her. Perhaps she had.

"I survived and am none the worse for wear." She stepped back. "Do come in. The fog is making it chilly out there." It wasn't yet so thick as to make it difficult to see, but wisps of it were floating in.

Crossing the threshold, he shut the door behind him. Now

that they were both standing inside, the storage room seemed incredibly small. Perhaps it was just that his presence over-whelmed the space. She'd noted it before, the manner in which he dominated his environment with such ease, as though it was his right to be in command. "I'm sorry. I don't have any spirits on hand to offer you."

"I've had enough scotch for the night." She could feel the inten-sity of his gaze as it roamed over her, as if he was searching for wounds. "Your coming out was a success, then."

Statement, not question, and yet it demanded a reply. She gave a tiny scoff, hating that it sounded so hard and bitter. "No, not really."

Feeling the burn at the back of her eyes, she refused to give in to tears.

"What happened?" His tone was that of a man displeased, a man on the verge of calling others out to answer for their actions.

"My family had such hopes, but I fear they were rather dashed. I danced with my brothers, my brothers-by-marriage, the brothers or good friends of my sisters-by-marriage—always some relation in one manner or another. When they'd all had their turn, I wan-dered among the guests for several dances. Observed, but not ap-proached, not spoken to. Very much like an exhibit at the zoological gardens. Or some theater of curiosity. Come see the girl born out of wedlock—"

"Fancy, no."

He'd never called her by her given name before, nor had his palm ever cradled her cheek so lovingly. She wasn't quite certain which of those two occurrences were responsible for making her feel as though her heart were made of candlewax and slowly melting.

"People fear what they do not understand," he continued.

Slowly she shook her head, grateful his warm, gentle fingers stayed against her skin. "The worst was yet to come. Of a sud-den, gentlemen began asking me to dance. But I sensed they were simply going through the motions. So I began making inquiries."

If his thumb had not begun stroking the curve of her cheek, she might not have found the strength to confess the rest. "It seems my brothers were offering favors to those who took me on a turn about the room. I was beyond mortified because I'm certain everyone knew. The aristocracy adores gossip, and tonight I provided it."

"Those lords are fools, every last one of them. I would not have needed a bribe to ask you for the honor of a waltz."

She gave him a sad smile. "But you weren't there. And you're my friend."

Something—an irritation, an anger—flashed across his face. He looked up to the ceiling. His jaw tautened, relaxed, and as though he'd reached some conclusion, he lowered his gaze to her. "Waltz with me now."

Her laugh was soft, gentle. "We have no orchestra."

"We don't need one." His hand left her cheek, skimmed down her arm, and laced itself between her gloved fingers. He began leading her out of the storage room. "What is your favorite tune?"

"'The Fairy Wedding Waltz.' The first one I danced to at my first ball."

"I know it. If you had a pianoforte, I could play it for you."

"You play the pianoforte?"

She had expected him to take her upstairs to her lodgings, to her parlor where there was more room—although she quickly realized he wouldn't know that. Instead he stopped in the middle of the area that separated her counter from the walls of bookshelves that ran perpendicular to it, faced her, and released his hold on her. She nearly snatched back his hand. "My mother insisted. When I was a lad, I hated the lessons. But she told me if I practiced diligently, I would acquire very deft fingers. I've found they make me quite popular with the ladies."

The seductive way he looked at her made it difficult to draw in breath, and when she thought of his fingers doing more than touching her cheek as they had earlier, she had a strong urge to unfasten lacings and hooks and invite him to play a tune over her skin. Why was it that when she was with him, she wasn't content to be separated by a few inches? Why did her musings conjure up images of bared flesh and limbs entangled, kisses and embraces?

Bowing slightly, he held out his hand. "Miss Trewlove, may I have the honor of this waltz?"

She didn't know why she was more nervous than she'd been at the ball, why it was imperative she not trip over her feet, but dance to perfection. She wanted to impress him, to demonstrate that her lessons hadn't been a waste of Mick's coins. With a sigh to calm her rioting nerves, she placed her hand in his, taking comfort from the surety with which he wrapped his fingers around hers. His other hand came to her waist, and she placed hers on his shoulder, her posture perfect.

He began humming and, with the slightest dip, glided her over the floor, past the shelves that housed books on various countries, continents, and wildlife, around the edge of it, and up the aisle where one could find information on constellations, down a row where biographies brought long-ago personages back to life. They circled round and round, past romantic novels and detective stories, past Dickens, Brontë, and Austen. This waltz was better than any she'd had earlier because he took her along a route that encompassed all she loved and adored.

All night she'd longed to have a man look at her as though he'd waited his entire life to have her in his arms. Matthew never took his eyes from hers.

She liked thinking of him as Matthew rather than Mr. Sommersby. As they journeyed around the room, an intimacy swelled up between them, like an ocean wave leading a tempest toward shore. She was aware of everything about him. He carried the fragrance of bay rum, but beneath it was the very essence of him, and a hint of the scotch he'd had earlier. Before coming to her, he'd not bothered to tidy himself up with waistcoat, neck cloth, or coat. She rather appreciated that he wore only his boots, trousers, and a shirt, a few buttons free of their moorings so she had a clear view of his throat, a glimpse of the edge of his chest.

She was willing to dance in his arms until dawn. But he ceased his humming and slowed their steps until they were still and quiet, the only sound their breathing. Although he didn't release her, not completely. One hand remained on her waist, while the other slipped away from hers and came to light upon her cheek. He skimmed his thumb over her lips. Everything within her tightened, as though he'd taken that thumb over places that had never before been touched by a man.

"May I kiss you, Miss Trewlove?"

His voice was raspy, like that of a man lost in the desert who'd gone years without water. Her mouth was suddenly dry as well. She barely nodded, yet he noted it and slowly lowered his lips to hers.

A gentleness accompanied his actions, as though he feared breaking her—or perhaps he sensed that he was the first to ever take such liberties and sought to ease her into it. On her waist, his fingers jerked before closing more firmly around her. His other hand left her cheek and his arm circled her, pressing her steadfastly along the length of him until her breasts were flattened against his chest.

To her astonishment, his mouth opened slightly, and his tongue lapped at her lips before urging them to part. Then his tongue was stroking hers, over and under, rough and silky. With a deep groan, he took the kiss deeper until she felt its effects in her toes.

Oh God. She wound her arms around his neck before her knees gave out and she embarrassed herself by tumbling to the floor. Numerous times she'd caught her brothers kissing their wives, but she'd never understood what a wondrous compelling thing it was. How it warmed one throughout and caused tingles between one's thighs. How it made one long to have deft fingers working some sort of magic, and even as she wasn't quite certain for what precisely her body was reaching, she knew he possessed the means to assuage the yearnings that were building to a fevered pitch within her.

She was vaguely aware of him backing her up. Her bottom

struck something hard, the counter her addled brain realized. Then, with his mouth never leaving hers, he lifted her onto the polished wood, scandalously parted her knees so he could stand between them, nearer to her, and, with a low growl, began to plunder with more earnestness, exploring every hollow as though his life depended on his being able to describe her mouth in exquisite detail.

Aware of soft sighs and keening whimpers echoing around her, it took her a moment to realize she was the one making them. The sensations he was stirring to life within her were threatening to cause her to come undone.

He dragged his mouth over her chin, along her throat, and up to her ear, where he nibbled on the lobe before whispering, "May I have permission to kiss your breasts, Miss Trewlove?"

Dear Lord, she nearly melted into a puddle of desire on the spot. Scandalized, she knew what her answer would be. *No. No. Absolutely not.* "Y-yes."

His mouth slowly trailed along the décolletage of her gown, while his hand glided up to cup her breast, to squeeze, to plump gently. Hooking a finger in the silk, somehow he managed to free the orb until it was straining toward him. He took her nipple in his mouth and began to suckle. Pleasure jolted through her. With a small cry, she dropped back her head and wrapped her legs around him, pressing her most intimate spot to his. Good Lord. Her actions were met by the hard ridge of his desire, and she wanted nothing more than to rub against it with no clothing separating their skin.

His tongue swirled over the areola soothing what he'd tasted. She was vaguely aware of her fingers tangled in his hair, her palms pressed to his scalp, as he once more closed his mouth around her breast. It felt wicked, so very wicked, to have so much of her flesh within the heated, cavernous confines, stroked lovingly by velvet and silk. She'd never known a sensation so sublime, so intoxicating, so . . . necessary. Her entire body called out for him to continue, to go further—even as she wasn't quite certain what all the further might entail. Oh, she'd seen dogs rutting in the mews, and while she knew that was the eventual end of this journey, she hadn't thought the getting there would include such a vortex of pleasure.

Not that she had any plans to allow him to reach journey's end. They could only engage in the beginning, the start of the trek. As long as he was asking permission, and she remained in control, but every nerve ending, every muscle, every inch of flesh screamed for her to give in, to relinquish her hold on remaining proper and above reproach, to allow him to carry her to the ultimate climax. Her mewling grew louder, her sighs higher in pitch. She was fairly squealing with abandon.

A screech and hiss—

"God's teeth!"

His mouth was no longer working its magic over her breast, and she jerked out of her wondrous state as reality crashed in on her in the form of Dickens crawling onto her lap, seeming to claim her as his. As much as she loved him, at that particular moment she was a bit put out at him for his intrusion.

Shaking his hand, Mr. Sommersby moved back slightly.

"Did he claw you?"

"Poked me. Didn't break the skin."

"I'm so sorry." Lifting her cat, she gazed into the slumberous green eyes. "Bad Dickens." Then she set him aside on the counter, where he promptly leapt down and wandered off. "Let me see your hand."

"It's fine." Leaning in, he peppered kisses over her sensitive flesh before tucking her breast back into her clothing.

She could sense his retreat, and wicked girl that she was, she wanted him to remain. "You've left one completely unattended."

She could scarcely believe she'd been so bold as to utter such a thing.

He lifted his gaze to hers, one corner of his mouth curling up into an ironic grin. "Yes, but things are likely to get out of hand if I don't stop now. Your cat very likely saved your virtue."

"Why did you even begin it?"

"Because I spent the better part of my night imagining some lord luring you into a garden and doing just this. Because I want you, Fancy, but I like you far too much to ruin you for anyone else, not when your Season has only just begun."

Taking a small step back, he placed his hands on her waist, brought her down to the floor, and cradled her cheek. "Are you still intent on securing a lord as a husband?"

"My family will be devastated if I don't marry into the nobility."

"Perhaps you should consider what you want."

"I want them to be proud of me. I want all the effort and coins they've put into me not to have been for naught. Perhaps at the next ball, some fellow will dance with me of his own accord—and the rest will follow suit. Thank you for the waltz. It was a lovely way to end the evening."

He hesitated, and she thought he might pull her back into his arms. Instead he headed for the storage room. Opening the door, he glanced out, then leaned back in and brushed a soft kiss over her lips before stepping outside.

After closing the door, she pressed her fingers to her swollen lips. Would her family understand if she set aside their plans for her in order to embrace her own desires?

𝒻ancy took that kiss to bed with her and woke up still able to feel the press of his lips against hers. The first kiss he'd given her had been devastating in its complexity. The last kiss devastating in its simplicity. It was the sort of kiss that spoke of a far greater intimacy than that created by unbridled passion. It was the sort of kiss that branded one as belonging to another.

Those thoughts traveled with her in the coach as she journeyed to her mum's residence. When she arrived, she shook them off, thanked the footman for handing her down, and crossed over to the door. Opening it, she stepped over the threshold into the small abode where she had spent most of her youth when she wasn't off learning how to project the image of a proper lady.

"You're right on time, love!" her mum sang out from the kitchen. "I have your tea ready."

She shuffled in balancing a cup on a saucer in each hand, and Fancy was hit once again with how much she loved this woman whose brown eyes warmed and sparkled at the sight of her.

"Sit down, pet."

Fancy took one of the two chairs set before the fireplace while her mum took the other, placing the saucers on the low table between them. Settling back, she smiled as though nothing brought her more joy than visiting with Fancy. "Now, tell me everything."

"Ah, Mum, I wish you'd been there. Nothing I describe could do it justice."

"People came, did they?"

She rolled her eyes. "So many people. The ballroom was packed. I could hardly move through it. Gillie was so pretty and self-assured. She charmed everyone."

"As did you, I'd wager."

"I tried. Here, I brought you something." Reaching into her reticule, she pulled out her dance card and handed it over to her. "My dance card. The first several dances are blank because I was standing in the receiving line, but as you can see, I had quite a few gents dance with me."

Her mum didn't need to know why they'd danced with her. Her annoyance with her brothers was mollified a bit since their efforts gave her a card with names on it that she might not have had otherwise.

With a great deal of reverence, her mother stroked the elaborate dance card. "Oh, it's so pretty."

"Gillie did everything to perfection. The flowers, the orchestra, the footmen wandering around."

"Did any of the gents snag your attention? Were any of them worth a second look?"

Matthew. But how would she explain him to her mum? "The gentlemen were all quite nice, polite, respectful." They wouldn't dare be otherwise in fear of losing their boon.

"Handsome, I'll bet."

"Most, yes. But I'm more interested in how he treats me than how he looks."

"Did any of them make you laugh?"

She shook her head. "Not that I recall, no." Although Matthew had on occasion.

A dreamy expression came over her mum's face, followed by a faraway look, the past passing before her eyes. "My husband made me laugh. Oh, we had some good times, we did."

"And my father? Did he make you laugh?"

As though awoken from a pleasant dream, she gave a little

jerk and snapped her attention back to Fancy. "Of course, love. I wouldn't have been with him otherwise. Now, tell me more about these fellas you danced with."

"There's not much more to say. I had a fine time visiting with the gents, but none made my heart sing." She scooted to the edge of her seat. "Mum, what if the man capable of making my heart sing isn't a lord?"

Her mum's face went through a series of contortions as though she were striving not to let her disappointment show. "You have to follow your heart, naturally, but wouldn't it be nice if it led you to a dukedom?"

She had a feeling her mum didn't really realize what she was asking. Like so many, she'd placed the aristocracy as a whole upon a pedestal. "There aren't that many dukes, and Gillie already claimed one." Did she have to sound like a petulant child? "It's just . . . there's a gent who comes into the shop, and he's rather nice. I find myself thinking about him quite a bit. To be honest, Mum, the men I met last night all seem to run together. Not a one really stood out."

"You might meet someone at the next ball who does."

"I suppose. I haven't really given it much time, have I?"

Her mum studied her for a full minute before saying, "Tell me about the gent who comes into your shop."

What could she say that wouldn't give away she'd actually done things with him without a chaperone, had kissed him, had given him permission to do something he shouldn't have? "He likes penny dreadfuls. He's teaching my reading classes on the nights I can't be there. I've seen him give coins to children. And he's shown a great deal of patience with Dickens. When he's about, I feel as though my entire body is smiling. And he's made me laugh a couple of times." And wiped my tears.

"He sounds right jolly. Has he set his cap for you, do you think?"

She smiled, felt the heat warming her cheeks. "No, I think he's just friendly." Exceedingly friendly. "But I don't want to disappoint—"

Closing her eyes, she released a sigh. "It was one ball, one night." She opened her eyes. "I'm certain in time I'll meet some lord who will sweep me off my feet."

"As long as you're happy, love, that's all that matters."

AT EIGHT, TIMMY Tubbins had an honest, but dirty face with large, guileless brown eyes that, in all of Fancy's dealings with him, had never once not been steady as they held her gaze. Thanks to Matthew, as she examined the tattered book with several pages that had come loose of their mooring, she doubted the lad. "Where did you say you found it?"

"In Whitechapel, in the street, just lyin' there, abandoned loike."

"Not from a bookstall, where it could have been easily plucked from a cart or box?"

"No, Miss Trewlove. That'd be stealin', woodn't it? I ain't no thief."

He appeared truly hurt that she'd questioned the origins of his find, and she felt guilty about having done so. It was one of the better ones he'd brought to her. With a little loving care, she could restore it to its former glory, having become quite skilled at book restoration, hating the thought of the life of any tome coming to an end. "A shilling, then."

His grin caused two large dimples to form on either side of his mouth, and she suspected it was those dimples that had her believing him. He held up a hand that was slightly grimier than his face. "Deal."

She removed the coin from her till. Reaching into an onyx box, she retrieved a wooden token that Gillie had first begun passing around in an effort to feed those who would go without sustenance otherwise. Handing both items over to him, she suspected he'd purposely planned the timing of his arrival to ensure he had a free late midday meal that would keep his stomach from grumbling until morning. "Go to the pub and get yourself a bowl of soup."

He doffed his flat-cap. "Thanks, miss."

He rushed to the door, opened it, and then stepped back, holding it ajar as though he were a trained footman as three ladies walked past him, two scowling at him, while the third, Lady Penelope, reached into her reticule, pulled out a coin, and handed it to him. "Thanks, miss!"

He dashed out, slamming the door in his wake. Fancy grimaced at the sound as she moved away from the counter to greet her three new guests. "Good afternoon, Ladies Penelope, Victoria, and Alexandria. How wonderful it is to see you."

"You still remember our names," Lady Penelope said, smiling brightly.

"I'm not likely to forget them now. What brings you here?"

"You, of course. We so enjoyed visiting with you last night that we wanted to call upon you."

"We had no chance to speak with you again after Lord Dearwood took you out onto the floor," Lady Victoria said. "My word, you had so many dance partners that you must have worn a hole in the sole of your slippers."

"Not quite." Although she had come close.

"Lady Aslyn had informed my mother that if we wanted to call on you, we were to go to her residence at the Trewlove Hotel," Lady Penelope continued, "but when we disembarked from the carriage, Alexandria noticed the name of this shop—The Fancy Book Emporium—and we thought it must surely be yours! How cleverly you named it."

"We adore it," Lady Alexandria said. "It's a play on your own name, isn't it?"

"It is, yes, although not everyone understands that. Some think it needs an apostrophe and an *S*."

"That would absolutely ruin it."

"I thought so as well."

"So you actually own the shop," Lady Victoria said.

"No, my brother does. Because of the law regarding married women and property."

"Oh yes, dastardly thing."

"But other than that, it's all mine. I decide which books I'll carry. I arrange everything, create the displays. Would you ladies like a tour?"

Lady Penelope looked at her friends. They all nodded. "That would be splendid."

Fancy introduced Marianne to them—not certain she'd ever seen her clerk so starry-eyed—and while she watched the counter, Fancy took the ladies up to the reading parlor.

"Oh, isn't this lovely?" Lady Penelope said. "It's like a regular parlor only with lots of books."

"People can borrow them and read them in here."

With her delicate brow pinched, she looked at Fancy. "I thought you had a bookshop, which means selling books."

"I do. Downstairs. Up here is a lending library. But there is no subscription fee."

"How do you maintain it?"

"With donations."

Her brow smoothed out, and she seemed quite relieved. "Oh, I see. How clever you are. So people who can't afford books can read them."

"Exactly." She went on to explain about her classes.

"What good works you do, Miss Trewlove," Lady Penelope said, while her friends smiled and bobbed their heads. "You must find it all very satisfying."

"I do."

"What if you marry a man who won't let you continue with these endeavors?" Lady Alexandria asked.

"Well, I shan't marry a man who won't." Fancy had spoken without thinking. And yet, she knew she'd stated the truth. No matter how much she wanted to please her family, she couldn't marry a man who would make her unhappy. Could she? Would they ask her to make that sacrifice?

Lady Victoria appeared shocked. "You get to choose whom you marry? I don't believe my parents are going to let me. They care too much about his position—their position."

"Hopefully it'll work out that the man you love is the man they want you to marry."

"I don't know that I have to love him, but I would very much prefer to like him."

"We're all going to have splendid matches," Lady Penelope said.

"I'm certain we are," Fancy concurred.

"Oh, my goodness. Is that a cat on that shelf?" Lady Penelope asked.

Looking toward the bookcase to the right of the fireplace, Fancy saw Dickens lounging between Austen and Brontë. "That's Dickens. He keeps a watch over things for me."

"I love animals, but my mother would never let me keep one inside." She wandered over to the bookcase, lifted her arms, then glanced back at Fancy. "Will he scratch or bite?"

"No. He loves to be held."

Carefully, Lady Penelope shifted him from his perch into the cradle of her arms. "Isn't he a sweetheart? Does he stay here alone at night when you return to your residence?"

"I have rooms here, on the floor above."

The ladies blinked at her as though they were having difficulty deciphering her words.

"You live here . . . alone?" Lady Victoria asked.

"Yes. It's quite safe."

"You're so independent," Lady Alexandria said. "Living with my mother can be a nightmare at times. She has to know what I'm doing every moment of every day."

"At least you don't have a sister who is always poking around, trying to find your journal." Pressing a hand to her lips, she looked at Fancy with mirth reflected in her eyes. "I hide it in the fireplace flue. She doesn't like to get dirty, so I know she'll never look there."

Fancy had never really talked with others about their families. It made her realize how fortunate she was to have hers. "Would you all care to join me for some tea in the hotel gardens?"

"I like this room too much and hate the thought of leaving

Dickens," Lady Penelope said. "Would it be possible to enjoy our tea here?"

While the ladies settled in, Fancy dashed over to the hotel dining room, spoke with the majordomo, and returned to her guests. A short time later, the hotel staff delivered tea and cakes. The ladies stayed longer than they should have for a morning call, a full half hour, but Fancy enjoyed visiting with them, felt as though she was making inroads to being accepted.

Chapter 15

*F*riday night, sipping his scotch, Matthew sat in a large leather chair in one of several small sitting areas spread throughout the library at Dodger's. The footman who had brought him his drink had done so without making a sound. Gentlemen who were sitting about spoke in low voices, their mumbles barely audible. Everything was so quiet, so dignified, so refined. So blasted boring. Not at all like the lively affairs he'd been attending with Fancy.

He'd been avoiding her since the kiss. And he missed her like the very devil.

"Good God, Rosemont, where have you been keeping yourself?" Lord Beresford asked cheerfully as he took the chair opposite him. "Haven't seen you at any of the balls."

"I've been keeping myself busy elsewhere. After Elise's letter made its appearance, I discovered I'd returned to Society a bit too soon."

Beresford furrowed his brow. A few years older than Matthew, he'd yet to marry, although the rumors bandied about implied that he was quite taken with his mistress. "Sorry, old chap. I wasn't thinking. I imagine it's difficult to return to the gaiety after suffering such a tragic loss. Not easy to move on, I daresay."

"No, it's not."

"Although your countess certainly gave you permission. That was some letter she wrote. Quite shocking, really. Took me a minute to remember she was no longer with us."

He was more than ready for a change in topic. "Any debutantes catch your interest this Season?"

Beresford waggled his thick brown brows. "You've missed out on all the excitement. The Trewlove chit was introduced into Society."

One hand balled into a tightened fist, the other closed around his glass so firmly he feared it might shatter. He didn't appreciate Fancy being labeled a chit, not that he hadn't used the word himself on occasion in reference to other women, but she deserved a more respectful tone. It took everything within him not to launch himself at the man sitting across from him and introduce his jaw to his fists.

"Waltzed with her at the Thornley ball," Beresford continued. "She's a comely little thing."

Matthew set his scotch aside because he expected the glass to crumble in his hand at any moment. He hadn't expected the anger—or perhaps it was jealousy—to swell so forcefully within him when he imagined Beresford circling Fancy over the dance floor. "I heard rewards were offered to anyone who danced with her. What benefit did you receive?"

"The benefit of her company. Nothing else. I don't gamble so I have no debt. My stables are up to snuff, and my investments are sound."

He was at once happy for Fancy that she might have an actual admirer, while again experiencing a stab of jealousy that someone else might have an interest in her. "You were taken with her then?"

Beresford glanced around as though on the verge of doing something he ought not. Leaning forward slightly, he met Matthew's gaze. "She's a beauty, doesn't giggle or simper. Appears to be a woman of intelligence."

That was an understatement.

"She asked after my family and my hobbies. I've never had a woman ask questions of me. They generally just talk about themselves or the weather. She was quite a delight to be honest."

She was most definitely that.

"However, she's unlawfully born. Her father could be a murderer for all we know."

He almost revealed that her father was a war hero, but then he'd have to explain how he knew, and things could get a bit complicated from there. "I don't believe criminal tendencies are inherited."

"Still, tainted blood and all that. A man could lose some power and prestige taking her to wife."

Or he could gain it. "Thornley married her sister, a by-blow."

"He's a duke from one of the most powerful families in all of England. He can do whatever he bloody well likes and suffer very little for it. You and I are mere earls."

It was true that Thornley came from an incredibly formidable family, but Matthew could hold his own when it came to power, prestige, and influence. "Is that the reason you don't marry your mistress?"

A sadness coming over him, Beresford settled back in his chair. "Duty before love. They were the first words I was taught."

They'd been battered into Matthew as well. They were the reason he'd married a woman knowing her treachery would forever prevent him from loving her. When he was in Fancy's company, the past no longer mattered. She made him believe the potential for love hovered within reach, if he would but dare to grasp it.

FANCY TOOK GREAT satisfaction in watching people wander through her shop, taking books from the shelves, opening them, perusing a few words, putting them back. Or hugging them close and bringing them to the counter to purchase. This particular Saturday afternoon, more people were about than usual and helping them select books kept her mind occupied so she wasn't thinking about Matthew or the fact that she hadn't seen him since the kiss.

She had just finished helping a woman with her book purchase when the bells above her door jingled—and Matthew was dominating her thoughts once again because he stepped over the threshold and approached the counter. "Mr. Sommersby." She wondered why she had to sound so breathless when she'd said his name a hundred times already, whenever she saw him in her dreams.

"Miss Trewlove. How are you this fine day?"

Wonderful now that you've made an appearance. "Very well, thank you, and you?"

"At a bit of a loss. I'm in need of a book for my niece and was hoping you might have a suggestion."

"Oh, absolutely. How old is she?"

"Four."

Such mundane conversation, and yet she so enjoyed the rumble of his deep voice that she would happily listen to him reading *Debrett's* without growing bored. As long as words spilled forth from him, she really didn't care what they were. "If you'll come with me . . ."

He followed her to the back wall where they were partially hidden by the bookshelves running perpendicular through the center of the shop, shelves around which they'd waltzed. She knelt. "I keep books appropriate for children on the lower shelves here, so they have easier access to them."

He crouched beside her, balancing on the balls of his feet, and she couldn't help but notice how his trousers pulled taut against his thighs or how masculine it looked to have his elbows resting there, his hands clasped before him. He'd removed his gloves, and it took everything within her not to wedge her hand between both of his.

"You've been rather scarce," she whispered, her voice low, hushed.

"I decided a bit of distance between us was needed."

There certainly wasn't much between them now. She could feel the heat emanating from him, and the pull of her body toward his, as though he were the moon and she the ocean tides. Or perhaps she was the moon, but it didn't really matter when the attraction between them seemed so strong. "I thought perhaps you found fault with my eagerness the last time we were together."

"I found fault only with my own actions. Thank God for your cat."

She gave him a sly smile. "I've been cursing Dickens for interfering."

"You should be rewarding him for putting a stop to my antics. Things between us almost went too far, Miss Trewlove."

They had. She knew that. And she'd wanted them to. Whatever was wrong with her? Plenty of men were handsome, but no other made her feel as though she garnered all of his attention, as though he hung on every word she spoke, as though he cared about what she had to say. "After what transpired between us, it seems you should call me Fancy."

He'd said her name before, and she wanted to hear it again on his lips.

"Fancy." His voice was low, deep, hinting at secrets and seduction.

"Matthew." She'd never called him by name before, at least not out loud, not to his face.

He slammed his eyes closed, released a shuddering breath. When he opened them, they contained an intensity that led her to believe he found his name on her tongue as sensual as she found hers on his. "The book?"

The rasp of his voice alerted her he was searching for a distraction. A good thing as someone entered their aisle, turned the corner, and disappeared between two more sets of bookcases. "These here"—she skimmed her fingers over the spines—"all have illustrations. The stories are simple. This book"—she leaned partially in front of him, taking satisfaction with his hand coming to rest on the small of her back, steadying her—"has several of Aesop's fables in it. They're short enough to hold her interest while you read them to her."

"Your hair's come loose of your bun."

"Has it?" She lifted a hand, and he wrapped his fingers around her wrist, stopping her actions.

"Allow me."

She didn't move a muscle while his knuckles skimmed over her cheek as he captured the few rebellious tresses between his finger and thumb before gently, carefully tucking them away. "You have the softest hair."

"What a shame every strand of yours is in place."

His hand came around to cradle her cheek. "*Aesop's Fables*, you say?"

"Yes. Here." She pulled it from the shelf and handed it to him. "The illustrations are lovely."

"As lovely as you?"

"You can't tell me in one breath that things between us are going too far and then in the next flirt with me."

"It's only flirtation if the words aren't uttered with all sincerity."

She was vaguely aware of the jangle of the bells. "Matthew—"

"Miss Trewlove! Miss Trewlove! Ah, there you are."

Glancing over her shoulder, at the entry to the aisle, she saw Aslyn's maid, smiling brightly and breathless. Fancy quickly shoved herself to her feet, Matthew hastily following suit. "Nan."

"Lady Aslyn sent me for you. You have a gentleman caller. Well, two actually."

Fancy stared at the maid as though she'd spoken in a foreign language. "Gentlemen callers?"

"Yes, miss. Lady Aslyn is entertaining them until you arrive."

"Well, this is a surprise."

"Would you like me to help you change, maybe tidy your hair a bit?"

She suspected Nan thought she should have it styled a little more elaborately than in a simple bun. As for her clothing, it was serviceable. Both reflected who she was, and she wanted to be completely honest with any gentleman who might have an interest in her. Sometimes she wore plain attire and her hair had not been fiddled with for more than an hour to ensure that every curl dangled just right. "I appreciate the offer, Nan, but I don't think we need to go to such bother for afternoon tea."

The woman looked stricken but didn't say anything. "If you'll give me a minute to finish with this customer, I'll be right there."

"I'll wait by the door."

"Thank you." She turned to Matthew. "I have to go, but I think your niece will very much enjoy that book."

"Go boating with me tomorrow."

She opened her mouth, closed it. He was correct. They needed to keep distance between them. However, if they went out in a rather large boat and sat at opposite ends—

"I go to church with my mother in the morning."

"In the afternoon, then. Say one o'clock?"

She nodded. "I'll meet you at the park, shall I?"

"Bring a chaperone if you wish."

She gave him what she hoped was a saucy smile. "I think we've moved beyond that. See you tomorrow."

She hurried through the shop, toward the door. "I'll be back shortly, Marianne."

"Yes, miss."

She heard the excitement thrumming through her clerk's voice. "It's only tea, Marianne."

"With a couple of gents."

"You're not supposed to eavesdrop." Her words lacked conviction or sternness, so the shopgirl simply continued to smile.

"This will be the first of many such visitors," Nan said when Fancy reached her. "You mark my words."

"Let's not have me betrothed before dinner."

Nan laughed. "Ah, miss. You deserve to have the very finest, and these two are quite a feast for the eyes."

They were indeed, but then she'd thought the same thing when she'd first met them. They both came to their feet as she entered. "Lord Beresford. Mr. Whitley." Beresford was an earl, Whitley the eldest son of a viscount.

"Miss Trewlove," they said in unison, both bowing.

She took the chair Aslyn had discreetly vacated in order to move to a chair in the corner, so she could chaperone without interfering. Both gentlemen returned to their respective places on the settee. Tea had been prepared and poured, and everyone picked up their saucers and cups to take a sip. Once her cup was back in its place, Fancy said, "It was so nice of you gentlemen to call."

"I'd have come earlier if I'd known Whitley was going to be here at this time," Beresford said.

"I'd have come later," Whitley said.

She didn't have the impression the gentlemen disliked each other. It was more that they didn't want to share the attention. "What book are you currently reading, Mr. Whitley?"

"Well, I'm not reading. I'm having tea."

It took everything within her not to roll her eyes.

"Good God, man, she doesn't mean at this precise moment."

"Lord Beresford is correct. What book is on the table beside your bed or your favorite chair in your library? What book has a ribbon marking your place?"

"My books are all on shelves. I don't *read* them."

"You don't read books?"

"Haven't time."

How could a person not find some time for the pleasure of reading? "How do you spend your time?"

"Cricket. Polo. I've recently taken up marathon running. I prefer physical exertion to simply sitting about."

She supposed then she should be honored that he was simply sitting about here.

"And you, my lord, are you reading anything of interest?"

"*A Tale of Two Cities.*"

"Are you a fan of Dickens, then?"

"I am."

"A young lad brought me a rather dilapidated copy of *Little Dorrit*. I'm working to restore it."

"Is that a hobby of yours?"

"In a way. It goes well with my bookshop as I'll sell the book once it's been repaired. Would you gentlemen like a tour of my establishment?"

"You're not going to work in it when you're married, are you?" Mr. Whitley asked.

"Well, no."

"Then it would be a waste of time, would it not?"

It would allow him to get a better sense of her. As it was, she was beginning to feel he was a waste of time. "Well, this has been enlightening, gentlemen, but I must return to my endeavors."

Besides it was rude for a gentleman to linger more than fifteen minutes, and surely that much time had passed. She wasn't going to double it just because there were two of them. She rose to her feet, and they both stood. "It's been a pleasure, my lord, Mr. Whitley."

Beresford stepped forward, took her hand, and placed a kiss on her knuckles. "I do hope you'll honor me with a dance at the next ball you attend."

"It will be my pleasure. I look forward to it."

Mr. Whitley looked as though he had a strong urge to shove the lord aside. As soon as Beresford was out of the way, Whitley also took her hand. "Until our paths cross again."

He planted a kiss on the back of her hand. Because she was not wearing gloves, she could feel the spittle leaking between his lips. As soon as he released her, she placed her hand behind her back and discreetly wiped it on her skirt, hoping she never had occasion to feel his lips pressed to hers. Still she returned his smile.

"My lord, sir, I wish you both a good day," Aslyn said, having approached. She led them into the hallway and called for a footman to show them out.

Once she returned, she lifted her eyebrows at Fancy. "Well?"

Fancy dropped into the chair. "Beresford seems rather fine, but Whitley. How can a man have no love for books? We would never suit."

Aslyn sat on the settee. "I have no advice when it comes to

courtship as my betrothal to Kipwick and my eventual marriage to your brother were quite unconventional when it came to the wooing. All I can offer is to follow your heart."

Unfortunately, her heart was leading her toward a man who would not be all her mother wanted.

"UNCA MATTHEW!"

"Poppet!" Bending down, Matthew swept his four-year-old niece up with one arm, laughing as she planted a rather wet and sloppy kiss on his cheek.

Leaning back, she squinted and pointed at the package he held in his other hand. "What's that?"

"A gift for you." Setting her back on the floor, he crouched and handed it to her, taking delight in her excitement as she tore away the brown paper—quite quickly and efficiently with those little fingers of hers—to reveal the book Fancy had suggested. He hadn't intended to ask her to go boating with him, but the realization that gents were calling on her had sent a primal and possessive need to claim her through him, and the invitation had come out before he'd been able to analyze the wisdom of it or give it much thought.

"A book!" Tillie exclaimed. "I love it!" Immediately she sat on the floor and began turning pages.

"Tillie! A lady does not sit upon the floor."

Glancing up at his sister, he smiled. Two years his senior, she'd been married nearly six years now and had yet to produce the heir. "Surely she is forgiven when it is her excitement over a book that prompted her actions."

"You spoil her."

"As though you don't."

Straightening, he went to her and bussed a quick kiss over her cheek. "You have more color in you today. I've been a bit worried. You were quite pale the last few times I visited." He remembered a time when he hadn't noticed things like complexion.

"Would you say I'm glowing?"

"I would rather."

Lifting her shoulders, she gave him a secretive smile. "I'm with child."

He took her hand, squeezed. "Ah, Sylvie, that's wonderful."

"Four months. I almost told you last time but wanted to wait until I wasn't taking a second look at my breakfast each morning. However, that seems to have passed now, so we're hopeful all will be well. Fairhaven is beside himself. I am praying for the heir. He says he doesn't care, but he's a marquess. Of course he wants a son to pass everything off to. Just as you do." She touched his cheek. "You look healthier of late. I'm pleased to see that."

"I am more of myself, these days." In part, thanks to Fancy Trewlove.

"I'm glad. I have a favor to ask before Fairhaven joins us." She moved over to her daughter and bent. "Come along, Tillie. The floor is no place for a lady. Let's retire to the parlor so we can sit properly."

"I've got her." He scooped her up into his arms, her delightful laugh warming his heart. He wondered if Fancy had been reprimanded in a similar manner when she was growing up, never allowed to truly be a child, but always cognizant of how one *should* behave instead of how one wanted to behave. He hoped her family hadn't been quite as strict as his sister.

In the parlor, he set his niece down on the corner of the sofa. She immediately opened her book. His sister lowered herself to a spot beside her daughter and lovingly brushed her fingers over her dark hair. He took a nearby chair, absorbing the tranquil sight, feeling an unwanted ache in his chest because his life had yet to bring him similar moments.

Her hand never leaving her daughter's hair, Sylvie looked over at him. "About this favor. I'm hosting a ball at the end of the month and it would be quite a coup for me if you were to make an appearance. As I've mentioned, you're all the talk. Some good should come from this sabbatical from Society you've taken."

Some good was coming of it. He was once again enjoying his

life. "I have no desire to step into the whirl that is the Social Season."

"But it will be the perfect opportunity for your foray back into Society. I have invited the most popular debutantes."

He already knew he wasn't interested in the ones who'd made an appearance at his door. "Would Fancy Trewlove be included on that list?"

Her head jerking back slightly as though he'd tweaked her nose, she blinked, blinked, and blinked again. "Not at the moment. I hadn't yet decided if I would invite her. How do you know of her?"

"Her bookshop is in the same area as the residence I'm leasing. As a matter of fact, I purchased Tillie's book from her this afternoon. I assume you met her at the Thornley ball."

"I did. I found her to be beautiful, poised, and confident. To look at her, you wouldn't know she was"—she glanced over at her daughter before lowering her voice to a whisper—"unlawful."

"It seems to me that term should be used for those who don't adhere to the laws, not those who have no say in how they are born."

Her entire body gave a little twitch as though his words had been tiny stones pelted at her. "That's certainly a novel thought. I'm not certain your avoidance of Society is to your benefit if it's filling your head with such odd notions."

He was ashamed to admit a time existed when he'd have judged Fancy by her origins rather than herself. "Invite Miss Trewlove to your ball."

His sister went so still he wasn't certain she continued to breathe. Very primly, she knitted her fingers together and folded them in her lap, her gaze sharp like a raven's. "Why would I do that?"

"Because I asked."

"She's not accepted."

"An invitation to your affair will make her so."

"What is she to you?"

"A friend. She's been kind to me. She wishes to move about in your world, and I want to make it easier for her to do so." He didn't particularly like the thought of other men taking her in their arms for a turn about the dance floor, but he wasn't selfish enough to deny her what she wanted.

"Usually when a gentleman says a woman has been *kind* it's because she spread her legs for him."

The fury that rent through him nearly made him tremble. "Such talk is beneath you, Sylvie."

Her cheeks burned red. "You're asking me to put my reputation on the line."

"I'm asking you to show a kindness."

"Will you attend?"

"No." He stood. "I don't believe I'll be staying for dinner."

Rising, she placed her hand on his arm. "I don't want to have a row with you. You're my only brother. I'll think about inviting her, if you'll think about coming."

He nodded. Perhaps by the end of the month, he would have won Fancy over to such an extent that he'd have told her who he truly was. In which case, he would claim every one of her damned dances at the ball.

$\mathcal{I}$f Matthew wanted to keep distance between them, he'd certainly selected the perfect boat for ensuring his goal. It was long with a flat bottom. Holding a white lacy parasol that Mick had given her a couple of years earlier, Fancy sat at one end, while Matthew stood at the other, impressing her as he stayed balanced while dropping the pole into the water and then pushing it back, guiding the craft through the stream.

"I assumed we were going rowing," she said. Matthew had been waiting in a curricle for her near the park entrance. It seemed this gentleman of leisure had his own conveyance available to him, but wherever he stored it made it inconvenient to retrieve on short notice. But he'd made arrangements to have it on hand for this planned excursion.

"I prefer punting," he said.

"It's such an odd-shaped rowboat." He'd rented it from a gent who'd had several boats available. Occasionally they passed another spot where it appeared boats were being let or could be returned if one had enough of the river.

He grinned. "It's a punt, not a rowboat. Hence, the punting, not rowing."

"Oh. Have you ever fallen into the water?"

"Once, when I was first learning how to control the pole."

While others were about, most were in rowboats. Before shoving off from the shore, he'd removed his jacket and rolled up his sleeves. In spite of how much of her he'd seen, she realized now that she'd viewed very little of him. She was rather taken with his forearms, the ropy muscle and sinew, the raised veins indicating the strength that resided there. She liked the way the punt glided along the water, almost as though it sat on top of it. It was a smooth and relaxing motion, and she rather enjoyed her view of Matthew. "Did your niece enjoy the book?"

"She did. She especially loved the illustrations."

"Did you read to her?"

"Not this time. I ended up not staying for dinner."

"So . . . you and your wife . . . you never had children?"

"The strain of our relationship made that possibility very unlikely."

"Do you want children?"

"With the right woman, yes."

"What would make the right woman?" she dared to ask.

He'd discarded his hat as well, no doubt because the breeze would have blown it into the river, so no shadows kept his gaze hidden from her. His eyes were even more green in the sunlight, more intense, and she had the feeling he could see clear through her, knew she found him far more fascinating than any other man she'd met thus far.

"A luscious mouth made for kissing." His voice was low but still it traveled on the wind to her. "Sultry eyes that belong in a bedchamber. A raspy voice that whispers wicked things in my ear."

With a scoff, she rolled her eyes. "I think you've just described Lottie."

He laughed, a deep rich sound, and she thought it was the sort of laugh that would make him the right man. "I think every man wants his wife to be a tart in the bedchamber."

Leaning forward, she placed her elbow on her thigh, her chin in her palm. "Truly?"

"Don't you want your husband to be a bit of a scoundrel when it comes to bedding you?"

She couldn't believe they were discussing this topic on the river, in the open where anyone might hear—even if presently no one was within hearing distance. She looked toward the trees. "I'm not certain I know enough about it to determine precisely what I want." She peered up at him. "I suppose when it comes down to it, in or out of the bedchamber, I want to feel I can be as open with him as I am with you."

"Do you feel that way about the gents who called on you yesterday?"

She shook her head. "One of them I have no interest in at all. He has no appreciation for books. The other . . . was nice enough, I suppose. I'm not certain I have patience for this courting thing. I want an instant rapport, and thus far that has escaped me." *Except when it comes to you.* Not that she was going to confess that to him. "Do you really only care about a woman's mouth, eyes, and voice?"

"In truth, I'm more interested in her actions, the manner in which she treats people, the things she cares about, the things she doesn't. The other attributes I named would be a nice addition but not a requirement."

"Are you looking to marry?"

His gaze shifted until it appeared he was looking past her, not so much to ensure they had no collision with another boat but because the water provided a calming effect over his thoughts. "I hadn't really contemplated it. When I met my wife, I was quickly smitten, and she took advantage. I was young and stupid. I am neither any longer and a good deal more cautious." His gaze came back to her. "Or at least I'm trying to be."

"I worry that some lord will pretend to be smitten with me in order to win my hand, but all he really wants is my dowry. I want love but know it's not what those among the aristocracy generally seek. Financial or political advantage holds much more sway. My family can definitely provide a financial advantage, and now that they've married into the aristocracy, I believe they'll have some political influence. I want a man who cares nothing at all for any of that. So he mustn't be impoverished. He must have his own power and influence, and not look to me to provide it. Even as I begin listing out my requirements, I realize I'm doing exactly what I don't want him to do. Ticking off what I believe will make him perfect."

"No one is perfect."

But Matthew Sommersby came close. "In the end, I just want to be loved."

"I suppose that's what we all want." He grinned. "That and a spot of tea. Hungry?"

She laughed lightly. "I'm a bit peckish."

He nodded toward the shore. "We'll pull over here, enjoy a bit of a repast."

MATTHEW SECURED THE punt to a low-hanging bush, delivered the blanket and wicker basket to a spot beneath a willow tree, and returned for Fancy. She looked like sunshine in her yellow frock, like a lady of quality with her white parasol, like a country lass with her straw bonnet. With one foot in the boat, he sought to steady it as he offered her his hand. "Hold on to me to balance yourself."

As she placed her hand in his, he closed his fingers around hers and became the support for her as she gingerly rose to her feet, the punt rocking slightly with her movements. "It's all right," he cooed. "I'm not going to let you go over into the water."

"I have absolute faith in you."

He was completely taken aback by how much her words meant to him. When she began to wobble slightly, he placed his free hand on her waist. She froze. Their eyes met. He could gaze into those brown depths for the remainder of his life and never fully uncover all the various facets to her. She was elegance and poise, a perfect fit for the aristocracy. She was adventurous and fun, perfect for the world she now inhabited. She would forever be a part of both, of where she'd come from and where she was going. He had little doubt she would succeed in whatever she attempted. She would wed a lord.

And their paths would cross at future balls and affairs, because Sylvie was correct. Eventually he would have to return to Society, find a woman to marry in order to gain his heir and secure the line. He had closed off his heart, decided it served no useful purpose when it came to his determining whom he would take to wife. But now with this woman putting all her trust in him, he realized he'd been more foolish with that assertion about involving his heart than he'd been when he allowed Elise to so effectively seduce him. Whether he desired it or not, his heart was becoming involved, was nudging him toward Fancy Trewlove. He could have her so easily if he told her the truth, but he wanted to earn her, without the advantage of his title.

"Easy now, don't move," he murmured. Slowly releasing his hold on her hand, he lowered his to her waist, so she was now bracketed between both his hands. "Put your hands on my shoulders."

When she did so, he tightened his grip on her, lifted her up, and swung her over to the bank. She was as light as the branches of the willow beneath which they'd soon be sitting, and he was reluctant to let her go, but as her feet came to rest on the ground, he loosened his hold and brought his own foot from the boat to the shore.

"It's odd to be standing on land after being on the water," she said softly. "I feel as though we're still moving."

"It'll pass, but you can hold on to me until you're feeling more steady."

It seemed the most natural thing in the world to offer his arm and have her wrap both of hers around it, fairly snuggling up against him. As he led her toward the tree, he kept his steps small and realized it had become a habit for him to do so whenever they walked together. How many other aspects of his life were dictated by his desire to ensure she always felt comfortable in his presence? How often did he do something simply because he knew it would please her?

How was he going to feel when a gentleman called on her, not for a cup of tea, but for a stroll in the park? He didn't want to think of her arm intertwined with another's. Didn't want to contemplate her gazing up into another's eyes.

When they reached the tree, she eased away from him and together they spread out the blanket. After they'd settled on the wool, he opened the wicker basket.

"Are you truly going to make tea?" she asked.

With a grin, he pulled out a bottle of red wine. "No, too much trouble."

As she laughed, she untied the ribbon on her bonnet, removed the hat from her head, and set it down near her side. He handed her a glass. "Proper stemware."

"I didn't think you'd like drinking from the bottle." He brought out a platter and removed the cloth covering it. "It appears we also have some cheese, bread, apples, and grapes."

"Did Mrs. Bennett prepare all this?"

"She did." Stretching out on his side, he rested on an elbow. "I didn't realize she couldn't read until I saw her at your class. I don't know how she manages her household."

She studied her wineglass for a moment. "I think people who can't read find a way to remember things. My mum was never a very good reader. She had a basic understanding of most of the letters, I think, but she still struggles. Yet she raised six children. And we've all turned out fairly well."

"Is she the reason you teach reading?"

She nodded. "I hope to have an actual school for adults in a building, very much like the ragged schools. Not only to teach them reading but to introduce them to some skills that might help improve their income, their lives. I just have to secure a husband willing to embrace all I hope to accomplish."

"It's all worthwhile. I'm sure you won't have any trouble there."

"I can only hope." Reaching out, she snatched up a small chunk of cheese and popped it into her mouth. "I'm curious. How did you become a gentleman of means? How do you make your way?"

After the kiss they'd shared, she had every right to ask. "I inherited a good deal from my father. I have some property." Not everyone who owned property was a noble. "Have a few tenants working the land. I meet occasionally with my man of affairs to discuss ways to make the property more profitable." How to ensure his income could cover all the maintenance costs associated with having an earldom, an estate, a manor house. "I'm also keen on investing, and I'm rather good at it."

"So you've never actually *worked*?"

"It takes a great deal of effort, insight, and skill to manage property, people, and money. I would have thought your brother would have taught you that." Not to mention his duties in the House of Lords, not that he was ready to tell her about that portion of his life.

"I didn't mean to insult your efforts." She took a sip of her wine, glanced up at the tree. "The gentleman I marry will no doubt partake in similar endeavors. Or perhaps none at all. Lords don't generally engage in labors. I can't imagine what he will do with his day."

"Don't underestimate what they contribute. They have their duties in the House of Lords. They provide work for laborers and farmers. Think of the people in this country who are employed as servants. A good many of them work in noble households. Lords always have some matter with which they must deal. It's not as though they loll about in bed all day. They have responsibilities. Sometimes it's a heavy burden."

"You truly do have respect for the aristocracy."

He hadn't meant to go on about it, but it was imperative she realized she was seeking to marry more than a title. While her siblings had married into the aristocracy, with the exception of Thornley, none of their spouses were active participants in it any longer. Granted, for the women, their choice of husband had created scandal, and the aristocracy was not a forgiving lot, but still they were seldom seen in the thick of things. Straightening, he set his glass aside and edged over until his hip was close to hers, with her facing one way, he the other so he had a better view of her. He cradled her face. "You will be responsible for tenants, farmers, laborers, servants. They'll come to you when they have problems, when they are ill. You'll manage a manor house, perhaps more than one. It depends on how many titles or estates he has. You'll oversee his London residence. Wherever you go, you will represent him, people will associate you with him. I know you're up to the task, but just take care in the choosing. He will be as much a reflection of you as you are of him."

"I'm well aware. I'm not going to make a hasty decision. I fully understand the responsibilities I will take on as the wife of a lord. Managing my shop as much as anything has helped prepare me for them. I intend to be a great help to my husband, ensuring he never regrets taking a chance on me."

"Any man who regrets having you at his side would be a fool. I think you're too smart to marry a fool."

"I'm not as smart as you think. I probably shouldn't be here with you."

"Why are you?"

"Because I like you a great deal. I enjoy your company. And while all my lessons have prepared me to oversee my duties and responsibilities, I've had no lessons whatsoever in how to entice a man into wanting me. As I've mentioned, my family has worked very hard to keep me pure and away from those with wicked intentions. As a result, I feel somewhat . . . unmoored when it comes to being alone with a man. I don't know how to properly kiss—"

"I found no fault with your kiss, sweeting."

"It seems to me, though, that perhaps I should practice a bit more, simply to ensure I've mastered the technique."

He skimmed his thumb over her lower lip. "If you practice at balls or with other gentlemen, you're going to gain a reputation that will not serve you well. I suggest you have but one tutor, one who will keep the lessons secret."

"Have you someone in mind?" The hushed words came out slowly, seductively, and his body reacted as though she'd brushed them over his skin.

"You're not quite as innocent as you seem, are you?"

"I've read some books banned under the Obscene Publications Act, so I know a few things, but reading is never as educational as doing. Does my boldness frighten you, Mr. Sommersby?"

Her eyes held a challenge that he intended to accept. "Not at all, Miss Trewlove."

He'd begun slowly before. This time, he offered no preamble. He simply took possession of her mouth as though it belonged to him, and damned if at that particular moment, he didn't feel as though it did. As though she belonged to him. Every facet of her. Her heart, her soul, her body. Ah, yes, especially her body as she twisted toward him, her breasts pressing up against his chest, her leg swinging up and over his thigh, trapping him within her skirts. Her hands glided over his shoulders, one resting at the nape of his neck, the other sliding along his arm and then ducking under it to splay across his back. Wrapping himself around her, he lowered her to the ground.

She tasted of rich wine and something more, something unique to her. Her soft sighs were sweeter than the trill of the birds in the trees or the rustle of the leaves in the breeze. As much as he longed to unbutton her bodice, strip her bare, he showed restraint because he was well aware that at any moment someone could happen upon them. This spot was popular among boaters. With luck, any intruders would be strangers and a kiss they could laugh off. To be caught doing more . . . he wouldn't risk bringing that shame to her. No matter how his body ached to possess her fully.

He didn't want her practicing with anyone else, exploring another's mouth. She was daring as she stroked her tongue over his, as she drew his into her mouth and suckled. His low growl echoed between them as he dragged his hand down her back to her bottom and pressed her close so she could know the affect she had on him.

Tearing his mouth from hers, he trailed his lips along the underside of her jaw. She released a tiny mewl. "Do you like that?"

"Yes."

He took her lobe between his teeth, nipped, then soothed with his tongue. Another mewl. "And that?"

"Yes. I thought only mouths were involved in kissing."

"How boring would that be?" He made a sojourn along the column of her throat. "If no possibility existed for us to get caught, I'd kiss every inch of you."

"Every inch?"

Raising up, he looked down on her and grinned. "Every inch."

She blinked. *"Every?"*

He kissed the tip of her nose. "Every."

"Is that proper?"

"Probably not. But I would enjoy it and would ensure you did as well."

"Would you want me to kiss every inch of you?"

"Only if you wanted."

She licked her lips. "Would you think me wicked if I did?"

"Ah, Christ." He buried his face in the curve of her neck. Never in his life had a mere thought caused him to ache with such need, but the vision of her mouth moving over every inch of his flesh—

She squirmed beneath him.

"Please lie still."

"You're poking me."

"That's my body signaling that I want you."

"Oh."

"You sound surprised."

"I don't know if I've ever been wanted before."

"I rather suspect you have."

"Why?"

"Because, Fancy, you are a delectable delight."

She laughed lightly, her entire body shaking beneath him. God, he loved the airy sound of her laughter, like the chimes at Christmas.

"How do we make it so you don't want me?"

That wasn't going to happen. Even if he took her fully, he'd want her again. He knew that with certainty. But also knew what she was asking. "To distract myself, I'm going through Aesop's fables."

More laughter from her. "I don't know that there is one that applies to this situation."

No, but she'd distracted him. Taking a deep breath, he shoved himself off her and stood, turned away from her, and adjusted himself. "We should probably call it an afternoon."

He hadn't heard her get up, but her arms came around him and she pressed her cheek to his back. "Kissing is like reading, isn't it? The more you learn, the more comfortable you become with it, the more you want to do it."

"I'm glad you found it enjoyable."

"You're a very good tutor. If you ever make a bad investment and need funds, I think you could make a living giving kissing lessons."

Laughing, he spun around and wrapped her in his embrace. "At the moment, the only person I'm interested in kissing is you."

Chapter 17

The following afternoon, using a thin but sharp blade, Fancy was carefully removing the leather cover from the book Timmy Tubbins had brought her when Marianne rapped on the doorjamb. Looking up from her desk, she wondered why her clerk's brow was furrowed so deeply and her mouth pinched. "Is something amiss?"

"There's a gent here what wants to talk to you."

"*Who* wants to talk to me."

"The gent. The gent what's out here."

She squeezed her eyes shut, opened them. Marianne was sharp but had grown up with very little education. Although her grammar had improved greatly since coming to work at the shop, challenges still presented themselves. "It's the gent *who* not the gent *what*."

Marianne appeared even more flummoxed. Fancy waved her hand dismissively. "Never mind. We'll discuss it later. Send him in."

She rose to her feet. Not even half a minute later, a slender man of rather short height—she doubted the top his head would reach the shoulder of any of her brothers—entered, holding his hat and a satchel in one hand. "Miss Fancy Trewlove?"

"Yes, sir. How may I be of service?"

"It is I who am here to serve you." Confidence shimmering off him, he came nearer and set his things on her desk. "My name is Paul Lassiter. I'm a solicitor. One of my clients wishes to make a donation toward helping to finance your lending library and your efforts to educate those adults who have yet to learn to read."

"Oh." She hardly knew what to say. Until that moment all her donations had come from her family or their spouses' families or friends. Once she married, hopefully, she would be able to tap into a host of beneficiaries.

He opened his satchel, removed a package wrapped in brown paper secured with string, and set it before her. Slowly, she loosened the bow and folded back the covering to reveal a stack of notes.

"Five hundred pounds," he said.

She jerked her gaze up to meet his. "Who is this client?"

"Someone who wishes to remain anonymous."

Someone? A man? A woman? Could it be Lady Penelope? She'd certainly perked up when she'd learned the library was maintained with donations. Or was it someone else? "Why would this person be so incredibly generous?"

"A believer in your cause." He picked up his hat and satchel. "Have a good day, Miss Trewlove."

"Wait. I . . . I'm having a difficult time absorbing this. You can tell me something about this generous soul, surely. Have we met? How did he—or she—learn of my cause?"

"I've done what I've been hired to do. Simply make good use of the funds." He gave a short bow before walking out.

She sat there in silence for several long minutes before getting up, closing the door, and placing the money in her safe. Then she headed out into the shop. "I'm going to see my brother, Marianne. I shan't be long."

"Very good, Miss Trewlove."

Once she entered the hotel, she charged up the stairs until she reached the top floor where Mick had his offices. She opened the glass door that had *Trewlove* etched in it and smiled as Mr. Tittlefitz came to his feet behind his desk while she stepped over the threshold. "Miss Trewlove, how may I be of service?"

"Is my brother available?"

"For you, miss, I'm certain he is." He hurried over to the door that led into Mick's inner sanctum, gave a brisk knock, shoved it open, and peered inside. "Your sister wishes an audience."

An audience? Good Lord, he acted as though her brother were a king. She couldn't make out the words but heard the rumble of his voice. His secretary opened the door farther ajar and stepped back. After passing through the portal, she heard the door echo a quiet *snick* as it was closed in her wake.

Mick was already standing. "What's wrong?"

"Nothing. I don't think." She approached the massive desk. "A solicitor just visited me. An anonymous person has donated five hundred pounds to my cause. I'm unsure what precisely to do with it."

With a loud and unflattering scoff, he crossed his arms over his chest. "You didn't seem to have any trouble figuring out what to do with the money I gave you."

"That's different. Your money comes in manageable increments and doesn't make me feel guilty. But this—I don't know who sent it. Did you mention my endeavors to anyone?"

"Only in passing to an investor or two."

"Do you think it could have come from one of them?"

He lifted a broad shoulder. "Possibly. What does it matter, Fancy? Besides, once you marry, you'll be asking all sorts for contributions. You'll have more donations than you'll know what to do with. I'm certain some will be anonymous."

"Why? Why would he not want his contribution acknowledged?"

"Perhaps he likes to do good deeds without credit. Or he worries if his generosity is known, others will hold out their hands. Accept the gift with gratitude."

"But I don't know who to thank."

"If he wanted thanks, he'd have given you his name."

"I don't suppose you can find out who he is."

"Sweetheart, I wouldn't even if I could. On occasion I've done things for others in secret simply because I don't want them feeling beholden to me. Perhaps he feels the same. But whatever his reasoning, it needs to be honored."

She sighed. He was right. Still, she couldn't help but wonder about her mysterious benefactor. "Well, I suppose I should get back to the shop and determine how to make the most of the contribution I received."

"When you marry a lord of the realm, you'll receive a good many more, I suspect. Moving about in that world will have grand advantages, Fancy."

Not if the man didn't love her.

"I remain optimistic, Mick, that I'll find happiness there." Approaching him, she gave him a hug. "Thank you."

THAT EVENING, WHEN Fancy walked into the reading parlor to prepare it for the students' arrival, she was surprised to find Matthew looking up at the painting above the fireplace. "Hello."

He turned and smiled at her, genuine pleasure reflected in his green, green eyes. "Hello."

It wasn't that she was feeling off-kilter, but it seemed they should be greeting each other with a kiss or an embrace instead of this awkwardness. "I don't have a ball to attend tonight."

"I know, but I enjoyed teaching the other night and thought you might welcome my assistance. I have nothing else pressing."

"I'd like that very much, and I'm fairly certain Lottie will as well."

He laughed. The joyous sound that vibrated from deep within him made her chest feel as though it were expanding to encompass the world. "Perhaps I could take the gents and you could take the ladies."

"I think that's a rather splendid idea." She eased up until the hem of her skirt touched the toes of his boots. "I'm glad you find these efforts worth your while."

"Maybe I'm just using it as an excuse to spend more time in your company."

"I'm glad of that as well." Based upon the sudden warmth of

her cheeks, she was fairly certain she was blushing. "The most astonishing thing happened this afternoon."

"Indeed?"

"A solicitor came to see me on behalf of someone who wanted to make an anonymous donation to my lending library and other efforts. Five hundred pounds."

"How will you use it?"

He said it so calmly as though it wasn't an astronomical amount. "For books and slates and other supplies. I can hardly countenance that I have so much to work with. I've been striving to determine who could have been so generous."

"Perhaps you should simply accept your good fortune."

"I suppose you're right. A fortune that is increasing because now I have another teacher."

A teacher who was proving to be a distraction. He'd taken the gents to a far corner, but still his voice carried to her ears whenever he spoke. It was as though she noticed every aspect of him. He sat forward, his elbows resting on his thighs, the primer clasped between his hands, his brow furrowed as he concentrated on reading along with Mr. Davidson.

Matthew represented what she wanted in a husband. Someone who took an interest in the things that mattered to her. Someone who wanted to do more than spend time with her at balls, operas, and theater. Someone willing to give his time to improving the condition of others. Someone who looked up from his book and captured her gaze as unerringly as Robin Hood's arrow hit its target—at least according to the serials about his adventures that her brothers had read her. It seemed she would never tire of the intensity with which Matthew observed her. Even though across the room, she felt as though he were beside her.

When the lessons ended, she felt a twinge of jealousy when Lottie sauntered over to Matthew and trailed her hand up his arm. He said something to her, and her throaty laugher echoed throughout the room. Fancy was tempted to grab the woman by the hair and pull her into the hallway—or at least inform her that she was no longer welcome to take classes here. But she wasn't going to be as petty as all that. Lottie was striving to better herself. Fancy needed to respect that.

"If it's any consolation, she was flirting with me earlier."

With a huffed laugh, she turned to Mr. Tittlefitz. "Why would I care if she's flirting?"

"I don't think you care that she's flirting. I think you care with whom she's flirting."

"I have no claim to him."

He gave her a pointed look that indicated perhaps he knew that she wanted to have such a claim. But she wasn't at all certain how her family would feel about him. If only she didn't love them so much.

"I didn't realize he was going to be helping out on the nights you are available," he said.

"Neither did I, but I think it worked well and each of the students had more time to read aloud."

He nodded. "Well, I'd best be off. I promised to walk Marianne home again."

She smiled. "Thank you for that. I worry about her less when she's in your care."

As always, when receiving any sort of compliment, he blushed. "I enjoy talking with her. She makes me laugh."

She felt the tiniest of tightenings in her chest. "Does she?"

His blush darkened. "I mustn't keep her waiting. I'll see to things Wednesday when you're not here."

Watching him go, she sensed a shift in the air around her and knew Matthew was now at her side. Swerving her attention over to him, she realized they were alone in the room, that Lottie had disappeared. "Lottie seems to be taken with you."

"She's taken with all men whom she judges to have a few coins in their pockets."

"I have the impression you have more than a few."

"I have enough to see me in good stead." His gaze roamed over her face and she wondered if she wished it was his fingers taking the journey. She certainly wouldn't have minded. "I didn't hear you ask Tittlefitz to escort Marianne home."

"He'd already informed me that it was his intention to do so."

"Your matchmaking may be bearing fruit."

She tilted her nose up in the air as haughtily as possible. "I am feeling somewhat satisfied that my efforts are going well."

"I suppose you'll focus on your own matchmaking now."

Running her tongue over her lips, she took gratification when his gaze dipped to her mouth. "The next ball is Wednesday. After having two gentlemen and three ladies call on me, I'm not dreading it as much as I might have. It could be fun."

"Avoid going for turns about the garden."

"Do you think a gentleman would take advantage?"

"He might."

"We're alone now and you're not."

"But I want to, and because I do, I'm going to bid you good night."

"Where I'm concerned you don't have to be so honorable."

"Lords set high standards for the women they want to marry."

And if she decided she didn't want to marry a lord? She didn't pose the question to him. Just because he was drawn to her, wanted to kiss her, didn't mean he wished to marry her. Perhaps she was in danger of following her romantically inclined heart toward a man who saw her as only a woman to bed, not wed. "As well they should. Still, where's the harm in a kiss?"

Lifting up on her toes, she placed her hand at the back of his head and took his mouth as though it was her right to do so. He responded in kind, cradling her in one arm, bending her over slightly, bettering the angle so the kiss deepened. She had a strong urge to ask him to go to the ball, wait for her in the garden. She could join him there so he could ravish her—but in such a way that when she returned to the ballroom no one would be the wiser.

She couldn't imagine anyone else kissing her like this, with so much passion and yearning, giving so much of himself to the endeavor. His groans mingled with her sighs, creating the perfect music for a waltz. She feared having waltzed with him in her shop, he had spoiled her for waltzing in a ballroom. Would she be able to dance with any other gentleman and not be able to reminisce about how wondrous it had been to dance within his arms?

At her first ball, she'd been comparing other men to him, but now she had so much more to compare. Punting, a picnic, the taste of wine on his tongue. The taste of scotch. The taste of him, dark and rich and so very flavorful. She might even be detecting a hint of toffee. She couldn't stop herself from smiling with that thought.

He drew back, his eyes heated by passion and desire. "What do you find so humorous?"

"I think you ate a toffee earlier."

"You've gotten me addicted to the damn things, and I can't have one without thinking of all the sensual movements of your mouth while you suck on one."

"I enjoy sucking sweets."

"Ah, Christ." His growl echoed around her, his hold on her loosening so quickly she nearly lost her balance. He took two steps back, then two more. "I have to leave now before I convince myself that you know exactly what image your words were going to create in my mind."

Her words had been spoken with all innocence, but his reaction now had her remembering how he'd suckled at her breast and she wondered if she could bring him pleasure in the same manner. "Are there parts of you to suck?"

"God, Fancy." He spun on his heel and headed for the doorway.

"Have I offended you?"

"No, but you have reminded me how innocent you are."

She hurried after him as he descended the stairs. "Did Lottie offer to suck something for you?"

He spun around so fast, she nearly ran into him and sent them both tumbling down the stairs. Narrowing his eyes, he studied her for a full minute before saying, "She did as a matter of fact."

"Will you go to her now?"

His gaze grew soft as he tucked his bent finger beneath her chin and stroked his thumb over her lips. "No."

"She made you laugh."

"She said something funny. I can't even remember what it was now. But I remember every word you've ever spoken to me."

As though he hadn't just captured a corner of her heart, he continued on down the stairs. She hastened to catch up, but his legs were so much longer that she arrived at the foot of the stairs just in time to hear the door *snicking* back into place. After turning the lock, she lowered the light and fairly floated up the stairs. Sometimes he would say the most touching things, almost poetic in their simplicity.

After changing into her nightgown, she took her book from the table beside her bed, walked to the window and pulled the draperies aside, smiling at the sight of Matthew, a shadow surrounded by light in the window across the way. Settling onto the bench, bringing her feet up, and adjusting the pillows behind her back, she opened her book, pretending to give it attention while peering to the side over at him.

As he had the other night, he dragged a chair over, sat, and held an open book at eye level.

With a sigh of happiness, she began to read, feeling as though they weren't separated by a mews but were together in the same room, or at least the same world. It was calming and peaceful, something she'd miss when she no longer lived here.

Chapter 18

$\mathcal{S}$he had just moved beyond the Duke and Duchess of Hedley after greeting them and thanking them for hosting the ball and including her when she spotted Aiden and Finn, along with their wives, waiting for her. Mick and Aslyn were still conversing with the duke and duchess.

"You're here early. I didn't expect to see you until at least half ten," she teased as each brother leaned in and brushed a feathery light kiss across her cheek.

"We wanted to catch you as soon as possible, before the gents started asking you for dances," Aiden said. "We've let it be known no further incentives from the Trewlove brothers are to be had."

"Thank you. I truly appreciate it, although you're far more optimistic about gents asking me to dance than I am." Still, she was relatively certain Lord Beresford and Mr. Whitley would sign her dance card.

"I have a reason to be optimistic. Regarding the offer I made the gents at the last ball . . . You should know three of them told me not to tear up their vowels. Seemed they enjoyed dancing with you."

A spark of joy swept through her. "Truly?"

"I told you that once they spent time with you—"

"But that wasn't the way to make it come about."

"I'll concede your point." Reaching into his jacket pocket, he pulled out a folded scrap of parchment. "The names, in case you wanted to look at them more favorably."

She clutched it in her hand, unable to stop her broad smile. "Oh, Aiden, I do believe you've made my night."

"Don't give him too much credit," Finn said with a grin. "It'll go to his head. I'll let you know if anyone takes me up on my offer so you can look at them unfavorably."

"No one has taken you up on the offer regarding horses and breeding?"

"Not so far."

"Looks like some good news is being shared here," Mick said as he and Aslyn joined the group.

"It seems not all the gents are collecting on the offers made last week," she told him. "Has anyone come to you for advice?"

"A couple of gents did." He shrugged. "But they are already married. I should have put a few stipulations on who I was willing to assist."

"Are we having a family gathering?" Gillie asked as she and Thornley entered their circle.

Fancy explained the news her brothers had shared.

"That's jolly good to hear, although I had confidence in you and knew you wouldn't need the bribes," Gillie said.

"I appreciate your faith."

"Hand over your card, let us claim our dances," Mick said.

"No." She gave them a gentle smile to lessen the harshness of her decision. "I'm not dancing with anyone tonight to whom I'm related. I'll make exceptions for your friends or your families"— she looked at each of her siblings' spouses—"but I'm not dancing with you four gents. I'm quite certain I'm going to need those dances for other gentlemen."

Gillie gave her a hug. "I like your confidence."

Taking a deep breath, she slowly released it. "Let's see how long I can maintain it."

To her surprise, it wasn't at all difficult to maintain her confidence. Once her family wandered off, gentlemen began to approach her and within five minutes she had half a dozen dances claimed. She'd even been introduced to two lords who had not attended Gillie's ball.

The Marquess of Wilbourne was the first to take her on a turn about the dance floor. She was grateful for the waltz because it allowed them to speak more intimately. She told him about her bookshop and her efforts to teach adults to read. "An investment in the future." She didn't ask for a donation. Instead she asked his opinion on how she might expand her programs, where he thought she might have success teaching in other areas of London.

She gave her undivided attention to each lord who asked her for a dance. One gentleman was silver-haired and slightly bent over, a walking stick propping him up. Rather than sweep her over the floor, he barely moved her from the spot where they'd begun, but when the tune drifted into silence, he patted her hand. "I'd heard you were a delight, Miss Trewlove. Thank you for indulging an old relic."

She smiled warmly. "It was my pleasure, Your Grace."

"Ah, if I were but forty years younger."

As he shuffled her off the dance floor, she didn't rush him. Her next partner commented on her graciousness in dancing with the elderly duke. "I didn't do it for the praise. I simply find that it's not that difficult to be kind."

She had been dancing for nearly two hours when she finally found herself with an unclaimed dance and actually welcomed a moment to sit for a bit and rest her feet, but on her way to the wallflower corner, the flaxen-haired trio stopped her.

"My goodness, Miss Trewlove, but you're popular tonight," Lady Penelope said. "I've been dying to have a word ever since we arrived, but you've been on the floor the entire time."

"I think I'm still a bit of a curiosity."

"Are you implying they're all cats?"

She laughed. "No. I'm just not quite sure what to make of their interest."

"Have any gents called on you?" Lady Victoria asked.

"Two. Lord Beresford and Mr. Whitley."

Each of the ladies grimaced.

"Wet-mouthed Whitley," Lady Alexandria said, and then she brightened. "Oh, that's how I can remember his name."

"You already remember his name," Lady Victoria pointed out.

"Yes, but if I should ever forget it . . ."

Lady Penelope rolled her eyes. "Has he ever kissed your hand, Miss Trewlove?"

Fancy nodded. "Yes."

"He's very nice but the . . . spittle not so much. I wouldn't settle on him, if I were you."

"I don't know that we'd suit. He doesn't read."

"He's in fine form, though. Very good at polo."

She was vaguely aware of the music drifting into silence again and then spotted Lord Beresford striding toward her. "It's been a pleasure, ladies."

"Do say hello to Dickens for me," Lady Penelope said.

"I will."

Lord Beresford arrived, offering her his arm with a flourish. "Ladies. Miss Trewlove, I believe this is my dance."

"It is indeed sir."

As they circled the floor, she found herself thinking that no one danced as wonderfully well as Matthew did.

IT WAS LATE when they finally arrived back at Mick's hotel, and she was safely ensconced inside her shop. After lowering the flame in the gas sconce, she headed for the stairs where a pale glow filtered down from above. Halfway up, at a tiny landing, the steps made an abrupt right turn and the light became a bit brighter. Mr. Tittlefitz must have left it on so she wouldn't be stumbling about in the dark.

At the top of the stairs, she could see it wasn't a light in the hallway, but rather one coming from the reading parlor. The secretary must have simply forgotten to turn it off.

Walking into the room, she came to a stop at the sight of Matthew sitting in a chair by the fireplace, so lost in a book he hadn't heard her arrive. She was taken aback by the joy that struck her, as though she'd traveled the world, alone and forgotten, to suddenly arrive at the place where she belonged. She imagined the pleasure to be found in looking up from her own book to see him so near. He still wore his jacket, neck cloth, and waistcoat. She had an urge to divest him of the cumbersome clothing, and yet he was relaxed, as though accustomed to wearing them late into the evening.

"I'm surprised to find you here," she said softly.

Slowly, as though not at all startled by her appearance, he lifted his gaze while closing the book and setting it aside. He came to his feet, and as always, she was surprised by how elegantly he moved, gracefully, as though accustomed to being watched and determined to project a confident mien. "I decided to make use of your library while waiting for you. How was your evening?"

She crossed over to the settee near his chair and lowered herself to it, grateful when he again took his seat, studying her with those incredibly green eyes. Removing her dance card from her wrist, she extended it toward him and watched as he scrutinized it.

Dickens jumped onto the settee and curled up on the other end. After removing her gloves, she buried the fingers of one hand in his fur and waited for Matthew's response.

Finally, he looked up, met and held her gaze. "Nearly every dance claimed."

She couldn't stop herself from smiling. "And my brothers weren't making any offers."

He leaned back and brought one booted foot up, resting it on his knee. Such a relaxed, masculine pose, as though they were settling in for the evening. "Were you impressed by anyone?"

"The Marquess of Wilbourne was rather charming. Lord Beresford, who called on me last week—"

"Beresford called on you?"

"Yes, he was one of two gentlemen who did. Do you know him?"

"I've read something about him in the gossip rags, I think."

That statement was a bit of a surprise. "You don't strike me as someone who would read the gossip news."

"I'll read anything. It was no doubt lying about at my sister's and I saw it there."

"Well, I don't give much credence to gossip, and he seems rather nice. Three of the young debutantes have welcomed me. I visited with them for a bit. The matriarchs are keeping their distance."

"Matriarchs are always disapproving and difficult to win over."

"My mum isn't. She was strict when I was growing up, but always managed to make me feel that I could achieve anything I wanted. Sometimes I think it might be easier to simply invite them all here so they can see who I really am. If I hosted an affair, would you come?"

He shifted in his chair as though suddenly uncomfortable. "I don't know."

She didn't blame him for his hesitation. If one wasn't groomed to move about among the aristocracy, it could make for an uncomfortable situation when every word, action, and expression was judged. Glancing over at Dickens because it was easier to look at him than Matthew, she confessed, "You were on my mind often tonight, particularly when I waltzed."

She heard his foot hit the floor, a moan of the chair. Then he was kneeling before her, taking her free hand in both of his. Why could she get no lord to look at her as he did, like the moon and stars revolved around her, that she existed for his pleasure and his alone?

"I thought about you. Nearly ran mad wondering with whom you were waltzing."

"Dukes, marquesses, earls, and viscounts. We conversed. I asked them questions, tried to get to know them better, worked to determine if they would ever make me laugh. My mum has advised me to find someone who makes me laugh."

"She's a wise woman, your mum."

"I can't tell if any of these gents are taken with me. Oh, they say the right things, do the right things, but I can't stop thinking about your favorite Aesop's fable, and I find myself wary of their compliments."

"You shouldn't be." He angled his head slightly and brushed his lips over hers. "They no doubt adore you as much as I do."

"Do you?"

"I very much would like to kiss you, Miss Trewlove," he whispered, his warm breath fanning over her cheek.

"I would very much like you to, but perhaps I should close Dickens off in my bedchamber."

"No need. He'll not interfere. The furry fellow and I are friends now. I fed him a tin of sardines."

Her laugh was cut off as his mouth claimed hers, and nothing else tonight had felt so right, so perfect. She didn't hesitate to part her lips, to give him full access to the confines within. This was what she wanted for the remainder of her life: the passion, the fire, the desire.

But finding it with him would be a blow to her family, and he'd certainly given no indication he wanted anything permanent with her. Yet where was the harm in enjoying pleasure, within limits? He'd already proven he wouldn't take more than she was willing to give. And his mouth moving so determinedly over hers did much to calm the doubts that plagued her in spite of what had been a successful evening. She sighed with wonder, with joy, that he could make her feel so treasured.

His arm snaked around her waist, and he gently pulled her off the settee and onto his lap. Supporting her back, he bent her over slightly, changing the angle of the kiss, taking it deeper. Of their own accord, her hands went to his head, her fingers becoming entangled in the thick strands of his hair. She desperately wanted him to be as grateful to have her in his arms as she was to be within his.

But his experience was so beyond hers. He stroked his hand

down her back and cupped her bottom with abandon, without hesitation, with a surety that announced more clearly than any words that he was familiar with the female anatomy, that he knew how to touch, how to press, how to stroke in ways that could drive a woman mad—in the best possible way.

While she was a novice, learning her way around a man's physique. But what a wonderful specimen he was. Muscled and toned, firm beneath her touch as her hands journeyed over his shoulders, his back. While pleasure was threatening to distract her, she was determined to come to know him a little more, to give to him as much as he was giving to her.

As she trailed the fingers of one hand along his bristly jaw, he groaned low and carried his mouth on a journey to her ear where he nibbled on her lobe before sweeping his tongue over the sensitive shell. How did one ever learn all the different areas where an intimate stroke would weaken knees? She felt as though her entire body was in danger of melting.

Suddenly she realized he was no longer supporting her, that she was spread out on the thick Aubusson rug, and he was nestled against her side, raised up on an elbow. Lifting his mouth from hers, he held her gaze as he trailed his finger along her décolletage, where flesh met silk. Back and forth, back and forth. Then he stopped, his fingers lingering over the swell that had been denied his attention after the first ball.

"Yes?" His voice was a tortured rasp, that of a captured man seeking to be free.

"Yes."

With a low growl, he set himself to the task of revealing what he wanted to claim. When silk, lace, and more were dragged down and her breast was free of all restraints, he lowered his head and took her breast into his mouth. Not just the nipple, but as much as he could, his tongue gliding over and around. Then he was sucking as though she were a hard confection to be worked over with patience and determination, enjoyed and appreciated.

She dug her fingers into his scalp, holding him in place, even as her hips tilted up, her feminine core pressing up against him as her body sought surcease. If Dickens interfered now, she would kill him.

She became aware of Matthew gathering up her skirts and petticoats with one large hand, pushing them up until they were a mound at her waist. Cupping her intimately, he released her breast, peppering kisses around and over it before capturing her gaze, his own smoldering. Slowly, deliberately, he inserted a finger through the part in her undergarments and slid it along her feminine core. She gasped at the wondrous sensation, could feel herself throbbing for him.

"Yes?" he asked.

She gave a jerky nod. "Yes."

He stroked her once, twice, three times, gave a dark, wicked chuckle when she released a tiny squeal. The entire time, he didn't take his eyes from hers, knew he was driving her to distraction, relished doing so. She wondered if on the morrow, people would look at her and be able to determine she'd been touched so intimately. It seemed sensations so profound, so intoxicating should leave their mark for all the world to see.

Smoothly, swiftly, he practically climbed down her body until his head was at the juncture of her thighs. With both hands, he parted the opening in her drawers, widening the slit until she could feel the breeze of his breath. Filled with promise, his gaze held hers for all of a heartbeat before he disappeared behind the gathered mound of her skirts.

His tongue stroked what his fingers had only moments before, and she cried out from the pure ecstasy of it. "Oh God!"

She wanted to tell him to stop, feared she'd die if he did. He suckled and soothed, tormented her with light caresses, then delivered stronger ones. She'd never known it was possible to feel so many different things at once. She was flying, yet grounded, on the verge of laughing, close to tears. She was straining to reach the top of a mountain—

And then she was soaring through the heavens, among the stars, but like her kite, still tethered, tethered to him. She was vaguely aware of him moving up, even as he straightened her skirts, attempted to return to her a bit of modesty.

He wore a self-satisfied smile that she suspected very much matched her own. "You breathed fire down there."

Chuckling low, he threaded his fingers through her still bound hair. "My waiting for you was done with the best of intentions, but I can see now that I am easily led astray when you are near. Yet I am loath to leave. But I know if I stay, come morning, you'll not be a virgin."

How she wanted him to stay, how she wanted to know him fully. But she knew the challenges that awaited ruined women. Her siblings had all been brought to her mum because of errors in judgment.

She brushed the tips of her fingers along his cheek. "I am tempted. But too high a price is paid for momentary pleasures." For her the payment would be the dashing of all dreams—hers and her family's. "I can't accept what you're offering."

"As well you shouldn't. The lords of London are fools if they are giving you any reason at all to doubt the sincerity of their compliments."

"Perhaps I'm the fool for seeking to marry one."

"You are probably the least foolish woman I've ever met." After kissing her breast once more, he tucked it back beneath cloth. Rolling off her, he stood, reached down, and brought her to her feet. "I should be off now."

Placing his finger beneath her chin, he tilted up her face and bussed his lips over hers. Something that should have been innocent, and yet she felt the touch clear down to her toes. It was as though her entire body was now attuned to his, that with his actions he had created a stronger connection between them.

Reaching over, he patted Dickens on the head. "Good kitty."

"I'll reward him with another tin of sardines."

Matthew didn't object when she slipped her hand into his and walked down the stairs with him. "I'll go out the back. Less chance of anyone seeing me."

At this time of night, few people would still be up, but she appreciated that he was taking such care to see her not ruined. When they reached the storage room, he unbolted the door, opened it, and stepped out. The thick heavy fog fairly enveloped him. He glanced back. "Sleep well."

She doubted she'd sleep at all, almost asked him to stay. He quickly became lost as he disappeared into the gray.

Shutting the door, she pressed her ear against it, striving to hear his footsteps, but they were muffled, distant. Before long, she heard no sound at all. Forever changed, she would always hold the memory of him doing deliciously wicked things to her. Why had he? Why had she let him?

Yet, always it seemed, there had been some pull between them, something deep within each of them that called to the other. She'd felt it the moment he walked into her shop—

She heard a scrape, a clatter. A muted footstep, followed by another. Her entire body felt as though it were smiling. He'd returned. Swinging open the door, she froze at the sight of the man standing there.

Not Matthew Sommersby.

Thick, chapped lips spread to reveal blackened teeth. "'Ello, daughter."

Chapter 19

Fancy stared at the rumpled man with his crumpled top hat pulled low, his greasy hair hanging in matted ropy strands down to his shoulders, his scraggly beard possibly serving as a home to lice or fleas. The fingers of his gloves were naught but frayed remnants, leaving his actual fingers—dirty and grimy—exposed. His tattered, worn clothing hung off his skeletal-like frame.

Swiftly, she moved to slam the door closed, but he stuck his booted foot over the threshold, stopping her from reaching her goal. He gave a hard shove on the door that caused her to loosen her hold and stagger back. Squaring her shoulders, she straightened and glared at him. "You're not my father. My father's dead."

"Is that what your mum told you, gel? Bless her. She never did seem to favor me."

Then how in God's name could he possibly be her father? It made her skin crawl to think of this man touching her mum. Her mother wouldn't have borne it. She wouldn't have allowed him anywhere near her. "You're lying. My mother never would have let you touch her."

"Ye'd be surprised wot a woman will do to keep a roof over 'er 'ead and that of 'er brood."

She was going to be ill, bring up her dinner all over his scuffed boots. "I would appreciate it if you'd take your leave now."

"Caw, gel, not so fast. I ain't got wot I come fer yet. Thought I'd 'ave to jimmy the lock, I did, but ye so kindly opened the door fer me. Imagine ye thought I was that bloke what just left. How would yer mum feel knowin' ye was entertainin' blokes late at night?"

She would be ashamed and devastated. Disappointed. Her entire family would be disappointed. "Sir—"

"Dibble is the name. She should 'ave told you that, at least."

Her father's name was Sutherland. David Sutherland. He'd been a soldier. A hero. He wasn't this vile, dirty creature standing before her. "You need to leave."

"Yer mum's been boastin', telling all and sundry, anyone what'll listen, about yer little shop 'ere. That 'n' yer introduction to the nobs." He smirked as his sneering gaze traveled the length of her, what little bit of her there was. Oh, how she wanted to smack that odious expression right off his face. "Says 'er little gel is gonna marry a lord. Wot she's been sayin' got back to me, it did. And I started thinkin' yer my little gel, too. Since ye 'ave such a posh life, I reckon ye can spare a bit of blunt fer yer father. Fifty quid tonight should do it. Ye wouldn't want me showin' up at one of your posh balls, would ye? Introducing meself around?"

At least he seemed to recognize that he was not someone with whom anyone would take pride in being associated. But surely it was all a bluff. How would he even know where she was going to be? And no servant in his right mind would allow someone so grubby to be allowed into the home of an aristocrat. "You're mad if you think I'll give you so much as a ha'penny."

"Ah, gel, don't be like 'at." His hand came up fast, before she could react, tightening around her jaw, lifting her head, threatening her ability to breathe because his foul stench was causing her to gag to the point of retching. "Don't force me to teach ye manners like I did yer mum. Ain't pleasant schoolin—"

"Get your bloody hands off her."

The growled words were feral, frightening, even to her. Dibble reacted instantly, snapping his head back in surprise, his eyes going wide, his grip loosening as he lurched around—

Matthew pounded a tightly balled fist into Dibble's face that caused blood to spurt from his nose as he staggered back and landed hard on the floor. Matthew was nearly a blur as he straddled the prone man, grabbed a handful of his shirt, lifted him slightly, and hit him again. Dibble grunted. Another blow and he went limp.

Breathing harshly, straightening, Matthew came to her and looked her over, concern reflected in his eyes. With a grimace, he gently touched her jaw. It was tender, and she suspected it was already showing signs of bruising. "Did he harm you anywhere else?"

"No." A lie. How did she explain the pain he'd caused her heart? "He claims to be my father."

"I thought your father died at war."

She nodded jerkily, shook her head. "My mother told me she loved my father, but how could she love that?"

"He could have been lying. Do you have any rope so I can bind him before going to fetch a constable?"

"No, but I have my kite string."

"I can make do with that. Will you fetch it for me?"

She ran up to her lodgings, got a pair of scissors, and cut the reel of string from her kite, then hurried back downstairs to where Matthew waited. When she arrived, he rolled the man named Dibble over onto his belly and held out his hand for the string. "I can tie him."

"Make it tight."

He brought Dibble's wrists together. She knelt and began wrapping the kite string around, over and under, his wrists. "He said his name is Dibble."

"You've never seen him before?"

"No."

"Fancy, he was probably lying. Part of a game he plays to dupe someone into giving him what he was seeking to obtain."

She desperately wanted that to be true, but he'd been so confident. "What do you think will happen to him?"

"The constables will lock him up in a cell. In a few days he'll go to trial for attempted robbery and accosting you."

She drew some comfort from his words, wanting Dibble locked up for being a nasty bit of rubbish if nothing else.

"There, that's good. Cut the string, knot up the ends."

As she tried to position the scissors, she realized her hands were shaking too badly. Matthew closed his hand over hers. "It's all right." Taking the scissors from her, he finished off the task. Then moved down to Dibble's feet. "I don't want him getting up and running off while I'm gone."

"I have a skillet. I could conk him on the head if he wakes."

"That's my girl."

When Dibble was tightly bound, Matthew cradled her cheek. "I won't be long. Close the door, bolt it in case he has friends. Don't open it until I call for you."

"You will be careful."

He gave her a cocky grin. "I will be back, I promise." Reaching into his pocket, he pulled out his handkerchief and stuffed it into Dibble's mouth. "For good measure, in case he wakes up. You don't need to hear his horrid words."

Then he was gone, and she was left alone with this vile creature. After bolting the door, she moved nearer to him, crouched, and studied his face, searching for any familiar characteristics, looking for any of herself in him.

It was impossible to know what his nose might have once looked like because it appeared to have been broken or smashed several times. She wondered if he was a boxer by trade. She couldn't imagine that he was a very successful one. She recalled his eyes being dark, but she was rather certain she'd gotten her eyes from her mum. Black hair, but so was her mum's.

His cheeks were rounded. Hers high and sharp. He had a mole on his jaw near his ear. She had no moles.

His eyes popped open, and she fell on her bottom in surprise. He began struggling with the bindings and groaning.

"You won't free yourself. You might as well save your energy."

To her astonishment, he went still and glared at her. He said something but she couldn't make out the words through the cloth. She scooted back until she felt the wall behind her. "I have no interest in hearing your lies."

Then she waited for what seemed like an eternity for Matthew to return. When she heard him calling for her on the other side of the door, she'd never known such joy. Nor had she ever seen him so authoritative as he ordered the constables about. They were deferential toward him, seeming to want to ensure they worked to his satisfaction. The first night she'd had the impression he was accustomed to being in command. But now here was clearer evidence that he was a man not only willing to take charge, but comfortable doing so.

Dibble protested the entire time as the constables replaced her meager bindings with iron manacles and chains around his wrists and ankles. None too gently, they hauled him out. When they were gone, Matthew looked back at her. "You're trembling."

"I'm just cold."

He closed the door, bolted it, strode over to her, and wrapped his arms securely around her. "It's all right, sweetheart. It's all right. You're all right. Let's get you up to your rooms."

"I have his chin."

Matthew went still for a heartbeat before tucking his finger beneath said chin and tilting her face back so he could gaze in her eyes. "Your chin is far more lovely, far cuter than his."

"Why would he come here and say what he did? Why would he claim to be my father if he's not?"

"Perhaps he's a swindler. What did he want?"

"Money. Money not to show up at a ball and tell people he sired me."

"Your family has been making a name for itself with their success and their marriages into the nobility. From time to time they make the gossip sheets. A couple of years back there was that article in the *Times* about your brother's hotel. A family of by-blows. The man was playing the odds that you might not know who your father was."

"I think he might have been telling the truth."

"Will you tell your mother about him, ask her?"

She nodded. "I'd planned to see her in the morning, to tell her about the ball. Mick's carriage will be readied for me."

"Shall I go with you?"

His kindness was her undoing as tears threatened. "No, it'll be best if I see her on my own. But I appreciate the offer."

With a nod, he dipped down and lifted her into his arms.

"What are you doing?"

"I'm going to carry you upstairs."

"I can walk."

"I know, but if I'm holding you, I can start warming you."

She settled her head into the curve of his shoulder as he began striding toward the stairs. "You're stronger than I thought."

"It doesn't take much strength when I'm carrying a cloud."

"I'm heavier than that."

"Not by much."

When they reached her rooms, he carried on through to her bedchamber—which was easy enough to determine as it was the only other room—and set her gently on the bed. With tenderness, he removed her slippers. "Will you trust me to loosen your lacings?"

She nodded. He came around behind her, and she was very much aware of his fingers working along her spine, not stopping with the gown but loosening the lacings on her corset as well. When he was done, he urged her to lay down and draped a blanket over her. He stretched out beside her, wrapped his arms around her, pressing her face to his chest, and began rubbing her back through the blanket and her clothing.

"I'll have you warmed in a jiff."

Her teeth were clattering from a cold deep within her that was threatening to turn her blood into ice. "I can't seem to stop trembling."

His lovely ministrations ceased briefly as he unbuttoned his waistcoat and shirt. "Slip your hands in here."

"I can't do that to you. My fingers are like ice."

"I can bear the momentary discomfort. What I can't bear is your suffering." Taking one of her hands, he guided it between the parted cloth, settling her fingers against his smooth, heated skin. She heard his sharp intake of breath, felt him stiffen.

"I'm sorry."

When she would have removed her hand, he held it in place. "It's all right. Now the other."

Doing as he bade, she thought the hottest of fires would not have thawed her so completely, nor would they have felt so welcoming.

"Better?" he asked quietly, and she did little more than nod. "Good."

He returned to rubbing her back, and her body grew warm, lethargic. She sank against him but her mind raced like it was a runaway mare desperate to escape the horrors that had befallen it. "If he sired me"—horrific images bombarded her—"I can't imagine that my mother loved him, that she would have welcomed him into her bed. He was so vile, so nasty."

"Perhaps he was a very different fellow when he was younger."

"Can one change that drastically in twenty years? He said she needed to keep a roof over her head. Why did she turn to him for help? What did he require of her?"

"Sweetheart, don't torment yourself with questions. Everything he said could have been a lie."

"Yet it contained a spark of truth." Her fingers had lost their chilling edge, so she slid her hands around his sides to his back, holding him close. "I can't bear the thought of what she might have endured at his hand."

"They can't bring charges against him for what he did so long ago, but I'll see to it that the magistrate knows and that his past actions be taken into account when sentenced."

"I supposed I'll have to testify—"

"I'll do it. No reason for you to even go to the trial. My word will suffice."

"But I'm the one he attacked."

"I saw it happen and can serve as a witness. You've lamented how the law treats women unfairly. The courts do the same. I don't condone the reality of it, but a man's testimony will hold more sway than a woman's. Trust me, sweetheart, the blighter will never bother you again. I'll ensure it, one way or another."

He sounded so confident, so in command, so certain he could bring about the outcome she desired. She wouldn't mind not seeing Dibble again, and yet she had a responsibility to ensure he never bothered her again. But she wasn't in the mood to argue about it at the moment. She would do what needed to be done when the time arrived. "How did you know to come?"

"As you're aware, I tend to look across at your window before retiring. I noted the back door ajar, pale light spilling out into the mews. I knew you'd closed it after I left. I wanted to reassure myself nothing was amiss."

"I was surprised by how quickly and efficiently you dispatched him."

"I've done a bit of boxing for sport, among friends. Some are more competitive than others."

She would enjoy watching him box, but then she took delight in watching him breathe. "I'm warmer now, if you want to leave."

"I'd rather stay."

The relief overwhelmed her, and she snuggled more closely against him. She'd always known dangers existed in the world, but until tonight none had ever touched her.

Chapter 20

To Fancy's surprise, within Matthew's arms, she'd slept. He'd stayed until dawn and then slipped out the back. No one seemed to be about, so her reputation was safe.

But as she traveled in the coach, her mind filled with the images of the horrid man who'd come to her door. His black teeth, his black, black eyes. While she knew she could have gone to Mick for help, for reassurance, for some unfathomable reason, she'd wanted Matthew. Not only because he required no explanation regarding what had happened but the comfort that he'd provided had seemed so much more intimate than what her brother would have given. Oh, certainly Mick would have held her and murmured words of reassurances, would have meant all he said and did, but she didn't know if he could have gently begun piecing back together her heart.

She should have been stronger, shouldn't have allowed it to shatter so easily by what might be false words. But what was broken, when repaired, became stronger.

At least that was the mantra running through her mind as she stepped out of the carriage, with the assistance of the footman. When Fancy stepped inside, her mum sang from the kitchen, "I've just put the kettle on."

This woman she loved so very much wandered into the living room and staggered to a stop. "Oh, my dear girl, whatever has happened?"

Fancy felt the tears forming and was powerless to hold them back as her mum's arms came firmly around her. "Mum, please tell me it's not true. Please."

Her mum went very, very still, so still Fancy wasn't even certain she continued to breathe. Or perhaps she simply couldn't because her daughter was holding her so tightly.

"What are you talking about, love?"

The slight tremble in her mum's voice, the hesitation as though she already knew the answer and hadn't wanted to ask the question caused Fancy's chest to tighten to such an extent, she thought it might cave in on itself. "A man came to see me last night. His name is Dibble."

Her mum's body jerked as though she'd been delivered a physical punch by a giant. Leaning back, Mum studied her face. "What did he do to you?"

"Nothing." Not wanting her mum to worry, she couldn't confess how for a few moments he'd terrified her, and she'd been afraid he would hurt her—until Matthew put a stop to that. "He wanted money, claimed to be my father." Based on her mother's reaction, she feared she had the answer she'd been seeking, but still she asked the question anyway. "He wasn't lying, was he?"

Her own eyes damp, her mum cradled her face with one hand. "I'm so sorry, pet."

"Did you love him?" She was well aware one didn't always have control over one's heart and the path it wanted to travel.

"Ah, no, pet. How could you think I'd love such a vile excuse for a human being? But from the moment I realized I was increasing, I wanted you."

She shook her head. "But I don't understand why you ever let him touch you."

Her mum stepped back. Her eyes grew damper before she finally shuffled to her chair and dropped into it as though a boulder had suddenly landed on her. "Sit down, pet."

Fancy didn't want to. Her body seemed to sense that at any moment she would want to flee and needed to be in position to run as quickly as she could. Still, she couldn't deny her mum's simple request, so she eased down onto the edge of the chair across from her, but couldn't relax as every muscle remained tense, awaiting a blow.

"He was the landlord, you see. While people paid when they left their babes with me to raise, it wasn't enough to last years. Not able to leave my five wee ones alone, my options were limited for working. I didn't read well and that put me at a disadvantage. Which is one of the reasons I'm so proud of you for your teaching."

She'd known her mum struggled with reading, had no memory of ever seeing her read, of ever having her read to her.

"So I made matchboxes and did piecework. Your brothers and sister, as they got older, they began working. But still coins were often scarce, and when I didn't have the money for the rent, well, he had other ways I could pay him."

Her stomach roiling, Fancy slammed her eyes closed. "He hurt you."

"He never raised a hand to me. Because I didn't love him, it wasn't pleasant having him touch me, but I couldn't have my children put out on the street, now could I? Don't cry, love."

Her children. Children who had once belonged to others, to people who had brought them to her to care for. And she'd raised them as her own. Opening her eyes, she swiped at the tears on her cheeks. "It was horrible, what he did. He needs to be punished."

"Your brothers saw to that. You growing inside me couldn't stay a secret for long, so I told them the truth. They were fourteen, big strapping lads. They took their fists to him. He never bothered me after that. Didn't even ask for rent money anymore. Course, Mick eventually bought the properties around here."

"Did Gillie know about my . . . about Dibble, as well?" She couldn't attribute the word *father* to him.

Her mum nodded.

"Why didn't you tell me the truth?"

"Because I never wanted you to be ashamed of where you come

from. I never wanted you to doubt that you were a welcomed addition to my life. I loved you from the moment I realized you were going to be."

Burying her face in her hands, she sobbed for all her mother had endured, for being forced to let that maggot touch her. And she wept for herself, because part of that man was inside her. Not a war hero for a father, not a grand love.

Her mother's arms came around her. "I'm so so sorry, love. After the lads saw to him, I thought he would stay away forever. No reason for you to know my shame."

Fancy jerked her head up. "Your shame?"

"For laying with a bloke I hadn't wed."

"Ah, Mum, the shame is his, not yours." Yet even as she said the words, she realized she felt a sense of shame as well. It hadn't been easy growing up born out of wedlock, but at least she'd believed she was the product of something beautiful. To know ugliness had been responsible for creating her made her want to weep all over again.

"We can debate that later. Once your brothers find out about his visit—"

"I don't want to tell them." She was still struggling with the fact that her siblings had all known such a horrible secret about her and kept it to themselves. To protect her, but at what point was there too much protection?

"He took money from you."

"No, he didn't. A gentleman who lives in the area happened by and put a stop to things, had him arrested."

"Thank the Lord for that. Still they need to know."

"I'm not ready for them to learn that I know the truth about my . . . sire." Her brothers had never referred to the men responsible for their existence as their father, but always as only their sire. She was beginning to understand why they'd chosen a more impersonal term. She didn't want to acknowledge any sort of intimate relationship with Dibble—and yet it was there all the same.

Mum was kneeling on the floor, her hands folded over Fancy's knee. "I'm ever so sorry, pet."

"You don't have to apologize, Mum. You did what you did to keep the others safe. I understand that."

Reaching up, she touched Fancy's cheek. "You're still my precious girl."

But now she felt sullied by the truth.

FROM THE MOMENT Matthew had left Fancy, he'd wanted to return to her, but suspected she needed some time alone with her thoughts and worries. So he waited until late morning.

When he walked into the shop, Marianne greeted him, but her smile was a little less bright.

"Hello, Mr. Sommersby."

"Miss Marianne. Is Miss Trewlove about?"

"She's tidying up the reading parlor."

"I'll go up, then. I need to have a word with her."

"Of course, sir."

He bounded up the stairs and entered the reading parlor. She was sitting on the floor, near the fireplace, several books stacked beside her as she wiped a cloth over the now empty shelf. He strode over to her and crouched down. "Fancy—"

"The thing about having a bookshop that one doesn't consider when deciding to have a bookshop is that there are so many shelves and so many books that need to be constantly dusted. After you've gone through them all, it's time to start over." She picked up a book, gently wiped the cover, and returned it to the shelf.

His heart ached for her. "You spoke with your mother. I'm going to assume she confirmed the truth of his words."

Without looking at him, she nodded and ran the cloth over another book. "He was the landlord, and she didn't have the coins for the rent."

He slammed his eyes closed. "Christ." Opening his eyes, he placed a hand on her shoulder.

She curled it away from him. "I bathed when I got home, and yet I still feel so dirty."

"Perhaps it's only the dust from the books."

She looked at him then and the sadness in her eyes would have brought him to his knees if he were still standing. "Oh, Matthew, the filth runs much deeper than that."

"You are not that man. He is no part of you."

"Did you ever look at your parents and think, 'they are no part of me?'"

In his world, lineage was so deuced important. Of course he'd never done that. He'd grown up aware that the very fact they *were* part of him was what made him special, made him *what* he was, if not who he was. "I concede your point."

"Normally, I would take great joy in being correct."

"But, Fancy, the people who are responsible for your existence do not necessarily determine the type of person you become. My father was a harsh man. Not once did I ever hear him laugh. The people who reported to him were terrified of him. They knew he could destroy their lives with a word. He gave me my eyes; he gave me my hair. But he did not give me my soul. I work with many of the same people he did, but I listen to their ideas and discuss ways to improve things. He was dictatorial, thought no one knew more than him. For him, all that mattered was his opinion. I recognize that I don't know everything, that it's worth listening to others' suggestions. In other words, I'm far more reasonable than he was." He touched his fingers to his chest. "That is me. I am different from him. You are different from your father. You are Fancy Trewlove, and there are aspects to you that have nothing at all to do with him."

"I doubt any among the aristocracy would agree. They care so damned much about lineage, about blood, about heritage. I had the disadvantage of being born out of wedlock but still had pride in my mum and the man she told me was my father. I felt worthy because of what I'd believed they'd shared. I'd always thought my father was the hero and it turns out he's the villain."

He hated that she was filled with such doubts. "But you're the heroine, the one who does such good for others."

"While I appreciate your sentiment, knowing the truth of who sired me, how could I in any way be an appropriate wife for a lord?"

"If they find the circumstances of your birth objectionable—something over which you had no control—they can go to the devil." His words caused her to smile slightly, but it was enough to cheer him. He wanted to tell her that he was an earl and her beginnings made him only admire her all the more. But now was not the time for her to learn that he hadn't been completely honest with her either. Not telling her he was the Rosemont of the damned letter hadn't seemed a bad thing when he'd first met her. But now that he'd come to know her, it was difficult to find the proper time to spring the news on her. She would look upon him differently, just as he now viewed her through different eyes and realized how incredibly remarkable she was not to be anything like the maggot who sired her. "In all honesty, Fancy, you need never tell anyone."

"Then it's not honest, is it? There's a deceptive quality to it. And if he's not convicted—"

"He will be. I spoke this morning with the barrister who will be prosecuting the case. With my testimony"—along with the weight and influence of my rank—"he has little doubt Dibble will be found guilty."

She studied him for a full minute. "While that's a relief, I still think I should also be a witness. I don't want Dibble to think I'm afraid of him. I want to face him, take satisfaction in bringing about his comeuppance."

"As much as I admire you for that, why put yourself through it when there's no reason?"

"I hate what he did to my mum. He took advantage of her, and his position gave him the power to do so. I'd like to see him gelded."

Although he hadn't expected her to be so vindictive, he didn't blame her for the sentiment. "I doubt they'll go that far, but he will be punished. Prison is not an easy existence."

"I know. My brother Finn spent time in prison. He never spoke about it, but it changed him, made him more somber." She picked up a book, dusted it, and set it on the shelf. "Do you view me differently now that you know the truth of how I came to be?"

"Yes."

When she jerked her gaze around to meet his, he cradled her cheek, grateful that this time she didn't withdraw from his touch. "I now know you to be stronger than any other woman of my acquaintance. Last night you were accosted, physically and emotionally, and you did not cower in the face of the truth. You are truly remarkable, and any lord would be fortunate to have you as his wife."

Any lord, including him.

Chapter 21

Later that afternoon, after Marianne had left for the day, Fancy stood at the counter, going through the post that had been delivered when a cream-colored envelope caught her eye. Her name was inscribed in elegant script on the vellum. Her fingers were trembling slightly as she turned the missive over, broke the seal, and unfolded it. The words flew at her, a jumble that hardly made sense.

Ball.

Fairhaven Hall.

Pleasure of your company.

She stared at the date. At the end of the month. In the evening. Of course, in the evening. Eight. The Marquess and Marchioness of Fairhaven requested her presence.

She could hardly fathom it. She wasn't related to them at all. But here they were wanting the *pleasure of her company.*

She remembered a time when she would have been overjoyed. Now all she could think was that she didn't belong, wasn't worthy of such an elaborately designed invitation. She shoved it back into the stack, carried the pile into her office, and crammed it all into a drawer, as though doing so would extinguish its existence.

Returning to the counter, she watched the clock tick off the minutes before she would lock her doors, determined to keep the shop opened until the proper time, even though she found it to be a chore. She hated Dibble for taking away her joy of work-ing, grateful he'd not moved beyond the storeroom, so she had no memories of him invading this section of her shop.

In spite of Matthew's earlier visit and his kind words, she was unable to shake off the gloom that had settled over her as she struggled to deal with how vulnerable she suddenly felt. Vulnera-ble and off-kilter. She wasn't as she'd always believed herself to be: the product of a grand love. She had devoured romantic stories because they represented a world that had come together to create her. While she knew her mum loved her, she couldn't get past the fact that she'd come to be because of ugliness, and that made her feel ugly. On the surface, deep down, throughout.

Her chest ached, her soul was battered. She wasn't deserving of all the dreams her family had dreamt for her. She felt like an imposter. Her past was a lie, and while she understood why her family had sought to spare her the truth, even loved them for it, she felt unmoored.

As soon as the clock struck six, she headed for the door. She'd nearly reached it when it suddenly opened, and Matthew walked through carrying two wicker baskets, one lidded, the other over-flowing with a cornucopia of flowers.

"Closing up for the day?" he asked.

"Unless you need a book."

"Not tonight. I thought you might like to join me for dinner."

"I'm really not in the mood for the pub."

"I thought you might not be." He held up the lidded basket. "So I've brought the pub to you."

Her heart gave a little squeeze at his kindness. "Oh, Matthew, I don't think I'll be good company."

"I'm not expecting you to be, but I also suspect you've not eaten today, and you do need to eat."

Only then did she realize he had the right of it. She had no ap-petite but didn't want to grow faint from lack of nourishment. "Is there enough in the basket for both of us?"

"Yes."

"Would you like to come upstairs, then?"

"I thought you'd never ask."

"You are going to behave."

His smile held a bit of deviltry. "Only if you want me to."

She couldn't help herself. She laughed, and oh it felt so good, especially as she'd thought she might never find the wherewithal to laugh again. Reaching around him, she locked the door and then closed her hand around the handle of the basket holding the flowers. "I'll take this."

"You might as well. They're yours."

"I've never seen so many in one place. Or such an assortment." A myriad of colors greeted her when she looked down. "You must have pleased many a street flower girl today."

Matthew had actually had his gardener snip them from the gardens at his London residence. He'd wanted at least one of every variety and every color. When he'd left her earlier, he'd had the sense that she was still struggling with the facts of her origins and he wasn't about to leave her languishing in self-doubt.

He followed her up to her rooms. Having paid them little heed the night before once he'd located her bedchamber, he was now surprised to discover how simple the parlor was. Although it wasn't precisely a parlor. It was a relatively large room that included a small kitchen, where she had set her basket on a square table. Joining her there, he placed his basket beside hers. He hadn't actually brought her the pub but rather had asked the cook at his proper residence to prepare something. The dear woman who had served the household for years had been thrilled with the opportunity to provide dishes that would be eaten by more than the servants. He did hope Fancy wouldn't think anything of the fare being a bit fancier than what was usually served across the street.

"I haven't a vase," she said. "Will you be offended if I use a pitcher?"

"It would take a good deal more than that to offend me."

She brought over a pale yellow piece and began arranging the stems in it. "Feel free to look around, make yourself comfortable. I won't be but a minute here."

Wandering away from her, he noted that the remainder of the area was devoted to comfort. A dark blue settee and a low rectangular table rested before the fireplace. On either side of them and nearer to the hearth were two plush chairs of robin egg blue with threads of yellow creating an assortment of swirls. She liked her yellow, it seemed.

The mantelpiece held a framed portrait of four tall men and one tall woman—all young, not much older than twenty if that, he'd wager—standing outside a tavern. The Mermaid and Unicorn, according to the sign hanging over the threshold. An older woman of small stature stood among them. Pressed up against her and nearly buried in her skirt was a tiny sprite who couldn't be much older than six or seven.

"My family," she said quietly, coming to stand beside him. "The day Gillie opened her tavern."

"I thought as much." Another nearby photograph, also framed, sat a few inches from the first. Based on the gown Lady Aslyn wore and the church behind the assembled group, he assumed it had been taken on the day she stunned London Society by marrying a man with no lineage. Fancy had been on the cusp of womanhood, her grace and charm shining through.

"Shall we eat before it cools?" she asked.

He'd taken it to the pub and asked Hannah to warm it for him, so he hadn't technically lied when he told her it came from the pub. At the table, he opened the bottle of chardonnay that he'd brought, poured them each a glass, and sat down with her to his left. He liked having her there. He wasn't surprised to find her china was patterned in yellow and blue. "You like yellow and blue."

Her smile was forced, didn't seem to quite belong on her face. "The combination reminds me of the sun and sky on the loveliest of days."

He found her to be so much like sunshine herself that she

brightened the dullest moods—until last night. Now, she was the one needing brightening.

His cook's chicken slathered in a tart orange sauce was one of her specialties and one of his favorite dishes, yet Fancy ate with the enthusiasm of someone who'd been given an old shoe to gnaw on. Even the wine, an excellent vintage from his cellar, held no appeal for her.

"I inherited coal mines in Yorkshire." It was a boring thing to admit, but he was unaccustomed to the quiet between them and wanted to bring forth her true smile.

His words seemed to pique her interest a bit, at least enough that she reached for her wine. "Where you grew up."

He nodded.

"Shouldn't you be off managing them?"

"I have an excellent foreman who sees to matters. He sends me reports. I do occasionally visit." More often when he retired to the country after the Season ended.

"Did you ever work in the mines?"

"A few times. Backbreaking labor, but it gave me an appreciation for the men who toiled within them."

"Do you use children in the mines?"

"In spite of my father's numerous faults, one of his redeeming qualities was that he didn't believe in child labor. Except when it came to me. He resented that I should have a childhood. Thought I should take on responsibilities as early as possible."

"My family would have kept me a child forever if they could have."

"They only sought to protect you."

"Because they all knew the truth about my father. I can't seem to stop thinking about him." She took a long sip of the wine, nearly emptying her glass. He promptly refilled it.

She ran her finger up and down the stem, and he couldn't help but think about how much he'd like her stroking it over his jaw. Only he wasn't here for his needs. He was here for hers. "He's not worth your thoughts."

"I know, and yet I hardly know who I am any longer."

He hated that the blighter caused her to have so much as a single doubt about herself. "You're Fancy Trewlove of the Fancy Book Emporium. Fancy Trewlove who is taking London Society by storm."

She gave a small laugh. "More like a gentle breeze."

"In the life of a Season, two balls hardly signifies. By its end, you'll have won them all over."

She looked at him, averted her gaze, sipped her wine. "Today I received an invitation to the Fairhaven ball."

So Sylvie, bless her, in spite of her protests had issued the invitation at his request. He would have to send her a gift. Although Fancy didn't seem as pleased as he'd expected her to be.

"I met the marquess and marchioness at Gillie's ball," she continued. "None of my relations are related to them. It's the first sign that I'm being accepted."

"And that's good, isn't it?"

"Normally, yes. But I've been reflecting on the Collinsworth ball, the next for which I have an invitation. I'm thinking of not going, of ending my Season."

He didn't like the thought of her flirting with other men but preferred even less that she would give up on something she'd worked so hard to attain. "You're intending to let him win?"

"No, I just . . . in a year or two I'll go back. Maybe. I've been ruminating about what you told me earlier. I could keep this secret, but I worry it would fester and that I would live in fear of it coming out. Would it not be better to admit the truth of things? Especially if I am to have any hope at all of having the sort of marriage I desire."

Weary of going through the motions of eating when his entire focus was on her, he shoved his plate aside and leaned toward her. "What sort of marriage do you desire?"

"One of love, respect, admiration. Honesty. Devoid of secrets."

"People seldom share everything."

"But this isn't some trifling thing, Matthew. It's the ugly truth of how I came to be." She rubbed her hands briskly up and down her arms. "I told you earlier how dirty I feel, tainted. I took yet another bath this afternoon and failed once again to rid myself of the filth. It inhabits me." Tears gathered along her lashes, and it was as though a storm pounded against him. "I'm ashamed. Ashamed that he's part of me. Ashamed that I haven't the strength to cast him off. That he continues to haunt me. How can I burden a husband, a family, with all that?"

He thought he knew her, understood, and he realized her devotion to those she cared for was far greater than any he'd ever known. She couldn't shake off what she'd learned of her father because of her realization regarding the price her mother had paid and her worry for those who had yet to become a part of her life. She humbled him with her unselfishness, with her ability to always put others first.

She was struggling to adjust to what she now knew of herself, thought herself different because she wasn't the result of a fairy tale, but of a nightmare. Yet she couldn't see that the heart and soul of her remained the same. Because the maggot had not only touched her but her world, and in so doing, he'd coated her with his filth, and it had gone so deep that she couldn't wash it off. But he knew how to rid her of it.

Shoving back his chair, he stood. "Where do you store your tub?"

Clearly taken aback, she blinked up at him. "I have a bathing room. Why?"

"I'm going to bathe you, and when I'm done, you'll be so clean your skin will squeak."

FANCY DIDN'T KNOW whether to be horrified, wary, or intrigued as Matthew draped his jacket over the back of the chair, removed his neck cloth, unbuttoned three buttons, rolled up his sleeves, made himself at home within her small kitchen area, and began heating water. She decided on intrigued with a hint of wariness. "You can't be serious."

Settling his hips against the counter, he crossed his arms over his chest, and she fought not to notice how the action made his forearms appear as though they'd been cut from stone. "When I came out of the mines, I was covered in grime, so much so that every crevice and fold was filled with dirt. It was the one thing about working down there that I abhorred. I became very skilled at bathing thoroughly, and when I was done the water was murky."

"But I'm not literally covered in dirt."

"No, but you feel as though you are. You've confided that your own efforts have failed to yield results. So where's the harm in letting me give it a try?"

"Through my clothing?"

Uncrossing those lovely arms, he approached her slowly as though she were a skittish mare that might bolt at any unexpected movement or sound. He stopped just shy of his chest brushing over her breasts, and her blasted nipples immediately puckered and strained toward him. He held her gaze with raw honesty. "My mouth has known a good deal of you intimately. You must know I will not take what you are not willing to give."

But without her clothing, could she refrain from giving him everything? She trusted him more than she trusted herself. Danger hovered, but if he could rid her of the awful sensation of being mired in muck, she thought she stood a chance of coming back to herself. Ever since Dibble's arrival, she'd felt lost, floundering. She wanted more than anything to be again on a steady course.

She nodded. With a smile of understanding and gentleness, he leaned in and bussed a tender kiss over her lips.

"Knowing what you do about my past, how can you stand to touch me?" she whispered.

"Because I don't see him. I see only you. And when I am done, you'll see only you, too."

He turned away from her, and it took everything within her not to grab him, pull him back, and walk into the circle of his arms. Not until she felt clean, although already she felt less dirty. Just because of the way he looked at her, as though she were as she'd always believed herself to be: worthy of love.

"I'll begin filling the tub."

She didn't wait for him to respond but went into her bedchamber and carried on through to the bathing room. She turned on the tap, watched the water come through the spigot. It was an improvement to how they'd taken baths at their mum's, dragging in the tub from the shed and filling it by bucket loads from the kitchen sink. Mick had been researching how to get heated plumbing into his buildings, but had been unable to make it available as of yet. She was rather certain a time would come when everything would be more convenient.

Hearing the tread of heavy footsteps, she backed up against the wall and watched as Matthew came in holding the huge pot and poured the steaming water into the bath she'd prepared. He made several more trips while she fluttered uncharacteristically nervously around her bedchamber.

Finally, he announced, "It's ready."

She wove her fingers together. "I think you made the water hotter than I did. I could just bathe myself."

"You've done that twice already today. It didn't help." He held up one hand, flexed his fingers. "I have magic here."

"The next thing I know you'll be performing on the street, competing with the Fire King."

He laughed, deeply and richly, then sobered. "I don't share them with just anyone. Only the most special of ladies."

Her heart warmed. He made her feel as though he cared for no one as much as he did her.

He set aside the pot he'd been holding. "I'll unfasten you."

Standing at the foot of the bed, she turned and grabbed the intricately carved poster, presenting him with her back. His hands were slow and steady as he loosened her lacings, while hers had begun to grow damp with the slightest bit of trembling in anticipation of his touch grazing over more than cloth. "You should probably remove your waistcoat and shirt so they don't get wet."

She didn't much like the hint of breathlessness in her voice, but when he pressed his mouth to her spine at the base of her neck, the hint disappeared completely as her ability to draw air into her lungs deserted her.

"What a wise woman you are. Can you handle the remainder of your clothing or shall I see to it?"

"I can handle it."

She mourned the loss of him when he moved away. "I'll give you a few minutes and then join you at the tub."

Nodding, she listened as his footsteps heralded his departure. Then she dashed to the tiled room, quickly shed her clothing, piled it in a corner, and sank into the incredibly warm water, hotter than she'd ever had the patience to make it. Carting in heated water had never been her favorite task, and she usually did it only long enough to get the water comfortable. She would have to rethink the value of the effort because this was lovely.

Hearing a slight scrape, a bump, she grew still and waited. She thought she should have been nervous, but she'd never not felt comfortable around him. And he had done deliciously wicked things to the most private and intimate places of her body. She wasn't hypocritical enough now to tell him he couldn't touch, especially when she loathed her very skin. She'd nearly scrubbed it raw that afternoon.

He was so quiet she barely heard him when he walked in. His waistcoat was gone but his shirt remained. He placed a stack of books against the wall and set a lamp on top of them. "You didn't let down your hair."

"It doesn't need to get wet. It takes forever to dry."

"Mmm. We'll see."

He disappeared and the light above went out, leaving her in a room barely lit with shadows dancing around. When he returned, the shirt had been discarded and she found herself staring at a smooth, finely chiseled chest as he crouched before her and offered her a glass of wine. She did wish he'd left the light above on. Some of the dips and shallows were lost to the shadows, and she couldn't see them as clearly as she'd have liked. Beneath the water, her fingers flexed in want of a touch. She had to calm them before lifting one hand from the water, focusing on the stem to wrap them around, rather than the breastbone over which they longed to trail.

"I've never had wine in the tub."

"It'll help you to relax. I always enjoy a bit of scotch while bathing."

"It seems rather decadent."

"Exactly."

She warmed at the low word that seemed filled with promise. Taking a sip of the wine, she positioned her arm so it rested on her breasts, providing them with a bit of cover from his wandering gaze. She didn't think anything farther down in the tub could be seen too clearly, although it was silly to be modest now when he'd seen everything so very closely the night before.

Had it been only a night since her world had collapsed around her? Perhaps she was being unfair to believe she could recover so quickly.

She watched, mesmerized, as he dipped one of her soft linen cloths in the water at the far end of the tub. His muscles flexed as he squeezed out the excess dampness.

"We'll start with your face."

Gently he touched the linen to her forehead. "And where will you end?"

He grinned wickedly. "With your toes."

Tenderly he skimmed the cloth around her face, along her nose, over her mouth, across her chin. Then he studied her as though he were to take an exam the following day and would be required to draw a likeness of her. "I see no evidence of him."

She nibbled on her lower lip before taking another sip of the wine.

"You don't have his chin," he said quietly. "You look exactly like the woman in the photograph behind whose skirt you were hiding."

Her smile was small, tentative. "My mum."

He nodded. "You're not as old, of course, but all the lines are the same."

"I've been told on numerous occasions that I'm her spitting image."

"Believe it."

"But he had to have given me something." She squeezed her eyes shut. "Maybe it's something deep within me, something that can't be seen."

"Your spleen perhaps."

With a choked laugh, she looked at him, at the twinkle in his eyes, and felt the tiniest spark of joy.

"Definitely not your heart, sweeting."

Although her heart was beginning to feel as though it wasn't hers any longer, was beginning to feel as though it might belong to Matthew. He reached for the milled soap, settled it in the palm of his large hand, and dipped it in the water, avoiding her raised knee, avoiding touching any aspect of her. Then he was rubbing it over the cloth, saturating it with the fragrance wafting up as a result of his actions.

He seemed at once intrigued and awed. "So this is why you always smell like oranges."

"That, and I have one every morning for breakfast. When I was little, I'd stick my finger in the pulp and dab it along my throat, like it was perfume."

"Imitating your mother putting on perfume?"

"No, she would never spend coins on something so frivolous. She'd put a spot of vanilla behind her ears. Mick brought her an expensive bottle of perfume once. It just sits on her dresser, never used. I think she believes it to be too precious because one of her children gave it to her."

"She sounds like a remarkable woman, your mother." With the cloth covering his palm, he glided it over her neck and shoulders, massaging as he went, and she feared she'd never be able to take another bath without reliving these sensations.

He took the cloth only to where the water lapped against her breasts. He didn't dip there, even though she wouldn't have objected. He closed his hand around her arm and lifted it from the water. She watched as his jaw momentarily clenched and his eyes shuttered. "You abraded yourself."

"I scrubbed too hard," she whispered, "but it made no difference."

"It's not harshness that'll do the trick. It's tenderness." He washed her arm with such deliberate care that she nearly wept.

Remarkably, when he was done, she felt as though the skin were pristine. Wherever he touched, she felt renewed, unsullied. Taking the now empty wineglass from her, he proceeded to wash her other arm. "You're very good at this."

"I've spent a lot of time thinking about doing it."

A jolt of surprise hit her. "You've thought about washing me?"

Folding her fingers over his hand, he brought them to his lips and pressed a warm kiss there, all the while holding her gaze, challenging her. "I've thought about doing a lot of things with you."

He'd left her other arm lying along the lip of the tub. Lifting her finger, she grazed the tip of it from his collarbone to the center of his chest and knew victory when his eyes slid closed.

HE HATED THAT this strong woman was doubting herself, hated even more that he was having to work so hard not to take advantage of the situation. His true motive had been to make her feel clean again, but when she touched him with little more than the tip of a finger, it was all he could do not to join her in the tub. He'd even keep his trousers on. He just wanted to take her in his arms and hold her close.

Instead he set that lovely hand back on the edge of the tub and moved behind her. "Sit up. I'll get your back."

"You're determined to wash all of me."

Every bloody inch, and for some spots, he wasn't averse to not using the linen, but rather his tongue. The water splashed in minute waves as she brought her knees to her chest, leaned forward, and wrapped her arms around them, placing her cheek against them, revealing the delicate expanse of her back. "I suspect you weren't able to reach here earlier."

"No, not all of it."

Setting the linen aside, he rubbed the soap between his hands until it nearly slipped from his grasp. After putting the soap within easy reach, he spread his hands wide and laid them against the center of her back. Slowly he glided them up and over her shoulders, down and across her hips. Her low moan caused him to smile. "Like that?"

"Very much. I have a feeling it's very, very dirty and is going to need you to go over it several times."

It was the most lighthearted thing she'd said since the early hours of the morning, and his chest expanded with pleasure and triumph. Easing up, he rested his lips against her ear, relishing the feel of the damp tendril that had escaped her bun catching in his whiskers. "Feeling cleaner?"

"Remarkably so. You touch me as though he doesn't matter."

"He doesn't. You are your own woman, Fancy. I knew that the moment I first walked into your shop and saw you." With the pads of his thumbs and fingers, he kneaded her shoulders and back, her skin slick and like silk beneath his touch.

She groaned. "I've never experienced anything like that before."

"The other ways I've touched you . . . have you experienced them?"

Turning her head slightly, she looked back with a mischievous smile on her face that brought him more joy than anything else in his life ever had. "I'd accuse you of taking liberties, but I'm afraid it would make you stop."

"I won't stop until you tell me to."

"Then we'll be here until dawn."

"The water will grow cold. It's already cooling."

"But you'll warm me, won't you?"

In ways he shouldn't. "I'll always warm you."

"Are you dirty, Matthew?"

His breath hitched, his lungs froze. Danger lurked on the horizon, and he ignored it. "I certainly can be."

She gave a little laugh, twisted slightly, and reached back for him. "I want your entire body to wash all of mine."

"Fancy, my resistance to you is weakening by the minute. I want you to know that to me you are no different today than you were yesterday. But if I shed my trousers and climb into that tub—"

She pressed her fingers to his lips. "I know. But I want to feel clean inside and out. I want to be clean all over."

SHE'D NEVER BEEN quite so brazen, so bold. But then neither had she ever wanted anything as much as she wanted him. Not just his hands, but every inch of him.

He made the past not matter, only the present, only the future. While she knew that lords wanted their wives untouched, she was no longer certain she was going to follow that path.

Not because of the man who'd sired her. Matthew had the right of that. Dibble was inconsequential, nothing to her. He'd planted his seed and moved on. He had no claim on her. And even if she disagreed with Matthew's assessment of her chin, she knew it didn't matter. The love that had surrounded her as she'd grown up had mitigated anything at all that had to do with the man who'd come to her door with his ugliness. She'd allowed viciousness to seep into her, but Matthew had countered it with tenderness and care.

And he was the reason she was questioning her future, that this moment felt perfect and right. She knew that no matter what tomorrow brought, she would not regret what she felt now.

She watched as he unbuttoned the fall of his trousers. As he shoved them down and stepped out of them, she caught sight of his feet and realized why he'd been so quiet entering earlier. He'd removed his boots. Lifting her gaze, she stopped it halfway up, having caught sight of something more. "Aren't you magnificent?" she asked, her voice low and raspy.

"Are you referring to me or my cock?"

With firm thighs, toned stomach, corded muscles, he reminded her of marble statues of the gods. "Do I have to choose?"

His laughter echoed around the room as he stepped into the tub, the water creating waves as he lowered himself and took her in his arms so the entire length of her was pressed up against him. "When we leave this tub, your hair is coming down."

She barely had time to smile and nod before his mouth captured hers and disintegrated the last bit of grime that had been clinging to her. Nothing mattered except for him, except for them.

His hand traveled along the length of her back, over her bottom, along her thigh, hooked beneath her knee and draped it over his hip so he could settle more intimately against her. And she welcomed the feel of him. The water had begun to cool, but now it seemed so much hotter. She felt hotter, warmed to the core.

He dragged his mouth along her throat and the heat traveled all the way down to her toes. "Feeling cleaner?"

"Inside and out."

Lifting his head, he captured and held her gaze. "Stay like that. Never let him inside you again."

"I won't. You make me feel invincible. You make me feel treasured."

"Because you are. You have so much to give, so much to offer."

"I want to give to you tonight."

Groaning low, he buried his face in the curve of her neck. "With such ease, you bring me to my knees."

"It's because of your position in the tub."

When he lifted his head, he was grinning and cradled her face with one large and very wet hand. "You're nervous."

"A little. You know the worst about me and yet still you're here."

"Because I also know the best about you, and it far outweighs the worst." This time when he took her mouth, he took possession of her heart as well.

He accepted her as she was. Her past didn't matter. With him she didn't have to pretend or put on airs or strive to meet expectations. It was what she'd always wanted, an honesty with a gentleman. And here she had it.

As his hands skimmed over her, she thought, *yours, yours, yours.*

As she glided her hands over his broad chest and wide shoulders, she thought, *mine, mine, mine.*

Then she shivered because as warm as he was, the water had grown colder. Immediately he noticed and drew back. "Let's get you out of here."

He went first, not bothering to hide his perfection from her as he reached for a towel. As she shoved herself to her feet and the water sluiced over her, his eyes darkened, heated, and she felt like a nymph who'd captured the attentions of a god. As she stepped out of the tub, he draped the soft linen around her and began patting it gently over her, gathering up all the drops. Going down to one knee, he saw to her legs and feet and she combed her fingers through his hair, awed that he would humble himself so before her, would see to her needs before his own.

"You must be cold," she said.

"I'm fine."

When he was finished, he grabbed another towel and wrapped it around her, while he briskly rubbed the first over his skin, not bothering to take the same care with his body that he'd taken with hers. The entire time his gaze remained latched on to hers. His actions slowed, stopped, the towel clutched in one hand where ribs gave way to stomach, the linen trailing down covering his most vulnerable areas, providing him with a modicum of modesty.

"Fancy, my intention truly was to only bathe you, to show you that what makes you Fancy Trewlove hasn't changed. I won't fault you if you'd rather I dress myself and walk out of here now."

With a smile she released her hold on her towel, acutely aware of its journey along the short length of her body until it pooled at her feet on the floor, noting how his hand fisted more tightly around his towel, his knuckles turning white. Reaching out, she threaded her fingers through his unoccupied hand and began leading him toward her bed.

ALTHOUGH HE'D OFFERED, with all good intentions, to walk out if she wished, he hadn't been sure how he'd accomplish that action when his body was straining with the need to be with her, to bury itself in her, to hear her cries as passion rode her. As she pulled him from the bathing chamber, he released his death grip on the towel and padded after her.

Never in his life had it seemed so important that he get it right, that he make it perfect—for her.

As they neared the bed, she let go of his hand, reached up, and began plucking the pins from her hair. His gut tightened as the waves of black silk cascaded around her shoulders, along her back, halting just shy of the dimple in her backside. Plowing his hand through the satiny tresses, he stopped her from climbing onto the bed, turned her around, tilted back her head, and settled his mouth over hers as though it belonged there. And damned if it didn't feel as though it did.

But then it had felt that way from the very first time they'd kissed. Everything with her always seemed right, seemed new and yet familiar.

Falling against him, she wound one arm around his neck, carried the other on a journey around his back as though she wanted him as close to her as he had an urge to be. She was warm softness from head to toe. While her skin didn't squeak as he dragged his hands over it, she felt untouched, pure, pristine, a goddess bestowing her attentions on a mere mortal. He'd never felt more humbled, more undeserving of something so exquisite. But he wasn't fool enough to give up and not work to be deserving. Especially when she was no shy miss but was taking her tongue on a journey that mapped out every nook and crevice of his mouth while still managing to occasionally return for a slow seductive waltz with his tongue.

She had no timidity about her when it came to any aspect of her life. Her passions guided her, and they'd led her into his embrace. He couldn't have been more grateful.

Lifting her into his arms, he placed her on the bed and followed her down.

IT WAS WICKEDLY wonderful to be tucked up beneath a man's body as he stroked and caressed sensitive areas that she'd never before realized were aching for a man's touch. The underside of her breasts, the expanse of her back, the inside of her thighs, the back of her knees. He was tall with long arms that could reach so much of her without having to stretch. Although it no doubt helped that when he went for her calf, she bent her leg so a portion of it rested against his hip, giving him easier access. They moved in tandem, each seeming to instinctually know what the other required. She'd never known such fulfillment, such an intense sense of belonging with another.

Oh, she belonged with her family, had never doubted that, but this was an entirely different level of acceptance, of discovering where she fitted, and she fit against him perfectly. And she knew that all their encounters from the moment he'd strode into her bookshop had been leading her toward this. Want. Need. Satisfaction.

Every other man she'd met had failed to make her even think about leaping onto a bed with him, but with Matthew the desire had always been hovering, just beneath surface, teasing and taunting. Here, at last, it was coming to fruition.

Once more his hand trailed down her thigh, beneath her knee, back up. Only this time, it went higher, took a detour, and his deft fingers parted her folds, stroked the tender flesh. She relaxed into the passion. She knew how the quest would end and had no reservations regarding where he would lead her.

"You're so wet," he rasped. "So ready for me." He slid his finger inside her, and lovely sensations swamped her. "And so damned tight."

"Is all of that good?"

She felt his smile against the curve of her neck. "All of that is wonderful."

Shifting until he was nestled between her thighs, he kissed the underside of her chin, her collarbone, the hollow between her breasts. Then he took her mouth even as he took her body, pushing into her slowly, gently, giving her time to adjust as her body stretched to accommodate him. She dug her fingers into his back, scraped them along his spine. When he was fully seated inside her, she wrapped her legs around him, held him.

He began to move, just short strokes at first, and then they lengthened, coming faster, with more purpose, more intensity. She felt the pleasure begin to swell, from where they were joined, outward to the tips of her fingers, the tips of her toes, even to the ends of her hair. Her cries mingled with his grunts, and she thought no symphony would ever sound as sweet.

Frantically her hands moved over him, over shoulders, arms, back, neck. She couldn't seem to get enough of him, needed more, as he plowed and she met him thrust for thrust. His mouth never leaving hers, he took the kiss deeper, as deep as her body was taking him.

Every nerve ending, every muscle tightened. An explosion of sensations ripped through her. Screaming his name, she clung to him, aware of his body tightening, his back bowing. He broke free of the kiss, his feral groan echoing around her, as he went still before collapsing on top of her and burying his face in the crook of her shoulder.

Chapter 22

$\mathscr{F}$ancy didn't know why she was at this blasted ball, striving to prove that Dibble held no sway over her decisions, when ironically she was only in attendance because of her misguided need to demonstrate what required no demonstration. Yesterday her sire had dominated her thoughts and today she'd thought of little else save Matthew and how it had felt to be held in his arms.

She hadn't seen him since he'd crept out of her residence near midnight, and she missed him terribly. Because no classes were being held tonight, she hadn't seen him before leaving for the ball, and there had been an unexpected emptiness in her chest. She wanted to ask how his day had gone, wanted to sit in a chair reading with him across from her, wanted to share his meal, wanted his mouth on hers, his hands on her skin.

She was always striving to prove her worth to the people crowded into this grand salon. With Matthew, she'd never had anything to prove. He accepted her as she was.

And she accepted him. His kindness to Dickens. His slipping coins to barefoot children on the street. Embracing her desire to spread reading to those who had never known it. His determination to see her sire imprisoned. His comforting of her during her darkest hours. His ability to reach into her soul and heart to mend the cracks that threatened to shatter all.

Arriving here tonight, she knew she should have been impressed with all that surrounded her: gaiety, stunning gowns, and jewelry. Knew she should have been overjoyed when handsome gents asked her to dance. Within twenty minutes of her arrival, her dance card was filled with the names of lords who wanted to take her for a turn on the dance floor.

As she danced with Mr. Whitley, she realized she wanted more than a gentleman's interest. She wanted his love. Whether the love came quickly or slowly, all that mattered was that the spark of it was there, so it could blossom into something remarkably fulfilling.

When she waltzed with Lord Wilbourne, she realized she was simply going through the motions, placing her feet where he led. There was no connection, no joy. Certainly, it was entertaining, but it was also lacking. She much preferred waltzing through her shop in the shadows.

She'd dreamed of a night like this, of having attention, of flirting, fluttering her eyelashes, blushing at compliments issued. She'd prepared for it since she was a little girl. Yet, somehow it paled, which made her feel guilty as Lord Wilbourne escorted her from the floor because the gentleman had wasted his time with her. This was not what she wanted. These men were not what she wanted. What she wanted was so much simpler, so much more rewarding: Matthew.

She'd barely taken a breath before Lord Beresford was at her side to claim his dance. "My lord."

"You've been kept quite busy tonight."

She smiled. A lady always smiled, no matter that her feet hurt, no matter that she wished to be elsewhere and would begin counting the minutes until she could leave. "It would appear so."

"I know you favor books, Miss Trewlove. I wondered if you'd seen the Collinsworth library."

"No, I've not had that pleasure."

"Might you allow me to share it with you, rather than claim my dance? His lordship has a rare assortment of tomes I think you'd find intriguing."

Her smile this time was genuine. "I would welcome a respite

from dancing, words I never thought to utter. And you've definitely discovered my weakness. I can never say no to perusing books, ancient or otherwise. But is it acceptable for us to go into his library?"

"People wander through it all night. I would be honored to introduce you to it."

"By all means, then. I'd be delighted to see it."

He offered his arm, and she tucked her gloved hand into the crook of his elbow. She wondered briefly if Aslyn should accompany her, but if other people were about in the library, Lord Beresford couldn't get up to any mischief.

As he led her up the stairs and into the hallway, she saw couples milling about, coming and going. A few acknowledged them with a nod or a smile, and she realized she was becoming more accepted. Men were now dancing with her; women were speaking with her. It seemed she was well on her way to winning them over, and yet it brought her little joy, not when her thoughts were occupied with a black-haired, green-eyed gentleman.

Beresford escorted her farther along the corridor. People were gazing at paintings or talking quietly. He turned down another hallway. No one was about, but that didn't mean no one would be in time.

He opened a door, and she slipped into the room of shelves, books, and a musty fragrance. They were alone, but she wasn't concerned, too enthralled by all the leather bindings. She didn't think it was as large a library as Thorne's, but it certainly housed a goodly amount of reading material.

"Over here," Beresford said, leading her to a large open book that rested on a pedestal.

She approached with caution and reverence. "Oh my word."

"The *Gutenberg Bible*." His voice was low, near her ear.

"It's beautiful."

"There are very few remaining. It's rare, Miss Trewlove. Like you."

Her breath hitching, she glanced back over her shoulder. "It's very kind of you to say so, but I'm not so rare."

Lightly, he touched his fingers to her cheek. "But you are. And I would very much like to kiss you."

Her gaze dropped to his lips. Not the correct plumpness, the correct shape. Not the ones she wanted pressed to hers. "That would be inappropriate, my lord."

"Come, Miss Trewlove. We are alone. No one is to know. You are curious regarding what it might be like between us, surely."

Three days ago, perhaps, but now she knew what she wanted. And it wasn't an earl or a marquess or a duke. It was Matthew. "Please, don't take offense, my lord, but actually, I'm not curious in the least."

His brow furrowed. "That does not bode well for our marriage."

Startled, she gave her head a little shake. "I don't recall you asking for my hand."

Grazing his knuckles along her cheek, his other hand landing solidly on her waist, he lowered his face until she felt his breath stirring tendrils of her hair. "But I shall, my sweet. You have won me over, Miss Trewlove. Where is the harm in a gentle pressing of our lips?"

Stunned by his declaration, she didn't move fast enough when his mouth grazed over hers—

The click of a door had her jerking back her head. She wasn't quite sure what she saw within the brown depths of his eyes: regret, satisfaction, embarrassment. An entire host of emotions seemed to be rolling through him as though he couldn't quite decide what he should be feeling.

"Fancy?"

She recognized the voice. Mick. And he didn't sound at all pleased. Placing her hands against Beresford's chest, she shoved slightly and turned to face not only her brother but her brother-by-marriage and their host. She had a feeling that Beresford might not have been quite honest about people flitting in and out of the library. She suspected the group had sought refuge in here to get away from the crowd in order to enjoy a bit of scotch and private conversation.

"Lord Beresford was just sharing with me your wonderful rare *Gutenberg Bible*," she said, wishing her tone didn't sound as though she'd been caught with her hand in the biscuit tin.

"That's not all he was showing you," Mick barked. "Beresford, tomorrow afternoon, my office, two. We'll sort this matter out."

Beresford gave a sharp bow. "Of course."

"We can sort it now," Fancy announced. "Nothing untoward happened." The touch of his lips barely even registered as a kiss.

"Tell *them* that." Mick jerked his head forward.

She swung around. Oh, good Lord! At least half a dozen people were on the terrace gawking at them through the window. She was rather certain they hadn't been there when they'd first entered the library, but she'd been so arrested by the rare book that she'd noticed very little except it.

Based on the way Beresford had positioned himself so she was blocked from their view, they no doubt thought he'd taken advantage and she'd let him. It was bad enough to be caught alone with him, but his nearness, his lowering of his head—

It wouldn't take much imagination to expect the worst, and the aristocracy was not lacking in imagination.

Her reputation was ruined. Her standing, what little bit she'd managed to obtain, was crumbling. She had an awful feeling that Beresford might have intentionally placed her in this comprising position. He had to have known her family would have heard of this, had to have known where it would lead.

She was vaguely aware of his taking her hand and pressing a kiss to her knuckles. "Until tomorrow, Miss Trewlove."

"Lord Beresford." As she watched him stride from the room, she realized with a bit of dread that she'd just bid farewell to her future husband.

"I'm assuming he used the lure of the Bible to get you alone," Mick said, his voice low, laced with understanding and perhaps a bit of disappointment.

How could he not be disappointed when she'd mucked things

up irrevocably? Beyond mortified and humiliated, Fancy was grateful for the dark confines of the carriage. "He said other people were touring the library. That it was done. I know I should have walked out when I saw no one else there, but it was a Guttenberg. I thought no harm would come from a quick look. And then suddenly he was so close, talking of marriage . . . I'm so sorry. I know I was foolish and reckless. I've ruined everything for which you and the others have worked so hard."

Unless she married Beresford. Her brothers would ensure he did right by her. She was going to become part of the aristocracy but not in the manner she'd planned: because of a grand love.

"Our goal was to see you happy and well cared for. I've no doubt he could provide you with the sort of life Mum wished for you, but will he make you happy?"

Perhaps if she didn't find herself constantly comparing him to Matthew, if she could relegate Matthew to little more than a youthful passion. Their paths would never cross. She wouldn't have constant reminders of how he'd made her laugh, comforted her, helped her to believe in herself again. She would have to forget him and all they'd shared. "We're each responsible for our own happiness, aren't we, Mick?"

It would make her happy to please her family, to ensure that all the advantages they'd given her had not been for naught. If she didn't marry Beresford, her Season would be done along with their dreams for her. Even now she knew tittering was going on regarding her morals, and her suitability as a wife was being questioned. She imagined a good many of the matrons viewed her as being no better than Lottie. They certainly wouldn't allow one of their sons to wed her if she turned Beresford away.

"At least he knows you well enough to have discerned you have no resistance when it comes to books."

She almost smiled at the truth—and irony—of her brother's words. It was her love of books that would now guarantee she wouldn't marry for love. Although perhaps in time, affection could develop between them.

"You seemed to get along well enough when he visited," Aslyn said softly, encouragingly.

"He reads, so that's a point in his favor. I've enjoyed our conversations." Still, she couldn't help but wonder if he possessed a deceptive streak. Had he planned for them to get caught? Was he in need of her dowry? Or had he been as taken aback as she when Mick had walked into the room, as horrified as she when she realized they had an audience? "What more do you know of him?"

"He comes from a good family. He's never been associated with scandal until tonight. I've always found him pleasant, good company, polite."

"I could say the same of Dickens." Except for the polite part, she supposed. He had attacked Matthew when he'd first gotten a tad too amorous. Yet she'd yearned for his attentions, had wanted all he'd been offering and more. She couldn't say the same of Beresford.

How the deuce had she managed to win the earl over when she'd waltzed with him three times and he'd called on her only once? Upon what did he base his feelings?

The remainder of the journey was spent in silence, which gave her a good deal of time to reflect on her future and what it would entail. And what it wouldn't.

It wouldn't include Matthew, wouldn't include a gentleman who could set her skin to tingling with a mere look, who could set her on fire with a touch. A man who occupied her thoughts nearly every minute of every hour. A man who had not turned away from her when he learned the truth of her parentage. A man who had sought to comfort and reassure her that he found no fault with her for matters over which she had no control.

Would Beresford be willing to take her to wife, to kiss her if he knew the truth regarding her father? He obviously had no issue with her illegitimacy, which was a point in his favor. Perhaps he would overlook that vile creature who had sired her. Or would she be better served to keep the truth from him? What sort of marriage would she have if it lacked complete honesty?

When the coach came to a stop, she was more than ready to escape the suffocating confines. Mick walked her to her door and placed a hand gently on her shoulder. "You should be there when I have words with Beresford. He'll treat you with respect or he'll deal with me."

She knew exactly what those words would be: a demand for him to marry her. "I'll do what must be done, Mick. I won't bring the family shame."

"I never thought you would, sweetheart."

Rising up on her toes, she kissed his cheek. "Tomorrow."

"Come to my office a few minutes early so we're all settled before he arrives."

With only a nod in response, she went inside, leaned against the door, and fought to absorb the quiet of the shop, but her mind was racing, and for the first time since she'd initially unlocked the door and stepped over the threshold into the empty building inside which she'd create a haven for booklovers, the place felt lonely. Matthew wasn't here waiting for her. She knew it as surely as she knew that in spite of her world falling apart tonight, the sun would rise in the morning and people would go on about their lives as though hers had not taken a momentous turn.

Knowing no classes had been held tonight, that Mr. Tittlefitz wouldn't have left him with the key and responsibility of locking up, she experienced a keen disappointment. After all that had transpired between them, considering how much he'd come to mean to her, she should have given him a key so he could come and go as he wanted, so he could make use of the reading parlor at his leisure, so he could wait for her whenever it was his desire to do so.

Although after tomorrow, she doubted she would see much of him. She would be betrothed and while it had not come about as she'd hoped—with a proper courtship and love—she certainly wasn't going to be disrespectful of Beresford. Just as she understood her responsibilities to her family, she recognized her duties to her future husband. She would do nothing to cause him or Society to question her devotion to him.

Shoving herself away from the door, feeling as though no strength remained to her, she climbed the stairs to her rooms, carried through to her bedchamber, and gazed out the window. Her chest tightened to such a degree that she feared it might crush her heart. He was there. Standing so still, his arms raised, spread wide as he pressed his hands against either side of the glass.

How many nights had she sat here reading and looked across to see him doing the same? How often had she peered through parted draperies and watched him gazing out? After tonight, she would have to keep the draperies closed in order to avoid the torment of viewing what she couldn't possess. After tomorrow, he could never kiss or touch her again. Could never hold her, stroke her, whisper in her ear.

She could never welcome him into her bed.

He would become little more than a customer who occasionally came to her shop for a purchase. How long before he read every penny dreadful and had no reason to wander through the aisles of shelves? How long before she was married and was no longer sharing her knowledge of books with her patrons, with him?

Because it didn't matter that nothing had happened between her and Beresford. In the aristocratic world, it mattered only what people thought. Perception was everything.

Matthew could never be her future, but he was deserving of a proper goodbye. One more night of memories that would see her through into her dotage, that he would hopefully look back on with fond remembrance.

Where was the harm in indulging in her yearnings, her wants for just a few hours? For a short time, she could pretend that the horror in the library hadn't happened, that her reputation wasn't ruined, that come morning her life wouldn't be dictated by Society's rules rather than her own heart.

To avoid bringing her family total humiliation and shame, she would have to give up what she desired. But not for a few hours yet, not until the lark heralded the start of a new day. Not as long as the nightingale sang.

Her decision made, she turned on her heel and headed back out, her steps beating a rhythmic and steady tattoo, growing stronger as the rightness of her actions reverberated through her. Just as she would have no choice tomorrow, so she had no choice now. She needed Matthew with the same urgency that she required breath in order to live. She would not consider the bittersweetness of having him once more, only to lose him. Her entire focus would be on now. Only now.

Up the street she went. Past the mews. Around the corner—

Straight into his arms. Never before had she belonged any place more than she did then, in his embrace, with her face against the soft linen of his shirt, with his heart pounding hard beneath her cheek.

"I had to put on my boots, or I would have gotten to you sooner. What happened, Fancy? What's wrong?"

"Nothing now." Not for hours yet, and when the wrongness arrived, she would deal with it. Leaning back slightly, she skimmed her fingers up into his hair, cradling his face between her palms. "Kiss me, Matthew. Kiss me as though it's the first time you ever have. Kiss me as though it's the last time you ever will."

"Fancy—"

"Please. I need passion and fire. I need you. Only you."

His mouth came down on hers, hard, greedily, hungrily. Yes! This. This was what she wanted, needed, required. With the first meeting of Matthew's lips against hers, the sparks were kindled, with the full taking of her mouth the fire spread throughout her body, down to her toes, to the tips of her fingers. The heat was consuming, glorious, all-encompassing as their tongues stroked and parried. As though she were clinging ivy, she intertwined her arms around his shoulders, his neck, and his hold on her tightened as though he needed them closer as much as she did.

With a low growl, he tore his mouth from hers, lifted her into his arms, and began walking toward his residence. "We need privacy for what's to follow."

"Are you taking me on an adventure, Mr. Sommersby?" she asked breathlessly, gliding her fingers over every inch of him she could reach.

His chuckle was dark, muted. "That is my intention, Miss Trewlove."

"I do so love your wicked intentions," she whispered before circling her tongue over the shell of his ear, nipping at his lobe.

Moaning low, he quickened his pace, carrying her inside and kicking the door closed behind them. Barely noting that the front parlor had no furniture whatsoever, she fought not to imagine how she might have furnished it for him, how she would have turned the cold space into a warm and welcoming lair where she would greet him each time he came in through the doorway. At some point, he would marry another who would hang paintings on the walls and snuggle against him on the settee. She didn't want to think about that, think that another would share this intimacy with him.

Up the stairs he carried her and into the room that she'd only ever viewed a portion of. It was simply furnished, but neat and tidy, the bed made—no doubt by Mrs. Bennett. Would the woman figure out that tonight he'd not been alone, that another had shared his residence, his bed, his body? When all was said and done, would another glass join the one that presently rested next to the low-burning lamp on the bedside table? Would her scent fill the room and mingle with his?

Lowering her feet to the floor, he once more took possession of her mouth as though it belonged to him and him alone. His lips were moist and full, and she loved the way they moved over hers, urgently and yet tenderly. Then he was trailing a path along her cheek, and his mouth came to rest near her ear. "It drove me mad thinking of you at that ball enjoying the company of other men."

She squeezed her eyes shut, not wanting to ruin their last night together, not wanting him to know yet that it would be their last.

"I don't even know why I went. You haunt me, and all I could think was that I couldn't wait to be with you once more. You know everything about me, the good and the bad, and still you seek out my company. I never have to pretend with you." She let all that she felt for him flood her eyes, her expression, her face.

"God, Fancy, I hate it every time you attend a ball. I sit up here torturing myself, thinking that you'll meet someone you'll prefer to spend your time with. He'll take you on picnics and boating—"

She touched her fingers to his lips. "No one will ever replace you in my heart."

Even as she spoke the words, she recognized the absolute truth of them. A man such as he had always been her dream. A man who could claim her heart, her soul, her body while still leaving the ownership of them in her care.

With a low growl, he once more took possession of her mouth, deepening the kiss until it was nearly impossible to tell where he ended, and she began. Heat swept through her, through skin, muscle, and bone. Sensations rose to the surface and danced along her nerve endings, causing little sparks to burst forth like the tiniest of fireworks.

She couldn't stop the little mewl of distress when he separated himself from her.

"Patience, love," he urged, his low voice sending shivers of need through her. Slowly, he trailed one finger along the line where silk met flesh, over the swells of her breasts. Puckering tightly, her nipples strained against the cloth. "I want you as you were last night, naked before me."

Those deft pianoforte-playing fingers made short work of removing her clothing and his, but then he was barely dressed. Shirt, trousers, boots. They came off so quickly, a heap of clothing on the floor.

"You're so beautiful," he rasped.

Reaching out, he pulled the pearl combs from her hair. As though appreciating the value of them, he carefully placed them on the table beside his bed. He began plucking the pins from her hair. What had taken nearly an hour to pile into place, he disassembled in less than a minute, and the long heavy tresses fell around her shoulders, along her back. "You are as lovely as the first ray of sunlight over the moors."

"Poetry?"

"Merely truth."

Lifting her into his arms, he carried her to the bed and set her upon it as though she were handblown glass that needed to be handled ever so carefully or it would shatter. Taking his hand, she pulled him down. "Make me soar." Higher than a kite, a balloon, a bird in flight.

Chapter 23

A twinge of guilt pricked at his conscience because he had yet to tell her the truth of his identity, and yet he couldn't deny the absolute pleasure it brought him knowing that she'd sought him out for simply being Matthew Sommersby. A man. Not an earl, not Rosemont.

Last night she'd needed reassurances. Tonight she was here because she needed *him*.

He considered telling her the truth of things now, but he didn't want to ruin the moment, didn't want to have to delve into an explanation that might cool the passion that was burning so fervently between them. Later. He would tell her later, when his blood wasn't rushing so forcefully between his ears, when he could think more clearly, when he wasn't distracted by those lovely breasts that were in need of his attention. She wanted him now without the title. Surely, she would want him with it.

Clearing his mind of all thought except pleasing her, he lowered his head and began peppering kisses over her breast. Kneading it, licking it, suckling it.

Her hands running over the corded muscles of his shoulders and back served to urge him on. His name released on a sigh caused his stomach to tighten, his cock to harden when he'd thought it could get no stiffer. This woman had power over him that no other had ever possessed. She could so easily bring him to his knees, and he'd not object. He'd go willingly.

Shifting his attention to her other breast, when he clamped his mouth around her nipple, he lifted his gaze to find her studying him, her brown eyes sultry and smoldering with desire. Good Lord, he nearly spilled his seed then and there. No other woman had ever looked at him as though she were contemplating devouring him and would thoroughly enjoy doing so.

He trailed his mouth down her stomach, surprised when she shifted, sitting up slightly, leaning back on her elbows. Raising his head, he quirked a brow at her. "Is there something in particular you would like me to do?"

"I like to watch you." She skimmed her foot along his leg. "Are you going where I think you're going?"

"Do you want me to?"

"Very much so. I want you licking every inch."

"You say the naughtiest things."

"Only with you."

She bent forward until she was able to capture his mouth with hers. He poured all that he was, all that he felt into the kiss. She undid him, every facet of him. So much for his plans of never again allowing his heart to become involved when it came to women. She had conquered it, mastered it. It was hers, completely and absolutely.

SHE ALMOST TOLD him that she loved him. Because she did. She'd begun to suspect she held these frightening and wonderful feelings toward him, but now she knew it with absolute certainty. But it wouldn't be fair to give him the words when she no longer had the freedom to bind herself to him for longer than this night.

Although she realized with startling clarity that she'd never had the freedom. Not in the rookeries, not to a lad who raced barefoot through alleyways. Not in the posher area that her brother had built, not to a commoner who enjoyed penny dreadfuls, who accompanied her on adventures, who tore his mouth from hers, pressed a kiss to each breast, and pushed himself farther down so his breath stirred the curls between her thighs.

She'd set her own dream aside in favor of her family's. And yet here she was, where she shouldn't be, taking the night and him for herself one last time. She couldn't leave him with the memory of only one night together, a night when he'd given her everything. She didn't want him doubting that to her he had been special. That the joys he brought her, she wanted to return in kind.

His tongue stroked her intimately. Still resting up on her elbows, with a sharp intake of breath and a low moan, she dropped back her head. Another stroke, a swirl, and she turned her attention back to watching him, only to discover that he was watching her. Intently. As though each of her sighs was a catalyst for his own pleasure.

"Touch your breasts," he said against the sensitive flesh.

And she did, skimming her thumbs over her hardened nipples, taking pleasure in his gaze darkening. He was caught between her thighs, and she was rather certain she'd felt him tense with her actions. Cupping his large hands beneath her bottom, he lifted her slightly and began to feast in earnest.

Winding her legs around him, their gazes locked, she held him in place while pleasure spiked. Oh, the wondrous sensations he caused to spiral through her. Instinctually, she knew no other would make her feel as he did: powerful, beautiful, magnificent. With him, she was everything she'd ever hoped to be, experienced all she'd ever longed to know. It wasn't only the physical, although God help her, she'd have been content with that and that alone. It was the manner in which he made her feel appreciated, treasured, capable. Comfortable within her own skin.

He accepted her fully as she was. With him, she didn't need a title, a ladyship. It was enough that she ran her bookshop and taught others how to read. With him, she didn't have to put on airs or select the proper utensil for whatever delicacy had been placed upon her plate. For him, she could spread her thighs and let him have his way with her.

And what a wonderful way it was. Taking in the entire glorious length of him, his bare back, buttocks, and legs only heightened her own pleasure. Removing one hand from her breast, she threaded her fingers through his hair, circling them over his scalp. She had an urge to close her eyes, to do nothing but feel, but didn't want to give up one moment of gazing on him, wanted memories of every aspect of their lovemaking. She would remember these bittersweet moments until she drew her last breath.

Then the pleasure increased, became a vortex of sensations swirling within her, tightening every muscle, collapsing until she was aware of little except his mouth working its magic, as though the little bud was a toffee he was savoring with licks, strokes, sucks. Her other hand was suddenly also in his hair, holding him there as her legs tightened their hold, as her thighs trembled.

"Oh God. Oh God." The climax ripped through her, untethering her from the world around her until she was soaring, falling into the depths of his gaze until she was lost—and then found.

Slowly, provocatively, never taking his eyes from hers, he prowled up the short length of her and took her mouth. She tasted her own saltiness on his tongue, inhaled her musty aroma along his bristled jaw.

Rising up, he gently probed her, and she wound herself more tightly around him. When he plunged deep, she sighed with the satisfaction of having him fill her once again, completely, absolutely. He didn't look away. She couldn't. She wanted to memorize every expression that crossed his features. He pounded into her with vigor and purpose.

She met him thrust for thrust, loving the way their bodies moved in tandem, in awe of the deeply binding intimacy. At that moment, he was hers, and she was his. Nothing would ever sever this bond, nothing would ever diminish it. She was capturing this moment in time so nothing and no one could ever take it from her.

Never again would she experience this closeness. Never again would she revel in such familiarity. Her heart was swelling to such an extent she thought it might burst through her chest. She loved this man, with all that she was, with all that she would ever be.

Tears welled in her eyes.

"Am I hurting you?" he asked, through clenched teeth, his breathing harsh and tortured.

"No. Never." *I love you. I love you. I love you. I always will.*

Within her, sensations once again began to mount—

Then she was soaring into the heavens.

With a grunt, he thrust twice more, before collapsing on top of her, his arms closing around her as he pressed a kiss to the curve of her neck.

She'd never known such bliss for having had this . . . or such sorrow at knowing she'd never have him again.

HE SHOULD HAVE withdrawn, should have spilled his seed elsewhere. If he'd gotten her with child, he would know no regrets because tonight she had become his fully and completely and he'd become hers. She'd brought him to his knees. Even though he hadn't been standing, she'd managed it all the same.

With her nestled against his side, his finger slowly drawing circles along her spine, he needed to tell her who he was, but not now. Not while she lay replete in his arms. He wanted to find a romantic way to break the news to her. Perhaps he'd take her for a ride in a hot air balloon. Up in the heavens, with the world at her feet, he would reveal the truth and promise her that even when she was on solid ground, he would lay the world at her feet. Anything at all that she wanted would be hers for the taking.

He loved her. The thought of once again falling should have terrified him, should have given him pause. Instead, he knew that nothing in his life had ever felt so right. In spite of his resistance, the hardening of his heart, love had found him. This remarkable woman had broken through the barriers, destroyed his defenses, and won him over.

Every word she voiced came from the depths of her soul. He'd never known anyone as open and honest. Not only with her words, but with her body as well. He'd never known all the aspects of any woman as thoroughly as he knew every facet of her. This woman in his embrace held nothing back, kept nothing hidden. He could only hope that she would understand why he'd kept a portion of himself hidden from her.

In the beginning it had been because he wanted an escape from Society. As he'd come to know her, the right time had never arrived. On the morrow, he would make it arrive.

Dragging his hand down her back, he cupped her bottom. "I already want you again." His other hand joining the first, grabbing her hips, he urged her onto him, straddling him. Then he cradled her face. "I think I shall always want you again."

She traced her fingers over his jaw, his lips, his nose, his forehead with such deliberation that it seemed she was striving to memorize every line, dip, curve, and hollow. "And I shall always want you."

Lowering her mouth to his, she took what he wasn't certain she realized she now owned. He understood that he would never find as much satisfaction with any other woman. Not that it mattered. He intended to never have another. From this night forward, she was the only one who would ever grace his bed, the only one he would ever pleasure.

When she lifted away from the kiss, he was surprised to see that she had a look of shyness about her. "What's wrong?"

She licked her lips. "I want to be wicked."

"You don't think being here is wicked?"

"More wicked. Like we talked about when we went boating."

He slammed his eyes closed. "Christ."

"I want to kiss every inch of you."

Opening his eyes, he spread his arms wide. "Who am I to deny you so simple a request?"

Her laughter floated around them, and he wanted to harness the sound and place it in a music box so he could listen to it whenever he wanted.

She pressed her lips to his forehead, and it was his turn to laugh. "You don't have to be literal with the *every* inch."

Holding his gaze, she gave him a stern look. "Shh. I'm counting how many kisses you're comprised of. So every inch it shall be."

And every inch it seemed it would be. His face, his throat, his arms, his chest. The dear woman even went down to his toes. Up his calves, over his knees, along his thighs. He'd never known the inside of his thighs were so sensitive, that a lick here and a nip there would cause his breath to hitch.

Then she stopped and studied his swollen cock. She had to know how badly he wanted her. The damn thing was practically begging for her touch. He reached for her. "Straddle me."

Moving beyond his reach, she shook her head. "I'm not done yet."

Resting back on his elbows, he waited, his nerves taut, his muscles fairly trembling with need. Leaning in, she puckered and blew air along the entire length of his shaft. He groaned low in anticipation. Then she gave him the wickedest, sauciest, most sensual of grins, her eyes dark and smoldering.

When her lips touched the head of his cock, he nearly exploded. "Jesus."

Her tongue slowly circled the incredibly sensitive skin. When she closed her mouth around him, he dropped back on the pillow, lost in the sensations. She took her time, tormenting him as though she'd been born to do so. He threaded his fingers through her hair because he needed to touch her, needed a deeper connection than simply feeling her wedged between his legs.

She was keeping every wicked promise with which she'd ever teased him. He shouldn't have been surprised. Again, with her, there was the open honesty. She never said what she didn't mean. With her, he'd always known exactly where he stood.

Her mouth was so hot, so wet, so damned skilled. He knew she'd been a virgin when he took her the night before, had felt her body give way to him, but she pleasured him now like the highest paid courtesan. No, better than that. She wasn't doing it for money. She was doing it because she wanted to. She was here now because he meant something to her. She'd not uttered the words, not told him that she loved him, but how could she give so much to him if she didn't?

Pushing himself back up, he watched as her mouth slid along the length of his cock. "I'm close to bursting, Fancy. Straddle me now. I want my cock inside your sweet haven."

Offering support, he eased her up and assisted her as she slid down, enveloping him completely. Blanketing her mouth, he tasted himself on her tongue. Sitting up, with one arm under her bottom, the other clasped against her back, he guided her as she rode him hard and fast, her hands stroking his shoulders, his back, as though she couldn't get enough of him.

Her sighs and mewls heightened his own pleasure. "That's it, sweetheart. Come for me again."

"It feels so good." She buried her face in the curve of his neck. Her arms tightened around him. She shuddered, trembled, cried out, and the muscles of her core squeezed—

He hung on to her as the cataclysm rocked him to his core. Dropping back to the bed, he brought her with him. Lethargic, weakened, he still found the strength to hold her to him. He belonged to her now, heart, body, and soul. He would forever remain hers.

JUST AS DAWN began lightening the mews, Fancy awoke, aching, sore, and tender, but feeling marvelous all the same. She'd had him twice more before they'd finally drifted off to sleep.

Matthew rested on his side, facing her, his hand cradling her hip. He was so beautiful, still lost in dreams, as night began easing away, unveiling him for her eyes and her eyes alone.

A sadness swept through her because she would never again awaken in his arms, in his bed, with his scent wafting around her. Never again would she see his spiky, sooty lashes resting on his high cheekbones. Never again would she see his hair sticking up on one side or note the heavy bristles coating his jaw.

She was tempted to wake him, ask him to take a razor to his

face, so she would have that memory of his mornings. To watch him wash up and dress. Although she thought her favorite memory would always be of him divesting his clothing. And hers.

She had no regrets regarding their coming together, not last night or the night before. Men did it all the time: took women and left them. Why couldn't a woman do the same?

But it wasn't the same. Already there was an ache in her heart for the emptiness that would consume her when she left here. The thought of leaving him hurt so badly. It made it difficult to breathe, caused her throat to tighten and tears to threaten. Love was supposed to give one strength, and yet she felt so weak. She didn't want to leave him—ever. She wanted to stay here until their hair turned silver. She wanted to kiss every inch of him again . . . and again and again. Wanted him kissing every inch of her. She wanted to feel him moving inside of her with purpose and strength. She wanted what she couldn't have.

All because of a silly desire to see a rare and precious book. Because for the briefest tick of a clock another man had touched his mouth to hers and it had meant nothing. But still, it would change the course of her life. It would take her from Matthew.

Giving him up would be the hardest thing she'd ever done.

He alone held the power that made her heart and body sing. He was a rare find. Like the books she loved most of all, he offered a unique glimpse into something that shouldn't be taken for granted. It was more than love. It was a soul-deep connection that made everything right and good.

Hearing the creak of a wagon's wheels, she squeezed her eyes shut. The real world was beginning to move about and would soon be invading this fantasy one, causing it to fade away until it too was naught but reality. She couldn't hold on forever.

She had to let go.

Carefully, gingerly, she began easing off the bed. His hand clamped around her hip.

"Mmm," he murmured, opening his eyes narrowly and peering at her. "Where are you going?"

"I have to leave before too many people are about." Leaning in, she kissed his forehead. "I can't be caught leaving a bachelor's residence at dawn."

"Stay awhile longer." He gave her a wicked grin. "I'll make it worth your while."

He would, she knew he would, but it would make it all the harder to leave. "I can't."

WITH A GREAT deal of reluctance, Matthew let her go, rolled onto his back, shoved himself up slightly, and placed his hands behind his head, watching as she began gathering up her clothing. He wanted to watch her doing that every morning for the remainder of his life. He loved her, to the depths of his soul. "Don't open the shop today. Let's do something together. We'll take the train to Brighton. No, we'll take a flight in a hot air balloon." *I want to tell you who I am. I want to ask you to marry me. You can have your dream of marrying for love. Your family will have theirs of seeing you become part of the aristocracy.*

Straightening, she wrapped a hand around the bedpost and stood there in all her naked glory. He wanted her breast back in his mouth, her legs wrapped around his waist. "I can't."

"Then I'll purchase all the books in your shop, and you'll have nothing to sell and no reason to unlock your door to customers."

She gave a huff of a laugh, her smile not nearly as bright as he'd expected his words to make it. "You can't afford to do that."

"I can." She stared at him, her eyes slowly blinking. He climbed out of bed, took two strides to reach her, and cradled her face between both his hands. "Spend the day with me, Fancy."

Tears welled in her eyes as she placed her hands over his, threaded their fingers together, and brought them to her lips, pressing a kiss against his knuckles. "I want nothing more."

As her warm breath wafted over his skin, the affection he held for her intensified. They would have this day and all the days that followed.

"But it wouldn't be fair."

She lifted her gaze, and he realized the tears weren't brought on by his fervent desire to have her with him, but by something else, something that caused her sadness, was crushing her, and dread slithered through him.

"I did something rather foolish last night."

"You regret coming here?"

Quickly, she shook her head, loosened her tight hold on his fingers that was causing them to ache, and cupped his jaw in her hand. "Never. The moments spent with you were the most beautiful, wonderful of my life. I'll never forget them. I'll never forget you."

Her words made no sense whatsoever. It was almost as though she were striving to say goodbye, to end things between them when they'd only just truly begun. "What are telling me, Fancy?"

"Oh God, Matthew, this is so hard."

Tears were rolling down her cheeks now, and it took everything within him not to gather them up with his thumbs. But something was wrong, terribly wrong. "Just spit it out. We've always spoken honestly with each other."

With a nod, she licked her lips. "At last night's ball, I was caught in a compromising situation with Lord Beresford."

Suddenly it was as though the ocean had entered his head, the roar of waves crashing against his skull, drowning out all thought. "Beresford?"

"I told you about him calling on me. He's an earl—"

"I know who the bloody hell he is."

Releasing his hold on her, he stepped back, the anger shimmering through him, the betrayal slicing at him. He'd thought her different, but she was just like Elise, just like Sylvie, just like his mother. She wanted a title and was willing to do anything to get it. He'd almost offered the conniving wench his.

"Mick is meeting with Beresford this afternoon." She extended a hand imploringly. "I have no choice but to marry him."

In order to gain her damned title. Under his breath, he released a harsh curse and turned away from her. She'd have her lord. If only she'd waited—

What a fool he'd been to think she'd valued him over a title. That was all she wanted of the man. For Christ's sake, she'd lured Beresford into a trap and then come to Matthew's bed. "Get out."

"Matthew, it wasn't my intention to hurt you. I just wanted one more night with you. You are so special to me."

He swung around. "Someone so damned special that you placed yourself in a compromising situation in order to capture your damned lord?"

She looked as though he'd struck her. "You think I wanted to be found in a compromising situation?"

"It's what women do. They lure a man in and then they set their trap. My mother, my sister, my wife. They all gained their husbands through deception. Why should you be any different, especially when you were groomed your whole life for the role?"

"This is not what I wanted. How can you possibly believe—"

"Because I know the most innocent of women can be conniving in order to gain what they want. But you fooled me into believing you were different. You won me over, heart and soul. I am completely besotted. I didn't want you to open your shop because I was going to take you off somewhere and ask you to marry me."

With a gasp, she fell to her knees. "No."

"Would that have been your answer because you wanted your title more than you wanted me?"

Additional tears fell. She was trembling. He wanted to take her in his arms and comfort her. More fool was he.

"Matthew, I love you, but you must see that I can't marry you. My marrying Beresford would be a dream come true for my family. Do you really want to marry a woman of scandal, a woman who was caught alone with another man? Even though you and I weren't married at the time, it will still follow me, follow you. Your business associates, whoever they are, what if they hear of it? How will that reflect on you?"

Her words were a cudgel hitting against his chest. He'd never wanted anything more than he'd wanted her heart. He knew he would never love anyone to the extent he loved her. But once more he'd misjudged the honor of a woman. He edged past her without touching her. "Just get the hell out."

He didn't wait for her to leave but headed down the stairs to begin preparing to get the hell out himself. He was more than ready to return to his residence in Mayfair and to leave Miss Fancy Trewlove and his heart behind.

Chapter 24

With her undergarments bundled in her arms, the lacings on her gown undone, and tears streaming down her face, Fancy ran to her shop, not caring if anyone spotted her. Her heart was breaking. She'd found the love for which she'd always dreamed, only to lose it because of an error in judgment. And Matthew blamed her, believed she'd tricked Beresford.

How could he think that of her? After all they'd shared, all they'd confided in each other, how could he believe the worst of her?

When he strode from the room, her damned pride had refused to allow her to chase after him. She should not have to explain herself. He should know that she was the one tricked.

Not that it mattered what he thought, because it didn't change the truth of things. Even if he still wanted her, she couldn't bring shame to her family by rejecting Beresford. Her reputation was on the cusp of ruin and only marriage to the earl would see her accepted in Society.

When she reached her rooms, she plopped down on the settee. Dickens leapt up and settled in her lap. Combing her fingers through his fur, she gazed at the photographs of her family on the mantel. What if she didn't want Society? What if she wanted Matthew?

She'd never had a row with anyone before, but people had rows all the time and overcame them. If she explained what had hap-

pened at the ball, would he believe her? Could her heart with-
stand the battering if he didn't?

He'd wanted to marry her.

In the face of his anger over what he obviously viewed as a betrayal, she'd barely been able to absorb the words he'd thrown at
her. Not exactly the way she'd always envisioned a proposal coming, but now his words reverberated through her. He loved her.
Oh, he hadn't used that term, precisely, but he'd admitted she'd
won him over. And he'd wanted her to become his wife.

Dickens hissed, and she realized she'd been hugging him
tightly as though he were Matthew. She released her hold and he
darted away, leaving her arms empty, as empty as her life would
be without Matthew. How in the world was she to reconcile what
she wanted with what was best for everyone else? At what point
did she put her own needs and desires first?

Glancing over at the mantel clock, she saw that she was an hour
away from opening her shop. Her world was falling around her,
but she couldn't let her beloved shop go to hell as well.

She prepared her bath, and when she sank into the warm
water, all she could think about was Matthew's gentle touch as
he'd washed away her imagined grime. As the tears began to flow
in earnest again, she buried her face in her hands. Everything she
did, everywhere she looked were reminders of him. He made her
laugh, feel special, hunger for passion. He'd defended her against
Dibble and was going to see the man sent to prison. He'd shared
happy times and sad. He'd been her rock.

With wet hands, she swiped at her tears. How could her chest
ache this badly, as though her heart were being physically rent
from her?

Would she find any comfort at all with Beresford? Would he
make her laugh? Would she come to love him in time?

Matthew certainly didn't seem to like the earl. She shook her
head. That made no sense. He'd meant he knew of the earl, didn't
know him personally. She'd mentioned his calling on her, and apparently he hadn't liked that at all. Matthew had been jealous. But

then if he'd been caught in a compromising situation with another woman, she'd have been jealous as well. Although she certainly wouldn't have immediately assumed that he was the one who led the other to ruin. It had hurt her deeply that he had such a low opinion of her. But then she remembered his wife had been a trickster. His sister and mother as well, it seemed. No wonder he'd found fault with her when they'd first met, but had she not proven herself to him? Or had he been so hurt by the thought of losing her that he'd been unable to think clearly?

Her mind was a fog of confusion, of questions, of anger, of hurt. She needed time to sort it, but the minutes were ticking away.

SHORTLY BEFORE TWO o'clock, with her head held high, she walked into Mick's office. He stood before his desk, arms crossed, Aslyn beside him. On one side of his desk was Aiden, Selena, Finn, and Lavinia. On the other side stood Thornley and Gillie. Beast was leaning against a bookcase. He loved books almost as much as she did.

Obviously, Mick had let everyone know about the unfortunate incident, and they'd all gathered to lend their full support.

Mick cleared his throat, released a deep sigh. "Last night, I was remiss in asking you exactly what happened. Would you like to tell us?"

She lifted a shoulder. "He told me Collinsworth had some rare books and offered to show them to me. He said other people would be in the library but no one else was. I know I should have left right then." She met each gaze. "I'm sorry I didn't."

"When I walked in, it appeared you were locked in an embrace—"

"He held me, yes. He wanted to kiss me. But I wasn't having it. However, I know that based on the way he was standing, leaning toward me, to those in the garden, it had to look as though he was. And that's what people will believe, what he will let them believe. But regardless of what didn't happen, it doesn't change the fact that I was alone with him. And because of that, if I don't take him to husband, I will be ruined."

"Do you want to marry him?"

Oh God, this was difficult. "You all have worked so very hard to get me to this point. I will do what I must."

In the hush of the room, he studied her for a full minute. "That's not what I asked, sweetheart. Do you *want* to marry him?"

"I've thought of nothing else all morning. I've struggled with it. Nearly strangled my cat, I held him so tightly." She thought a little levity might help, but it didn't. This was a serious affair, and she had to take it seriously. It was her future, her life. "I don't want to disappoint you all or Mum, but I'm going to. I can't marry him. I'll just be miserable if I do."

Uncrossing his arms, he pushed away from his desk, strode over to her, wrapped his arms around her, and placed his chin on the top of her head. "You're not going to disappoint us. We just wanted to know if we needed to take our fists to him if you wanted to marry him and he wasn't going to step up and do the right thing."

Unshed tears clogged her throat as she wound her arms around his back, held him close. "I don't think fists will be necessary. I can handle it."

He tucked his finger beneath her chin, tilted up her head, and gave her a warm smile. "We know you can."

More tears threatened. She was going to be a blubbering idiot before Beresford appeared. "I'll be a woman of scandal. Society won't have me."

"That just makes you one of us, then, doesn't it?" Aiden asked.

She looked past Mick to her grinning brother. "I've always been one of you."

He winked at her. "That you have."

A knock on the door had her heart skipping a beat, her stomach tightening. Mick pressed a quick kiss to her forehead. "Give Beresford whatever answer you want, Fancy. We stand behind you."

No, she thought, they stood beside her. They always had.

Mick strode back to his desk, leaned against it, and once more crossed his arms. "Yes?"

Mr. Tittlefitz peered inside. "Lord Beresford is here and requires an audience."

"Send him in," Mick ordered.

Taking a deep, shuddering breath, Fancy turned and faced Beresford as he entered, and she wondered why she'd never before noticed how arrogant and entitled he appeared. Mr. Tittlefitz closed the door. She was rather certain the lord jumped slightly at the sound of it *snicking* into place. He gave her a nervous glance, and she suspected he hadn't expected to be facing an army of Trewloves. He gave her a perfunctory bow. "Miss Trewlove."

"Lord Beresford."

He looked past her, took a step to walk around her. And she knew with absolute certainty that her decision was the correct one. She moved in front of him. "Your meeting is with me, my lord."

He blinked, looked to the window, the ceiling, the floor, finally back to her. "That's not really how it's done, Miss Trewlove."

"You will find, my lord, that we are a family that seldom does things in the manner they are usually done. I am, however, curious. Was it a coincidence that an audience was present to see us alone in the library?"

The earl cleared his throat. "I might have mentioned to Mr. Whitley I was going to show you the rare Bible."

"Do you know what my dowry entails?"

"I do. I find it quite satisfactory."

"I bet you bloody well do," Aiden fairly snarled.

She gave her brother a sharp look, and he mouthed, "Sorry."

She gave her attention back to Beresford. "In a situation such as ours, my lord, wedding bells soon ring."

"Indeed they do, Miss Trewlove. I shall assume I have your family's blessing, and—"

He started to lower himself. How could she embarrass him by refusing him once his knee hit the floor? "No."

He stopped, half-bent over and looked up at her. "I beg your pardon?"

"Please straighten yourself, Lord Beresford."

He did as she requested, his eyes never leaving hers. Taking a deep breath, she released it slowly. "I'm sorry, Lord Beresford, but I can't marry you."

Lord Beresford gaped, actually gaped. "If you don't accept my offer, you will not be welcomed among the aristocracy. You will be ruined, dear girl."

"I'm well aware."

"I was willing to overlook your unlawful birth, but now you are asking me to overlook the scandal that your refusal will create. You will be fodder for gossip."

"Better fodder for gossip than a wife with regrets."

"If you deny me now, I shan't be calling on you. No lord will call upon you."

"Then, Lord Beresford, I must say I am more than happy with my decision."

"You have to marry me."

"She's given you her answer," Beast said. "Now, off with you."

With a huff, a glare, a jutting out of his lower lip, Lord Beresford stormed from the room, slamming the door in his wake.

"I might have had to disown you if you married him," Finn said. "What an oaf."

With a soft smile, and a great sense of relief, she faced them. "Thank you for . . . well, everything. Your love, your support, your understanding. I love you all so much."

"What now, Fancy?" Gillie asked.

"During all these years, while you've *guided* me, you never once asked me what my dream was."

"What is your dream, sweetheart?" Mick asked.

She gave him a smile that caused her jaw to ache. "My dream is to marry a man I love, a man who loves me. And I'm going to make that dream come true."

CROSSING THE STREET, she felt free, liberated, excited about the future, couldn't wait to reconcile with Matthew, to reassure him that she loved him, wanted to be his wife. She was done with the aristocracy.

Later when she went to tell her mum about the decision she'd made, she would ask Matthew to accompany her. She wanted them to get to know each other. She was relatively certain that once her mum saw how he called to Fancy's heart, she would not only understand her daughter's decision, but would applaud it. Her mum had been with a man she loved and one she hadn't. She understood the rewards and the horrors.

She strode past her shop, increased the length and speed of her steps until she reached Matthew's residence. Smiling brightly, she inhaled deeply, and lifted the knocker, taking satisfaction in the bang as it fell back into place. Mrs. Bennett should be done with all her chores by now, shouldn't be about to see Fancy fling herself into Matthew's arms when he opened the door.

Except he didn't.

She lifted the knocker three more times. Waited. Balled her fist and knocked. Nothing. Sliding over to the window, she raised a hand to shield her eyes and peered in through the window. She knew there was no furniture in the front parlor. She could see a portion of the passageway into the next room but couldn't see any furniture. Surely, it was just the angle.

She knocked one more time and then tried the door. Locked. A fissure of disquiet went through her. Had he packed up and moved away? She shook off the absurd thought. He was no doubt just having a meeting with his man of affairs. Maintaining his income required his attention. He would return shortly. She would come back later, see if he might join her for dinner at the hotel dining room.

Her steps were much slower as she made her way back to the shop.

Marianne greeted her with a bright smile. "Did your meeting with your brother go well?"

She hadn't told her clerk the particulars. Rumors would circulate among the upper echelon. No reason for them to be spread elsewhere. "It went perfectly. How was business while I was away?"

"We had a couple of customers who purchased five books between them."

"I don't suppose one was Mr. Sommersby."

"No, miss. Were you expecting him?"

She shook her head. "No. I'm going to be in the office seeing to some business." Once she was settled in her chair behind her desk, she began working to reassemble the book Timmy Tubbins had brought her. It helped to distract her from wondering when Matthew would return, although it couldn't stop her from running various conversations through her mind. Where to begin, what to explain, what to omit. How best to get them back on an even keel.

At half five, the bells jangled. After the quiet of the afternoon, her heart gave a lurch of nervousness mingled with a speck of joy. Could it be Matthew? Had he spent the day tearing apart their encounter that morning, analyzing every word said, striving to determine how everything had gone so wrong and what was now needed to make it right once more? She wasn't certain she knew precisely what to say, how to greet him, but was confident when she set eyes on him, everything would fall into place. Love had that sort of power.

But when she stepped out into the shop it was to see Mr. Tittlefitz leaning on the counter talking with Marianne.

"Hello, Mr. Tittlefitz." They both gave a startled jump like they'd been caught doing something they ought not. She certainly knew how that felt.

"Miss Trewlove, I was just asking Marianne if she'd like to go with me to the music hall this evening."

Fancy couldn't help the swelling she felt in her chest. She'd known these two were right for each other. With a raised eyebrow, she looked at her clerk, who was blushing profusely.

Marianne lifted a shoulder shyly. "I told him I'd be delighted."

"Then you must be off to get ready."

"I don't want to shirk my duties."

"No duties to shirk. No one's about. Off with you now— No, wait right there." She dashed up the stairs to her bedchamber, went to her vanity, opened a drawer, and pulled out a pair of silk gloves that she had yet to wear. When she returned downstairs, she offered them to her clerk.

"Oh, Miss Trewlove, I can't take them. They're far too lovely."

"I have another pair." Several in fact. "They'll make you feel elegant on your outing."

"If you're sure . . ."

"I am."

Her clerk took the gloves and stroked them. "I've never had anything so fine. I'll wash them and bring them back—"

"They're yours to keep. Who knows? You may have other occasions to wear them."

"Thank you, Miss Trewlove. You're always so generous."

"Nonsense. I hope you both enjoy your evening."

"I'll walk you home," Mr. Tittlefitz told Marianne.

"I'll just get my reticule."

She disappeared into the office, and Fancy turned to her brother's secretary. "I'm so glad things are going well between you and Marianne."

"She's a lovely lass. I'm sorry Mr. Sommersby won't be assisting any longer with the lessons. I'd begun to like him."

Fancy's stomach dropped down to her toes as a wave of dizziness along with a spot of dread hit her. "Why will he no longer be helping?"

He seemed taken aback by her question. "I assumed he'd spoken to you about his plans. He's moved on."

Trying to make sense of his words, she stared at him. "What do you mean he's moved on?"

"He brought me the key to his terrace just before noon. Told me he wouldn't be staying for the remainder of his lease, had already packed everything up and moved out. Odd thing. He'd paid for two months in advance. Said I was to use his remaining balance to assist anyone struggling to make their monthly rent."

"What's this, then?" Marianne asked, clutching her reticule.

"I was just explaining to Miss Trewlove that Mr. Sommersby won't be helping with the lessons any longer."

"He doesn't have to live here to help us," she said.

Mr. Tittlefitz looked at her sadly. "He told me he wouldn't be returning to the area."

She could barely think for the blood rushing between her ears. She'd left him believing she was going to marry Beresford, because at the time she'd thought it was her only alternative. She'd given him no hope, no reason to believe that they had any chance of being together. But she certainly hadn't expected him to pack up so quickly, to be gone in the span of a couple of hours. Her chest was in danger of caving in on itself. "Did he happen to say where he was going?"

"No, miss."

Maybe he was going to live with his sister. She didn't even know the woman's name. How could she find him to let him know that she wasn't going to marry Beresford? She knew so much about him, yet so few intricate details. "You two should be off now, making the most of your evening."

After they left, she wandered through the shop, and everywhere she looked she had memories of Matthew. Waltzing around the shelves, tucking her hair behind her ear, lifting her onto the counter and kissing her senseless.

That night, she sat in her window nook, looking across the way at his darkened residence. Where had he gone? How could she find him? He needed to know that she loved him with every fiber of her being, that she wanted to marry him, wanted to make a life with him.

Waiting in vain for light to spill forth from his window, for him to return to her, she'd never felt lonelier in her entire life.

Chapter 25

*U*sing a linen cloth, Fancy dried the platter that her mum handed her. It was the last of the dishes that needed to be washed after the luncheon they'd shared. It was Sunday, but not the first one of the month, so the rest of the family hadn't gathered here, for which she was grateful because she had things to say to her mum and would rather say them privately. Besides, her mood was melancholy and wouldn't serve anyone any good. She probably shouldn't have bothered her mum, but she'd needed a little distraction.

She could barely recall Saturday. She'd had customers but seemed to have forgotten where she'd shelved books, had been useless in helping anyone find a story they might enjoy reading. In her office, she'd intended to continue working on restoring *Little Dorrit*. Instead, she'd merely stared at nothing, striving to determine how she could find Matthew. She'd asked neighbors if anyone had seen him moving out. For her trouble, all she got was one account of three wagons and a coach pulling up, and liveried footmen hauling out furniture. No markings on the coach or wagons, but still—liveried footmen. Had she misjudged his means? Surely, he'd not been serious when he'd told her he could afford to purchase every book in her shop.

"All done with that," her mum said now. "Let's pour ourselves a bit of brandy and then you can tell me what's troubling you."

"Why would you think I'm troubled?"

"Because, ducky, you've hardly spoken a word and you look as though you just learned that every book in England was tossed into the sea. So let's settle in to have a good talk."

When they were sitting in the chairs beside the empty hearth, Fancy took a large swallow of the brandy and let it spread its warmth through her. Afterward, she slowly ran her fingers around the rim of the snifter. "At the last ball, I was caught alone with an earl. And it's just not done. To make matters right, he asked to marry me. I told him no."

"Did you kiss him?"

She furrowed her brow. "The earl? No. Why would I?"

"It's like that story, *The Frog Prince,* I remember Gillie reading to you. If you don't kiss a fella, how will you know whether he's the prince or just a frog?"

She laughed lightly. Her mum must have been sipping brandy when Fancy wasn't looking. "That's just a fairy tale."

"Have you not kissed that fella that's helping with your lessons?"

She felt her cheeks grow warm. "Well, yes, I have."

"Is he reason you didn't kiss the other bloke?" She leaned forward. "Maybe the reason you didn't want to marry the other bloke."

Feeling tears forming she blinked them back. "I love him, Mum. His name is Matthew Sommersby. He's kind and generous. He makes me laugh—just as you told me he should. I enjoy being with him." She gnawed on her lower lip, unable to believe she was really going to confess this to her mother. "And I really like when he kisses me."

Smiling with satisfaction, her mum settled back in the chair. "Sounds like he's a prince, then. A lot of frogs in this world, Fancy. When you find yourself a prince, you need to hang on to him."

"Oh, that's just it, Mum. I lost him."

"How did you manage that, pet?"

She took a sip of the brandy, relishing the warmth chasing away the cold that had started to spread through her. "He told me he loved me, wanted to marry me. But I told him I was going to marry the earl."

"Why did you tell him that?"

"Because I thought I was. I thought I had no choice. I worried I would disappoint you if I didn't. Your dream for me is never going to come true. Now I'm a scandalous woman, so I won't be invited to any more balls. I won't have an opportunity to meet a lord whom I'd like to marry." Not that she would have if she'd attended a thousand balls. Her heart was taken, would forever belong to Matthew.

"Hold on, pet. I'm hearing a lot of words and trying to make sense of them. Do you want to marry a lord?"

"I want to marry a man who loves me."

"As well you should. You know none of us ever wanted you to marry a man who didn't."

She finished off her brandy, took a big sigh. "Mum, what if I only wanted to manage my bookshop? What if I never marry?"

"Pet, I want you to do what makes you happy."

"But you've always wanted me to have a fancy man and live in a fancy house and have a fancy life."

"Aye. A man who loves you, sees you as his moon and stars. A house where you walk in the door and feel like you've come home. A life where you're happy and have everything you ever dreamed of—or if not everything, a good bit of it. You define what is fancy to you, and that's what I want you to have."

A tightness loosened in her chest with the realization that she wasn't going to be disappointing her mum. "I'm glad I didn't marry the earl, then."

"But what about your Mr. Sommersby?"

Sadness once more engulfed her. "Before I could tell him that I wasn't going to marry the earl, he moved away. I don't know where or how to find him."

"You need to talk to Beast, then. That lad has a knack for find-ing anything."

MONDAY MORNING FANCY awoke with a ray of hope. After re-turning from her mother's the day before, she'd penned a letter to Beast asking for his help, which she intended to hand off to Lottie that evening. Of all her brothers, Beast was the most mysterious. She didn't even know where he resided. While she was relatively certain her mother knew how to get in touch with him, she had decided to handle the matter in her own way.

Glancing at the mantel clock, she saw that it was nearly nine. In all the days that she had managed the shop, she had never not opened the door when the hour struck nine. In spite of her lack of focus on Saturday, she threw back the covers, climbed out of bed, and prepared herself for the day. On the dot of nine, she unlocked her door, went to the counter, lifted her cup of tea, glanced at the calendar, and froze.

It was the day that her sire was to go on trial. At ten. Matthew would be there, giving his testimony. He wouldn't break that promise, surely. She could see him, find an opportunity to speak with him, and at least let him know that she wasn't marrying Beresford. Perhaps they could begin anew. Or at least begin where they'd left off before they had their row.

Marianne wouldn't arrive for another couple of hours. As much as she regretted closing up her shop, she saw no help for it. After retrieving her reticule, she locked up and rushed along the streets until she reached the boardinghouse where Marianne lived. With the landlady's permission, she dashed up the stairs to Mari-anne's rooms, knocked briskly, and when a sleepy-eyed Marianne opened the door, she apologized. "I have something I have to do. Here's the key so you can get into the shop."

"Should I go in early?"

"If you'd like, but don't feel you must. I'm sorry this has come up so unexpectedly. I don't know how long I'll be, and I just want to ensure the shop is opened at some point."

"I'll change out of my nightgown and get right over there."

"Thank you, Marianne." She turned for the stairs, stopped, turned back. "I apologize. I was so distracted on Saturday that I didn't ask how your outing with Mr. Tittlefitz went."

Her clerk pressed a hand to her lips. "He kissed me, Miss Trewlove, and it was ever so lovely."

Reaching out, she squeezed Marianne's hand. "I've always thought the world of Mr. Tittlefitz. I'm glad he's making you happy."

"Oh, he is. Now off with you. Don't worry about the shop. I'll see that it's well cared for."

Feeling the tears welling, she blew Marianne a kiss and then raced down the stairs.

She had little trouble finding a hansom cab, but the traffic was horrendous, and it was several minutes after ten before she entered the courtroom where Dibble was on trial. The room was packed, no seats to be had. She didn't know why people cared so much about seeing the proceedings for someone they didn't know. Or maybe they did know him. Perhaps he had many friends.

Although based on his sneer as he stood in the dock, she doubted it. Then she realized he was glowering at Matthew who was striding toward the witness box. To see him again stole her breath. He exhibited such confidence and an almost regal bearing. She could tell he'd already managed to gain the respect of almost everyone in attendance. When he stepped up to claim his place, he looked over the courtroom, and she knew the moment he spied her standing at the back of the room because he went as still as death.

He didn't look as though he'd slept well, and she wondered if he'd been worried about his testimony or if perhaps he was regretting how things had gone between them when they'd last seen each other. She offered him a hesitant smile and wished she had some way to communicate to him that she had complete faith in his ability to see her sire put away. And that she desperately missed him and needed to speak with him.

"If you will please state your name for the court?"

He jerked his gaze to the wigged and robed man standing before him who had made the announcement. "Matthew Sommersby."

The man said something sotto voce. Matthew didn't appear pleased. He glanced over at Fancy, cleared his voice. "Matthew Sommersby, Earl of Rosemont."

The tiny cracks that had appeared in her heart when she discovered him gone deepened until her heart shattered.

HE WATCHED FANCY walk out of the room, and it took everything within him to remain in the witness box and give his testimony. She wasn't supposed to be here. He never should have told her when the trial would occur. He'd done it to bring her peace of mind, to reassure her that it would happen, and justice would be served.

As soon as he was done, he strode out of the courtroom and into the hallway, searching for her. But she was nowhere to be found.

All for the best. What was there to say?

She'd made her choice. She'd chosen Beresford.

And he'd made his. He hadn't told her who he was.

AS HE HAD every night since he'd returned to his residence, Matthew lounged in his library and sipped his scotch. And as he had every night since his return, he thought of Fancy.

Only tonight, he couldn't escape the vision of her startled expression when he'd been required to give not only his name but his title. He'd known the court would insist on a full identification because his position among the aristocracy lent credence to his words, would help ensure that Dibble was adequately punished for the harm he'd caused, not only recently, but years ago. Even if the ancient news had not been brought to light in the courtroom, he knew it and had insisted the man not be let off lightly. The toad's day in court had been merely for show.

Matthew hadn't meant for her to find out the truth of him

in such a public setting and with no warning. He'd considered writing her a letter because he had known once she married Beresford, their paths would undoubtedly cross. He had intended to be polite, but cold, not to let her see how her trickery had wounded him to the core not only because he had so misjudged her but because it had meant he couldn't have her for the remainder of his life.

He'd fallen in love with her, damn it. Felled without realizing it. Wanted her as his wife.

But she'd grown impatient, wanted her lord.

Seeing her today had been at once a joyous and sorrow-filled moment. The sight of her still caused his heart to expand; the truth of her caused him to realize that when it came to women, he was an awful judge of character. He never would have expected Fancy Trewlove to use underhanded means to gain what she'd wanted. And he'd begun to believe she had a care for him, that if he asked for her hand, she would choose him, not knowing he had a title.

But now she knew, and he still wanted her. With everything within him. If she had known who he was, if she had sought to have them discovered in a compromising position so he would have had to marry her—he wouldn't have cared, because he would have had her in his life.

WITH HER LEGS drawn up, Fancy sat in the window seat with her cheek resting on her knees and gazed at the darkened windows across the way. Since Matthew's departure, she ended every night in the same manner.

No, not Matthew. Rosemont.

Was she destined to have those she loved keep the truth of things from her?

All day, she'd pondered why he hadn't told her, and now in the still of the night, she remembered his reaction when the letter had fallen from her pocket, recalled him telling her how his wife had tricked him. Remembered Gillie's ball where Lady Penelope and her friends had risked speaking with her because they'd wanted to know if he'd been invited. Learning how so many ladies had called on him. He'd come here to escape who he was.

She'd wager every book in her shop that she had the right of that.

She understood a little better his reaction when she'd told him about being caught in a compromising position with Beresford, but the understanding didn't make her hurt any less. He'd accused her of duplicity, hadn't even bothered to give her the benefit of the doubt. Although neither had she corrected his misassumption. She'd been too stunned by it, to be honest.

But now to realize he'd held a part of himself from her, she had to wonder if she really knew Matthew Sommersby.

"GOOD MORNING, JAMES."

"Miss Trewlove."

"I'll see myself to breakfast."

"Very good, miss."

Following a fitful night's sleep, it was nice to engage in a familiar routine, and she was quite looking forward to having breakfast with Mick and Aslyn. As usual, when she walked into the dining room, he set his newspaper aside and stood. "How are you this morning?" he asked.

She forced her brightest smile. "Looking forward to a new day."

After selecting various tempting offerings, she joined her brother and Aslyn at the table. "How are you, Aslyn?"

Her sister-by-marriage reached out and squeezed her hand. "I'm doing well. You know I very much admire you for how you handled Beresford."

"I doubt anyone else does—at least anyone outside the family. But it hardly matters. I'm more than content with my decision." She looked to her brother. "Is there anything in the newspaper regarding Dibble's trial?"

She should have stayed to hear the testimony, the verdict, and the sentence—if there was one—but following Matthew's revelation, all she'd wanted was to leave. At the time, nothing had seemed more important to her sanity.

Mick went so still, he could have been mistaken for a statue. "Dibble, you say?"

She gave him a sympathetic, understanding smile. "I know he's my father, Mick. I spoke with Mum. She explained everything."

"When was this?"

"After he barged into the shop."

Fancy knew there were some who were terrified of her brothers, feared facing their wrath. Based on the fury that visibly washed over Mick's features, she clearly understood why.

"He *what*?"

She told him everything about that night. Well, everything except for the way Matthew had tended to her. Even though he'd done little more than hold her, she doubted Mick would appreciate it, which was no doubt part of the reason she hadn't told him about Dibble before.

"Lord Rosemont came to your rescue?" Aslyn asked, clearly dumbfounded by the knowledge, repeating what Fancy had shared.

"He was leasing a residence. Only I didn't realize until yesterday who he was, until he gave evidence at the trial. I didn't stay. Don't ask the reason." Nodding toward the *Times* crumpled in Mick's hand, she was surprised he hadn't turned the newspaper back into pulp. "Is there anything?"

He exchanged a glance with his wife, before pinning Fancy with his hard-edged stare. "I think there's something you're not telling us."

"With all due respect, Mick, it's none of your business."

"Does it have anything to do with why you turned down Beresford's offer?"

Lifting her cup, surprised to find her fingers not trembling, she took a sip of her tea, set the cup back on the saucer. "You are not to confront him."

She supposed that was answer enough because he cursed

harshly before rattling the paper and beginning to scour the pages. "Guilty," he finally barked, then looked at her. "Ten years in Pentonville."

A sigh of relief rushed out. "Thank God."

"Why didn't you come to me, Fancy, and let me know what was happening here?"

He sounded truly hurt, and for that she was sorry. "You've taken care of me for so long, Mick. It's time I took care of myself. And Matthew"—she pressed her lips together, squeezed her eyes shut, opened them—"Rosemont had seen to the matters I couldn't."

"Rosemont," he ground out, narrowing his eyes. "Perhaps I should have a word."

"No. And don't you try and work your way around this by asking one of the others to see to him. None of you are to interfere."

"So there is something between you with which to interfere."

She rolled her eyes. "Leave off."

Beneath his breath, he grumbled something about irritating sisters being too independent by half. She took it as a compliment.

"I will be having a word with Dibble, however," he said sternly, in a voice that would brook no argument. "If he survives those ten years, when he gets out, I'll be waiting for him."

"I don't have a problem with that." She shook her head. "I don't even know his first name."

"I'm not certain he has one. Never doubt, Fancy, that in spite of the circumstances, you were wanted."

"I know. Still, I wish they'd been different for Mum. That it had been as she told me. For her sake."

"She did love her husband."

"But she was only a little older than me when she lost him. So many years alone." She couldn't help but wonder if she was facing the same future.

Mick returned to his newspaper, Aslyn to her porridge. Fancy took another sip of her tea and cradled her cup like it was a tiny bird to be protected. "May I borrow your carriage tonight?"

He jerked his attention back to her. "For what purpose?"

"Is it not enough to know I have a need for it?"

He looked to the ceiling as though answers resided there. "When did you get so stubborn?"

"You're going to the Fairhaven ball," Aslyn said quietly, approval lacing her voice.

Forcing her stomach not to knot up at the thought, she nodded. "I need to face them one last time, leave Society on my terms, not theirs."

"Did we receive an invitation?" Mick asked, although she doubted that he'd stand on the formality of an invitation if he was determined to go.

"We did," Aslyn said. "That's why I know of it."

With a nod, he settled back. "Then we'll accompany you."

"I need to do this on my own, Mick. None of you are to go." Because she knew if she received a cut direct—of which she no doubt would receive many—her siblings would see the offender pay for the slight.

And she needed to stand alone in order to make her own statement: Fancy Trewlove was a woman to be reckoned with.

Chapter 26

*H*aving given in to his sister's pleadings, Matthew found himself at her damned ball wishing he was in his own residence, tossing back scotch, rather than waltzing with Lady Penelope. All of ten and seven, the girl was too flighty by half and talked constantly about subjects in which he held no interest: flowers, weather, her shopping expeditions. But then he'd experienced the same thing from the five ladies with whom he'd danced prior to her.

He'd not had a chance to visit with any of the gentlemen in order to catch up on the latest manly news, because the moment he'd entered the ballroom, the ladies had swarmed to him like bees in search of nectar.

Above the din of music and conversation, another arrival was announced, and he was grateful it was a young married couple who had no daughter in tow. Keeping his promises to all the ladies who had called upon him before he'd taken his sabbatical, he'd signed his name to a slew of dance cards and did his best to at least pretend interest, to offer compliments and a bit of flirtation, in spite of the fact that he was bored silly.

But then he'd felt that way ever since he'd walked out of his terrace. He'd gone nowhere—not even to his favorite club—and done nothing of any consequence except see Dibble sent to prison. Other than that, he roamed his empty residence with no purpose, a kite no longer tethered in danger of crashing and being destroyed at any moment. Every morning he opened the newspaper and searched for the announcement of Fancy's betrothal, knowing that seeing it would flay his heart, would confirm that she would never belong to him.

He couldn't sleep, thinking of her with Beresford, contemplating how he might have handled things differently from the beginning, how he might have ensured that she was his. He barely ate, nothing tasting as fine when he wasn't sharing the meal with her. He couldn't even take pleasure in reading because doing so reminded him of glancing across the mews to see her sitting in her window with book in hand. Every damned thing reminded him of her. He couldn't draw breath without thinking of her.

As he now circled the floor with the young lady in his arms, he caught snippets here and there.

Beresford.

Miss Trewlove.

Scandalous.

Why I never.

It seemed the couple was on everyone's tongue, except for the ladies with whom he danced, but then they were more interested in impressing him by sharing everything at which they excelled rather than gossiping about the latest scandal, one that would be put to rest by night's end.

"I'm so glad you've decided to return to Society."

He hadn't, not really, but he was so hungry for the sight of Fancy that he'd placed himself in the precarious position of having to cross paths with her and Beresford without giving away that his heart refused to release its tenacious hold on her. She and Beresford were bound to arrive together at any moment because the earl wasn't fool enough not to accompany her and use this opportunity to demonstrate his devotion and respect for the woman whom he was to marry. It was the first ball to be held since the Collinsworth affair. It was imperative that Beresford see his lady accepted and where better to begin than with the Fairhaven ball?

"Am I boring you, my lord?"

His dance partner's quietly spoken words jerked him from

his reverie. "My apologies. It appears I'm out of practice when it comes to entertaining a dance partner." Especially when his mind was distracted with musings of Fancy. He didn't know what he would have said to her if he'd managed to find her outside the courtroom. But he'd had a need to hear her voice, gaze into her eyes, and assure himself that she was happy with her decision that had landed her Beresford instead of himself. Although he still had a devil of time envisioning her succumbing to trickery in order to gain her place in Society.

"I've been unable to decide if you're anticipating the arrival of another debutante or planning your escape."

He arched a brow at her. "I beg your pardon?"

"I notice your gaze keeps wandering to the doorway at the top of the stairs."

"I find the announcement of arrivals distracting, and my gaze naturally leaps—"

"It's more than that." Perhaps the chit wasn't as flighty as he'd first thought. "I think you're looking for someone in particular."

"You would have the wrong of it."

"You're an awful liar."

He gave her a pointed look. "It does not serve a lady well when in search of a husband to call a prospective suitor a liar."

"That might hold if you were in search of a wife—which you are not—and I were in want of a husband—which I am not."

"Every unattached woman here is in want of a husband."

"Not I. I want to be as independent as Miss Trewlove."

Even as his heart tightened at the sound of her name, he scoffed. "Miss Trewlove. So independent she tricks a lord into marriage."

Her delicate brow furrowed as she blinked repeatedly at him. "Are you referring to the Beresford debacle?"

"Debacle? She got what she wanted. She's marrying a lord."

"Whoever told you that?"

She did! But for some reason, his mouth wouldn't form the words. He was trying to recall exactly what Fancy had told him.

"I know she was caught in a compromising position. I know she tricked him—"

"Absolutely not. She's a lady of integrity. She'd never do such a thing. Lord Beresford arranged the entire artifice, shame on him. Told my brother, as they are best mates, and a couple of his friends to gather some ladies on the veranda near the window that looked into the library. Then he got Miss Trewlove into the room and promptly kissed her. Knowing the lady as I do, I rather suspect she wanted only to see the rare Bible in Collinsworth's possession, not be accosted by Beresford."

He nearly tripped over his feet and hers. He couldn't keep circling the floor as though everything were right with the world. With his hand on the small of her back, he guided her beyond the chalk circle to a vacant spot at the wall. "Are you sure of this?"

He squeezed his eyes shut. How could he even doubt it when Fancy was the most open and honest woman he'd ever known?

"Absolutely. My brother told me Beresford was in want of her dowry. It's rather substantial. I gave my brother a good piece of my mind, I tell you, for going along with Beresford's underhanded means. A lady should have a choice."

He opened his eyes. "I know for a fact that the next day, Beresford met with her brother, to arrange the marriage."

"That's what he hoped to accomplish, but Miss Trewlove refused him. Then and there. Good for her, I say."

Everything within him stilled. "You know this how?"

She sighed. "Several hours after the meeting, Beresford arrived at our residence, deep into his cups, bemoaning his misfortune, and my brother consoled him. I was listening at the door, as I'm wont to do. It's the reason Lord Beresford isn't in attendance this evening. He's mortified she wouldn't have him. I'm surprised you'd not heard all this. It was on everyone's tongue for days."

He could hardly blame Beresford for escaping into drink. Fancy was a diamond of the first water, and in spite of all his machinations, he had failed to gain her hand. But she'd told him she was going to marry the earl. Somewhere between his residence and her brother's office, she changed her mind. Because he'd confessed to wanting to marry her? Or had she simply decided to place her own dreams ahead of her family's?

"I've not been moving about in Society much." He'd been holed up in his residence nursing his wounds, self-inflicted to be sure.

Lady Penelope angled her head thoughtfully. "I'm left with the impression, my lord, that you, also, are acquainted with Miss Trewlove, even though you've not attended any balls."

In her tone, he heard no accusation, no search for gossip, merely interest. "I visited her bookshop."

"Isn't it the loveliest? Have you met Dickens?"

"I have."

"He's such a sweet—"

"Miss Fancy Trewlove!"

The majordomo's booming voice echoed throughout the ballroom, bombarded Matthew's soul. He swung around to see Fancy in an exquisite golden gown standing at the top of the stairs. Alone. Not a brother or sister in sight.

Standing tall, proud, and so beautiful in her glory that she fairly brought him to his knees.

"Will you excuse me, Lady Penelope?"

He barely heard her "Of course," because he hadn't waited for her response but was already frantically heading for Fancy, determined to ensure she was no longer facing this crowd of gossipmongers alone.

FANCY HAD NEVER been more nervous in her life, or more sure of herself and her place in the world. She intended to prove that these people held no sway over her, did not determine her fate. She alone was mistress of her own destiny.

It had taken her a while to realize that. She'd done what her family asked of her for so long, occasionally slipping in a few of her own desires—her bookshop, her adventures, falling in love—that she'd lost sight of the fact that she was responsible for her own happiness, that she chose her own path. Sometimes she agreed with the dreams her family had for her, and sometimes, she had to go her own way. They'd given her the strength to stand on her own, and tonight she was putting it to use.

The announcement of her name was still booming around her when she took a deep breath and began her descent. She was well aware of couples stopping mid-waltz to stare at her, fought not to stare back, focusing her attention on the Marquess and Marchioness of Fairhaven, who waited at the bottom of the stairs. Then a stirring off to the side caught her notice, and she saw a dark-haired man pushing his way through the throng as though his life depended on reaching his destination, reaching her.

Her feet coming to a halt, she wrapped her fingers around the banister so tightly she feared she'd leave indentations. He broke free of the crowd and bounded up the steps. Dressed in evening attire, he'd never looked more devastatingly handsome, but she hardened her heart, refusing to greet him with so much as a pinch of gladness.

He stopped two steps down, which gave her the advantage in height, made it so much easier to meet his gaze head-on. "Fancy—"

"I didn't expect you to be here." He'd been at no other balls. Why would he be here?

His lips, that had done such wicked things to her, twisted into an ironic but slight grin. "Lady Fairhaven is my sister."

She remembered the lady's green eyes and black hair. How had she not seen the resemblance? But then she'd not been look-ing for him among the aristocracy. Still, she glanced around, imagining him visiting his sister, enjoying dinner. "Your niece is here, then."

"In the nursery upstairs. I read one of Aesop's fables to her be-fore she fell sleep. I thought of you."

A time existed when she'd wanted to meet his niece, would have enjoyed watching him read to her. A time when knowing she was on his mind would have brought her joy.

"I never think of you." She made to move past him, and he stopped her with a gloved hand to her arm, and she was grateful it wasn't skin to skin. She didn't know if she'd have had the strength to resist his silken touch.

"You're not a skillful liar."

He had the right of that. She thought of him nearly every minute of every day. "Unhand me."

"You haven't your reticule filled with books."

"I'm very good at shoving."

Slowly he unfurled his fingers. "Come somewhere with me so we can talk."

"No." She intended to do little more than walk through the throng, stare them all down, and be on her way. She started her descent and he moved in front of her, barring her way.

"You rejected Beresford. You're ruined. They'll turn their backs on you. You'll receive cuts—"

"I'm well aware of what I'll be forced to endure, but I shall leave Society on my terms, not theirs. I was invited to this ball, and so I have come."

"At least let me accompany you."

He offered his arm, and she merely shook her head. She only possessed so much strength when it came to refusing him, and if she touched him, her resistance was likely to crumble into a heap at her feet. She despised the way her heart pounded and her body strained to be nearer to him as though he were her North Star. "I'd rather you didn't, Matthew." Momentarily, she squeezed her eyes shut. "Pardon my slip. I mean, Lord Rosemont."

She started down, aware of him not following, further noting that music no longer played, that all eyes had been upon the drama playing out on the stairs. She'd wanted to face them all head-on but hadn't expected to do it all at once.

"I love you, Miss Trewlove."

In spite of the gasps and tittering, his voice echoed around her, his words slamming into the very fabric of her being. But this time, they seemed more intense, larger, more profound. Staggering to a stop, every muscle tensing, she slowly turned to face him. "Don't do this, Matthew, not here." So publicly. She hated that they had an audience, but in the aristocratic world, everything always seemed to be on display. "It will not go well."

"Because I hurt you. Because we hurt each other." He went down one step, then another. "If not here, if not now, then where and when?"

"Never. You didn't tell me who you were." She'd lowered her voice, but still it seemed to echo up the stairs.

"You know *who* I am, Fancy. You just didn't know *what* I am." He spread his arms wide. "Now you know. How am I different?"

How did she explain that he was more? Or at least he should have been. But all she saw standing before her was the man. The man who had eaten a meat pie with her on the steps, had looked at a naughty photograph, had come to her aid, had kissed her senseless. Who had introduced her to passion and shown her how to soar. "Why are you doing this?"

"Because from the moment I met you, you captured my heart with your kindness, your generosity, your openness, your acceptance. You are the most gracious, unassuming woman I've ever known. For me, you were never a passing fancy. I don't believe that can be said of all the gents here."

She knew he was referring specifically to Beresford. Was he in attendance? She hoped so. She wanted to face him as well. Matthew was saying all the right words, but he'd once said the wrong ones. "You believed me capable of deceit."

His eyes closed, his jaw clenched. Several heartbeats passed before he finally opened them. "I was blinded by my past. I don't excuse my accusations or my actions—and I know now that Beresford sought to compromise you. But he didn't count on you having the strength of will to reject a life or a gentleman you didn't favor." Another step down. "That took courage, Miss Trewlove. As well as an understanding of your own worth. A good many ladies could learn a great deal from you."

Another step nearer. One more and his feet would land on hers. One more and she would have no choice but to wrap her arms around him to avoid tumbling backward. *Take that step, a* corner of her heart pleaded. *Give me an excuse to touch you once again.*

"Tell me that you don't love me."

She hadn't expected the command. She could no more lie to him than she could to herself. He'd told this entire assembly that he loved her. How could she do any less? "Before Lord Beresford offered to show me the library, I had decided that I wasn't going to attend any more balls, that I didn't want to be part of the aristocracy because you weren't there. And afterward, when I realized to spare my family shame, I would have to marry him, I knew that never again would I know a moment of joy because you would no longer be in my life." The tears burned her eyes, and she blinked them back. "I love you so much that I can barely remember a time when I didn't."

The depth of emotion reflected in his green eyes weakened her knees. With one hand, he cradled her cheek. "I desperately want to kiss you, Fancy."

"I desperately want you to."

"Will you give me leave to call on you?"

She shook her head. "No, but I will give you leave to marry me."

His grin was devilishly wicked, filled with promises. "For you, Fancy, it must be done right."

Moving past her slightly, he went down a step and then lowered himself to one knee and took her hand. "Miss Trewlove, will you do me the great honor of becoming my wife?"

"I have a scandalous reputation, my lord."

He pressed a kiss to her gloved hand. "Then you're perfect."

She laughed as joy filled her heart, her soul. "I love you, Matthew. Yes, yes, I want to be your wife."

Shoving himself to his feet, he cupped her face between his hands. "Now they can't object."

And he claimed her mouth, her heart, her soul, there on the stairs, while the London elite looked on. Scandalous, a kiss such as this, so deep, so thorough, with her arms intertwining around his neck and his around her back, bringing her in so close that light couldn't make its way between them. He tasted as she remembered, rich and dark, decadent.

When he pulled back, he pressed his forehead to hers. "I think a waltz is in order."

Taking her hand, he escorted her down the stairs where the marquess and marchioness waited. When she would have curtsied, he stayed her actions with his palm gently placed on her back. "Fairhaven, Sylvie, I believe you've met Miss Trewlove."

"Indeed we have." Placing her hands on Fancy's shoulders, she leaned in and bussed a quick kiss over her cheeks. "It seems congratulations are in order. I cannot tell you how thrilled I am to see Rosemont looking so happy. And even more thrilled that such a public proposal was issued at my ball. My affair shall be the talk of the *ton*."

Matthew said something low to Fairhaven and with a nod, he walked off. Then Matthew leaned toward Fancy. "There is nothing my sister likes more than being the center of attention."

"Oh, there are things I like more but they are best seen to behind closed doors." She tapped her fan against Fancy's arm. "Whenever Rosemont visited of late, he always mentioned you. I can see why. It seems you've thoroughly enamored him."

"It is he who has enamored me."

The lilting strains of a tune started up. "The Fairy Wedding Waltz."

"If you'll excuse us, Sylvie, my betrothed is in need of a waltz."

As he was escorting her to the dance floor, three flaxen-haired misses stepped in front of them. Lady Penelope hugged her. "We're so happy for you, Miss Trewlove."

"The proposal was so romantic." Lady Victoria waved her fan as though the very thought of it warmed her.

"I daresay, proposals in the garden are going to go by the wayside," Lady Alexandria said. "I won't settle for anything less than a public proposal in a ballroom."

"I hope you all receive proposals very soon, but only from gentlemen you love."

The ladies giggled and waved as Matthew offered their excuses before leading her onto the dance floor, taking her in his arms, and sweeping her over the polished parquet.

"I don't know if I'll get used to hearing you referred to as Rosemont," she told him.

"I love you, Fancy. Call me anything you like."

"Whenever I attended a ball, I imagined you being there, waltzing with me. You're everything I ever dreamed of wanting."

"Don't stop dreaming, Fancy. For I intend to help you realize all your dreams."

She had an entire list, although she suspected he knew most of them and would guess the rest. They'd always been so attuned to each other.

She wished her mum had been here tonight, but she would tell her all about it in the morning. For now, she became lost in the music, the movement, the eyes of the man she loved.

BERESFORD STUDIED HIS cards, fighting not to groan and alert everyone that his luck continued to be ghastly. He was still struggling with the fact that Fancy Trewlove had preferred scandal to marriage. The moment he'd heard of her incredible dowry, he'd set his sights on acquiring her as a wife. He hadn't cared about her lack of a pedigree. He'd cared only about the coins she'd put in his coffers. Year after year. That she was interesting, gracious, and comely had been a boon. Even more so was the fact that he enjoyed her company. He didn't know if he would have ever come to love her—his mistress had held his heart for years now—but he'd already developed a bit of affection for her. He certainly would have worked to ensure she never regretted marrying him.

He shouldn't have arranged to be caught in a compromising situation, but he'd panicked when he saw how much attention she was garnering from other lords. And then when Rosemont—a man presently outside of social events—had implied a knowledge of her, Beresford had decided action was needed. Because if or when Rosemont returned to Society, he couldn't compete with the man, not when half the ladies of London were going on and on about the damned letter his wife had written. It had been bad enough listening to his sisters wax on about it, hearing them sighing over the earl.

So he'd made an error in judgment, tried to force Miss Trewlove into accepting him. The devil of it was that her rejection had only served to make him respect and want her all the more. He wondered if he would stand any chance at all with her if he courted her properly. Of course, now she was not only tainted by her birth, but by scandal. Even if he was the reason behind the scandal—

"Stand up, Beresford."

The whispered words carried enough venom to paralyze him. It took him several heartbeats to recover. When he finally did, he glanced up to find Rosemont glaring at him with an intensity that sent a cold shiver of dread racing up his spine. "Why?"

"Because I never strike a man when he's sitting."

"And why would you want to do that, old chap?" Although he had the unsettling thought that he knew.

"To defend Miss Trewlove's honor. I know you sought to take advantage of her, and I require satisfaction for my betrothed."

"You're going to marry her?"

"I am."

Beresford glanced around. No smiles greeted him. Only somber faces and hard stares. He'd not been discreet enough with his plans. There was no hope for it. He was going to have to take his punishment like a man or lose the respect of his peers. Shoving back his chair, he stood and tugged on his waistcoat. "I'd appreciate it if you'd avoid the nose. I have a rather fine no—"

The blow hit it directly, causing blood to spurt and his eyes to water, and sent him staggering down to the floor. Scrambling for a linen, he finally located it in his pocket, pressed it to his nose, and glared at Rosemont. "I do hope you're satisfied."

"I am. I'll send you an invitation to the wedding."

The bugger probably would.

Chapter 27

The next afternoon, Fancy sat in Aslyn's parlor watching as her hostess prepared yet another cup of tea for her—her third since her arrival. Matthew had been impatient to get her siblings' blessings. Earlier they'd shared a midday meal with her mother and gained hers. But he'd understood the importance of acquiring everyone's blessing. When they'd arrived at Mick's office, missives had been sent out to the others. Matthew and Mick were together in his office now, although surely everyone else had arrived by now.

"Don't look so nervous," Aslyn said as she passed her the saucer and cup of tea. "I'm certain Lord Rosemont will receive a blessing to marry you from each of your siblings."

"It doesn't matter if he does or not. I'm going to marry him."

Aslyn smiled. "Good for you."

"I just don't know what's taking so long."

"I'm sure they're putting him through his paces."

"The only thing of any consequence is that he loves me."

"And you him."

She smiled. "I do, Aslyn. So very much."

"I'm going to assume Lord Beresford was not the first gentleman you might have spent time with, without benefit of a chaperone."

She studied the elaborate rose pattern on the delicate china cup. "No."

"Mick kissed me before we were married."

She snapped up her head. "Oh, I knew that." She arched a brow. "Possibly more than a kiss?"

"A lady never tells."

She supposed not, although it certainly was tempting to share everything with Aslyn, to let her know how wonderful Matthew was. She glanced at the clock on the mantel. "Whatever can be keeping them? It's been two hours. They should all be here by now. Matthew should have asked for their blessing, they should have said yes, and someone should be coming for me."

"It takes time."

"Not this much time. I've no doubt they're making it difficult for him." She leapt up from her place. "Well, I'm not standing for that."

Turning on her heel, she headed for the door.

"Fancy!"

"I won't be long."

Once in the hallway, she crossed over to Mick's offices. Mr. Tittlefitz immediately came to his feet. "Miss Trewlove."

"Mr. Tittlefitz. I assume they're all still in there?"

"Yes, miss."

"As it's my future they're discussing, I don't think they'll mind my popping in." She reached for the door and jerked slightly when it opened without her pushing on it. She stared at the man who it appeared was striving to take his leave. "Mr. Lassiter."

"Miss Trewlove."

"What in heaven's name are you doing here?"

Matthew appeared in the doorway, edged passed Lassiter, and settled a hand on her waist. "He's my solicitor. I wanted to get the settlement agreed to as I intend to get a special license and marry you as quickly as possible."

"Your solicitor." Turning into Matthew, she wound her arms around his neck. "You wouldn't also happen to go by the name anonymous, would you?"

"I have many clients, Miss Trewlove," Mr. Lassiter said.

"I'm sure you do."

"It's all right, Lassiter. A man shouldn't keep secrets from his betrothed."

"You got their blessings?"

"I did. Each and every one of them."

She gave him her sauciest smile. "Matthew Sommersby, are there any other names you go by that I should know about?"

"The man who will always love you."

Rising up on her toes, she captured his mouth, not caring one whit that they had an audience.

THREE WEEKS LATER, Fancy stood in the vestibule beside Beast, waiting rather impatiently as her brothers and brother-by-marriage escorted their wives to their places on the first pew, where her mother was already seated. Fancy was excited, thrilled, anticipating the day, anticipating life. The church was packed to the rafters.

"You don't have to do this, you know," Beast said quietly, with teasing lacing his voice.

With a small laugh, she looked up at him. "Oh yes, I do. I love him so much, Beast. I've never been happier."

"That much is obvious, sweetheart."

Her brothers strode back up the aisle, all so handsome and confident, not at all intimidated by those filling the pews: the earls, marquesses, dukes, countesses, marchionesses, duchesses. But then why should they be when their family was slowly expanding to include so many of them? When they reached her, they each gave her a hug and a peck on the cheek.

"Ready?" Mick asked.

She smiled brightly. "Absolutely."

"No doubts?" Aiden asked.

"None whatsoever."

"You've not known him long." Finn, who had met his love when he was barely a man, gave voice to his worries.

"I've known him long enough."

Beast, having already said his piece, merely gave her a nod and a warm smile.

"Can we get going?" she asked. "I'm anxious to begin the remainder of my life."

Mick offered his arm, and she took it. Then he gave a signal and the organist began playing her favorite waltz. It wasn't traditional, but it was special to her and Matthew.

Mick started leading her down the aisle, her other brothers following. Out of the corners of her eyes she was aware of people standing, but her entire focus was on the man at the altar waiting for her. It brought tears to her eyes to see so much love reflected in the green of his. He was so frightfully handsome in his gray trousers, white waistcoat, and navy coat. When they were near enough, he winked at her.

"Who gives this woman away?" echoed through the church.

"Her brothers," Mick responded, and then he was placing her hand in Matthew's, and she thought it had never looked as though it belonged anyplace more.

MATTHEW SEEMED UNABLE to recall a single moment of his first wedding, but knew he'd never forget a single second of this one. The other had been a chore, a test of his willingness to endure an unpleasant task. Today none of his thoughts centered around himself. They were all focused on Fancy and ensuring he gave her a day of fond memories—not necessarily to see her through to old age because he planned to give her a good many more before then. But he did want their public commitment to each other to hold a special place in her heart. He didn't know if his voice had ever sounded more clear, more sure, so strong as it did now while he recited his vows. She was all that mattered. And he'd nearly lost her.

Never again would he doubt, never again would he hesitate. Where she was concerned, he'd always trust his instincts.

She was lovely in her frothy white gown with its wisps of lace and tulle that reminded him very much of a confection, but beneath it all was a woman of steel and determination. When he placed the ring on her finger, he'd never been more sure of anything. She was his, and he was hers.

Then he was leading her down the aisle to begin their life together as man and wife, earl and countess, lord and lady.

AFTER SIGNING THE registry in the vestry, Fancy and Matthew fairly dashed to the white open carriage with the four white horses waiting for them. Once they were seated, they began waving at the crowd exiting the church. The driver set the vehicle in motion at a rather slow pace. When the church was no longer visible, Matthew slipped his arm around her shoulders. "Hello, Lady Rosemont."

Then he took her mouth as though he owned it. She never wanted to stop kissing him. She ran her fingers up into his hair, knocking off his black top hat. He didn't seem to care that it might have landed in the street, as he groaned low and took the kiss deeper. It was so wonderful to finally have this again. They'd taken a respite from each other in order to build the anticipation for the wedding night. He wouldn't be taking her virginity, but she still wanted it to be memorable, and so they'd abstained.

Now he was hers. Completely. Absolutely. Unquestionably.

They were traveling to his Mayfair residence, Rosemont House. He'd offered to take her to it before, to show it to her, but she'd preferred to wait, so everything today would be an introduction to her new life. Besides, she was aware that a good many brides didn't see their homes until after they were wed.

The carriage turned through the open wrought-iron gates onto a long tree-lined drive that circled around in front of a massive manor house.

"Welcome home, Lady Rosemont."

With a smile, she glanced over at her husband. "It's beautiful."

"You can change anything you want inside or with the gardens. Could probably have your brother change the façade if you don't like it."

"I love it." The rich history of it. He had a past here that encompassed those who had come before him. Their children would know that past.

The driver brought the carriage to a halt. Matthew reached down to the floor and retrieved his hat before disembarking. Reaching back, he handed her down and bussed a quick kiss over her lips before tucking her hand in the crook of his arm and turning toward the broad steps. As he led her toward them, the wide wooden door opened, and the butler stepped out. Based on his clothing, she assumed he was the butler. She recognized him.

Still she waited until they reached the top of the steps, in order to see him more clearly and to confirm her suspicions.

"My lord, my lady," he said with the voice that had once wafted through her shop.

"Jenkins," Matthew said. "Fancy, our butler."

"Mr. Jenkins."

"Just Jenkins, if it pleases you, my lady. The staff are queued up to make your acquaintance."

But before that, she had something else to say. "You made a visit to my shop."

He darted a glance to Matthew before once more meeting her gaze. "Yes, my lady."

She squeezed Matthew's arm as she searched his beloved face. "The book of Shakespeare's plays was from you," she said softly, in awe, delighted that her husband blushed. "Wherever did you find it?"

"In our library."

Our. Everything with him had become *our.* Although it hadn't been *our* at the time. "Why give it to me?"

"I thought it would find a place in your heart." She recalled telling him that she didn't worry about people returning books for that reason. "And it just seemed it should belong to you. You're going to take delight in our library."

She most certainly did. He escorted her to the grand room right after she was introduced to all the servants who had been lined up in the foyer waiting to meet the new Countess of Rosemont. Books, books, books. Everywhere she looked. Walls of books. Floors of books.

"Have you any idea how many are here?" she asked.

"No. We should probably have them catalogued."

"Indeed. I'll get the staff started on it immediately."

Snaking his arm around her waist, he drew her near. "Not until after we return from our wedding trip."

They were spending the night here. Tomorrow they would leave for Calais.

He lowered his mouth to hers, and she was glad he'd passed his hat and gloves off to Jenkins, so her fingers had the freedom to muss his hair without running into any obstacles. While she'd been imagining them settled comfortably into one of the various seating nooks in this room and reading in the evening, she'd also begun considering how lovely it would be to make love among the books. On the desk, on the various settees, standing against a shelf, her fingers caressing leather spines while he caused wild sensations to riot through her.

Dragging his mouth along her throat, he growled low. "I can't wait to have you all to myself. I'm going to peel off your clothes layer by layer—"

"Oh yes." Her words released on a moan seemed to incite him further.

"I'm going to lick every inch of your skin."

"And I yours."

"Every inch?"

"Every inch."

With a tortured-sounding groan, he pressed his forehead to hers. "I wonder if we have time to go upstairs before breakfast."

Family and close friends would soon be arriving for the wedding breakfast. That list had been small. They couldn't prevent anyone and everyone from attending the church ceremony, but Fancy had wanted what followed to be more intimate, so her mum would be comfortable in the surroundings. "Will you be able to put me back together, so I don't look as though I've been ravished?"

"Absolutely not. Besides, where's the harm in being ravished on your wedding day?"

"We could just do it here. Save us some time."

"I do hope you're not considering what I think you're considering," a sharp voice stated succinctly from the doorway.

With a grunt, without taking his arm from around her, creating the image of a united front, Matthew turned to face his sister. "Sylvie."

"Your guests are arriving. You should be in the foyer to greet them." Quickly, she crossed over and gave Fancy a glancing kiss over her cheek. "You look lovely, m'dear. It was obvious to all sitting in that church that you've made Matthew exceedingly happy. With my help, you'll soon be embraced and loved by all."

"I'm happy enough that you've accepted me. As for the others—"

"Posh. You shall have it all. Now, if you'll excuse me, I need to dash off and make sure all is ready for the breakfast." She'd taken charge of arranging it.

After she'd disappeared into the hallway, Fancy said, "I like your sister."

"She likes you." He tucked her hand into the crook of his elbow. "I suppose we'd best greet the others."

Rising up on her toes, she kissed the underside of his jaw. "Mmm. But later, you're going to be all mine."

THE BREAKFAST HAD gone on for what seemed hours. Everyone offering their wishes, enjoying a scrumptious assortment of food, visiting, laughing. Matthew had taken Fancy and her mum on a tour of the house. Halfway through, her mum had started to cry.

"I'd always dreamed of you living in a posh house, but caw, not this posh. It's more than I could have ever dreamed for you."

How could she explain to her mum that the house meant little to her? It was the man who made her heart sing, the man who was important. Having Matthew was all that truly mattered.

"You can come live with us," Fancy told her.

"Ah, no, ducky. This place isn't for me."

"But you will come visit."

"Yes, love."

She'd extracted the same promise from each of her siblings as they look their leave with their families and friends. Until finally, it was only she and Matthew who remained in Rosemont House.

Now as she stood in her bedchamber, she thought she shouldn't be so nervous. After all, it was Matthew who had led her in here and closed the door. It was simply the thought of so many dreams realized. Not only hers. But her family's as well.

"It's customary for a husband to give his wife jewelry on the day they marry," he said as he ambled over to a vanity, picked up a long, slender black velvet box, and extended it toward her. Inside had to be a necklace, but one so large that it would dwarf her. Still she would wear it every day for the remainder of her life.

"I don't want us doing things because it's customary. I want us doing things because we want to do them."

"I *want* to give you this."

She opened the hinged lid and stared at the scrolled vellum. As she lifted it out, he took the box from her. She unrolled her gift and read the words, surprised, pleased . . . overjoyed. If it meant what she thought it meant. "It's a deed to a property. The address is—" She looked up at him, her brow furrowed. "It's the bookshop."

"Your brother is a hard bargainer."

"You purchased it?"

"I did. In your name." He shook his head. "The law will say it's mine, but it's yours. I have Lassiter working to find a way to circumvent the law so no matter what happens, the property is seen as belonging to you. Do with it as you will."

Tears burned her eyes. "You know me so well. There is no gift I would have treasured more. I won't spend all my time there."

"I shall hope not. You'll need to host dinners and such in order to convince people to donate to your efforts to teach adults to read."

Smiling brightly, she pressed the scroll to her chest. "I own my own bookshop. Even my eldest brother wouldn't give me that." She flung her arms around his neck. "Oh, Matthew, thank you."

She kissed the underside of his jaw. "Thank you." She kissed his chin. "Thank you."

Then their mouths met, and the vellum fluttered to the floor, as passion rose up, hot, bold, and wild.

"Matthew?"

"Yes, my love?"

"I don't want to wait to have children."

Straightening, he cupped her face between his hands and smiled warmly. "I shall endeavor to accommodate your wishes."

He kissed one side of her mouth and then the other before settling his lips against hers. When she parted them for him, he slowly, tenderly, mated their tongues, an ancient ritual of dancing and sparring. No rush. No hurry. As though they had all night. As though they had the rest of their lives.

While she hated to admit it, she'd felt a spark of guilt when they'd come together before, had worried about being a fallen woman. But now she experienced nothing but pure, unadulterated joy. They were legal. Any children she gave birth to would be legal. They would not be looked down upon because of the circumstances of their birth. They would know their father as the good man he was. They would be surrounded by aunts, uncles, and cousins who loved them.

Without breaking away from the kiss, she began loosening his buttons.

"Anxious, are you?" he teased against her lips.

"Very much so. We need to put your deft fingers to work."

Chuckling low, he did just that, and in short order, their clothes were strewn about the floor and they were strewn about the bed, a tangle of limbs, bodies gliding and sliding as mouths kissed, bit, and suckled. It seemed impossible that her skin could be more sensitive to his touch, and yet it was, as though it had learned that the movements of his fingers signaled that pleasure was waiting in the wings and would be arriving at any moment.

"I can't sleep when you're not in my bed, in my arms," he rasped as his tongue laved the peak of her breast.

"Then you should sleep well tonight." She nipped at the curve where neck met shoulder, then sucked passionately, knowing she would leave a mark, but wanting some evidence that she was there, and would be again. Night after night. Day after day.

"My parents slept in separate bedchambers. I don't want that for us."

"Neither do I." Tossing back the thick waves of her hair, she straddled him. "I've waited for you my entire life. Why wouldn't I want to sleep with you?"

Spreading his fingers on either side of her face, he brought her down for a kiss, plunging his tongue sure and deep, circling and stroking. Sliding his hands down her back, he pressed her to him, and rolled until she was on bottom, he on top. He gazed down on her with so much love reflected in the green depths of his eyes that she nearly wept. A corner of his mouth hitched up. "Fancy Sommersby."

"Today you gave me your name. I gave you my heart."

"I think you gave me your heart before."

She nodded. "And you gave me my shop."

"That's just the start of everything I'm going to give you."

"I've married a man of means."

"Considerable means."

She gnawed on her lip. "Could you really have purchased all the books in my shop?"

His smile was one of confidence, and yet there was a boyishness to it, an almost embarrassment. "Every single one." Lowering himself, he kissed the tip of her nose and lifted himself back up. "So I know you didn't marry me for my fortune. And you didn't fall in love with me because of my title."

"If I list all the reasons I fell in love with you, Matthew Sommersby"—she tilted up her hips—"we may never get to the fun part."

"I love you."

She would never tire of hearing those three words, nor of giving them back. "I love you."

As he claimed her mouth, the teasing vanished, replaced by an urgency as sensations began to sweep through her. As he pushed into her, filled her, she wrapped her legs around his hips and held on as he rode her with a ferocity that matched her own desires. The world faded away until it was only them, the two of them, locked in a passionate embrace, hurtling toward the storm that would erupt in ecstasy.

And when it came, they were flung through the tempest together, both crying out with the strength of their release.

When she came back into herself, sated and replete, she whispered, "I love you."

The words came back to her in a deep and lethargic voice.

Smiling, she let sleep take her.

THE FOLLOWING MORNING, as the carriage carried them away from the residence, Fancy nestled up against Matthew's side. It was her favorite place to be.

Their trunks had been carted to the docks earlier for loading onto the ship, and soon they'd be in Calais for their wedding trip.

"Content, Fancy?"

"Very. I think you may have gotten me with child."

He laughed. "Sometimes it can take a while."

"I want to give you your heir."

"I would be happy with a girl, especially if she favored her mother in looks and temperament."

"I suppose we could have one of each."

"Eventually, I suspect we'll have several of each." Tucking his finger beneath her chin, he tilted up her face and brushed a kiss over her lips. "I can't resist you."

"I hope that holds until we are old."

"I don't see why it won't."

Straightening, she glanced out the window at the unfamiliar scenery, the absence of buildings. "Matthew, I thought we were heading to the docks."

"No, our vessel is waiting for us elsewhere."

"Where?"

"At England's edge, near Dover."

"I'd not expected that."

"It's the best place for us to depart."

"I'll take your word for that as I'm so untraveled."

Leaning in, he nipped her ear. "Trust me, you're going to love it."

She had no doubt of that because he would be with her.

After all the excitement from the day before, she must have been more tired than she realized, wasn't even aware of drifting off, but suddenly Matthew was nudging her shoulder. "We're here, sweetheart."

Covering her mouth, with a yawn, she straightened away from him. "Sorry."

"You've nothing for which to apologize."

The carriage had come to a stop. He opened the door, leapt out, and reached back for her, handing her down. And that was when she got her first real look at where they were. She could see green and cliffs and nothing else save—

"That's not for us, surely."

"It's for you," he said, his voice thrumming with excitement. "It's our vessel."

In wonder, she stared at the hot air balloon.

So MANY TIMES, before she knew of his title, he'd thought of taking her in a balloon, but had wondered how to explain a common man having access to such a remarkable creation.

"We're taking this to Calais?" she asked, hesitantly.

"We are."

"Across the sea?"

"That is where we'll find Calais."

She turned to him. "What of our trunks?"

Trust a woman to worry over her clothing, not that he planned for her to be wearing much once they were settled in the cottage he'd let. "They're on the ship, and Jenkins will see them delivered to us in Calais."

"You present me with the most wonderful surprises."

He could say the same of her, as she leapt at him, flung her arms around him, and kissed him with exuberance. Making her happy had become his favorite thing to do, and it was so easy.

Stepping back, she smiled brightly. "Oh, what a grand adventure this is going to be. Shall we give it a go?"

He introduced her to Mr. Green, the balloonist and pilot, who he'd flown with before and trusted to get them to their destination. Then he lifted Fancy up, settled her in the gondola, and joined her.

"Oh, this is wonderful," she exclaimed a few minutes later. "So much better than flying the kite."

He couldn't disagree with her assessment, not when her arms were wrapped tightly around his waist as she peered out over the gondola's edge at the rapidly receding ground. Soon they were floating out over the sea, leaving England behind.

She looked up at him. "You spoil me."

"Whenever possible."

If he were skilled at working the mechanics that kept the gas filling the silk balloon so they stayed aloft, he might have dispensed with having the balloonist in the gondola with them. But it was more important they have a safe journey, even if they had company.

Gently Matthew turned Fancy around and held her gaze. "Whenever I'm with you, Fancy, this is how I feel. As though I'm floating on air."

He lowered his mouth to hers, kissing her tenderly but thoroughly while the nearby clouds looked on.

Epilogue

*F*ancy walked gingerly amidst the debris scattered over the ground. Erecting buildings was such a terribly messy business, although she did enjoy the scenery, especially when it was her husband walking about shouting orders, overseeing the construction. He'd taken a personal interest in ensuring all was done to her specifications. The building was a gift to her, would be a gift to a good many others. When finished, it would be a school where classes would be held for adults during the day and at night. Not only reading and writing would be taught, but other skills as well, skills that might lead to jobs with better working conditions.

She found it incredible when she thought of all that had transpired over the past few months. She and Matthew spent most of their time in London, occasionally visiting his country estate when he needed to check on matters. She loved the time spent at the estate but was always anxious to return to Town so she could pop into the bookshop easily to ensure that Marianne—now Mrs. Tittlefitz—was having no issues with the shop or customers. She was doing a splendid job of running things. Business was increasing, and they'd hired two additional staff members to assist her.

Fancy had hosted her first ball, and all had gone well. She was accepted by most of the aristocracy, in part due to her marriage to such a fine and respected earl. Lord Beresford had made it clear that he was at fault when it came to what transpired in the library. Lady Penelope's friendship had also gone a long way to seeing her accepted. The woman she'd first judged as being flighty had turned out to be far more cunning than anyone gave her credit for.

Especially when it came to raising funds for charitable endeavors. She and Fancy had begun hosting readings—some done by the authors themselves, some by actors. The fee they collected from people who attended was used for the lending library or classes.

Matthew caught sight of her, scowled, and began trudging toward her. She did so love watching the way he moved.

"You shouldn't be here. Not in your condition."

With a smile, she ran her finger along his bristled jaw. "I still have two months yet before this little one is to arrive, and I was walking carefully."

He sighed. "You are such a stubborn minx."

"You love me for it."

"I love you for a thousand reasons."

He demonstrated his love every day, every night. She looked over at the building. "It's coming along nicely."

"They should be finished by the end of the month. You'll want to start interviewing for your teachers and staff."

"I've decided to hire someone to watch children while the mothers have lessons. I suspect there are many women who can't come because they have little ones to look after."

"We can do something with the back garden, so the children have a place to play, run about."

"I knew you'd embrace the notion, come up with an idea for improving it. Now if I can just decide what to call it."

"I had an idea this morning. What do you think of the Fancy Center for Adult Learning? No apostrophe S. A play on your name."

"That makes it sound as though it's all mine, when it's really ours. What do you say to the Rosemont Center for Adult Learning?"

"I say I'd like very much to kiss you, Lady Rosemont."

"I do wish you would, Lord Rosemont."

And he did.

Author's Notes

The primer in this era contained the fairy tale of Cinderella, but it was spelled Cinderilla. It was only later that the spelling became Cinderella.

In addition, *Mr. William Shakespeares Comedies, Histories, & Tragedies* does not contain an apostrophe as originally printed.

It WWhenIt was not until the passage of the *Women's Property Act of 1882* that married women were allowed to own and control property.

Boating was an extremely popular pastime during the Victorian era. One company in particular set up stations along the Thames where people could lease rowboats and punts. They could then travel upriver, disembark at another station, and be returned to their original starting point.

The first balloon to fly from England to France was in 1785. It landed in Calais.

As for the Fire King, he was based on a real Victorian street performer who revealed how he managed to swallow fire, and the moment I read his personal account, he filled my imagination with possibilities. I have a feeling we haven't seen the last of him.

Acknowledgments

I'm not certain why I struggled so much writing this story, but from the beginning I couldn't seem to make it work. Eventually it became a Frankenstein project, scenes hobbled together as I came to better understand the characters. As a writer, I am always amazed by how a word, thought, or experience can open up a world of possibilities within my imagination.

I owe a great deal to the three people who played a role in bringing the story to life. My editor, May Chen, whose insights helped me to understand where I'd gone wrong; Addison Fox, who helped me see my heroine more clearly; and my son, Alex, who read the draft and offered suggestions for improving the depth of the story and also said, "I can't believe you didn't have him tell her, 'You were never a passing fancy.'" And thus, a different hero came to be.

$\mathcal{L}$orraine Heath concludes her breathtaking
Sins for All Seasons series with the
story everyone has been waiting for

$\mathcal{B}eauty\ \mathcal{T}empts$
$the\ \mathcal{B}east$

$\mathcal{B}$enedict "Beast" Trewlove has long
haunted London's dark and treacherous
underworld, offering protection to
those who need it. But when he comes
to the aid of a mysterious beauty, he
discovers she is a danger to his heart.

Coming Fall 2020

Prologue

The frantic knocking woke Ettie Trewlove from her first restful sleep in days. Her three lads, each only a few months old, were teething, which made them a grumpy lot, but tonight for some inexplicable reason they were sleeping like the angels they normally were.

The rapping continued. With no hope of it stopping unless answered, she tossed back the covers and climbed out of her bed. After turning up the flame in the lamp on the bedside table, she carried it with her to light the way as she passed by her dear boys, smiling at the way they snuggled against each other in the small crib. They'd soon be outgrowing it, and she'd have to make other accommodations for them.

Shuffling to the door, she opened it a crack and peered out, surprised to see a woman, a little younger than her own twenty years, standing there, a blanketed bundle cradled tightly in her arms. Until tonight, only men had made the deliveries.

"Are you Ettie Trewlove, the woman who takes in bairns born out of wedlock and sees them well cared for?" Hope and fear wove themselves through her thick Scottish brogue.

Ettie nodded. A baby farmer by trade, she took in by-blows no one wanted, for a few pounds each, sparing their mums the shame and the challenges to their lives that their presence would have brought them. "Aye."

"Will you take my lad? I've only a few shillings to leave with you, but you won't have to keep him long." With wide, dark eyes, she glanced around quickly. "Just until it's safe. And then I'll be back for him."

A few shillings would see him fed for only a couple of weeks, and she had three others in need of food. Still, she set the lamp on the table beside the door, opened it wider, and held out her arms. "Aye, I'll take him."

The young woman eased aside the blanket and pressed a kiss to the sleeping babe's cheek.

"What the devil did you do to him?" Ettie asked in dismay.

The stranger jerked up her head, held her gaze. "Nothing. He was born like this. But he's a good boy, will give you no trouble a'tall. Please don't turn him away. You're my last hope for protecting him from those who would see him harmed."

Ettie knew there were those who believed children born out of wedlock were born in sin and should be denied breath.

"I don't blame babes for things that aren't their fault." If she did, she wouldn't have found herself with three born on the wrong side of the blanket. Now four. She wiggled her fingers. "Hand him to me."

Taking care not to wake him, the lass—the light caught her fully, showing her to be more girl than grown—gently placed the lad in Ettie's waiting arms. "Promise me you'll love him like he was your own."

"'Tis the only way I know how to love a wee one."

With a tremulous smile, she pressed the coins into Ettie's palm. "Thank you."

Turning away, she took three steps before looking back over her shoulder, tears now glistening in her eyes. "His name is Benedict. I *will* come back for him."

The words were spoken with fervent conviction, and Ettie

wasn't certain who the lass was trying to convince: Ettie or herself.

She darted into the heavy fog and quickly disappeared into the shrouded darkness.

And Ettie Trewlove kept her promise. She raised the lad as though he were her own and loved him as only a mother could.